JOURNEY TO THE ELDEROAK

JOURNEY TO THE ELDEROAK

DAUGHTER OF THE EARTH TRILOGY
BOOK 2

K.M. GORDON

K.M. GORDON

MY DEAREST READERS

I'm assuming you've read book one of the Daughter of the Earth trilogy, so this will not be news to you. But just a friendly reminder that this is a fantasy book with a world on the brink of war so it does include violence and other challenging scenes. It is no more significant than Whispers of the Elderoak, but if you would like detailed content warnings, you can find them on my website at www.km-gordon.com.

Please take care of your mental health and take a break should you need to.

I hope you enjoy the next part of Ava's journey and thank you from the bottom of my heart for your love for this trilogy. I'm honored to share Journey to the Elderoak with you.

All my love,
K.M. Gordon

To those who question themselves. The over thinkers. The worriers. Those who just want to be accepted.

You belong.

THE FAE OF EORHAN

The Kingdom of Monterre (Earth)
Capital city: Mosshaven

Thorne Everwood - *King; brother to Ava Everwood; animal companion: eagle named Skye*

Ava Everwood - *Princess; younger sister to Thorne; animal companion: cat named Luna*

Casimir Undergrove - *general of the armies; animal companion: bear named Aro*

Quinn Ashbluff - *captain and second in command of the armies; animal companion: panther named Bastien*

Raine Verlice - *captain and third in command of the armies; brother to Fanya; animal companion: wolf named Sabriel*

Jorrar Farrow - *chief advisor to the King; husband to Kai; animal companion: owl named Percy*

Kai Farrow - *head healer; husband to Jorrar; animal companion: deer named Ivy*

Fanya Verlice - *sister to Raine; owns a bakery in town; animal companion: squirrel named Coco*

Pax - *orc soldier who guards Ava's rooms*

Zeph - *fae soldier who guards Ava's rooms*

Gisela - *captain of the ship Song of the Wind; animal companion: raven named Pascal*

Desmond - *advisor to The King; animal companion: snake named Arda*

Vivienne - *advisor to The King; animal companion: fox named Hazel*

Remy - *hobgoblin; former fellow prisoner with Ava.*

THE KINGDOM OF SAXUMDALE (STONE)
CAPITAL CITY: CAIRNHOLD

Soren Greatstone - *Queen; wife to Astrid*

Astrid Brightsong - *Queen; wife to Soren*

Corvus - *steward to the Queens*

THE KINGDOM OF FROSTHAVEN (ICE)
CAPITAL CITY: ONDING

Velaria Silvershield - *Queen*

Eros Silvershield - *King (deceased)*

THE KINGDOM OF IGNEOTHENIA (LAVA)
CAPITAL CITY: TORVAK

Aelerion Graysong - *King; husband to Thalia*

Thalia Graysong - *Queen; wife to Aelerion*

Maeryn Blackbeam - *general of the armies*

THE KINGDOM OF CAELESTIA (ASTRAL)
CAPITAL CITY: BOREALIS

Orion Starbringer - *King; husband to Seraphina; father to Jareth*

Seraphina Starbringer - *Queen; wife to Orion; mother to Jareth*

Jareth Starbringer - *Prince; son to Orion and Seraphina; heir to the Caelestial throne*

WHISPERING BOG
ELDEROAK
MONTERRE
MOSSHAVEN
EMERALD MOUNTHINS
OAKSHIRE
GREYWOOD FOREST
PORTAL FROM AVA'S FARM
DAEMON

AN
BOREALIS
CAELESTIA
OSTHAVEN
ONDING
IGNEOTHENIA
TORVAK
SAXUMDALE
CAIRNHOLD

1

The cry of gulls pierced the salty air, wind whipping Ava's braid down her back as she walked through the picturesque port on the coast of Monterre. The sun had just made it over the cluster of wooden buildings lining the cobblestone streets, painting the seaside town with a warm glow.

"Nervous?" Raine asked from beside her.

Ava gave him a flat look. "What do you think?"

His blue-gray eyes danced. "You've been living here for almost six weeks now. It's about time you do something princess-y."

"Right," she said with a sigh. "And training my ass off every day for the Elderoak journey isn't enough, so the king thought to send me to speak to another kingdom without him?"

"Your brother wouldn't have sent you if he didn't believe you were capable," Casimir said as he walked on her other side. "Besides, we know the queens well. We'll guide you."

"It's good practice, dainty human," said Raine, using the nickname he had given Ava upon her arrival in their realm of Eorhan.

Her thoughts caught on Raine's last word. Human. A month

and a half after arriving in Mosshaven, the capital of her kingdom, she was still human. Training to prepare for a harrowing journey to a magical tree where her true fae abilities would be unlocked. Because she was the sole person with portal magic running through her veins who could banish the daemon queen, Deidamia, back to her realm. The daemon queen she hadn't even known existed until everything fell apart months ago back on her grandfather's farm.

She was still in disbelief that this was now her life.

"At least I get a break from that awful obstacle course," she said, glancing at Casimir.

"You still have to complete it when we return."

Casimir, the general of her kingdom's armies, had created a grueling training routine for Ava. She'd spend the morning running laps and working her way through a horrific military-style obstacle course she was still struggling to complete. Then, she'd work on weapons training—swords with Casimir, daggers with Quinn, one of the army's captains and second in command, and archery with Raine, another one of their captains.

They rounded a corner, passing a tavern, clothing repair shop, and an inn. A lively market thrived in the square and the shouts of merchants selling their wares cut through the upbeat music winding its way through the tavern's windows.

They ventured closer to the docks, preparing to board the ship sailing for Saxumdale, the stone kingdom. Ava's stomach was in knots at the thought of meeting with the queens, asking for their help to fight Deidamia and her daemon armies. This would be her first attempt at diplomacy since learning she was the lost princess of her kingdom.

And she was terrified.

"Are you hungry?" Casimir asked, always seemingly concerned with her nutrition.

"I'm fine." But her stomach growled with betrayal.

"You're a terrible liar," he chided. "Wait here."

Ava stopped and looked at Raine.

He pushed his platinum hair behind his shoulder and smiled. "Do you two still argue all the time?"

She rolled her eyes, hands on her hips as she looked up at him. "A little. But we're friends now."

"Friends?" Raine raised a brow, waiting for her to elaborate.

"Yes. *Friends,*" she emphasized.

And they were. After their initial arguments upon her arrival in Mosshaven, Casimir had apologized, surprising her, and they'd worked through it. Though he still got irritated with her on occasion, and she with him, he seemed to be amused rather than upset.

Casimir returned, handing Ava a paper wrapped pastry. He then held up a bright orange fruit unique to their kingdom. "They had your favorite, so I got this too."

Her eyes brightened as she took the fruit in her other hand. "Thank you."

Then he would go and do something like that. Remember her favorite fruit. Say something kind. Tease her. And her heart would do a somersault in her chest.

"Why didn't you get me anything?" Raine interrupted.

"You didn't ask."

"Neither did Ava. I seem to recall her distinctly saying she *wasn't* hungry, but you didn't listen and—"

Casimir glared at him. "Let's go. We need to board soon."

He turned and walked toward the docks, Ava and Raine hurrying to catch up. She placed the fruit in her pocket for later, while she unwrapped the pastry and took a bite, the sweet filling melting in her mouth.

Raine leaned in and whispered sarcastically, "Friends huh? Friends who remember your favorite fruit?"

"Are you going to be like this the whole trip?" Ava whispered back harshly.

"Yes," Casimir said.

"So how are your lessons going?" Raine asked, changing the subject. "Learning anything interesting?"

After Ava trained in the mornings, she'd been spending time with Jorrar, the oldest and wisest advisor to the king. He'd been teaching her about fae culture and any other information she would need to know now that she was living in her homeland. The homeland where her parents had ruled as King and Queen of Monterre before dying and leaving it to her brother, Thorne.

"I learned that all of you are old."

"Early one hundreds is far from old," Raine said. "I'm practically a teenager."

"You sure act like it," Ava quipped.

Casimir chuckled quietly. "Still hard to get used to, isn't it?"

"It is. Though you all look close to my age, it's strange when I remember how old you really are."

"Remember if you'd been born here, you'd be around one hundred now so technically, when you think about it, we're practically the same age," Raine said.

"Right..." Ava replied.

She'd learned that time in Eorhan moved roughly three times as fast as the human world, so even though Ava was thirty-two, she'd been 'missing' from her kingdom for close to a century. It was all still difficult to wrap her mind around, especially since after she became fae, she'd live just as long.

They approached the docks lining the bay. Several ships sat idle on the shimmering water, preparing to trade the goods Monterre was known for—healing balms, herbs and certain produce other kingdoms were unable to grow. They stopped before the largest vessel, crew members scurrying back and forth, loading crates of supplies.

Raine led the way up the wooden ramp, boots echoing as Ava followed. She had dressed in a pair of tan pants with roses embroidered on the hips and a white cotton tunic tucked into her wide leather belt. The pants were tighter than what she typically wore, almost like leggings, and showed off the curves of her body she had finally regained after being starved in the daemon camp.

Casimir followed behind her and she may have swished her hips a little, knowing how good she looked in those pants.

"Welcome to The Song of the Wind," said Raine as they stopped on the deck. "This is Gisela, the captain." He gestured to a pale-skinned fae with ice blue eyes and white hair. She was dressed in navy pants, a white shirt with a blue vest, leather belt, and a sword at her side. On her shoulder was a large black raven eyeing them pointedly.

"Nice to meet you, Your Highness," Gisela said as she approached, scrutinizing Ava. "This is Pascal," she added, gesturing to her animal companion.

The raven tilted its head at Ava, released an enthusiastic caw, and flew off to perch on one of the nearby masts. She ached at the fact that they couldn't bring their own companions onto the ship. It was much too risky being on the open water should something happen.

"It's nice to meet you too."

"These two already know the rules." Gisela jerked her thumb toward Raine and Casimir. "But you haven't been on one of my ships so let me lay it out for you. I'm in charge. Period. I don't care that you're the princess or he's the general." She jerked her head at Casimir. "Those ranks mean nothing on my ship. You do what I say, no questions asked. Especially if we come across difficult weather or enemies. Is that understood?"

"Yes," Ava said. "Absolutely."

"Good." She clapped her hand on Ava's shoulder. "Then we won't have a problem." She turned on her heel and walked across the deck, barking orders at the crew as they prepared to sail.

"She's terrifying," Ava said.

"You have no idea," whispered Raine.

Crew members lowered the sails at each of the four masts of the large ship, readying for departure. Wooden railings carved with intricate vines and leaves surrounded the deck and depictions of the sacred Elderoak tree were prevalent on the vessel—embroidered on the sails, carved into the base of each mast, and integrated into the steps leading to the upper deck.

"Come on," said Raine. "I'll show you where we're sleeping."

Ava followed, Casimir silent next to her, as they turned left and walked to the stern of the ship. Crew members nodded greetings as they passed, and they stopped before two doors framed by twin sets of stairs leading to the helm where Gisela now stood.

"Anchors aweigh!" she called out, preparing to set sail.

Raine pointed to the door on the left. "Captain's quarters," he said, then to the one on the right. "Royalty quarters."

He stepped forward and turned the handle, entering with Ava and Casimir close behind. It wasn't a large space, but it was opulent and cozy with a small wooden desk in the corner and a window on the back wall overlooking the ocean. The window was cracked open, the sea breeze swaying the ruby velvet curtains and cooling off the room. Off to the right was a large bed in an alcove against the wall with its own set of curtains for privacy.

Ava took it in and froze. "Umm...where are all the beds?"

Raine's hand clamped down on her shoulder as he laughed under his breath. "It's a ship. Not everyone gets their own fancy room. We must share. You're lucky we get this. Most sleep below deck crammed together."

Ava glanced at Casimir who looked almost as nervous as she was. "Raine and I will sleep on the floor," he said, strolling around the room.

"Oh, I probably won't be sleeping in here much." Raine winked at Ava. "Gisela and I have a lot of catching up to do. On that note, I'll see you two later." He turned and left the room, shutting the door behind him.

Ava walked to the set of open windows and leaned her elbows on the frame. Moments later Casimir appeared next to her. "Sorry. We should have warned you," he said, his gaze fixed on the ocean.

"It's okay."

"I'd go sleep down with the rest of the crew, but Thorne ordered us to keep a close eye on you."

She turned and looked at him. "What? You think I'm going to get myself into trouble?"

"No. But being at sea comes with its own dangers. We don't know if Deidamia has any ships. If she learns we're out here, she could send her army after us. If something happens in the middle of the night, someone needs to be close."

"I guess that makes sense." She sighed as the ship began to move. "What now?"

"We explore the rest of the ship, so you know where everything is, introduce you to more of the crew, and relax. We'll resume training tomorrow."

"We're training on the ship?"

Casimir gave her a wolfish grin, his chestnut hair blowing in the wind, framing his golden eyes. "Oh yes. You don't get a break, princess."

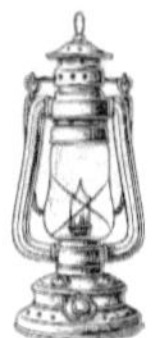

2

Raucous laughter echoed through the small dining quarters below deck as Casimir sat on the long wooden bench for dinner. Surrounded by dark wood, the space was lit with oil lamps along the walls, no windows to allow in natural light.

They had to eat in shifts since the space only fit a dozen crew members, give or take. The two guards stationed outside the castle suite he shared with Ava, Pax and Zeph, had come along and now sat at the end of the table. Half a dozen crew members took up the rest of the space, drinking and singing songs.

They'd been at sea five days now, with another five to go if all went according to plan. Each morning, Casimir supervised Ava's training. Being at sea didn't mean they could stop their regimen and he'd gotten creative with her workout routine to ensure she continued to gain back her strength.

Raine hadn't stayed the night in their room once, rekindling his past fling with Gisela, and Casimir slept on the floor without a word. He could tell Ava felt guilty about it but when she volunteered to trade places last night, he had refused. He would never let her sleep on the floor.

"So, how do you like being at sea?" Zeph asked Ava from across the table, her blue hair bright against her pale complexion.

"I love it," Ava said from beside him. "The ocean is peaceful."

"No issues with seasickness?"

Ava shook her head. "Not like this wimp." She nudged Casimir with her elbow. He tried not to show how affected he was by just that little touch, clearing his throat.

"You get seasick, general?" Zeph asked.

"I have to take a daily tonic," he grumbled, sipping his ale.

"Cas hates being at sea," Raine blurted as he set his fork down. "We offered to send someone in his place, but he said, 'wherever Ava goes, I go,' or some bullshit," he finished in his gruffest voice.

"What does that mean?" Pax said, looking in between Ava and Casimir, the orc's dark eyes full of curiosity.

Casimir tensed. "It means I'm responsible for keeping up with her training."

"Sure, it does," said Raine.

He stood from his seat, shaking his head and mumbling under his breath, as he left the dining quarters and ascended the stairs to the deck. He stepped into the night and made his way to the railing, leaning on his elbows and staring at the vast black ocean reflecting the innumerable stars overhead.

Why did he insist on going everywhere Ava went? Was it truly because of his role as her mentor? That was part of it. But the truth was he wanted to be near her. Needed to.

Someone approached from behind, but he didn't have to turn around to know who it was. He'd recognize the smell of Ava's lavender soap anywhere. She always smelled so fucking good.

Ava stopped beside him, staring out at the view. "The ocean is beautiful."

"It is."

They remained silent, listening to the soothing sound of the waves. Sporadic laughter erupted from below as the sailors drank the night away, trading stories and singing more of their seafaring songs. Ava was standing so close to him, their arms were almost touching, but neither of them moved or acknowledged the fact.

"Too bad you get seasick," she continued.

"I'll be fine."

She shot him an annoyed look. "You know, you've been really irritable the last couple of days. Like extra Casimir-y."

He turned toward her. "Extra Casimir-y? That's a new one."

"It seemed to fit. Why have you been so grouchy since we boarded the ship?"

He cleared his throat and searched her face. Her stunning green eyes were lit by the moonlight, framed by full lashes matching her strawberry blonde hair.

"Just a little back pain from sleeping on the floor," he said. "I'm old, remember?"

She crossed her arms and looked up at him. "Right..."

A strand of hair came loose from her braid in the breeze, and it took every bit of strength not to reach for it and tuck it behind her ear. He was grouchy because he had to sleep alone in a room with her, his asshole best friend leaving them behind. With the woman who'd been driving him mad since the day they met. Who he wanted so fiercely it was as if he couldn't breathe when she was near.

Ava shifted on her feet. "You can—I mean, if you want... sleep in the bed with me," she blurted.

His eyes widened as he went still. Dammit, he wanted to. Of course he did. But when he'd been assigned to train her, he set boundaries for himself. While he flirted with her on occasion, he wasn't going to make a move. Not yet. It was too soon and there was too much going on with the impending war. It would be a distraction for both of them.

But there was that fucking voice again in the back of his mind. The one that always seemed to laugh at his efforts to resist her. Reminding him it would be futile. That fate had other plans.

Ignoring it, he whispered hoarsely, "I don't think that's a good idea."

"Right," she said, fidgeting with her braid. "You're right."

Casimir studied her for a moment longer before clearing his throat. "Well...goodnight," he said as he turned and headed to the cabin, cursing himself the entire way.

Ava groaned as she leaned over, hands on her knees, after finishing her morning laps. She closed her eyes, welcoming the breeze as it brought a tinge of cool air to her sweat-soaked face.

Steps sounded as Casimir approached, stopping before her.

"I can't...believe...you're making me...run on the ship," she panted as she opened her eyes.

"I had to ensure we took advantage of the stairs."

"I hate those stairs," she said, rising.

"Wait until we get to Saxumdale. Everything is carved into the mountain. Stairs everywhere."

"That means you'll carry me, right?" She grinned.

"No," he said, chuckling.

She scoffed and tried to shove him playfully, but he was so strong he didn't even move an inch with her effort. Instead, he snatched her wrist and tugged her closer.

"Nice try," he said, eyes roving over her face. "You must do better than that if you mean to push me over."

"We haven't started hand to hand combat yet," she whispered. "Maybe you should teach me."

He leaned closer, lips hovering near her ear. "You'd like that, wouldn't you?"

A shiver went down her spine as he leaned back and looked down at her, a challenge in his eyes. She swallowed, unable to break his stare, as he watched her a moment longer before letting go and turning away.

"Alright, let's learn," he called over his shoulder as he strode to the straw mats laid out on the deck.

"Wait...now?" She hurried to catch up.

Casimir stood in the center of the makeshift ring and turned to face her, tying his hair back with a leather strip. "Yes, now."

Ava joined him in the ring, shifting on her feet. Why was she so nervous? Probably because the very large, very attractive and sometimes flirty general of her kingdom's armies was about to get more hands on than they had so far in the last six weeks of her training. Sure, he coached her on the sidelines through the obstacle course and taught her how to wield a sword, but this was different.

Shaking out her arms, she rolled her neck back and forth. "Okay, what do I do?"

"Try to punch me."

"I don't really know how to throw a decent punch."

"I figured, but I need to see how you do it so I can fix your technique."

She steadied herself. Pulling her arm back, she shot her fist forward, aimed at Casimir's chest. He caught her hand, freezing her punch in the air.

"That was worse than I expected it to be."

"Gee, thanks."

"You're welcome. Now, let's fix your arm position. You need to keep your wrist straight or you'll break it." He lifted her arm and adjusted it, holding her elbow at a ninety-degree angle with her forearm parallel to the ground. "Punch like this." He moved her arm forward, keeping everything aligned. "Try it," he said as he stepped back.

She punched the air several times, practicing the move. Despite the muscle she'd gained the last couple months, it felt awkward and weak.

"Better, but it still needs work. Now, you need to adjust your stance." He walked around and came up behind her, placing his hands on her hips, and she tried to ignore the way her body heated at his touch. And the way his fingers dug into her hip bones with the subtlest pressure. And the way he smelled. And...

"Ava, are you listening?"

"Yep!" Her voice came out higher pitched than she'd intended. "I'm an excellent listener. Your best student."

"Mmm hmm," he said, giving her the tiniest squeeze as if he could read her mind. "Pay attention. Place your feet shoulder width apart, like when you're wielding your sword. Put your foot slightly forward, the one on the same side as the arm you'll punch with." She did as he instructed. "You'll face your opponent at a slight angle. Keep your fists at chin height and your elbows close to your body."

"Okay," Ava said, her voice coming out hoarse.

"Now throw a punch when I tell you to. Keep your core tight and rotate your hips. Ready?"

She prepared herself.

"Now." Ava punched the air again, Casimir turning her hips in time with her strike. "Again."

She repeated the motion several times, Casimir not releasing her as he coached her through the moves. Once she had the movement down, he let go and walked back to face her again.

"Punch me as hard as you can," he instructed.

Ava balked. "Where?"

"Here," he pointed to his stomach.

"Uhh…"

"You can't hurt me," he said with a smirk.

"Rude."

She frowned but he only shrugged. "Just being honest. Punch me."

"Alright." She shook out her arms and resumed the stance.

"Stop hesitating and punch me, princess."

"Okay okay." She launched her fist at Casimir's abs.

He didn't even flinch when her hit landed. She looked at him, smiling broadly down at her, his eyes lit by the morning sun. She always forgot how tall he was until they were close like this. At a curvy five foot nine, she wasn't short or small, but Casimir was a giant. At least half a foot taller than her—likely more. And he was large. Broad shoulders and his body made of muscle; he dwarfed her.

"That was weak. Punch me as hard as you can."

She repeated the gesture, but he remained still as if nothing had even touched him.

"Oh, come on. I know you're stronger than that."

She let out a frustrated sigh and this time put all her weight into the punch. It landed in the center of Casimir's stomach, and he released a small grunt.

"Better?" she asked, backing away.

"That might actually leave a tiny bruise," he said.

"Oh, you poor baby."

He chuckled. "Now try to punch me in the face. I'm going to show you how to dodge it and take someone down."

Ava's fist flew through the air, but faster than she could comprehend, Casimir ducked, swept her legs out from under her and had her on her back, straddling her. And he'd done it without knocking the breath from her lungs.

"How did you do that?" She gasped.
"I'll show you."

3

*A*va ran a hand over her face and groaned, tossing and turning in bed for the hundredth time. They'd be arriving in Saxumdale tomorrow and she was much too anxious to sleep. The silence from her otherwise empty cabin didn't help.

Half an hour later, she was still awake when the door opened and closed, and she turned to find Raine taking off his shirt and boots.

"Scoot over," he said as he approached the bed.

She sat up. "What? What are you doing? Where's Casimir?"

"He got roped into the sailors' games. So, I'm on Ava duty tonight and I'm too good-looking to sleep on the floor. Move over," he repeated.

"I never said you could sleep in bed with me."

"I'm not asking permission." He pulled the blankets back and climbed in bed.

"Oh my god, you're serious."

"Absolutely." He settled in beside her. "We can snuggle if you want. I mean, I'm no Cas...but you can pretend I am if it makes you feel better."

She rolled her eyes and smacked his shoulder as she scooted to the wall, pulling her pillow with her. "I hate you."

He turned his head and gave her a huge grin. "No, you don't."

She stared at the ceiling. "What is this 'sailor's game' you mentioned?"

"It's some tradition they have the night before port. They pull out a bunch of straw mats and beat the shit out of each other."

Ava turned and propped her head on her hand. "Seriously? Why aren't you participating?"

"Because I'm not barbaric. Besides, I need my beauty sleep."

"No romping in bed with Gisela tonight?"

"She's out there with the rest of them. We'll get back to it later. On that note, I'm going to sleep now. Goodnight."

Raine was snoring within minutes.

Though Ava tried to fall asleep, her mind wouldn't stop racing. Add in Raine mumbling in his sleep and his horrible habit of hogging the whole bed and the covers, she gave up and glared at the ceiling. It seemed she would be meeting the queens with zero rest.

Raine groaned and rolled over, throwing his arm across her. "Ughhh," Ava said as she moved his arm and shoved him to the other end of the bed. He didn't even wake up. "This is stupid."

Abandoning her attempt to sleep, she climbed over him and got up. Throwing on a tunic and a pair of pants, she pulled on her boots and left the room.

The cool breeze whipped the sails above as the sound of cheering floated through the night sky. Following the noise, she walked to the circle of spectators at the middle of the main deck.

Ava stood at the back and raised up on her toes, trying to get a glimpse of what was going on in the center of the crowd. Fists were raised in the air in front of her as they cheered the fighters on, but she couldn't see much over the tall fae. Some of the crew noticed her and parted, allowing her closer. Now, standing at the inner edge of the circle, she had the perfect view.

A burly muscular woman was facing off with Eamon, the cook. They both had their shirts off, the woman wearing a bandeau similar to Ava's, and she had Eamon in a headlock on the ground. The crowd chanted as they counted to ten, then she released him. Eamon remained on his hands and knees, gasping for breath. The winner stood, raising her fist in the air, and the crowd went wild.

Ava scanned the spectators for Casimir. He stood at the edge diagonally from her, zeroed in on the mat, not having noticed her arrival. Shirtless, his arms were crossed as usual, his unbound hair framing his intense eyes as he watched the winner choose the next two fighters. His chiseled physique glistened with sweat, apparently having already fought, and her eyes caught at the way his biceps bulged against his chest.

Two male sailors, equally huge, took center stage next and removed their shirts while taunting each other. Energy contagious, Ava found herself cheering alongside the rest of the crew as they began their match.

"Princess?" Pax's gruff voice cut through the noise as he pushed through the crowd to stand next to her. "What are you doing out here?"

"Hey, Pax." Ava smiled. "I couldn't sleep so I thought I'd see what all the fuss is about."

He laughed. "It's risky being in this crowd. You might get chosen to fight next."

"Really?" It hadn't even crossed her mind.

"Maybe. Though I don't think the general would allow it."

For some reason, that annoyed her and she frowned, returning her attention to the circle. They watched two more rounds of fights and now Zeph was facing one of the crew members Ava had eaten dinner with. He threw a punch which she dodged, giving him one of her own to his gut. He blew out a breath with a grunt and staggered on his feet. Zeph darted behind him, wrapping her arm around his neck in a choke hold.

The crowd cheered as she tried to bring him down to the mat, but he managed to get free of her hold, whirled around, and had her on the ground, arm behind her back within seconds. The fight hadn't lasted more than a couple of minutes and Gisela declared him the winner.

They shook hands and the sailor turned, scanning the crowd for the next victims. His eyes landed on Pax and pointed at him. "You," he said. His eyes moved and landed on Ava.

Shit.

"And the princess." He gave her a feral grin. "I know you're a feisty one. Let's see what you got."

Casimir's eyes snapped to hers and widened, discovering her presence at last, as he marched her way.

"What are you doing out of bed?" he whispered harshly.

"Raine was snoring and I couldn't sleep. I wanted to see what all the commotion was about."

"You can watch, but you're not fighting," he ordered.

"Are you coming, princess?" Gisela yelled from the center of the ring where Pax was waiting, a look of blatant discomfort on his face as Ava and Casimir continued their argument.

"Give us a minute!" Casimir barked at her, not breaking his gaze from Ava.

"Why can't I try?" she said. "You know Pax won't hurt me. It'll be good practice, especially since you've been teaching me moves like this."

He stared down at her.

"You know I'm right," she urged.

"You're meeting the queens tomorrow. You need to rest. You spent almost the whole day training."

"I'm so anxious about tomorrow, I can't sleep anyway. It'll help me work off some of my nerves." She gave him a pleading look, pushing her bottom lip out just a little.

He narrowed his eyes, glancing at her lips. "What is that?"

"What?" she looked at him innocently.

"That look. Are you...pouting?"

"Nooo...I'm asking nicely. Please."

"Fine," he said as he jerked his head to the ring. "But don't expect that to work again."

She gave him a triumphant smile and could have sworn his lips twitched, suppressing his own amusement, before she turned and joined Pax on the mat.

Gisela addressed the crowd. "Since this is the princess's first time, I'll go over the rules," she shouted. "No kicks or punches to the groin. No kicking or punching when your opponent is on the ground. No head-butting. No strikes using your knee or elbow. And no punching in the face since Ava is meeting the queens tomorrow." She gave Ava a grin. "First one to keep their opponent on the ground for ten seconds or until their opponent taps out, wins."

Ava glanced at Casimir, who had reclaimed his spot at the edge of the ring. He grabbed Pax's arm and pulled him close, whispering something in his ear. Pax nodded, a flash of fear on his face, and took his stance back in front of Ava.

"What did he say?" she asked.

He stepped closer so no one else heard him. "He said if I hurt you, he'll strip my rank and make me clean the dungeons with one arm because he'll break the other."

She looked at Casimir again, who was observing her so intensely she felt exposed beneath his stare.

Turning away, she whispered back to Pax, "As the princess, I technically outrank him, so I'll make sure you don't lose your title."

He laughed and they backed away from each other, taking their fighting stances.

"Shirts off, you two," called the captain.

"Ava—" Casimir started but was interrupted by Gisela.

"Other than leaving her pretty face alone," Gisela said, clapping her hand on Casimir's shoulder. "She gets no preferential treatment."

Pax removed his shirt and tossed it on the ground, revealing his green skin. The orc was huge, bigger than Casimir, with rippling muscle. There was no way she'd last long in this fight.

Taking a deep breath, she looked at Casimir defiantly and didn't break eye contact as she removed her tunic and tossed it aside. Her breasts were bound tightly, no different than wearing a sports bra, albeit a strapless one. Casimir's pupils enlarged almost imperceptibly as his eyes flicked down and back up again, but he regained his composure and was back to looking irritated.

She smirked at him and looked back at Pax. "Don't go easy on me."

"Yeah right."

"Alright, enough chit chat," said Gisela. "Get on with it."

The crowd cheered and Ava shook out her arms as Pax crouched and grinned at her.

What the hell was I thinking fighting an orc soldier?

She tried to ignore her racing heart and focus on the moves Casimir had taught her. Pax lunged forward, quick as lightning. He wrapped one arm around her torso and moved behind her, ducking his head at the middle of her back.

He gripped her as they pushed each other in the center of the ring. Ava yelped at his strength and tried to get one of her legs under his to topple him, but his feet were planted too far away. She reached one arm behind her and wrapped it around his back. Well, she tried to, but he was so wide she couldn't reach all the way across. With her other hand, she yanked his arm with all her strength. Twisting, she used the angle and momentum and rolled him onto his back clumsily, almost falling on top of him.

The crowd cheered, not caring that Pax was being easy on her, they just wanted a fight. He grinned as he hopped to his feet, ready to go again. Ava darted forward and tried to land a punch on his side, but he grasped her wrist and twisted it against her back, moving behind her again. She winced as her arm screamed in pain, but ignored it, trying to decide on her next move.

"Pax..." Casimir growled from the sidelines.

Pax loosened his hold and Ava stomped on his foot, causing him to release her arm. She pushed herself away and whirled toward Casimir.

"Keep your mouth shut and don't distract me," she snapped, then faced Pax again.

The crowd cheered.

"You heard her, general," said one of the sailors. "Princess says stop interfering."

Casimir grumbled as she prepared for the next move. Pax lunged and Ava tried to dart away, but he grabbed her legs and yanked them out from under her. She landed on her back with a thud, leaving her breathless.

"Shit," she wheezed.

The captain started counting to ten, but Ava wasn't ready to concede. Sailors shouted, "Get up! Get up! Get up!"

Zeph's voice cut through the noise, "It's not over yet, Ava!"

Just as Gisela made it to six, she was on her feet again. Pax advanced toward her, but this time she ducked at the last second and threw herself on the ground, crawling in between his legs. Before he had a chance to whirl around, she jumped on his back and wrapped an arm around his neck, putting him in a headlock.

She wrapped her legs around his torso, digging her heels

into his ribs. He yelped at the pressure and the crowd went wild, chanting, "princess!" Confidence soared as she jammed her heels into his ribs.

"Ouch, you little shit," he said as she repeated her actions.

He spun around, trying to loosen her hold but she pulled her arm tighter and kicked him as hard as she could. Grunting, he yanked her arm down so fiercely, she cried out as he leaned over and threw her over his shoulder.

"Fuck!" she yelled as she was flipped onto her back and landed on the mat.

She gasped, trying to catch her breath.

Gisela counted to ten and Pax was declared the winner, cheers of the crowd echoing in the night. He approached and held out his hand. She grasped it and let him pull her up, still panting.

"Did I hurt you?"

"I'll be sore, but I'm fine," she croaked.

Relief washed over his face. "Great job."

Ava made her way to Casimir as Pax picked the next two to fight. His arms were still crossed, and he was holding her tunic as she took her place next to him, watching the next round.

"You should put your shirt back on," he whispered.

"Why? I'm too hot and sweaty right now," she said as she watched two sailors square off.

"Because it's very distracting," he mumbled under his breath.

"None of the sailors are even looking at me. They're quite respectful. So, who's getting distracted?"

He edged closer to her and leaned in. "Me."

A shiver went down Ava's spine as she glanced at him, but he had straightened out and was watching the fight as if he'd said nothing.

She moved closer, standing in front of him, and leaned back so her bare shoulder and upper back brushed against his shirtless chest. He tensed at her touch and she could have sworn he stepped forward a little.

"Maybe I won't put it back on then," she whispered.

A low rumble vibrated in his chest but he remained quiet as they watched the fight end after one of the participants passed out from too long of a choke hold. The game finished with two more matches and both of them inched closer to each other over the course of the night.

There was something about this trip; something that made her want more connection with him. Maybe it was the ease of being around the sailors, their casual nature allowing her to feel less proper and more normal. Or maybe it was being some-where different than Mosshaven. A new routine not involving the obstacle course which constantly taunted her.

It was now the final duel and Ava was barely able to pay attention, leaning almost her entire weight against Casimir. His hand moved to her shoulder and his thumb traced slow circles on the back of her neck, causing her to shudder.

"Are you cold, princess?" he asked, lips brushing the edge of her ear.

"No."

"Hmm..." he said as his fingers brushed the side of her neck. "Am I making you nervous?"

Yes. "No," she breathed.

"Liar."

They remained quiet as the last fight ended. The crowd dispersed, everyone heading to their own sleeping quarters, and Casimir removed his hand from her neck.

"It's late," he said, handing over her shirt. "We need sleep."

The ship was quieter now, the pitch-black sky painted with millions of stars. She put her tunic on. "I don't think I'll ever sleep with Raine in there. He talks in his sleep. *And* he's a horrible bed hog. I shoved him and he didn't even wake up."

"He's a heavy sleeper."

"You don't say."

"Come on." He turned and headed to their cabin. "I'll kick him out. You need sleep for tomorrow."

She followed him across the deck, entering their room. Casimir marched to the bed, yanked the covers off and patted Raine's face several times until he woke up.

"What's going on? Are we under attack?" Raine scanned the room, confused.

"Get out," Casimir ordered. "You're keeping the princess awake."

Raine stumbled out of bed, grabbed his shirt and boots and mumbled as he left the room, saying something about indecisive generals and interrupting his beauty sleep.

"Thanks," said Ava, laughing.

Casimir turned around, his back facing her. "Change into your sleep clothes and get in bed."

He walked to his pallet on the floor and made sure not to look her way as she changed. Once she was back in her nightgown, she climbed into bed and scooted under the covers as Casimir made himself comfortable on the floor.

"Did you really threaten to break Pax's arm and make him clean the dungeons if he hurt me?" she asked, staring at the ceiling.

"Yes."

"Why?"

"No more questions, princess." Casimir rolled over. "Goodnight."

4

*A*va adjusted the long sleeves of her dress as she evaluated herself in the mirror. The sage green bodice hugged her curves, sprinkled with subtle beading flowing down the forest green skirt.

They had arrived at their destination early this morning and she couldn't shake the uneasiness in her gut at the prospect of representing her whole kingdom. Turning away from the mirror, she crossed the room and opened the door to the suite, stepping into the crisp morning air.

When she saw the view outside, she froze.

"Wow," she whispered.

Raine and Casimir stood by the railing near the gangplank being lowered as Gisela shouted orders to the crew. Ava strode toward them and stopped next to Raine, looking out at what lay before her.

Saxumdale.

Islands covered in towering flat top mountains surrounded them, the tallest disappearing into the clouds. The dark gray stone was peppered with trees, but it was far from the green she was used to in Mosshaven. The white trees here were twisted and grew precariously on cliffs along the stone giants, their bright yellow leaves cascading down the draping branches. Tiny white flowers bloomed among their roots, covered in bees and other insects.

They had docked at the largest island, but there were no signs of a city or castle aside from a few stone buildings carved into the side of the rocky face.

"Where's the capital?" she asked.

"Cairnhold is *inside* the mountain," said Raine.

She looked at the behemoth before her. "I've never seen anything like this."

Casimir led them down the ramp and onto the mainland. Dock workers buzzed about, speaking with the captain as they unloaded crates of goods. Saxumdale specialized in mining and their main export was iron ore, vital in forging weapons and other tools throughout Eorhan. Monterre would be taking back a large shipment to increase weapon production for the war and had brought produce, healing balms and their own goods to trade.

Winding their way through small buildings and the flurry of activity in the dock, they stopped before the mountain. A tall man with dark gray rock-like skin—all the Saxumdale fae had stony complexions in varying shades—approached them. He wore royal blue robes and his black hair rested perfectly on top of his head. Four soldiers followed behind him in iridescent armor made from kreovite—a rare mineral deposit only found in their kingdom. When the sun hit their armor, its charcoal color changed from a deep blue to violet. A stunning example of how skilled their armorers were. Ava had learned in her lessons with Jorrar that it was stronger than most other armor, yet lighter, allowing their soldiers to move with ease. Another reason they needed Saxumdale's help with the war.

"Welcome to Saxumdale, Your Highness." The man stopped before Ava and bowed.

"Thank you," she said, trying to keep her voice steady.

Raine and Casimir flanked her, taking on their roles as her guards, with Pax and Zeph behind them. They were all dressed in their usual leather armor, complete with swords.

"My name is Corvus," he continued. "I'm the steward for the queens. I'll be escorting you to the castle."

"It's lovely to meet you," said Ava.

Corvus turned and led the way, two soldiers flanking him while the other two waited for Ava's group to follow, bringing up the rear.

"Do you remember everything I told you?" Raine asked from beside her.

"Yes."

"Recite it to me."

As they walked along the base of the stony mountain, they came upon a wide archway carved with ancient symbols leading into the rock.

"First, we'll be presented to the queens. That's when I introduce myself and deliver the letter from Thorne," she recited as they entered the archway. "That's not the time for war talk. Then we will be shown our living quarters to rest and prepare for dinner. Dinner—dessert specifically—is where I will start the discussion of war."

"Good," said Raine.

They continued through a short tunnel with floating lanterns near the ceiling, and emerged into a sprawling city carved into the hollowed-out mountain. Ava gasped as she took in the space, in awe of the lively metropolis.

Stone streets wove through rocky buildings; taverns, shops, and blacksmiths lining the roads. No sunlight entered here, everything lit by orange flames in lanterns throughout the city. Though there were no plants or greenery to be found, it was beautiful in its own way. A city proud of its architecture and brilliant engineering.

They walked over a stone bridge, lanterns on the railings lighting the way, and crossed a flowing stream leading to the ocean through a hole in the rocky mountain. Children sat on the bank with wooden fishing poles, shrieking with laughter as one made a catch and reeled it in, beaming at his prize and showing it off to his friends.

A blacksmith hammered a beautiful dark iron sword nearby, the heat of the forge oppressive as they passed. Ava fanned her face at the sudden change in temperature, unable to look away from the smith's astounding skills.

After winding through town, the group paused, reaching the base of stone stairs carved into the side of the mountain.

"Where's the castle?" Ava whispered.

Casimir pointed to a level high above them.

She craned her neck and her eyes caught on the thousands of steps they'd have to take to reach the top. Corvus had already begun to climb, his guards behind him.

With a deep breath, Ava followed.

IRON TORCHES FLICKERING with bright orange flames framed the double stone doors of the throne room. The colors of Saxumdale were full of blues and purples, integrated into their armor and clothing, like the browns, golds and greens of Monterre. Guards flanked the doors, their shimmering armor accentuated with deep violet capes.

They'd climbed so many steps it had felt almost endless, then wound their way through countless hallways before reaching the throne room. Ava's legs ached with exhaustion, and she longed to soak in a hot bath before dinner.

The castle walls, ceiling, and floor were made from the dark stone of the mountain, rugs in the kingdom's colors adding a bit of warmth to the space. In lieu of artwork, there were statues and carvings integrated into the structure of the castle. Carvings of old kings and queens, of swords and weapons and other motifs.

"Are you ready?" Raine leaned in and whispered as the guards prepared to open the doors.

"Yes."

"Don't do what you did last time you met a king." He winked at her.

She huffed in response. Last time she met royalty, her own brother, he thought she was threatening him, and she almost got herself into trouble. She wouldn't make that mistake again.

The doors opened and they entered the long, narrow throne room. Tapestries hung from the walls with depictions of stone fae in battle and posing with their weapons. Braziers lined the walkway, casting an eerie glow as their flames danced among themselves. A navy-blue rug led them to the dais, where two stunning women were seated upon deep black stone thrones carved with tall spires along the back. Ava had learned in her studies their names were Astrid and Soren and they'd been ruling this kingdom for the last eighty years after their former queen was killed in battle.

"Presenting Ava Everwood, Princess of Monterre, sister of King Thorne Everwood," the steward announced. "Accompanied by General Casimir Undergrove and Captain Raine Verlice."

Ava clutched her skirt and curtsied as the rest of them bowed.

"Welcome to Saxumdale," Astrid said, brushing her black curls behind her shoulder. She had light gray stony skin, dark blue eyes and was dressed in a deep purple gown. "How did you find your journey?"

"It went smoothly. The weather was kind to us," Ava responded.

"I'm glad to hear it," Astrid said warmly.

Soren scrutinized Ava with hazel eyes, her shoulder length red hair bright against the stone crown resting upon her head with a glowing purple crystal in the center, matching the one her wife bore. Her cerulean gown shifted as she crossed her legs.

"I've been intrigued to meet this long lost fae but still human princess I've heard so much about," Soren spoke. "How are you adjusting to your new life?"

Ava cleared her throat, trying to ignore her nerves. "It hasn't been easy, but I've fallen in love with Monterre. Everyone's been welcoming."

"Thorne is a kind ruler," Soren said. "You're lucky to have him as your brother."

"I am."

"Did you bring the goods he promised?" Astrid asked.

"Yes, we did. They were being unloaded when we left the ship. I also have a letter from Thorne."

"Oh?" said Soren.

"Yes."

Casimir retrieved the sealed envelope from his pocket and handed it to Ava. She held it out and the steward took it and walked to the queens, delivering it to Astrid.

Astrid opened the letter as Soren leaned over to read it alongside her. They both frowned, then smiled, and Astrid attempted to hide a small laugh. Ava tried to make sense of their reactions, unsure what the letter contained.

"Interesting," Astrid murmured. "Alright. I'm sure you're tired from your journey. Why don't you rest and get cleaned up and we'll meet at dinner to discuss what you came here for."

Ava curtsied once more, thanking the queens for their time, and followed her group out the door.

5

The fire crackled as it consumed the wood beneath its orange flames, warming the small stone bedroom assigned to Ava. The bed was made in deep violet fabrics, and layered rugs brought a cozy feel to the space.

Ava stood before the full-length mirror, unable to take her eyes off the dress she wore for dinner. It was customary in Saxumdale for guests of the royalty to dress in the style of the kingdom, she just hadn't realized their style was more revealing than she was used to.

The dress she wore was a deep navy blue with off-shoulder sheer sleeves that draped down her arms, leaving her shoulders and back bare and exposing the scars she bore as a result of her torture by the daemon queen. Gold lace detailing wove through the snug bodice, ending in lush fabric skirts that parted into a slit. Her hair was braided around the crown of her head, sprinkled with matching blue jewels.

A knock sounded on her door and Raine's voice called out. "Are you done yet? Hurry up, I'm starving."

Ava ran her hands along the skirt. "I'm done...I'm just not ready to come out yet."

"I'm coming in," he said, barging into her room.

Raine paused. His eyes moved over her attire appreciatively. He put his hands on his hips and grinned. "Well, fuck."

She threw her hands up. "I know, right? It's...a lot."

He walked around her in a circle and chuckled. "Your ass looks amazing. Please, oh please walk in front of Cas as much as possible because you look sexy and he's going to lose his mind."

Ava crossed her arms and glared at him. He was dressed in a violet tunic lined in gold, black pants and boots.

"Well, you look good too," she admitted.

"I know," he said, flicking his hair behind his shoulder. "Let's go." He gestured for her to walk ahead of him.

"Oh no you don't," she chastised. "You go first. I don't want you staring at my ass all night."

He laughed and turned on his heel, heading toward the door as Ava looked at the ceiling, mumbling and hoping she didn't trip and make a fool of herself. She emerged into the opulent living room, decorated in a similar style to her bedroom. Plush fabrics softened the space, and a large balcony overlooked the city on the far wall, framed by navy velvet curtains.

Casimir rose from his chair and took a step forward, but halted as he took her in.

"That's the dress they gave you to wear?" he asked, voice low and hoarse.

"Ridiculous, isn't it?"

He shook his head as his eyes trailed down her figure. "That's not the word I would use," he murmured.

"This is getting awkward so I'm going to go find Gisela," interrupted Raine. "I'll see you two at dinner."

They didn't acknowledge him as he left the room, unable to break eye contact. Casimir looked devastating in a dark blue jacket with silver buttons and thread lining the seams and hem.

His black pants ended in ebony leather boots and his hair was left unbound.

Breaking the silence, Ava blurted, "You look handsome." She fidgeted with her skirt. "I feel ridiculous in this dress, and I'm going to trip in these stupid heels. How are we supposed to talk about war dressed like this?" she rambled, as she often did when she was nervous. "And now everyone's going to see my scars, and they're going to think—"

"Ava," Casimir interrupted as he crossed the room and stood before her, placing his hands on her shoulders. "You are beautiful. Fuck what everyone thinks about your scars. They're badges of courage. Okay?"

His thumb gently brushed her skin and she nodded. "Okay."

He stayed there for a moment before he turned and placed himself at her side, holding out his elbow. "Let's go to dinner, princess."

She looped her arm through his and let him lead the way.

AVA SAT between Raine and Casimir. Gisela was seated beside Raine, laughing every time he whispered in her ear. Astrid and Soren sat across the stone table with their steward to their right. Several guards were stationed along the wall, including Pax and Zeph, monitoring dinner.

The dining hall matched the rest of the castle. Dark stone walls carved with intricate designs encased the room, lit by an iron chandelier covered in flickering lights. A large tapestry hung on the far wall, depicting dozens of stone fae women with swords, appearing as though they were battling each other on top of one of the flat top mountains.

Dinners here were not casual like back in Mosshaven it

seemed, and staff brought out each course at a predetermined time. The food was delicious, mostly seafood due to Saxumdale's location, and they were finishing the main course of pan-roasted fish with herbed butter, roasted cabbage and a rice side dish full of spices Ava had never tasted before.

Ava waited for dessert as she picked at her dinner and sipped her white wine, trying not to fidget. Most of their conversation had revolved around her adjusting to her new life, and Soren explaining how things worked in Saxumdale.

"I've noticed you looking at our tapestry," Soren said.

Ava set down her fork. "It's stunning. What's happening in the picture?"

"It's how the new queen is chosen. Every hundred years, or sooner if the previous queen meets an untimely death, women who deem themselves worthy compete for the crown. We call it the Sovereign Rite."

"Only women?"

Astrid nodded. "*Only* women."

"I like the sound of a kingdom ruled by women," Ava said. "So, which one of you won?"

"We both did," Soren said, her hazel eyes bright. "The rite is brutal. Violent. When we reached the top, we were prepared to kill each other."

Astrid reached over and grasped her wife's hand. "The goddess we worship, Umis, reveals a cerodinite crystal at the top of the mountain, which is what you see in our crowns." Ava looked at the purple stone glowing atop Astrid's head. "Whoever reaches the top is deemed worthy to rule. This time there were two crystals."

"Umis wanted you both to rule," Ava said.

"Yes. It had never happened before," Astrid explained.

"That's amazing."

The staff cleared the plates in preparation for dessert and

the conversation switched topics, but Ava's anxiety returned and she got lost in her head, knowing the official talk was coming. Shifting in her seat, she tried to go over what she wanted to say in her mind, hoping she wouldn't stumble over her words.

"Ava?" Soren asked from across the table, startling her back to the conversation.

"I'm so sorry, I didn't hear you. What was that?"

Astrid suppressed a smile as Soren responded, "It's alright. I said that dress is stunning on you. I knew it would be perfect."

"Thank you."

"Your Highness," Corvus said. "I'm so sorry but I noticed some brutal looking scars on your back."

Ava's hand moved to her lap, and she fidgeted with her dress. "Yes," she answered. "What about them?"

"Well," he hesitated. "How did you get them? Would you be willing to tell us the story?"

Casimir tensed. "No, she will not," he said, sudden anger in his voice.

"I apologize. I meant no offense." Corvus held up his hands. "I was only curious. I should never have brought it up."

"It's alright," Ava said, as the dessert was being served. It was time. "While I won't go into detail about how I got my scars," she looked at the queens, "it leads us to an important discussion. Where do you stand in this war, Your Majesties?"

"Are you saying your scars are related to the war?" Astrid asked.

"Yes. And while we're here to honor our trade agreement, we've also come to ask for your help."

The queens watched her. "Go on," Soren said flatly.

"Our army is preparing to fight against the daemon forces. But we can't do it alone. With your strength and skills in mining and weapons, we could use your help."

"Have you discussed this with any other kingdoms yet?" Astrid asked.

"No, but we plan to approach Caelestia as well."

Soren leaned back in her chair and took a sip of wine, looking at Ava over her silver goblet. "Our kingdom has remained safe from Deidamia's forces due to our location. Why should we risk our army to help?"

"Why wouldn't you?" Ava asked, taken aback. Surely, they weren't going to refuse.

"You tell me, Your Highness," said Soren. "You came to make your case. So, make it."

Ava's confidence waned. She couldn't believe she was doing this poorly already.

"I—um." She took a deep breath. "I would think the presence of Deidamia would be enough of a reason for you to join our cause."

"It isn't," Soren said.

"What?" What the hell was she supposed to say now? She paused, thoughts churning.

As she was about to speak again, Astrid said, "We'll think on this and discuss it again tomorrow over dinner. It seems you need more time to gather your words."

"But—" Ava started.

Soren raised her hand. "Begging does not suit you, princess. Let's eat dessert and enjoy the rest of the evening."

Ava nodded, silent once more. Embarrassment churned in her stomach as she replayed the queen's words in her head. She'd made a fool of herself. She didn't plan ahead thoroughly. Wasn't prepared. She spent the rest of the evening silent as she picked at her lemon tart, barely able to stomach one bite.

AVA PACED BAREFOOT in the living room of the suite. She still wore the gown, but she'd tossed her shoes the second they returned to their living quarters. Raine disappeared into his room with Gisela, and Casimir sat on one of the armchairs with a goblet of wine, watching her wear a hole in the rug.

"I don't understand what I did wrong," she said. "I thought you all were friends with them."

"I think they're being hard on you on purpose," mused Casimir.

"Why would they do that? Is this some sort of test or something?" She walked to the fireplace, turned, and walked the other direction.

"Probably."

Ava stopped and looked at him, placing her hands on her hips. "Why would they do that?"

"I don't know." He shrugged. "But think about what you want to say tomorrow, and it'll be fine. They'll agree."

"What should I say?"

"You have to figure it out for yourself."

"What?" she said, exasperated.

"This is a learning experience for you. Practice."

She pinched the bridge of her nose as she looked at the ceiling. "I can't do this."

"Yes, you can."

She sighed and plopped on the couch, crossing her legs, baring her skin through the slit in her skirts. She leaned her head back, spread her arms along the back of the couch and closed her eyes, taking a moment to think.

After a couple of minutes, she lifted her head and looked at Casimir. He swallowed thickly when she met his gaze. As if he'd been watching her.

"I should go to sleep," she said.

He nodded but neither of them moved.

A low moan sounded from Raine's room followed by giggles and a squeal.

"Dammit. Now I'll never sleep," Ava huffed.

"Me either," grumbled Casimir. "Do you want to go for a walk?"

"Sure. Let me get out of this dress."

Ava rose from the couch and went into her room. Minutes later she emerged in a casual tunic and pants, her boots in hand, and she reclaimed her seat on the couch to put them on. Casimir was still dressed in what he wore to dinner, and it was hard not to admire how beautiful he looked in the glow of the fire.

Feminine moaning sounded from Raine's bedroom, followed by, "Yes! Right there." Then a low growl and grunt from Raine.

Ava stood and placed her hands over her ears. "Make it stop."

He laughed and pounded on Raine's door. "Quiet down, you're disturbing the princess."

"She's just jealous she isn't getting any!" Raine yelled and the moans resumed.

Her face warmed at his comment, and she rolled her eyes, attempting to hide it.

"Let's go," said Casimir.

He held out his arm for her yet again. She looped hers through it without hesitation and they walked down the torch-lit stone hallways.

"They have a beautiful garden," Casimir said. "I think you'll love it."

They wove through the castle, passing a few guards here and there who nodded as they strode by. After ten minutes, they arrived at a set of double stone doors, opening into a stairway.

"More stairs? I don't know if my legs can handle any more stairs," Ava groaned.

Casimir stopped in front of her and gestured to his back. "Hop on."

"What?"

"Come on, I'll carry you."

"Like a child getting a piggyback ride?" She laughed.

"I've never heard that term, but yes?"

"Okay..."

He knelt lower and she climbed on top of him, wrapping her arms around his neck. He grasped her thighs and pulled her higher as he ascended the stairs.

"This is ridiculous," she said with a small giggle, and he released a laugh of his own.

She almost let out a groan at the way he smelled, a comforting aroma of cedar and sage. She breathed it in, unable to control herself as she toyed with a strand of his hair. He cleared his throat but didn't stop her as they continued to climb.

"Your hair is surprisingly soft."

"I purchase only the highest quality shampoo," he said.

"Really?"

"No."

Ava scoffed. "You know, sometimes you can be funny."

"Oh? When I'm not being extra Casimir-y?"

She laughed. "Exactly."

Reaching the top, he set her down and she turned away to take in the space, astounded by the beauty. They were at the top of the mountain, with an opening in the ceiling revealing hundreds of stars in the night sky.

The area was packed with trees, shrubs and dozens of night blooming flowers. Large white blossoms were opening in the moonlight and Ava approached one and watched it in fascination. Gravel paths wove through the same trees that grew on the cliffs outside, and soft white lights glowed along the walk-ways. Each and every bloom in the garden was a bright white.

"It's a moon garden," Casimir said from beside her.

"It's beautiful."

They wove through the trees, silent save for the waterfall at the far end of the space, until they reached a balcony carved into the side of the mountain. Stark white flowers reminiscent of wisteria hung along the ceiling, framing the vast view. Ava reached the stone railing and laid her hands along it as she looked across the ocean.

Casimir stopped beside her, placing his elbows on the balcony, his arm brushing against hers. "I knew you'd like it."

They stayed silent for a while as Ava's mind drifted to the impending war.

"So, what's next after we return?" she asked.

"You continue your training and hopefully visit the Elderoak soon. Jorrar's searching our archives for any information that wasn't destroyed by your father."

Right. Ava had learned her father, the former King of Monterre, had gone mad, burning texts and firing librarians before he was killed on the battlefield, making it difficult to gather any information that might assist Ava in her task.

"And then?"

"Once you have your full powers, you'll begin learning how to use your magic as we prepare to march on Deidamia's army."

"Why aren't we doing that now?"

Casimir turned to face her. "Monterre alone doesn't have enough forces. With two kingdoms already under her control, the rest retreated long ago."

"Why?"

"I was very young when Deidamia and Andras disappeared, but rumors say Caelestia was the first to abandon the war, forcing the others to follow suit before their losses were too great. Everyone became so concerned with their respective kingdoms, they stopped working together. We need time to rekindle that."

"Will we have enough with Saxumdale's help?" Ava asked.

"Probably not. We will need to approach Caelestia."

"How big is Deidamia's army?"

"We aren't completely sure. I tasked Quinn with gathering a team to assess their forces. We must determine the numbers in the two conquered kingdoms as well."

"And once I get my powers, we still need to get the book back so I can learn how to make a portal to banish her."

"Yes."

The book. The one she'd found at her grandfather's farm months ago. It was in the daemons' clutches and until they retrieved it, they wouldn't know how to open a new portal to send Deidamia back to her realm. Another daunting endeavor in the long list of tasks they had to complete to defeat their enemies.

Someone cleared their throat behind them, and they whipped around, Casimir taking one step in front of Ava with his hand on the pommel of his sword.

Corvus.

"I'm sorry I didn't mean to startle the two of you. I hope you're enjoying our famous gardens," he said, his hands clasped behind his back.

Ava took a step forward. "Did you need something, Corvus?"

He waved his hand. "Oh no, no. I was just on my nightly walk. Enjoying the breeze of the evening. But I did want to apologize again for what I said earlier this evening. I shouldn't have brought up what's obviously a sensitive topic for you."

"Thank you," Ava said.

"Have you figured out what you want to say to the queens tomorrow?"

"You'll find out tomorrow, I suppose," she replied.

"Alright then. Have a good evening." Then he was gone.

For some reason, Corvus mentioning her scars again gave her an idea. An idea on how to get the queens to listen.

"Ava," Casimir interrupted her thoughts. "I see those wheels turning. What are you thinking?"

"I think I know what I want to say tomorrow," she answered.

"Alright," he said. "Let's hear it."

6

$\mathcal{A}$va sat at the dining table, finishing the last bite of the main course and waiting for dessert to arrive.

She wore a dress that put as many of her scars as possible on display. The deep purple fabric was cinched around her waist, the open back showing each and every scar she had from being whipped. It also had a slit on the right side where she could reveal a particularly brutal one on her thigh if she so chose.

Staff collected their plates and brought out the berry tarts moments later. Though Ava had practiced her speech in the moon garden with Casimir for hours the night before, she wasn't fond of talking in front of groups and tried to hide her dread.

Remember what you practiced last night, she encouraged herself. *You can do this.*

"Your Majesties," she began, looking directly at the queens. "I've thought over our discussion from last night. As you know, my brother sent me here to ask for your help in the war."

Soren and Astrid watched closely.

She went on, "I'm aware you may think I'm naïve. I've only

44

been in Eorhan a few months and I'm not well versed in the ways of the fae. While both my parents were fae, I'm still human. I imagine it's hard having someone like me make a case for your kingdom to risk itself in a war." She paused and took a breath.

"I wasn't here when the daemons first arrived. I didn't experience the original wars. But since the day I arrived in Eorhan, I've endured more horrors than I ever could have imagined. I spent weeks in the daemon camp surrounded by soldiers and horrific creatures. I watched a daemon soldier snap the neck of a prisoner right in front of me and laugh. That same daemon infiltrated Mosshaven a couple of months ago with a team of soldiers and serpents. They killed citizens right in front of us." She gestured between Casimir and Raine on either side of her. "They will not stop until they get what they want. The scars you've noticed are from my imprisonment in Deidamia's war camp. Where I was tortured for weeks."

The room was silent, everyone's attention on her.

"But I *survived*," she said. "This is just a taste of what they'll do. You think your kingdom is safe? We thought the same, but Deidamia has proven nowhere is safe. I don't know how to be a princess. I don't know what to do at royal balls or meetings. But what I do know is this: I would rather be the kind of royalty who dies fighting against evil, than sit back and hide in my castle while innocents are killed. I will be on the *right* side of history." She paused for a few moments. "Which side will you be on?"

That was it. Her speech was done, and her heart would not stop pounding. Casimir gave her an encouraging nod, but the Queens remained quiet, scrutinizing her.

Soren broke the silence. "You're right. You don't know the ways of the fae. And you aren't well versed in court politics."

Ava swallowed, waiting to be berated for her speech.

"It is strange to have a human practically demand our help,"

Soren continued. "Regardless of who your parents were or who your brother is."

"But we're impressed at your boldness for asking and will gladly assist Monterre in the war," said Astrid, taking over. "We are also not the kind of royalty to sit back while innocents are killed."

Ava blew out a breath, sitting back in her chair. "Thank you."

"Ava," Soren said. "We have a confession."

She gave them a confused look.

Astrid smiled warmly. "The letter your brother sent. He instructed us to be hard on you. To initially refuse. We were always going to say yes but he wanted you to rise to this challenge."

"What?"

"It was a test," Soren said. "And you passed."

Ava huffed a small laugh as she shook her head.

"We've known your brother and these two"—Astrid gestured to Raine and Casimir—"for over fifty years. We'll always be on the same side as Monterre. I'm sorry we put you through all that worry."

"It's alright," Ava admitted. "It was good practice for the more challenging kingdoms, I suppose."

"Indeed," said Astrid. "Caelestia will be almost impossible and much crueler. Anyway, our answer is yes."

Ava relaxed, tension leaving her body. She'd done it. She'd made the difficult speech and hadn't stumbled on her words once. Even though the queens would have said yes anyway, it unleashed a bit of confidence in her. Perhaps she could do this after all.

THE REST of the evening had been spent discussing plans for Saxumdale's armies. Ava listened as Casimir took charge, slipping into his role as the general as they discussed war strategy. The planning had started; something was being done. She'd learned war was often slow—not always full of battles and fighting, but meetings and strategy and seeking allies. They had a lot of work ahead of them as they endeavored to rekindle their relationships with the other kingdoms.

Exhausted and eager to be home, Ava had crashed into bed upon returning to their suite, Casimir and Raine following suit, but a sound had awoken her a few moments ago and she rolled over to glance around the dark room.

Before she had a chance to rise, something cold pressed against her neck and a voice sounded in the dark. "Don't. Move."

A stone dropped in her stomach when she recognized the voice. Corvus. And he had a dagger to her throat.

"Get up," he said. "Don't make a sound."

She did as he instructed, hands trembling as she folded back the sheets and stood in the bedroom. He moved behind her and gripped her arm, pressing the dagger harder into her flesh. The warmth of blood trickled down her neck as the edge of the blade cut her skin. Ava gasped at the stinging sensation, hoping he hadn't cut too deep.

"If you scream or struggle, my assassins in the others' rooms will slit their throats in their sleep."

Fuck.

"What do you want?" she whispered.

"Oh, I think you know, Ava dear."

Ava dear. It was what Andras, Deidamia's second in command, used to call her.

"Andras sent you?"

"Mmm. You're a smart one."

"You're bringing me back, aren't you?" she asked.

"Here's what's going to happen. You will come with me outside. There's a boat waiting to take us to Deidamia's camp. If you don't cooperate, I will not hesitate to kill your friends."

Her mind raced as she tried to figure out an escape plan. She refused to go back. Did Astrid and Soren know Corvus was working for Deidamia? Surely not. She had to warn them. Maybe he was bluffing. Maybe there was no one waiting to kill Raine and Casimir. But she couldn't risk it.

"What if someone sees us?" Ava said, trying to stall.

"I've already taken care of that. Walk," he ordered as he pushed her forward.

He removed the dagger from her throat and tightened his grip on her arm as he positioned the weapon at her lower back. "One wrong move and this dagger goes right in your side."

They entered the living space, but it was empty. Quiet. She begged for Casimir or Raine to wake and notice something was amiss, but didn't hear anything and wouldn't risk their lives by making noise.

Corvus pushed her into the hallway, turning right. No guards or soldiers were around. No one to help her. Where was everyone? She scanned the darkness for a solution, a way out.

He led her through a side door with a hidden staircase and shoved her forward. "Walk."

Perhaps she could trip him and run. But what if he stabbed her in the process? He was much stronger than she was. She needed a distraction.

Reaching ground level, they emerged through another door into a cave under the mountain with a small dock leading to the ocean. Two soldiers waited next to a boat, eagerly watching. Ava's eyes drifted to a set of chains in one of their hands and was almost overwhelmed with fear as her mind returned to the time she'd been put in shackles and thrown into a prison wagon.

She couldn't fight off three of them and the panic she was keeping at bay threatened to overwhelm her.

She scanned the area and her eyes caught on a familiar raven. Gisela's.

"Go get help. Hurry," she pleaded in her head, though she doubted it could hear her since she could only directly speak to her own animal companion, Luna.

It tilted its head and cawed, flying away. Maybe it had understood. Or maybe it recognized her and saw she was in danger. Either way, she hoped it would somehow bring assistance.

As they approached the boat, Ava squirmed, trying to get away before he got her on board. Corvus yanked her hair back and pushed the dagger harder, piercing her flesh. She gasped and stopped moving. He hadn't cut deep, but the warmth of blood seeped into her nightgown as he pushed her forward, freezing and barefooted.

Corvus shoved her onto the boat, her knees smacking the wooden floor so hard, she cried out. She pushed herself up, scrambling away, but one of the soldiers grabbed her ankle and yanked her back. She screamed and gripped the rail, her fingernails digging into the wood.

With a swift kick to the soldier behind her, she slipped from his grip and clamored over the side of the boat, landing in the icy water with a splash. She inhaled sharply, muscles tensing at the frigid temperature.

Oh, god it's so damn cold.

Once she got past the freezing shock she began to swim to the other side of the channel when a desperate idea hit her. If the raven had truly understood her, maybe another creature would. Like the mice who helped her escape Deidamia's camp. It was worth a try.

Ava screamed inside her mind, asking for help from any nearby animal who could hear.

"You imbecile!" Corvus called from shore. "Get her back!"

"Please! Please, hear me! I need help!"

Ignoring the numbness creeping in, she continued her frantic swim. A splash sounded behind her and she glanced over her shoulder to see a soldier closing in. Kicking her feet harder, she pushed herself to near exhaustion, desperate to evade his pursuit.

Reaching the other side of the channel, Ava clung to the wall, searching the water for an escape route. The soldier on the shore began to yell, pointing at the water with fear in his eyes.

His companion paused, following his wide-eyed stare, face going slack as he screamed, "Ocean drake!"

No idea what an ocean drake was, Ava remained in her spot, scanning the black water. The soldier had turned around, frantically swimming back to shore, when a giant tail covered in shiny cerulean scales, erupted from the waves and slammed into the boat, demolishing it and throwing his partner into the water.

He screamed, trying to escape, swimming past the now lifeless body floating on the surface.

"It's coming after me! Oh—" His pleas were cut off as a monstrous head erupted from below, clamping down on the soldier's arm with jagged teeth, and dragging him beneath the waves.

Had his creature heard her cries for help? Would it eat her too? Bright blue scales shimmered as the snake-like animal swam through the blood from its kill.

Hypothermia loomed as Ava's muscles started to lock up. Cold and losing feeling in her extremities, she needed to get out of the water. Now. She pushed off the wall and swam, but the ocean drake appeared below and pushed her above the surface.

It was letting her ride it.

"Oh my god, I can't believe this is happening," she muttered as she gripped a set of horns on top of its large head.

Her fingers ached, almost numb, as it swam her the short distance back to shore. She climbed off and collapsed onto the stone floor, breathless. Rolling over, she looked at the creature who was studying her with bright reptilian eyes.

"Thank you," she whispered.

It gave her a subtle nod and disappeared below the surface. It was gone.

After allowing herself a few moments to catch her breath, she climbed off the ground and looked for the door leading inside.

She glanced down at her hands, noting the pallor of her skin. The tips of her fingers were tinted blue, and she couldn't control the violent trembling. Spying the door, she padded toward it when someone grabbed her by the hair and slammed her head into a nearby stone wall.

Pain burst through her forehead as the warmth of blood trickled down her brow. She cried out and crumpled to the ground, fighting through the sudden dizziness.

"How did you call that ocean drake?" Corvus seethed.

Shit. She'd assumed he'd been killed in the attack from the creature. Scrambling to her feet, she searched for something she could use as a weapon and turned to face him.

His expression was full of rage.

She bolted for the door, but rocks erupted in front of her, blocking her path. How was she supposed to fight against someone with magic? She turned, running a different direction but Corvus used his magic yet again, this time raising the floor beneath her feet. Her hands hit the ground as she stumbled over the obstacle, scraping her palms raw.

Back on her feet, she sprinted away, but Corvus was faster and blocked her path, back handing her across the face. On the ground again, her head spun as her vision blurred, the ceiling fuzzy above her.

"Andras only said to bring you in alive," he snarled. "He didn't say you had to be conscious."

She groaned, clutching her face as she searched for anything to help. He lunged for her, but she rolled at the last second and snatched a sharp rock that had broken loose from Corvus' magic.

As she was about to rise, he landed on top of her, hands on her throat. Ava raised her arm, like Quinn had taught her, and slashed with perfect aim despite her still shaking hands.

Blood gushed from Corvus' throat, the sticky liquid warm against her cold skin, painting her nightgown red. She screamed as he clutched his throat and leaned back. Ava scrambled out from beneath him, still clutching the makeshift weapon. He gurgled and gasped, trying to form words. She rose and backed away, unable to tear her eyes from the gruesome scene. With a few more wet breaths, he collapsed face first, twitching before he stilled.

He was dead.

7

She killed someone. Oh god, she actually killed a person. Not an animal, not a monster, but a living breathing person. And not just anyone, but the steward to the queens of another kingdom. What had she done?

And the way he died, the gurgles and gasps; the blood pouring from his throat. Just like Eleanor. Her best friend who had died in almost the same way.

Her fingers ached as her grip tightened on the rock, barely able to feel the sharp edges cutting into her palm. Her trembling increased, hypothermia and the rush of adrenaline coursing through her veins. She couldn't move. Couldn't do anything but gape in shock at the body on the ground, blood dripping along the cracks of the stone floor like a macabre painting.

Barefoot in her nightgown, she stood frozen to her spot.

Shouts sounded and the door burst open, boots echoing in the cave as people ran to the scene. Multiple voices floated around her, but Ava could hardly make them out. And she couldn't look away from Corvus.

Casimir appeared before her and gripped her face.

53

"Ava," he said. "Ava, look at me."

"Oh, fuck is that Corvus?" Raine's voice sounded behind Casimir.

"Come on. Eyes on me," Casimir tried again.

Her eyes flicked to his. Panic was written on his face as he took her in.

"Are you hurt? What happened?"

"I—he…I don't—I k-killed him," she barely got out through the chattering of her teeth. She was so cold.

"Okay. Everything's alright. You're safe now," he said. "Your lips are blue. We need to get you warm." His voice was gentle as he stroked her cheek and pushed her hair behind her shoulder. He reached down and pried open her hand. "Give me the rock, princess." She let go and he tossed it to the ground. "I need to take your wet clothing off. Right now."

His statement barely registered but she nodded, unable to control her violent shivering.

"Everyone close your eyes," Casimir demanded, then turned to Pax who was inspecting the scene. "Give me your cloak. *Now*."

Pax did as he said, and Casimir draped the cloak over his arm as he eased the nightgown over Ava's head. She was wearing nothing underneath, but his eyes didn't wander, staying on her face the entire time. He threw the cloak around her and pulled it tight.

"Handle this, Raine," he ordered as he scooped her up.

"On it."

He gripped her as he climbed the stairs, whispering she was safe, he was here. That he wouldn't let anyone harm her. She nuzzled into his warmth and closed her eyes, gripping the cloak.

"I'm c-c-cold," she whispered.

"I know. Hang on. We're almost there."

They made it to the suite and Casimir set her on the couch

before rushing into his bedroom and returning with several blankets. He pulled the couch as close to the fireplace as possible and removed his shirt before sitting down. Reaching for Ava, he unwrapped the cloak, but kept his eyes away from her nudity as he pulled her into his lap before wrapping them both in several blankets.

He pushed her hair out of her face. "I'm sorry but you need body heat. It's the fastest way to get you warm." She didn't care. Barely even noticed her nudity as she nestled into the crook of his neck, still trembling. He was so warm. She inhaled and sighed into his soft skin.

"Where are you injured?"

Her muscles were so tense her whole body ached as she tried to remember. "I think...he stabbed me. I don't think it's deep...and my head? I think. He—he hit me."

Casimir tensed, gripping her tighter. "He hit you?"

"Yes," she whispered. "Slammed my head in-into the wall."

He cleared his throat. "Okay. We'll get your injuries addressed once you're warm," he said, attempting to hide the obvious fury in his voice.

"I—the blood. I have to wash it off. So much blood. Oh, god I killed him..." The words came spilling out. "They were going to kill you. I couldn't—the chains. The blood. I called for help. Then—then it came. It helped me. I did what Quinn taught me." She tilted her head to look at him. "I did it. I slit his throat...Oh...oh no. I killed him..."

"Shhh...you did well, princess," he murmured as he laid her head back down on his chest, pulling her closer. "You did exactly what you were supposed to do. You're still in shock. Let's get you warm and then you can tell me what happened."

The door opened and Zeph walked in, stopping in front of them. "Raine's handling everything. Meeting with the queens now." She looked at Ava. "Is she okay?"

"She will be," Casimir said.

"General," Zeph said tentatively. "The queens are upset. We need to know what happened. They're saying killing a member of their court is an act of war."

"Tell them a member of their court attacking our royalty is an act of war," he snarled back.

She held her hands up. "Understood," she said as she turned and walked toward the door.

"Find me some hot tea," he called after her.

"On it."

Ava had stopped shaking, leaning into Casimir's warmth. Feeling was returning to her fingers and toes and her body temperature was rising. She inhaled his scent again and closed her eyes while his hand tenderly stroked her hair.

They remained silent for a long time before Zeph returned with a tray, setting it down on the table in front of the couch, poured a cup and handed it to Casimir.

"Raine's on his way up," she informed. "I'm sorry but they need answers."

Casimir nodded and Zeph left again.

"Drink this," he said softly as he held the teacup for her.

Ava lifted her head, and he tilted the warm liquid into her mouth. Her shock had worn off and she was finally warm. But she didn't want to move from Casimir's lap. Didn't want this to end. The tender caresses and sweet words. She always felt safe with him. Even when they argued, even when they'd first met. Somehow, deep down, she knew he wouldn't hurt her. And safety was what she needed since the day she'd stepped foot in Eorhan.

Raine walked in and sat in a chair across from them, worry in his eyes.

"Ava. We need to know what happened."

"When she's ready," Casimir said.

"Cas..." Raine began.

"I'm ready." Ava sat up, remaining in Casimir's lap.

He pulled the blankets tighter around her. She took a deep breath and told them everything.

"Wait...hold on," said Raine. "You called an ocean drake? And it didn't eat you?"

She had moved from Casimir's lap and was leaning against the arm of the couch, wrapped in blankets and clutching the tea in her hands. Her legs were draped over his and his hand rested on her shin, thumb moving in slow circles as she spoke.

"No. It carried me to shore."

"How?" asked Raine.

"I think Ava has extra abilities with animals," said Casimir. "You've seen how all our companions responded to her. Remember how friendly Aro was when they first met?"

"Right. And when I was at Deidamia's camp, there were these mice that seemed to understand me too. They led me to a cave where I hid out the first night. You all can't do that?"

"No," said Raine, crossing an ankle over his knee. "We can only communicate directly with our companion. Sometimes certain animals are calm around us, but no one can summon random wildlife like that."

"How did you find me?" Ava asked them.

"Actually, it was Gisela," said Raine. "She said her raven told her something was wrong and to head to that specific dock. She came and woke us."

"I saw the raven. He was there."

"Incredible." Raine rose from his seat. "Alright, I'm going to smooth things over with Astrid and Soren. Once they learn Corvus was working for Andras this whole time, our alliance will be fine."

Raine left the suite and Casimir turned to her. "Let's get you cleaned up and I'll treat your injuries."

She rose and kept the blanket wrapped around herself, following him into her bedroom and adjoining bathroom. He ran the bath, checking the water temperature and pouring in a floral scented oil. Once the tub was filled, he turned toward her.

"I'll be right here in your room if you need anything," he said and left.

Dropping the blankets, she was about to step into the deep stone tub when she caught a glimpse of herself in the mirror. Dried blood caked the hair above her forehead where Corvus had smashed her head into the wall. She had a black eye, already starting to swell, and a split lip. Corvus' blood coated her shoulders and had splattered her arms and legs. Bruises were already forming on various parts of her body, her knees were scraped, and everything hurt.

She turned away and climbed into the tub, sinking below the water as she tried not to replay the events of the last couple of hours in her mind. But as she scrubbed her battered arms, the dam broke and she released her tears with a sob.

8

———

*C*asimir was on his feet in an instant when he heard Ava start crying. He wanted to respect her privacy, knowing she would feel vulnerable unclothed and bruised. Fuck privacy. He refused to let her sit there by herself and sob.

When he entered the bathroom, he found her sitting in the tub with her head in her hands, shoulders shaking as she wept. He knew exactly what was going through her mind. The first time he had to take a life, he threw up for half an hour and cried until he fell asleep. War was a terrible, terrible thing. And it had barely even begun.

He fought against his fury at the thought of Ava being put through this. Of this beautiful woman having to face more death, more trauma. It wouldn't end with tonight; it was only the beginning, and he would do everything in his power to ensure she was ready.

But what he wanted to do was keep her tucked away from anyone who wished her harm. Wanted to hold her. Protect her. Kiss her.

He knelt next to the tub and brushed the hair from her face. She looked at him and the way her green eyes filled with tears, split his heart in two. If only he could resurrect Corvus to kill him all over again. Ever so slowly.

He grabbed the washcloth floating on the water, lathered it with soap, and washed her back while she cried. Her fair skin was already peppered with bruises. Bruises on top of the brutal scars left by the daemon queen. It took every effort to contain his rage as he ran the cloth across her shoulders.

"Shh," he whispered as he scrubbed the blood off her arms. "I have you."

But she didn't stop crying. He reached into the water and lifted her ankle, washing the length of her leg. Then, the other. He cleaned her stomach and chest, careful not to touch her with his bare hands, and moved to her neck and face, wiping away the blood as she sniffled.

"Lean back," he whispered.

She did as he said, lowering herself into the water to wet her hair, and rose again. He poured shampoo into his hands and lathered her hair, scrubbing thoroughly as she closed her eyes, still crying. She leaned back again, and he rinsed it.

Casimir stood and handed her the washcloth. "Can you do the rest?"

She nodded and he turned to grab a towel while she finished. When she was done, she rose and he dried her off before wrapping her in the towel and leading her to the bedroom. "Let's get these injuries fixed."

He dug through the wardrobe and found a nightdress. Dropping the towel, Ava raised her arms and he lowered the dress over her, keeping his gaze away from her body. With the gentlest touch, he took her hand and led her to the bed, propping her up with pillows.

"I'm going to get the medical kit. I'll be right back."

Raine was sitting in the living room when he entered.

"How is she?" he asked.

Casimir looked at him. "How were you the first time you killed someone?"

"Not good," he said with understanding.

"Is everything taken care of with Soren and Astrid?"

"Yes. We're still leaving tomorrow and they're sticking with their agreement to help. They're devastated. They never imagined Corvus would have done anything like this. He was right there under their noses this whole time."

"It doesn't bode well for the rest of this war," Casimir admitted. "There could be spies anywhere."

Ava had stopped crying by the time he returned, now staring at the wall, numb and exhausted. He spent the next twenty minutes dabbing balm on her bruises and stitching the cut on her forehead. Thanks to the numbing agent their head healer, Kai, had packed, Ava hardly winced as he threaded the needle through her split skin.

"I need to see the stab wound," he said.

"Okay." She rolled to her side, and he lifted her dress.

It was deeper than he'd realized but at least it had stopped bleeding.

"This needs stitches too," he said.

She nodded and he applied the numbing agent and stitched the wound closed.

After seeing to her injuries, he slid into bed next to her, nestling into the blankets and pulling her close. She laid her head on his bare chest and draped her arm across him. He tightened his grip and ran his fingers through her hair. This was perfect. She was...perfect. The way she fit flawlessly into his arms, the scent of her lavender shampoo, the contented sigh she released as she nuzzled closer.

He knew this was probably crossing the line. It was much too soon, but the moment he got word something had happened to her, he didn't even think it through. The only thing he could focus on was getting to her as fast as possible. And when he saw her standing there, wet, trembling and covered in blood, his very soul ached. Like his heart was being torn from his chest.

He pulled her a little tighter, continuing to run his fingers through her hair, humming quietly. Within minutes, her breathing evened out and she was asleep.

"I'll always protect you," he whispered quietly so she wouldn't hear.

9

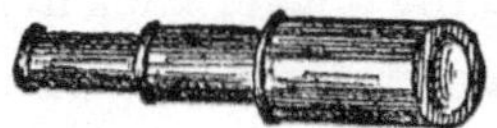

*A*va whirled, avoiding Zeph's advance with a dagger, but she didn't get behind her in time and Zeph used her leg to sweep Ava's feet from under her and had her on the ground in seconds.

"Dammit," Ava muttered as she pushed herself up to try again.

Boots sounded on the wooden planks of the ship as Casimir approached. "Maybe it's time for a break."

"No." Ava looked at Zeph. "Let's go again."

They'd been back at sea three days now and so far, there had been no signs of the daemon army. After the close call with Corvus, Ava was determined to improve her dagger skills and had insisted Zeph teach her more techniques. And maybe she was working out her anger and trauma on the mat.

Though she was terrified of the Elderoak journey, she was ready to get past it, to be free from this task hanging over her. Ready to have the increased speed and agility that would come along with being fae. She was fed up with being in this weaker human body where she couldn't defend herself against these stronger opponents. It made her too vulnerable; too weak.

Zeph lunged at Ava again and she whirled around, quicker this time, positioning herself behind her. She had her arm around Zeph's waist and a dagger at her throat, but knew Zeph had slowed her speed. She'd never be able to fight off someone who was actually trying.

"Good," Zeph said. "Now you need a break."

Casimir had claimed a spot against a pole, arms crossed as he watched.

"Fine." Ava placed the dagger back in her belt and stretched her arms above her head, heading to Casimir.

"How are you?" he asked.

Ever since Corvus had tried to kidnap her, he'd been especially observant. Cautious. Always checking on her. But they'd both pulled apart emotionally. Since he took care of her, bathed her, and let her sleep in his arms. There had been no more subtle touches or flirting and he was back to the gruff exterior as he monitored her training.

What she wouldn't give to be in his arms again. To burrow into his scent until she fell asleep. And she had a vague memory of him saying something about always protecting her, but she'd been half asleep. Surely it had been a dream.

She shoved the thought away as she stopped before him.

"I'm fine," she said.

He raised a brow as if he didn't believe her. "Let's head to dinner."

They walked toward the dining space and sat down at the small table. Pax and Raine were already seated, laughing with the other sailors mid meal.

A bowl of hearty stew was passed to Ava and she took a bite, starving after her intense workout. Though the cook on the ship was good, they didn't have the variety she was accustomed to in Monterre, limited to what they could store and keep fresh on the water. Tired of eating the same thing day after day, she was ready to be back home.

"Thank you for helping me," she said to Zeph, as she plopped down next to her.

Ava missed training with Quinn like she had back in Monterre and craved connection with another woman on the ship. Zeph obliged and had been helpful these last couple of days. She wasn't constantly asking Ava if she was alright, wasn't hovering like Casimir was, and she needed that.

"Absolutely." Zeph smiled, her purple eyes bright in the dim dining space.

"I can show you more moves later," Pax chimed in. "Show you how to flip someone over the way I did to you."

Ava laughed. "That hurt, by the way." She took a sip of wine before continuing. "But I need the practice. After dinner?"

"Yes!" Raine shouted as Ava flipped Pax on his back for the third time.

They had drawn a small crowd around the mats as he taught her more hand to hand combat moves. Even though he was massive, he'd shown her a technique to take down almost anyone, no matter their size. She had to duck low, get the angle right, and use momentum. It was basic physics and once she got it down, she was able to flip him almost every time.

A few others had joined, letting her practice on them, and she managed to take them down as well. She reached out to help Pax up and he gave her a huge grin.

"Great job. But now, we all need to go to bed," he said.

She agreed as the crowd dispersed, and crew members put away the mats. Ava strolled to the bow of the boat and leaned over the rail to watch the ocean. She closed her eyes, inhaling the salty air, and listened to the waves crashing against the hull. They'd be home in a few days.

She let out a deep sigh and opened her eyes to Casimir standing next to her.

"You've got to stop sneaking up on me like that," she chastised, calming her racing heart.

"Sorry. I just wanted to see if you were doing alright."

"You've been asking me that a lot the last several days."

"Well...I remember how it felt the first time I took a life. I didn't handle it well and I want to make sure you're okay."

She turned away and looked back over the horizon, the reflection of the moon rippling on the water. "Honestly? I'm not great. I thought throwing myself into training harder would help."

"Has it?"

"A little. But I can't stop picturing him dying in front of me." She shook her head. "It keeps reminding me of—" Eleanor. But she couldn't bring herself to say it out loud.

"Of what?"

"Nothing. Never mind. How'd you get over your first kill?"

"It's not something you get over. You must remember you did it out of necessity. Self-defense. It wasn't calculated. It wasn't in cold blood. You had no choice."

"I know. But that doesn't make it any easier."

"No, it doesn't." He turned to her and she met his gaze. "But the harsh truth of this is, it won't be the first person you kill, Ava. This is war. When it comes down to it, it's kill or be killed. You must figure out how to reconcile that."

"How?"

"I can't tell you that. It's different for everyone. But if you don't figure it out, it will eat you alive. And the first step is talking about the things you've been through."

She knew he was referring to what happened before she met them. Her torture and other traumas. But she still wasn't ready.

"Oh." She tilted her head. "Like you talk about your past?"

His face fell and he turned back to the ocean. "Point taken."

But Ava knew she was right. He kept pushing her to talk about her traumas and yet she knew he was struggling with his own. Why he'd initially been so cold toward her when she arrived in their world. And he obviously didn't talk about it either.

They remained silent a while longer before she spoke again. "Thank you..." she whispered.

"For?"

"For what you did that night. When Corvus...you know." She fidgeted with her braid. "Thank you for taking care of me."

They both kept their eyes forward, but Casimir reached over and took her hand, interlacing their fingers.

They remained there, holding hands, Casimir's thumb brushing the top of hers. She wanted to stay there forever. Just the two of them. No war. No fighting. Only peace and comfort.

His presence steadied her as she watched the ocean, taking in the reflection of the stars, like thousands of crystals dancing along the sea. She knew she had to focus on her preparations for the Elderoak journey. It was foolish to get distracted by the man with golden eyes who was always watching her. The man who was supposed to be her teacher. But in this moment, she didn't care. She'd let herself enjoy it and get back to business when they returned.

Her eyes continued to take in the magnificence of the ocean, her heart at peace.

"It's beautiful," she whispered.

Casimir hummed beside her, leaned in, and said into her ear, "Absolutely breathtaking."

She cleared her throat and almost turned to look at him when her eyes caught on something strange on the water. Dark areas where there was no reflection; no moonlight or stars.

She squinted, trying to look closer. Shapes on the water.

"What is that?" she whispered.

"Where?"

She pointed. "There. Do you see?"

Casimir scanned the horizon, his eyesight much sharper than hers. He tensed beside her and his grip tightened on her hand.

"What is it?" she asked again.

"Ships."

10

The emergency bell rang as a sailor shouted from the crow's nest, "Enemy ships ahead!"

Fear dug its claws into Ava's gut. They had found them. In the middle of the ocean. How did they even have ships? They must have taken them from one of their conquered kingdoms. She turned around to face Casimir, eyes wide.

"Get down below."

"Please don't make me hide," she pleaded. "I have to fight. I don't want to be helpless anymore."

He ran a hand through his hair, warring emotions on his face.

"If I'm hiding below deck, I'm a sitting duck. They already know I'm here. If any of them get wind of me hiding, I won't be able to fight my way out. I'll be cornered."

A long pause, then he relented. "You're right. Go get your armor on. Hurry. I'll be right behind you."

She sprinted across the deck to their sleeping quarters, darting in between crew members. The ship was a flurry of activity, Gisela shouting orders as they prepared for battle.

She threw open the door and dug through the wardrobe for her leathers. Raine burst in as she was securing the belt.

"Do you need help?" he asked, already dressed and armed.

"Make sure I did it right."

She couldn't get her heart to slow down as Raine adjusted the straps. He yanked on the armor, ensuring its fit.

"It's okay to be scared," he said, putting his hands on her shoulders. "Channel your fear into anger. Be angry they tried to take you. Protect your kingdom."

She nodded.

"You'll be with me and the other archers since that's your best skill. Listen to my instructions. Focus on what you're good at, which is not daggers. No offense."

"I know. Thanks."

As he released her, Casimir barged in and swiftly donned his own armor. After dressing, he marched over to her and grasped her face. His golden eyes were filled with worry and determination. "Please be careful."

"You too." Her throat was tight, her pulse racing.

He turned and left the room.

The deck was organized chaos. Orders were being given, soldiers and sailors splitting into teams. Raine led the way to the starboard side, the captain having turned the ship to allow more room for the archers.

There was no outrunning them; they had to stay and stand their ground.

"Stay next to me," Raine said.

She took a shuddering breath, squinting through the dark and using the moonlight to aid her vision. The ships had drawn closer, and bile rose in her throat as she counted four.

"Raine," she whispered. "How are we supposed to fight four ships?"

"With everything we've got," he said with false confidence.

"Can't you make giant vines and sink them?"

He looked down at her and grimaced. "Now probably isn't the best time to tell you we can't use our magic at sea."

"What?"

"It's earth magic, dainty human. We must be on land since we draw from the earth. It's the same with Saxumdale."

"So no one can use their magic?" she asked, panicking. Deidamia and Andras had magic. Did any of the daemon soldiers? She couldn't remember. Either way, this would not be an evenly matched fight.

"We've got a few hybrids on board who can," he said.

"Hybrids?"

"Has no one taught you this yet? Dammit." He shook his head. "Hybrids are fae who have parents from more than one kingdom. They usually inherit both types of magic. Gisela's one. Her mother was from the ice kingdom so she can wield ice on the ship."

"Okay." She turned back to the approaching enemies. "Okay. It'll be fine."

"It will," he replied, though she knew he was as nervous as she was.

Rowboats were lowered into the ocean with a splash, each one filled with daemon soldiers. They were close enough now Ava could make out their individual shapes on the water.

Her first real battle. There was the attack at the pub a couple of months ago, but she had zero training then and had spent most of the fight helping the injured. Until she'd found Raine's sister cornered by a soldier and stabbed him in the shoulder. That soldier had grabbed Ava and almost taken her back to Andras, but Raine killed him with an arrow through the throat.

And now she was about to do the same thing. This wasn't practice and these weren't straw targets. They were living, breathing soldiers who she had to kill with her bow.

Ava closed her eyes, steeling herself. She could do this.

Protect your kingdom, she told herself. *Defend your friends.*

Raine shouted orders. "Archers, ready your bows! Pick a target but do not release until I give the signal!"

Ava had never seen him in his role as captain. Had never been around when he was leading a group of soldiers. His humor was replaced by aggression, determination.

He turned to a small group of crew members without bows. "If you have usable magic, stand in between the archers and aim it at their rowboats. Take out as many as possible." Addressing the whole group again, he finished, "We must prevent them from boarding our ship or we'll be overrun. Don't let them board!"

Raine rejoined Ava. "Get ready."

She retrieved an arrow from the quiver on her back, squinting into the darkness until she found the shape of a soldier.

"A couple more minutes and they'll be close enough to shoot," he said.

"Alright. Where's Casimir?"

"He's in charge of the soldiers who'll be fighting in close contact if they end up boarding. Plus, he has a couple of the stronger hybrids with him on the upper deck to focus on the larger ships."

She nodded, not taking her eyes off her target.

"He'll be okay," Raine whispered. "Don't get distracted worrying about him."

"I know."

Ava reviewed the steps in her head to keep calm. Draw, aim, release. Grab another arrow. Nock it in place. Find your next target. Repeat. Draw, aim, release. New arrow. Nock it. Target. Again and again, she repeated it.

"Archers draw!" Raine called.

Ava drew her bow along with the group. She focused on the

daemon soldier she had set in her sights and took a deep breath.

"Release!"

She let go. The fletching brushed her cheek as it speared toward her target, piercing his neck. He toppled into the water along with dozens of other soldiers.

"Find your next target!" Raine shouted beside her, reloading his own bow.

Ava pulled back, aiming at another daemon in the same boat.

"Release!"

She released again, this time hitting him in the eye. They repeated the process, taking down as many enemies as possible while magic shot across the water. Ice burst from the extended hands of a crew member beside her, freezing a rowboat. Another directed a ball of starlight—likely astral magic—at the frozen boat and it shattered along with everyone on board.

The two of them alternated, ice and starlight, as they took down boat after boat. They were making headway as Ava focused on the enemies who weren't being destroyed by magic. The daemons rowed with vigor, but the team of archers kept them at bay.

She kept going, breathing in a bit of relief that no one had boarded the ship. She could do this. Focused and determined, her aim was perfect.

As her confidence soared, a crew member shouted from the crow's nest, "Incoming!"

"Ava," Raine barked. "Look up. New targets. Shoot them down."

Her eyes moved to the sky and her heart leaped in her throat when massive shapes appeared in the night, headed straight for their ship. Two dozen winged creatures. She glanced down to the sea to find dozens more rowboats drawing closer, as if they'd appeared out of thin air.

The first group was a test of their defenses, but now they were unleashing their entire force. They didn't have enough archers. They'd be overrun.

"Archers! Shoot down the monsters! Magic wielders, keep focusing on the boats!"

Ava aimed at the sky and released an arrow at one of the creatures. A blood curdling scream erupted from its wide mouth as a hole was torn through its wing, but it clumsily flew on, trying to reach their ship. She aimed for the other wing, her arrow tearing a bigger hole, and the being plummeted to the water with a splash.

One down. Many more to go.

Ava continued, ignoring her panic and following Raine's instructions. The monsters would be here in seconds, and they'd only managed to take down a few. Once they reached the deck, they'd be so focused on fighting these creatures, the daemon soldiers would board. Probably what they'd planned all along.

"Raine!" she shouted over the noise of beating wings and shouts of soldiers. "There aren't enough of us!"

"Keep bringing them down," he ordered.

She followed his instructions, but the flying beasts were much more difficult targets, avoiding her arrows as they neared the deck. A massive shape swooped low, and Ava ducked just in time. It grabbed the sailor beside her, talons piercing his shoulders, and rose higher before releasing him. His body smashed into the deck with a crunch.

Raine turned to her, wide-eyed as another creature dove. He shoved her to the ground, protecting her with his body, and gutted it with his sword.

"We need to move." He grabbed her arm. "Fall back!" he shouted to the archers. "Get to the center of the ship and take down the beasts!"

They sprinted to the middle of the deck where Casimir and

a group of soldiers had their swords drawn. Ice blasted through the air from Gisela, but the monsters dodged it with ease.

One of the winged abominations landed with a thunderous boom, the ship vibrating beneath Ava's feet. Moonlight illuminated the menacing creature as it stood on two legs, long arms ending in sharp claws, its bat-like wings spread wide. Black skin hung from its frame and a wicked grin revealed jagged teeth. Over eight feet tall, it took a step forward and swiped at a nearby soldier, gutting him in seconds.

Ava loosed an arrow, piercing its shoulder, but it only served to anger the monster. It crept closer and swiped again but the group ducked. Raine took off, shouting for Ava to follow, as Casimir snuck behind it.

Another landed with a shudder, pulling Ava's attention away, as three crew members lunged for it and took it down with their swords, while Raine shot an arrow into its eye.

Ava glanced back to where Casimir had been, but he was now running in another direction, the first monster a pile of ash on the deck. She swore he was glowing, but there was no time to think about that as daemon soldiers climbed over the edge of the ship.

They were being boarded.

Ava rushed to the railing and looked over the water. The ocean was overrun with rowboats. There had to be nearly fifty. She aimed her bow at the soldiers climbing up the side and took them down as fast as possible. Raine appeared beside her to help, and they felled as many enemies as they could.

It still wasn't enough.

More daemons clamored on board. Shouts and screams surrounded them as swords clanged behind her. They were fighting for their lives now. Would they even make it? Ava looked around, ignoring the fear working its way through her as she tried to think of some way to help. They couldn't die now. Couldn't fail at the first large battle.

There must be something they could do.

A plan formed in her mind. It was risky. Stupid, even. But if it worked, it could ensure their victory. She had to try.

"I have an idea!" she yelled at Raine.

"What?"

"You're going to hate it, but I need to get in the water."

"Fuck no! You can't go down there."

She grabbed his arm and yanked, making him look at her. "The last time I called an ocean drake I was in the water!"

"Are you crazy?"

"We need to take those boats and ships out! I have to try!"

He ran his fingers through his hair. "Alright. But I'm coming with you."

"You need to stay here and fight," she said.

"Absolutely not. If you were fae I would, but you're still human. I'm not leaving you alone."

"Fine," she relented. "How do we get down there?"

"Follow me."

He sprinted to the opposite side of the ship, free from the enemy soldiers, Ava following. They reached the railing and Raine unrolled a rope ladder. "Don't make me regret this."

11

asimir dashed across the deck after burning the winged creature with starlight. There were still eight monsters left and they were taking down his men left and right, almost impossible to kill without magic.

"General!" Gisela shouted from the starboard side of the ship, where more daemon soldiers were pouring over the rail. Half their archers were dead thanks to those winged creatures, and they were no longer able to keep the enemy forces at bay.

He rushed over and his eyes followed her finger pointing to the ocean. More rowboats. There had to be at least two hundred daemon soldiers headed their way.

They were fucked.

"Can your starlight make it that far?" she asked.

"I don't know."

He was a formidable opponent in combat, one of the best, and his magic reserves were deep, but astral magic required significant energy and concentration. And it was draining him quickly.

"I'll try," he said.

They had to take out those boats. He raised his arms and

focused all his energy, imagining it erupting from his fingertips. Nausea wormed its way into his gut and he ignored how it felt as heat erupted through him. He loathed using this magic, a reminder of deep wounds from so long ago, but there was no time to balk as he focused on the task at hand.

Aiming at the group of rowboats, a ball of bright white light formed and he released it. Two of the boats burst into flames as the starlight hit them, the screaming soldiers jumping into the water. But there were dozens more, and as he prepared to send another below the waves, the sound of wing beats behind him turned him from his task.

The creature landed with force, causing the deck to quake. How many men did they have left?

It lunged and he dodged it with a roll to the side. Gisela shot a small spear of ice toward it, her reserves almost gone, but it was enough to distract it.

Casimir threw himself on the ground, grabbing its ankle and focused the last of his magic into the monster. His skin glowed, his muscles on fire as he forced the starlight into its flesh. Within seconds it was a pile of ash.

On his hands and knees, he gasped for air, trying not to pass out. He was almost drained. He knew the cost of using too much magic too fast. It wouldn't kill him, but fae who drained themselves too far became weak, vulnerable, often needing to sleep for days to recover. Though he could summon more, it would leave him defenseless, without the energy to even fight with his sword.

Gisela knelt before him.

"No more," he muttered.

"Me either." She looked at him, defeat written on her face. "General. I don't think we're going to make it."

"Then we die fighting," he said as he forced himself to stand, swaying on his feet. "We don't die cowards."

She helped steady him as the next wave of soldiers made it

over the side of their ship. Casimir drew his sword and threw himself back into the fray.

Ducking and parrying, he felled soldier after soldier. A daemon rushed him and he whirled, beheading him in seconds as another threw a dagger. He rolled, narrowly avoiding it, as Zeph appeared and speared the soldier from behind with her sword. Two more daemons attacked and Zeph threw her own dagger at one, finding purchase in his neck, before she disappeared back into the chaos.

As the soldier crumpled to the ground, the other lunged at Casimir. Barely able to block the blow aimed for his neck, their swords locked in an 'x' as he growled inches from the daemon's face. Freeing his blade and knocking the enemy's from his hand, he ducked and rolled, landing on his back. The daemon withdrew a dagger and pounced, landing on top of him. But Casimir was quicker and had his own dagger ready. He shoved it into the belly of the soldier and pushed the body off him.

Panting, he crawled to his feet and tried to gather his wits before the next group attacked. But there was no time as an enemy soldier appeared on his left. He whirled to block him but wasn't quick enough. A sharp pain exploded in his side and he let out a surprised yell as he lost hold of his sword. Crumpling to his knees in agony, he looked down to see a daemon sword protruding from his abdomen below his rib cage.

"Where is the princess?" The soldier stood before him.

Relief swept through him. They didn't have her, thank The Mother.

"Fuck you," he rasped, looking at his opponent.

The soldier unsheathed a dagger and grabbed Casimir's shoulder with one hand while he prepared to finish him off. He angled his blade, ready to slit Casimir's throat when a sword sliced through the air and the daemon's head rolled to the ground, his body collapsing.

Pax knelt before him. "You have a sword in your side," he joked, attempting to hide the fear in his eyes.

"Pull it out," Casimir grunted.

"I don't think that's a good idea."

"Do it. I can't heal if it's still in there. That's an order."

"Fine," Pax replied. "Ready?"

Casimir nodded and Pax gripped his shoulder with one hand as he pulled the sword straight out with the other. Casimir cried out and pressed his hands on the gushing wound. The agony almost overwhelmed him as he remained kneeling, begging himself not to pass out.

He could heal from this with time, but it would be almost impossible while he was still fighting. And if he got any other major injuries, it could kill him.

"Another group of rowboats is approaching, general," Pax informed him.

"How many men are we down?"

"I don't have an exact count. But too many."

Casimir leaned his back against the side of the ship and tried to breathe through the pain, staunching the blood flow the best he could.

Hope was a curious thing. One moment it was there, bright and shiny, reassuring you through the darkest of times. The next moment, it was slipping away and laughing that you even dared to grasp it in the first place. And now, it was gone.

And where was Ava? Worry gnawed deep within, not having seen her in a while. He would never forgive himself if she was harmed or recaptured. Though he trusted Raine to keep her safe, *he* wanted to be the one to do so. He should be there to protect her.

Shouting interrupted his thoughts and alarm worked its way in as he turned to look at Pax, bracing himself for the worst. But they weren't screams of fear, they were shouts of joy. Cheers. His soldiers were celebrating.

"What's going on?"

"I don't know," Pax said as he scanned the ocean. His eyes widened and a slow smile spread across his face. "Unbelievable."

"Help me up," said Casimir.

Pax pulled him to stand and put Casimir's arm around his shoulder, propping him against his side.

Casimir's eyes skimmed the sea. Why was everyone cheering? He continued to search when he saw it. Well, he saw *them*. Three ocean drakes were winding their way through the boats, smashing them with their blue spiked tails.

He shook his head in disbelief. "How?"

"There." Pax pointed at a fourth ocean drake, much bigger than the others.

Two figures were riding it as it swam toward the larger ships, shooting arrows at daemon soldiers as they passed.

Ava and Raine.

The remainder of their forces whooped and hollered as they prepared for the next wave of soldiers. The ocean drakes made quick work of the rowboats, smashing them and pulling the remaining soldiers under. Daemon blood painted the water black as the creatures ripped apart the enemy forces.

His heart soared as he watched Ava ride the monstrous being, fearless as it used its spiked tail to break the hulls of the big ships. Once the rowboats were destroyed, the other three drakes joined it in finishing off the large vessels. The last few daemon soldiers who'd made it on the deck were cut down and all the flying monsters were dead.

Pax was laughing with relief. "I can't believe it," he kept saying as he shook his head.

But Casimir could. He knew what Ava was capable of when she pushed past her fears. Unable to take his eyes off her beautiful face, he watched as his princess led the creatures that saved them.

12

*R*ough fibers dug into Ava's palms as she climbed the rope ladder, not yet able to celebrate the victory. Not until she knew Casimir was alright. With each step of her booted feet, her heart beat louder in her ears.

Please be okay, she urged.

She was still in disbelief that she'd summoned those creatures again and rode on one, finishing the battle and ensuring their victory. Would animals come to her aid any time she called, or was it only in the direst circumstances?

"Ava," Raine called out from below.

"Yes?"

"Prepare yourself," he said, voice serious. "Though we may have won, I'm sure plenty of our men still died. I don't know what we'll find up there."

"Okay." Dread washed over her. "Can I ask you a question?"

"Sure."

"Am I going crazy, or did I see Casimir glowing earlier?"

Raine cleared his throat. "Umm...I don't think he'll want to talk about that."

"What? I'm not crazy?"

"Well, I didn't say *that*."

"I'd punch you right now if I could reach you."

"I know."

"Well?" Ava asked, hoping for more detail.

"All I'm going to say is Cas doesn't talk about it. It reminds him too much of Elara."

"Who's Elara?"

"This conversation ends now. If you want to know details, ask Cas. Though I suggest you don't. He doesn't handle that topic well."

"Okay, fine."

Elara? Glowing? Did Casimir have other magic too? Was he a hybrid? Questions swirled about in her head as she realized she knew nothing about him. He'd never spoken of his past and other than Raine's brief explanation about him being orphaned in the war and raised by Raine's father, he was a closed book.

Was Elara a family member? Or maybe an ex? At the thought of him being with anyone else, a wave of jealousy appeared, which was absurd. Of course he hadn't been celibate. She'd been with others too. But for some reason the thought of anyone else flirting with him, or feeling the warmth of his body, made her suddenly insecure.

They reached the top and a familiar large hand appeared over the rail. With a huge sigh of relief, she grasped it and let him pull her to the deck. Casimir and Pax stood before her, the latter with a huge grin on his face. Dozens of sailors cheered behind them.

"Princess! Princess! Princess!"

She scanned the group and gave them a smile as Gisela interrupted the celebration.

"Alright, you bastards. Time to get to work and clean this ship up!" She looked at Ava and winked as if she knew how much she disliked being the center of attention.

She turned back to Casimir, who was looking at her with

awe, but something was wrong. Bags under his eyes contrasted the pallor of his skin and he didn't appear to be able to stand, leaning on Pax for support. Her eyes trailed down his body and caught on his hand pressed into his side, drenched in blood.

She rushed forward. "You're hurt. What happened? What do we do?"

"I'll be fine," he said, voice rough and weaker than usual.

Ava looked at Pax for confirmation. "He's right. He'll be as good as new. We just need to get him to one of the healers."

Two out of the three healers they'd brought had survived and were already bustling about as dozens of injured lay moaning on straw mats.

Ava pretended to be unbothered, doing her best to hide the worry on her face, but inside she was terrified. He was hurt. Significantly. As much as Casimir himself and Pax tried to downplay it, it looked horrific.

"Okay, then," she said with a shaky breath. "Let's lie him down."

Raine was already giving the crew instructions while Pax walked Casimir to an open mat a few yards away. He grunted in pain as Pax lowered him.

"I'm going to go see who else needs help," Pax told her.

Ava sat next to Casimir on the floor, crossing her legs.

His hand slipped from the wound and blood seeped out. Jumping to her knees, she leaned over and placed her palms on it, applying as much pressure as she could manage. Casimir groaned as she pressed harder into his side.

"You promise you won't die from this?"

He let out a small laugh and winced. "I promise."

Pax's voice boomed across the deck. "We need a healer for the general!"

"Be right there," someone called out.

"What happened?" she asked, blood oozing between her fingers.

"There were too many of them and I was stabbed with a sword," he said. "Not a very exciting story. I'd rather hear about your adventure in the ocean."

"When I realized we were being overrun, I remembered how I had called that creature a few nights ago. I didn't even know if it would work but we went down there and tried it anyway."

"And it worked."

"Yes. Yes, it did."

"That was risky," he said, his voice gravelly. "Did Raine even try to stop you?"

"He did. But I got in his face and made him listen."

He looked at her for a long time, searching her face. "You're amazing."

She gave him a small smile as a healer arrived.

"You can let go, Your Highness." The man knelt beside Casimir and opened a small apothecary bag.

She removed her hands and moved to his other side as the healer placed his own hands upon the wound. It was deep; almost all the way through his back. The healer pressed hard and chanted softly.

"Fuck," Casimir said, closing his eyes.

Ava grabbed his hand and squeezed. "Breathe through it," she murmured as she reached out and brushed a strand of hair from his face. He tightened his grip and hissed through gritted teeth. She had the sudden urge to hold him, to take care of him. Like he had for her. "I'm here," she added, stroking the top of his hand.

The healer released his magic and ripped open Casimir's tunic. Ava tried not to gasp at the brutal wound revealing layers of muscle and fat.

"I need to stitch you up, general," said the healer. "I can find some numbing balm to help with the pain."

"No," Casimir barked. "Hurry and do it. Save it for the other injured."

"Oh, come on," Ava chastised. "Don't be so stubborn. That's deep and it's going to hurt."

"No numbing balm," he said, irritated. "Do it. Now."

The healer began to work, cleaning the injury before he prepared the sutures. Within minutes he was stitching each layer of the wound. Casimir's eyes remained closed, his jaw clenched so hard surely his teeth would shatter. She stayed by his side in silent comfort as he went into a meditative state to focus through the pain.

"Is he doing his whole 'I don't need numbing balm, every wound is a reminder to be better next time' bit?" Raine's voice cut through the noise as he stood before them.

"Is that what this is about?" Ava asked as she looked at Raine.

"Oh, yeah. Cas is the king of self-inflicted punishment. He thinks it makes him stronger or some bullshit."

Casimir opened his eyes and glowered at his friend. "Fuck off."

Raine raised his hands in defeat, looking at Ava. "Let's leave him to his martyrdom or whatever."

"Go with him," Casimir said hoarsely. "I'm fine."

"Are you sure?"

"Yes. Go. I don't want you to see me like this."

"Fine." She let go of his hand and rose, glancing back at him one last time. His eyes were closed again as the healer finished his stitches. She looked at Raine. "Do you need help with something?"

They walked along the deck and Raine pulled her aside. "This next part is going to be hard," he said with compassion.

"What next part?" she whispered.

"You're the princess. You represent all of Monterre on this

ship. If Thorne were here, he'd be doing the same thing I'm about to have you do."

"Okay. What are we doing?"

"Making the rounds. Visiting the injured and being a steady presence as we assess the casualties. There will be some of our soldiers who are still alive but won't make it. They need comfort."

"And I need to be the one to comfort them?"

"Yes. It means a lot when royalty and leaders provide that. You can grieve, but you can't fall apart in front of everyone. Hold it together now and fall apart later. Casimir would be out here doing the same thing if he wasn't injured. And knowing him, he'll probably be up and about sooner than he should be to do exactly this."

She swallowed. "Alright."

Raine led her back to the wounded, starting with those who were under the care of the healers; the ones who would survive. She reminded herself of how her mother used to be a steady presence in the face of stress and channeled that serenity, shoving down her trepidation as she visited with the patients. Once Raine saw she was in the throes of it, he left her to do the same at the other end of the ship.

The ship was full of pained moans and whimpers, murmurs of healers and the uninjured helping the best they could. Ava knelt beside a soldier whose leg was being stitched, when the woman next to her asked for water. She retrieved it, helping her sit up to drink, before returning to comfort the soldier in pain.

She spent hours tending to the wounded and providing reassuring words, sitting with them as a distraction while their injuries were treated. Several asked to hear the story of how she called the ocean drakes resulting in their victory, and she obliged, describing how it felt to ride on such a fierce creature.

So much blood and gore. So much pain and suffering. It nearly overwhelmed her, but she shoved the horrors of war and her fear of what was to come away. Locked it in her box and focused on being present.

How much could that box hold before it became too heavy a burden? Before it burst and overtook her?

The sun was high in the sky by the time she reached an area of the deck where about a dozen soldiers lay. Pax was standing watch and when he saw her approach, his face fell.

"What?" she said.

He leaned in, whispering in her ear, "These are the injured who won't make it. The healers aren't here helping because there's nothing they can do."

A lump formed in her throat as she scanned the small group, when her eyes caught on a familiar face. Zeph.

No.

A blanket covered her torso, hiding the fatal injuries. Ava forced herself not to collapse in shock as she approached her guard and knelt, brushing a strand of blue hair out of Zeph's face with a trembling hand. She opened her eyes and gave Ava the faintest smile, her breaths coming in slow, short bursts.

"Princess," she rasped.

"Shhh," Ava said as she took her hand.

She glanced at Pax who knelt on Zeph's other side, trying to hide the devastation on his face. He was about to lose his partner, his friend who he'd been stationed with for decades.

"I don't think she has much longer," he whispered as a tear rolled down his cheek.

"Princess..." Zeph said. "Don't forget...what...I taught you..."

Ava squeezed her hand. "I won't."

"Promise?"

"I promise."

Her heart broke as she stayed seated on the ground, fighting against the tears threatening to spill down her face.

Zeph took a shuddering breath. "Will you stay...until the end?"

"We will," Ava said, her voice taught.

She held Zeph's hand while Pax stroked her face, humming a mournful fae song. Ava picked up the tune and hummed along, their voices intertwined in a forlorn melody. It wasn't long before Zeph took her last breath, right as the song ended. As if she'd been waiting to hear it before fading away.

Once she was gone, Pax recited their prayer, his deep voice cracking. "May the Earth Mother hold you and keep you. May you never know pain and sorrow. And may you bask in the sunlight of the afterlife for eternity."

Ava allowed her tears to fall but remained calm, remembering Raine's words. *Hold it together now and fall apart later.* And she couldn't lose it now, because Pax was falling apart across from her. The giant orc warrior let out a sob as he kissed Zeph's head and closed her eyes. His shoulders shook with silent tears as he bowed his head and didn't leave.

"I'll miss you, dear friend," he whispered through his tears.

Ava bit her lip and blew out a breath as another dying soldier called out to her, then another.

"Will you hold my hand, Your Highness?"

"Will you stay with me?"

Ava rose, gave Pax a squeeze on the shoulder, and went to the next soldier. She spent hours sitting with the dying warriors, comforting them in their last moments. At some point she saw Casimir doing the same thing, despite him barely being able to walk, but she was too numb to acknowledge him. Lost in a fog of grief.

They all wanted solace as they moved on to the afterlife; wanted someone to hold their hand, to sing to them. Ava committed Pax's prayer to memory and recited it to every man and woman who passed. She'd had a sense of camaraderie with these sailors and even though she hadn't known them long, the last couple of weeks on the ship had brought her close to the crew.

Zeph was gone.

She wished she'd gotten to know her sooner. Stationed at Ava's door since the day she arrived, they'd barely spoken other than cordial greetings until this trip. The cook from the ship's kitchen was gone. So were several other sailors she had laughed and joked around with at dinner. Ones who had cheered her on as she fought Pax in the ring. Sailors who treated her like a friend instead of royalty.

By the time the day was over and night had fallen, Ava found a quiet place away from everyone on the back of the ship. Hiding behind a stack of crates, she slumped to the ground and let herself lose control as she put her head in her hands and cried.

Exhausted and numb, she wept for her friends, for the future of their kingdom, and for what was to come. How many more people would they lose? Ava had already lost so much. Most of her family, her only friend back home. And now that she'd found her place, she feared she may lose even more.

She didn't know how long she cried, but at some point Raine appeared and sat beside her, silent. He reached over and held her hand and she laid her head on his shoulder as she let the tears continue to fall.

Raine cleared his throat, trying to hide his own tears as he laid his head atop hers in silent support. The two of them sat together under the night sky, and grieved until they had no tears left.

13

"Good," said Quinn as the dagger Ava flung hit the edge of the target at the other end of the training ring.

"I'm nowhere close to hitting the center," Ava lamented.

"At least you're hitting the target now."

A week after they'd arrived back in Mosshaven and she was still struggling with daggers, despite Zeph's attempts to help on the ship. Ava much preferred the ease of the sword or bow and arrow.

Ava sighed. "Yeah, I guess."

Quinn crossed her arms. Her long black hair swished in its intricate braid as she scrutinized Ava. "What's up with you today?"

Ava shook out her arms. "Sorry. I haven't been sleeping well recently. I'm fine."

Quinn strode to the target, retrieving Ava's dagger.

What she didn't tell Quinn was that over the last week, she'd begun to have nightmares. The trauma she'd experienced at the hands of the daemons was starting to make itself known, cracks in her carefully constructed box threatening to reveal her grief and fear that she still scrambled to shove away.

Quinn turned around, mischief in her upturned brown eyes. Before Ava could prepare herself, Quinn had her in a hold with a dagger to her throat faster than seemed possible. Though a couple of inches shorter than Ava's tall frame, Quinn was much stronger and quicker. Plus, she was fae and Ava was still human.

"Shit," Ava muttered.

"You weren't prepared. That's what happens when you're tired and lose focus." Quinn tightened her grip on Ava's arm and pulled the practice dagger tighter to her throat. "Now get out of this hold. And don't hold back this time. Hurt me."

Ava shoved down the memory of Corvus in this same position, and used her free hand to yank down on Quinn's forearm. It took all her strength, and it was obvious Quinn allowed it. She ducked under Quinn's arm and twisted it against her back pressing hard until her grip loosened on the dagger. Ava plucked the dagger from Quinn's hand and pointed it at her as she kept hold of her arm.

"Good," said Quinn.

Quinn swept a leg back, catching Ava's own and yanking it forward, landing her on her back. The dagger fell to the ground and she wheezed as the air was knocked from her lungs.

"But not good enough," Quinn said, standing above her. "Once you get out of the hold, you need to get that dagger and back away as quickly as possible before your enemy can get a hold of you again."

Ava nodded, unable to speak as she continued to gasp for air. After a few moments, she crawled off the ground and stood. "I'm not fast enough as a human."

"I know, but you must do better than whatever *that* was. You think anything you might face on the journey will care that you don't have your fae abilities yet?"

"No."

"Okay then. You need to be faster."

"How?"

"Stop overthinking everything," Quinn said as she flung a dagger at Ava.

It hit her in the thigh and bounced off. They were using dull wooden practice daggers, but it would still leave a gruesome bruise.

"Dammit," Ava said as she rubbed her leg. "Casimir was right. You're the mean one."

Quinn grinned. "That's why I'm second in command. Now stop complaining. If that dagger was real, you'd be bleeding out right now. You're off your game today. Take five minutes for water and we're going again."

Ava slumped to the ground against the low stone wall which cordoned off the training area. Quinn was harsh but Ava appreciated it and enjoyed the connection with another woman, hoping their friendship would grow and she'd continue to connect with Raine's sister, Fanya, as well.

She took a swig from the water skin and observed the soldiers practicing in the other rings spread across the training field. Pax was squaring off with someone Ava didn't recognize, obviously working off his grief if the determination in his eyes was any indicator. They lunged at each other and parried with their swords, the peal of metal ringing as their weapons met.

"I'll never move that fast," Ava said to herself as she watched the orc.

"Sure you will, dainty human."

Ava turned to find Raine standing outside the wall, smiling down at her.

"Time's up," said Quinn. "On your feet."

Ava took one last drink of water and rose.

"Are you alright?" whispered Raine.

"I'm fine," she lied. "Just tired."

He narrowed his eyes as if he didn't believe her.

"Well, show me what you got," he said.

"Oh no you don't," barked Quinn. "Since you're interrupting, get your ass in here and help, pretty boy."

"Fine." Raine hopped over the stone wall with ease, stopping in the center of the ring. "How can I be of service?" He gave a sarcastic bow.

Quinn glanced at Ava, still standing on the edge of the ring. "Stay there."

She whirled to face Raine and flung a dagger at him much faster than she'd ever thrown one at Ava.

"Fuck," Raine yelped as he dodged the projectile.

Quinn had four more daggers in her hand and released them in quick succession, forcing Raine to pay attention as he evaded each throw. After avoiding the five blades, Raine shook his head and glared at Quinn.

"You could have warned me."

Quinn rolled her eyes and looked at Ava.

"You want me to do *that*?" Ava asked.

"Yep," said Quinn. "Get over here."

14

*A*va awoke with a start, drenched in sweat and gasping for air. She frantically glanced around her bedroom, heart beating out of her chest and hands trembling. It was still dark. Still the middle of the night.

Her cat companion, Luna, was alert on the bed, watching her with concern.

You're safe, Ava. It was a dream, Luna's voice sounded in her head.

"I dreamed I was at Deidamia's camp being tortured again. Then about Corvus and the ship attack," she whispered as she wiped her tears and sat up.

I know. But you're safe here. And the general is in the next room.

Luna climbed into her lap. Ava took a deep breath and caressed her soft white fur sprinkled with swirls of black.

"What time is it?"

Dawn is still several hours away.

It would be impossible to fall back asleep after that horrific nightmare. They'd been back in Mosshaven for two weeks now and though Ava tried to ignore her trauma, it seemed it was starting to make itself known as her nightmares escalated. Was this the beginning of her falling apart? There was no time for that.

Climbing out of bed, she wrapped herself in the plush warmth of her robe, as if she could protect herself from the lingering fears of her dream; the memories hovering at her mind's edge with every waking thought. Even sleep wasn't an escape any longer.

She entered the living room she shared with Casimir, embers still glowing and popping in the fireplace, and retrieved a book, settling herself in a plush brown chair beside the hearth. She pulled a blanket into her lap and opened the cover. It was a romance novel.

After an hour of reading the same chapter repeatedly, she set the book in her lap and allowed herself a bit of release. Unable to shake off the sensations of being whipped, the tears fell, tracing paths of sorrow along her cheeks. The scars on her back stung with the memories, the screams leaving her lips echoing in her mind. She couldn't stop the deaths from replaying in her head. Her best friend, Eleanor, being killed by Deidamia; Zeph taking her last breaths; the dead soldiers scattered about the ship.

Numb, she stared into the flames, no idea how much time had passed. It was just her and the glow of the embers, her sniffles the only sound in the quiet room, when Casimir's bedroom door opened and he emerged dressed for training.

Ava wiped her eyes and pulled the blanket higher.

Casimir froze. "What are you doing?"

"Nothing," she stammered. "I-I couldn't sleep and thought I'd read for a while."

He stepped closer. "You were crying."

"No, I wasn't. It's the shadows from the fire. They make my face look weird."

He sat down in the chair across from her and leaned forward, elbows resting on his knees. "You're a terrible liar."

Ava looked back at the fire. She could feel Casimir's intense gaze as he watched her. Whenever he looked at her like that, it felt like he could see into her soul. Like he knew exactly what was going on in her mind, though she desperately tried to hide it.

"Do you want to talk about it?" he asked.

"I need to get ready." She stood and walked to her room.

"Ava—"

"I'll see you at the obstacle course," she interrupted.

She swore she heard him sigh as her door clicked shut.

BIRDS CHIRPED overhead as Ava approached the next obstacle. The course stood in a large field surrounded by towering trees, their emerald leaves quivering as the breeze wound its way through the boughs. The sunlight was warm on her face as she evaluated her next move.

"Don't overthink it," Casimir instructed from the sidelines.

Dread crept its way in as she evaluated the obstacle before her. It was a balance beam about five feet off the ground. She had to run up a ramp to get to the top, cross the beam at two different angles, and jump to three separate platforms, each one lower as they led her back to the ground.

"Keep going," he called out.

"Shit, I'm going to fall," she mumbled to herself as she prepared to run.

"No, you won't."

Before she could change her mind, Ava sprinted up the narrow ramp.

"Good," Casimir encouraged.

Arms out beside her, she made her way across. Surprisingly, she only stumbled once and reached the end quicker than expected. Confidence boosted, she leaped, overshot the platform, and tumbled to the ground.

"Ouch," she breathed as she rubbed her hip.

Casimir appeared above her, and she rolled onto her back. "Are you alright?"

She groaned, rising to stand. "Yeah. This course is the bane of my existence."

"You get in your head too much and scare yourself. And you've been awake for who knows how long today. You're exhausted."

She sighed. "You're right."

They walked to the castle when he stepped in front of her. "What are you doing for lunch?" he asked, a sudden gleam in his eyes.

"Well, I was going to eat in my room and bathe before I met Jorrar in the library."

He smiled. A disarming smile she rarely saw, but it lit his whole face and made his gold eyes even brighter.

"Why are you smiling at me like that?" she asked.

"Because, I have an idea. It'll help you relax."

"I'm not tense."

"Well, you're tired and stressed. This will help." He led them back to their suite. "Bathe and change and meet me in the living room in half an hour."

"Wait, are we not doing swords today?"

"No. You're taking the rest of the day off."

15

asimir waited for Ava in the living room, having bathed and changed into a forest green tunic and brown pants.

He assumed she had a nightmare last night; could tell by the way she looked this morning and how she was more lost in her head today than usual. He'd been there before, having had nightmares about his own past, and knew what the trauma of war could do. And the war hadn't even begun in earnest.

He yearned to take care of her again. Like he had in Saxumdale. To hold and reassure her he would never let anyone harm her. But since they'd returned, they both fell back into their roles of trainer and trainee. And he'd pulled back because he could tell she was struggling and didn't want to cross a boundary.

Ava's door opened and he turned as she walked in. She looked stunning in a white asymmetrical dress with blue embroidery on the hem. Her long strawberry blonde waves were left unbound, and his heart skipped a beat when he looked into her bright green eyes.

She was so fucking beautiful.

"Ready?" Casimir asked, voice hoarse.

She nodded and he led them out of the suite. They made their way outside and headed to town before Ava broke the silence.

"Where are we going?"

"First, we're going to grab something to eat," he answered. "Then we're going to The Leaping Frog."

"What's that?"

He glanced down. "You'll see."

"I'll miss Jorrar's lessons if we're gone too long."

"I already let him know. We've got all afternoon."

Casimir's boots echoed on the cobblestone streets as they weaved their way through town, passing by a bookstore and potions shop built among the towering trees. Lanterns hung in the boughs where the sunlight didn't penetrate, and birds sang from their nests. Citizens passed them by, waving their greetings as they went about their daily errands. After a while, they stopped before a small restaurant with a sign labeled *Honeysuckle Teahouse*.

A bell rang as he opened the intricately carved wooden door, and they stepped inside. Ava inhaled a sharp breath as she took in the space, and he smiled to himself at her reaction.

"This is beautiful," she said.

"It's my favorite place," he replied, leading her to a table in the back.

Open windows along most of the walls allowed sunlight to illuminate the cozy eatery. Vines and flowers hung from the ceiling among hundreds of bundles of dried herbs, a comforting aroma of lavender and mint hovering in the air. Outside, a small stream wound its way through the shrubs and a group of russet-colored squirrels chased each other through the water.

They sat down as a woman with blue skin, long black hair and small horns approached to take their order.

"Hello, general," she said in an accented voice.

"Good afternoon, Sapphira." He gestured across the table. "This is Ava."

"Oh! Your Highness," she said, curtsying. "It's so lovely to meet you."

Ava gave her a smile. "Thank you. It's nice to meet you too."

"Would you like the usual, general?" Sapphira asked.

"Yes. Enough for both of us."

She walked away and Casimir turned to Ava.

"You brought me to a tea house?" she asked. "This is amazing."

He met her bright green eyes. "I know how much you love tea, so I thought it would be a nice distraction."

"How did you know I love tea?"

"I pay attention."

What he didn't say was he paid attention to everything she did; the contented sigh she always released at her first sip of tea at breakfast, or the way her nose crinkled when she was frowning at him. How she bit her lip when she was deep in thought or the way she twirled her hair around her finger when she was nervous.

She laughed. "Back home, I drank a lot of coffee. But you don't have that here, so I've been drinking tea. I do love it."

"What's coffee?"

"Well...it's a hot drink made from some type of dried bean from a tree. It's hard to explain. But it's brewed kind of like tea. You often mix it with milk or cream. I drank it every morning."

"What does it taste like?"

"Hmm...bitter, but smooth and nutty."

Sapphira returned and set down several teapots and a cup and saucer in front of each of them. "Your food should be ready shortly," she said before bustling off.

"What kinds of tea are these?" Ava asked, excitement in her voice.

"That one is cinnabark, apple and honey; this is blue blossom and seaspice; and this one is sun mint, silver flower and borage," he explained as he pointed to each one.

"Cas." Ava looked at him. "This is...this is really nice of you."

He smirked. "That's the first time you've called me that."

"What?"

"Cas."

"Oh." She tilted her head. "Is it?"

"Usually, you call me Casimir or general, or brute, or other colorful words..." Only his close friends called him Cas, but hearing it on Ava's lips did something to him. He longed for her to do it again.

She laughed. "Well don't get used to it, general."

He shook his head and smiled as he poured her a cup of tea and one for himself.

Sapphira arrived with the food and set it down before disappearing again, Casimir thanking her. The plates in front of them were covered in tomato and cucumber sandwiches, cheeses, fruits and pastries. The perfect compliments to the flavors of their teas.

"Eat." He took her plate and piled it with sandwiches.

"Bossy," she replied before she took a sip. "This is so good."

He set her plate in front of her and sipped his own tea, looking over his floral teacup at her. "You didn't eat breakfast."

"I—oh." She paused. "I guess I didn't. I was...distracted this morning."

He served himself some food. "Because of your nightmare?"

Her eyes snapped to his. "I never told you I had a nightmare."

"I used to have them too. I recognized that look on your face this morning."

Ava took a bite of a sandwich, remaining silent.

"Do you want to tell me what it was about?" he asked.

"Nope."

"Fine," he said, and changed the subject. "Do you like living in Mosshaven?"

"I've been here for I don't even know how long, and you're just now asking me this?"

"Two months and twenty days," he said.

"What?"

"That's how long it's been since you arrived in Mosshaven and met with your brother for the first time."

She narrowed her eyes and looked at him. "Okay...it's weird you remember that."

He lifted a shoulder. "I remember a lot. So, tell me how you like it here."

Her suspicion turned into a smile, genuine joy on her face. "I love it."

That smile had disarmed him the first time he saw it and he remembered the exact moment. It had been a couple of days after they found her in the woods. They were sitting around the fire and Raine had told Ava about taking her on a tour of the city. The relief and joy on her face had transformed her and though she was dirty and bruised, he'd been enchanted. It was the exact smile she was giving him now. One, he realized, he didn't often see on her face anymore.

"What?" she asked as she caught him watching her.

"Nothing. You were saying you love Mosshaven..."

She looked at him suspiciously but continued in between bites of food. "Yes. It feels like home, like I belong here."

"Of course you belong here," he said. "It's where your family's from. Even though you're still technically human, your fae nature recognizes the earth kingdom and your heritage."

"I've never really had that before. It's...well, it's wonderful."

They continued back and forth, talking about Mosshaven,

its people and the things Ava loved about it. When she was excited about something, this look of wonder came over her. Her eyes brightened and she gestured with her hands while explaining her passions. He found himself captivated as she gushed about the beauty of their kingdom and couldn't tear his eyes away for the entire meal.

16

"**W**here are we going now?" Ava asked as she walked next to Casimir.

They had spent a couple hours talking and eating while they drank their tea. She adored the teahouse and was taken aback by his excitement as he explained each tea while she tasted them.

And now, he claimed he had something else to show her, and she couldn't control her excitement and curiosity.

"You're impatient," he said. "We're almost there and you'll see."

They walked through the main road, turning onto a smaller cobblestone street winding through dozens of houses built among the trees. While some homes were at ground level, others were high among the boughs with stairs wrapping around the tree trunks leading to the front door. Lush flower gardens lined the houses on the ground and the citizens waved merrily as the two of them passed by. Children chased each other through the streets, laughing as they played their games while black and white spotted rabbits with silver eyes hopped along the road, pausing to munch on the bright green grass.

"This is beautiful," she said. "What is it?"

"It's one of the districts where citizens live. We'll be at our destination soon."

They continued through the neighborhood before stopping in front of a fenced-in piece of property with a sign that read *The Leaping Frog.*

Casimir opened the wooden gate and led Ava inside. They walked through a tunnel of yellow-leaved trees with purple blooms before the property opened, revealing a variety of enclosures, fenced in sections and large cages. It reminded her of a medieval-looking zoo.

"What is this place?" she whispered.

"It's a healing facility for animals," he answered.

She turned toward him, unable to stop the giant smile on her face and met his eyes. "Are you serious? Like a wildlife rehab? This is amazing!" She clapped her hands together. "Can I pet them? Can I feed them? Oh my gosh—"

Casimir grasped her hands and laughed. "Slow down. Let's go find the owner and he'll let you feed any animal you want."

He let go and they walked down the gravel path to a small hut built inside a giant old tree providing shade for part of the property.

"Durim!" Casimir called out.

The door opened and a short gnome with a brown beard and pointy green hat emerged and smiled as he greeted them. "Hullo, hullo! Are you here for your monthly visit, general?"

Casimir returned his smile. "It's good to see you. Actually, I brought the princess to show her around."

Durim turned to Ava and shook her hand as he bowed. "Your Highness! I'm honored to meet you."

"It's nice to meet you too."

"Well," Durim said to Casimir. "You know where everything is. Why don't you give her the tour yourself?"

"Alright."

"I have some work to do. But please, do let me know if you need anything," Durim said before wandering off.

Ava turned to Casimir. "Monthly visit?"

He rubbed the back of his neck, a subtle blush on his face. "I come once a month to volunteer."

The general volunteered at an animal rescue? All the fae in Monterre cared for animals, but she was amazed at the gruff general taking special interest in this.

"That's incredible. Okay, give me the tour. I want to see *everything*."

"Follow me."

He led her to a nearby enclosure and opened the gate. Shrubs, fallen logs and bright green grass filled the area with a small stream trickling through the space.

A large exotic feline chirped at the sight of Casimir and prowled up to them. Dark gray fur contrasted the black spots that shimmered when the sun hit its hide at the perfect angle. Its bright pink eyes evaluated Ava as she held out her hand, allowing the cat to sniff her, and a loud purr sounded in its throat as it relaxed and let her scratch behind its ears.

"This is Bale," Casimir said.

"I love him," she said as Bale plopped onto the ground and rolled around, begging for belly scratches. Ava obliged as she knelt. "So the big brute general volunteers at an animal rehab, huh?"

Casimir sat down across from her as another large cat plopped down beside him. "This is Willow." He rubbed her face. "Why is that surprising? We all care for animals here."

"Well, yes, but do the others come here to help on a regular basis?"

Casimir shrugged. "No, but they're busy. Thorne does finance this place though."

"You're the general. I'm pretty sure you're just as busy, if not busier."

"I make time."

"Why?"

"Because it's something I love," he explained. "Ever since I was a young boy, I've always found hurt animals and nursed them back to health."

Ava studied him, unable to look away at the kindness which always surprised her whenever he showed it. She didn't know why it was surprising; he was never cruel or mean, just calm and quiet most of the time. But underneath the gruff exterior, he was generous. Like the time he let her sleep in his tent even though he had just met her, or the fact that he noticed she struggled to eat when she was stressed. And the way he took care of her after she was attacked in Saxumdale.

"I used to do that too," she said quietly. "With my mother."

They sat in silence for a while, petting the two cats who were on cloud nine from the attention.

"So, the general loves tea houses and helping injured animals...What other things does the general like?" she asked.

"I like to read. You were actually reading my favorite book this morning."

"Seriously? That was a romance novel."

"Brutes can't like romance novels?"

Ava laughed. "You're a hopeless romantic, huh?"

He gave her his usual half smile. "Perhaps."

They remained quiet for a moment, unable to break eye contact when Bale got a burst of energy and pawed at Ava. He rose and head butted her so hard, she fell back onto the grass. The massive cat licked her face with enthusiasm, seemingly ready to play.

"Oh!" Ava exclaimed as she tried to push him out of her face.

Casimir let out a laugh as he reached over and pulled Bale

off. He stood and grasped Ava's hand to help her up. "He gets like that sometimes," he said, still laughing. "He likes you."

She laughed along with him as she wiped the drool from her face. "Then he's a good judge of character, I guess."

"Indeed," Casimir replied as he watched her. He cleared his throat and looked away. "Let's keep going. There are dozens more animals."

As they exited the enclosure and walked along the dirt path, Ava asked, "So why are the animals here and what happens to them? Do they get released?"

"Various reasons. Bale and Willow were orphaned and unable to live on their own. They'll have to stay here. Others have an injury or illness and once they can fend for themselves, they're released."

She couldn't stop smiling as they walked into the next cage. She was in heaven with all these animals, something she didn't realize she needed until today. A day to be Ava. Not the princess or the savior of Eorhan, training to defeat their enemies, but herself. The animal obsessed wildlife nerd she was back in the human world.

They stepped into the tree covered space and a strange creature flew toward them, landing at her feet.

"What kind of animal is this?" she asked.

It was the size of a large dog and covered in blue feathers. It had a black curved beak, a long feathered tail twitching like a cat, and four legs ending in taloned feet. Its bright blue eyes regarded her as it tilted its head and tucked in its wings.

"It's a finstrel," answered Casimir. "And his name is Eldar."

Eldar made a sound reminiscent of a growl and a bird call combined. Ava held her hand out, attempting to soothe him.

"Careful...finstrels can be dangerous. His beak and talons are sharp," he cautioned.

"He won't hurt me," she insisted as she stepped closer.

"Ava..."

She knelt, face to face with the sharp beak. "Hello, there. I'm a friend." She kept her hand extended.

Eldar approached with caution. His posture relaxed and feathers fluffed with delight as he nuzzled her hand, small happy chirps sounding in the back of his throat.

"How did you do that?" Casimir whispered.

"Do what?"

"Calm him." He looked down at her with wonder on his face. "He's attacked every single volunteer here at least once. Including me."

"I don't know," she answered as she continued to stroke Eldar's face and scratched under his chin. "I've always been able to do it."

"Like with the ocean drakes..." he trailed off.

"I guess so."

Casimir walked closer to Ava and Eldar tilted his head toward him. The animal made a strange sound, stepping in between them, as if trying to protect her.

"Whoa," Casimir said. "It's me. Remember me?"

Eldar narrowed his eyes and glanced back at Ava. She let out a giggle. "That big ol' brute isn't going to hurt you, silly boy," she said as she petted the top of his head. "He's quite sweet underneath all the grunting and frowning."

She chanced a glance at Casimir who was looking at her with a furrowed brow. "I don't grunt and frown *that* much."

She stood and turned toward him, crossing her arms and imitating his frown. "You're literally frowning right now, general."

He raised a brow. "Is that supposed to be me?"

Ava couldn't keep a straight face and broke into a smile. "Yes."

He lowered his voice to a velvety growl. "You didn't do it right, princess."

Ava cleared her throat. That voice. That was all it would

take for her to melt into a puddle right there. There was a tinge of humor in his eyes. As if he knew what he was doing to her.

She broke his stare, ignoring the warmth coursing through her body, and turned back to the finstrel who was nudging her thigh and begging for more affection.

They spent a while longer with Eldar before exploring the rest of the property. There were dozens more animals. Small birds, shiny snakelike creatures, glowing foxes and other small mammals. Casimir explained most of them were getting ready to be released and Ava was sad to see them go, while overjoyed at the purpose of this place.

They approached the final enclosure, a large aviary filled with small purple-leaved trees. White bell-shaped flowers grew among the grass and swayed in the breeze while bees visited each bloom to collect their pollen.

Durim was standing in front of the door. "Would you two like to help me release these three firefinches?"

Ava bounced on her toes. "Yes! I want to help. Oh, I'm so excited!"

Casimir chuckled as they followed Durim inside the enclosure. "You don't even know what a firefinch is, princess."

"I don't even care," she said. "It could be a giant worm and I'd want to help."

Upon entering, three creatures the size of a large songbird flew toward them and soared over their heads, releasing high pitched cries as they landed on a nearby branch. Raven black scales covered their four-legged bodies and each foot ended in small claws. Tall rabbit-like ears twitched and they regarded the group with giant turquoise eyes. Their pink and green leathery wings were iridescent in the sunlight, while antennae on their heads ended in bio-luminescent tips.

Ava put her hands up to her face. "They're beautiful!"

"I will give you each a piece of their food and they'll land on your hand. We can walk them outside to release them," Durim explained as he opened a jar filled with squirming worm-like insects.

The three of them held the worms flat in their palm and the firefinches shrieked and dove for them. The darkest and largest one landed on Ava's forearm and devoured its treat as Ava followed Durim outside a door at the back of the enclosure.

"Once they finish their worm, they should fly off whenever they're ready," he explained.

"Do they have names?" Ava asked.

"The one on the general's arm is Nymeria, the one on mine is Kirro, and yours is Titus."

"Hello, Titus," she whispered. Titus looked at her and chirped as he swallowed the last of his worm. "You are such a handsome boy."

Ava knew Casimir was watching her as she petted the firefinch who was cooing at her. She looked over at Casimir and Durim, whose creatures had already left.

"You can go now," she said to Titus. "It's safe."

But he wouldn't leave and crawled along her arm, chattering to her. He sneezed and a small burst of flames erupted from his mouth.

"Are you alright?" Casimir asked. "Did he burn you?"

"No." She marveled at the creature. "I'm fine. They breathe fire?"

"Yes," Durim said as he watched Titus curiously. "He doesn't seem to want to leave."

Ava spoke to Titus again. "You need to be free, little one." He climbed her arm and settled on her shoulder, nestling into her hair, and chirped. Somehow, she understood what he was saying.

Ava turned to Casimir and Durim. "Uhhh...he said he wants to stay with me."

Durim started. "You can understand him?"

"Yes. It seems so."

"Impossible," Casimir whispered.

She looked up at him. "What do you mean? You can't do that?"

"Not like that." He shook his head. "Some fae are better at communicating with animals than others but we can only actually speak to our companions. Could you hear him speaking in your head like with Luna?"

"No," she said. "I just somehow knew what he was saying."

Casimir observed her with wonder.

"What?"

"I've never heard of anyone being able to do that before," he said. "After the ocean drakes several weeks ago and now this... you definitely have extra abilities with animals."

"You're very special, Your Highness," said Durim. "If Titus doesn't want to leave, he can go with you."

Ava's head snapped to Durim. "What? Like a pet?"

"Kind of. But you must make it his choice," he explained. "I can supply you with all the worms you need, but he can hunt for the majority of his food."

She held out her hand and spoke to Titus. "Come here." He flew off her shoulder and landed on her arm, tilting his head as he looked at her. "You really want to stay with me?" He spun around and chirped. Ava turned back to Durim. "Are you sure it's okay?"

"Absolutely."

"Okay, you can stay."

Titus screeched with joy as he flew into the air and released a small burst of flames before landing back on Ava's shoulder and settling into her hair.

"He's excited," Casimir whispered as he watched the whole interaction.

"Of course he is," said Ava. "He has good taste, like Bale."

I hope you don't expect me to babysit, said Luna, startling her.

"*Can you hear my thoughts all the time?*"

Mostly. If that creature annoys me, he will make a tasty snack.

"Luna! You can't eat him!"

"What?" Casimir looked at her.

"Luna said she'd eat Titus if he annoys her," Ava replied. "I didn't know the animals basically eavesdropped on us."

"Oh yes. They can be quite intrusive when they choose to be."

"Does Aro do that to you?"

"All the damn time."

They said their goodbyes and headed back to the castle, Titus riding on Ava's shoulder.

"This was the best day of my life," she said, breaking the silence as they walked back through the neighborhood, the afternoon sun now high in the sky.

"Really?"

"Yes," she said with a huge sigh. "I don't think I've ever felt so happy. At least not in a long time. Thank you."

"If I knew all it would take to see that side of you was a bunch of animals, I would do it every day."

"What side of me?"

"The free side," he said. "The giddy one. The side of you that truly lets go because you're in your element. Where your smile isn't haunted by the grief in your eyes."

She glanced at him as they continued along the road, framed by shops and restaurants. "Well, maybe I need to go there more often."

"You can come with me whenever I go for my monthly visits."

"I can? That would be wonderful. I can be with the animals. And help them. And apparently, they like me so that would be a help to Durim—what?" She caught him looking at her in amusement.

"I like it when you do that," he said.

"Do what?"

"Get excited and ramble."

"Why?"

"It pleases me," he said, eyes burning.

Her heart skipped a beat. "Well...I'm glad I could please you, general," she said, voice hoarse.

17

Casimir sat at the round council table, maps of Eorhan spread out before them with figures to mark Deidamia's forces. He observed the argument ensuing between his king and one of his advisors, Desmond. Thorne was tapping his fingers together in his usual tell, his temper on a tight leash, while Desmond pushed to move on Deidamia's army sooner rather than later.

"Remind me why he's still on the council," Raine whispered beside him.

"He may be brash," Casimir whispered back, "but he's loyal and one of the few who was around during the first wars. We need his insight."

Raine grumbled under his breath, taking a sip of tea.

A breeze from the wide balcony wove through the space, blowing the vines hanging along the ceiling. A wooden chandelier made of tree branches held candles to light the space and the walls were decorated with tapestries in their kingdom's colors of green and gold.

"I insist we march on the daemon queen within the next month," Desmond said, his face red with irritation stark against his short white hair. His animal companion, a cerulean blue snake, slithered around his neck as he spoke. "We must take her by surprise."

"That's asking for half our forces to be wiped out," Thorne replied. "We need more allies first."

"Besides," Quinn interjected from across the table. "Until Ava has her magical abilities to banish Deidamia, we'd be losing men for no reason. Unless you've forgotten the daemon queen cannot be killed."

Desmond whipped his head to Quinn. "Don't presume what I have and have not forgotten. I've been around far longer than you, captain."

"Enough," barked Thorne. He brushed his long scarlet hair behind his shoulder. "I am not my father, Desmond. We will take the time needed to plan accordingly to ensure our success."

"You're right. You're not your father. He wouldn't have hesitated to immediately face this threat."

Thorne narrowed his eyes. "And that's what got him killed. I won't risk my people because you want to go barreling in without a plan."

"Do we have an exact number of their forces?" Vivienne, one of the other advisors, asked. Her dark blue eyes flickered with irritation at Desmond. Her own animal companion, a large red fox, sat dozing in the corner of the room.

"While they were in Saxumdale—"

"Getting attacked by daemons," Desmond interrupted Quinn, glancing at Casimir and Raine.

Casimir bristled at his tone but held his tongue, knowing it would stress out Thorne further should more arguments erupt. But he didn't appreciate the accusatory stare from Desmond, as if it had been Casimir's fault they were attacked.

Quinn ignored him and continued, "I was able to get the

numbers of their main camp. They have about a thousand soldiers, and hundreds of creatures."

"We have three thousand once we combine our forces with Saxumdale," Desmond said.

"I'm not finished," Quinn said. "That's not accounting for the thousands of daemons residing in Frosthaven and Igneothenia. Though we haven't been able to get an exact count, we estimate it's closer to five."

"If we can garner help from Caelestia," Vivienne said, "we'd get closer to that number."

"And no one has heard anything about where those who fled Igneothenia may be hiding?" Thorne asked.

Jorrar shook his head, his ebony skin warm against the morning light. "After their kingdom was taken over, they disappeared. No one knows where they are. I'll send Percy to look again. And see if he can gather any information from the other creatures."

"Please do. We need whatever forces they may have left."

Jorrar turned to his owl, seated on the back of his chair. After a brief silent conversation, Percy ruffled his gray and black feathers and took off with a hoot, disappearing into the trees.

"Your Majesty," Vivienne spoke. "I'd like to request we increase patrols in some of the outlying towns."

Thorne looked at Vivienne. "You have a sister living in Oakshire, correct?"

"Yes. With my nieces. Those towns aren't protected by our mountain range and are much more vulnerable."

Thorne looked at Casimir and raised a brow.

"I'll see if we can spare some soldiers to send out to those towns," Casimir said.

Vivienne nodded her thanks.

"Anything else?" Thorne asked, scanning the room.

"We've increased weapon production, thanks to the ore we

received from Saxumdale. They're doing the same. Right now we focus on keeping our kingdom safe, watching their movements and finishing our plan to retrieve that book from their camp," Casimir said.

"And Ava?"

"She's improving daily. If she pushes past her fears, she will complete the journey. I'm sure of it." Casimir turned to Jorrar. "Have you found any information about it yet?"

"Only that it's an annual occurrence. However, I can't determine when exactly. The text I found is mostly burned."

That demented king sure made things difficult for us, Aro, Casimir's animal companion, said.

"Yes, he did."

"How has she been since everything that happened in Saxumdale?" Thorne asked, concern on his face.

"She's fine," Casimir said.

You just lied to your king.

"I don't want him to worry about his sister."

But you're worried about her.

"And I'll handle it."

Thorne seemed to accept his answer and moved on, bringing their discussion back to the war preparations.

CASIMIR WALKED the halls of the castle, free of the arguing that barely accomplished anything. Desmond had relented, agreeing it was impulsive to make any moves before they bolstered their forces. He ensured he would oversee the weapons production, promising to keep it organized and efficient. Though old and cantankerous, Desmond flourished when he was given a task and Casimir knew he'd take this one seriously.

Vivienne had offered to help Jorrar search the archives for

more information on the Elderoak. Everything felt as though it was at a standstill until Ava became fae and they could retrieve the book from the daemon camp which would teach her how to use her portal magic.

Stepping outside, he found Ava alone in a training ring, flinging daggers at a target. Her aim had improved but he could tell she was still struggling with her technique.

"You're letting go too soon," Casimir said as he stopped next to the low stone wall.

Ava gasped and fumbled with the dagger in her hand. "You're always sneaking up on me."

"Sorry," he said with a laugh. "Are you ready?"

Her shoulders slumped. "The obstacle course…"

"Yes, but let's try something different first. I think it will help."

"Okay."

He led them away from the training field, but paused when they saw Aro asleep under a tree with Luna snuggled in his fur.

"Uh…" Ava said. "When did they start doing that?"

Casimir chuckled. "I just noticed this morning."

They walked toward the animals and stopped before them, Luna's feline snores blending with the whispering breeze. Sensing their presence, Luna opened an eye. When she noticed Casimir, she climbed off Aro and padded toward him, winding in between his legs and chirping. Titus appeared from his perch in the trees and gave a friendly snarl as he flew down and landed on Ava's shoulder.

I like that cat, Aro said.

"Well, it seems she likes you too."

You know why.

"I'm aware," Casimir replied.

But you won't tell Ava because you're scared.

"Since when did you become well-versed in the ways of fae relationships?"

Since the day you found her in the woods and couldn't stop obsessing over her, Aro responded.

"Stupid bear," Casimir muttered out loud.

Aro released a chuff resembling laughter as he ambled off.

"Having a fight with Aro or something?" Ava gave him a suspicious look.

"Or something." He grinned at her as he leaned over and lifted Luna, cradling her on her back. She licked his face.

Ava was astonished. "I've never seen Luna let anyone pick her up."

"She just likes me better."

"What do you think you're doing, Luna?"

Ava tilted her head as she listened to Luna's reply, her face blushing as she met eyes with Casimir, and looked away. He held back a smile at her discomfort.

Luna jumped from his arms, running in the direction Aro had gone.

"What did Luna say?" Casimir asked as they walked toward the woods.

"She said you need a bath."

"Uh huh."

They followed a dirt path weaving through the trees and he glanced at her again, noticing the weariness on her face.

"You look exhausted," he said.

Her brow knitted. "That's not something women want to hear."

"Oh?"

"Women want to hear things like 'you look beautiful,' not 'you look tired.'"

"You always look beautiful," he said, matter of factly.

She did. Every moment of every day. Whether she was wearing a fancy gown or covered in sweat and dirt, she took his breath away. Her stunning green eyes, the luscious curves of her body, the dusting of freckles across the bridge of her nose. He wanted to count them and kiss each one.

"I—" she looked at him, but he was staring ahead as they walked, keeping his expression unreadable. "Oh."

They made their way through a group of trees opening into a small clearing with a miniature obstacle course in the center. Several low balance beams, stepping stones and small pillars were interspersed throughout the grass.

"This looks like a children's playground," Ava said.

"It is."

"Okay..."

"You rely too much on sight. You need to learn what your body feels like as you make it through the course. It's about muscle memory."

"How are we going to do that here?" She looked around the clearing again.

He pulled a piece of fabric from his pocket. "The only way to get better at using your other senses is to remove the one you rely on the most."

"Is that a blindfold?"

He nodded. "Because I know you're going to ask," he said before she had a chance to say anything else. "I promise I won't let you trip and land on anything perilous."

"Does this mean you expect me to do the other obstacle course blindfolded?"

"No. I just want you to practice here and pay attention to your other senses."

Ava bit her lip. Fuck, he loved it when she did that.

"Fine. I'll do it."

Casimir walked up behind her and put the blindfold over her eyes, securing it with a knot. He could smell the lavender shampoo she always used, and it took every ounce of his self-control not to lean in and nuzzle her gorgeous hair.

"I've never let a man blindfold me before," Ava said, obviously trying to make a joke to ease her nerves.

He finished tying the ends and leaned closer, whispering low into her ear, "I'm honored to be the first one."

She let out the tiniest whimper as he allowed his fingers to brush along her neck and backed away. Her breathing had quickened, and she stood still, seemingly lost in thought. He tried not to laugh at how easily riled up she was with the brush of his fingers, the touch of his hand. What else could he do to make a sound like that escape her lips?

"Ava. You're already getting distracted."

"Maybe you should stop distracting me."

"Okay," he said. "I'm done distracting you...for now."

He liked flirting with her. Flirting was safe. It was easy. Soft touches, jokes, teasing each other. Poking at her to irritate her or make her nervous.

It was the rest that was difficult. Complicated. Feelings and words and deeper truths he was ignoring. Besides, she'd been through so much he didn't want to cross a boundary. And, admittedly, Aro was right. He was scared.

Scared of opening himself up; of pushing too soon and causing her more distress; of losing her like he'd lost his family.

"For now? What's that supposed to mean?"

"It means nothing," he answered. "Alright. Can you see anything?"

"No."

He took her hand and led her to the start of the small course. "Right in front of you is a low balance beam. I want you to feel around for it with your foot and make it across without falling," he said, letting go.

She followed his instructions and found the beam. Shuffling her feet, she walked, arms out as she tried to stay balanced.

"Arms down," he stated.

She grunted in frustration but did as he said. Moments later, her foot slipped. She found the beam again and continued forward but was unable to make it without sliding off. Every time her foot hit the ground, Casimir grabbed her hand and led her back to the beginning, instructing her to start over. It took her half an hour to get across the balance beam without fumbling, but she got the hang of it.

Next, he led her to the stepping stones and she struggled with this even more. "Memorize their locations when you make it to the next one."

"I don't know how to do that," she said. "I don't have the same senses you do."

"Try."

She did. Hopping to the next and only landing accurately about thirty percent of the time. But she lost focus, apparent exhaustion catching up with her. Leaping to the next stone, her foot slipped yet again, and she fell forward with a shout. Casimir was there in an instant, catching and steadying her on her feet.

Their bodies were closer than he'd intended, his hands resting on her hips. He wanted to pull her flush against him. Kiss her soft lips and comb his fingers through her hair. Run his hands along her body and touch every dip and curve until she begged him not to stop. But it wasn't just a want. It was a need. He needed her like he needed air to breathe, and it took every ounce of self-control he had not to act on it whenever she was around.

She reached to pull off the blindfold, but he grabbed her wrists, placing her hands on his chest. They remained pressed against each other, neither willing to break contact.

He leaned in and whispered in her ear, "I can hear your pulse racing."

She shivered at his words, and he cupped her face. His thumb traced her bottom lip and he allowed his gaze to rove over the delicate curve of her nose, the blush on her cheeks, her soft full lips.

"Ava," he groaned, stepping closer.

She sucked in a breath, as if she was waiting for him to do something. To make a move. But he knew he shouldn't while she was still learning how to cope with her trauma. So, he backed away with a sigh and disappeared into the woods, leaving her standing in the clearing.

Not yet, he told himself.

 bead of sweat trailed down Ava's face as she ran through the course. She had made it past the balance beam and platforms and was working on the last couple obstacles. Casimir coached her from the sidelines, urging her to focus and utilize her legs as she pulled herself up a fifteen-foot wall using a rope.

A week had passed since the incident with the blindfold and Casimir acted like nothing happened. He hardly even looked at her, even when they sat across from each other at dinner. She was sure he had almost kissed her. And she had wanted him to.

Putting it out of her mind, she tried focusing on the task at hand, but she was even more exhausted lately. The nightmares had increased, and between the lack of sleep and her morning training sessions, she was beginning to suffer the consequences. And, to be honest, she was in a wretched mood this morning. Not just cranky. She was angry. Furious.

Hands gripping the rope, she pulled herself higher and pushed with her legs.

"Don't get distracted," Casimir said.

"I'm not," she bit back, gritting her teeth as she gave another tug.

Finding a place for her right foot, she stepped higher but lost her grip on the rope and tumbled to the ground. She cursed as she rubbed her hands on her pants, wiping off the sweat.

"Yes, you are," he said as he stood before her and crossed his arms. "Try again."

She'd barely slept last night and could feel herself teetering on the edge of a breakdown. Tired and sore, she didn't have it in her to do anything else.

"No. I'm done for today," she said, remaining on the ground.

"You're not done unless I say you are."

"I have nothing left," she argued.

"Get up. Try again."

She stood and turned toward him. "No."

"Now, princess."

She shook her head and walked away, leaving the obstacle course, but Casimir appeared in front of her.

"Get out of my way."

"That's not how this works. I'm your general, and I'm telling you to get back on that course."

Her heart surged as the storm of anger churned in her chest. She closed her eyes and took several deep breaths, trying but failing to remain calm.

"And I'm telling you *no*," she seethed, opening her eyes again to stare him down.

"We don't have time for games, Ava. We're relying on you."

"You don't think I know that? That I think about it every waking moment? I'm *trying*."

"I'll tell you what," he said as he uncrossed his arms. "If you can get past me, I'll let you go early today."

"What?" She backed away.

He reached his hand out and made a 'come here' motion with his fingers. "Get past me. Take me down. Something."

"This is ridiculous. I'll go back and do the course."

"No. You're angry and you'll get distracted again. Fight me. Show me what you learned on that ship."

"You're a hundred times stronger than me. I'll never be able to get past you."

"Try. Or are you a coward?"

Her heart picked up speed. "Don't call me a coward."

"Or what...*princess*? Why don't you do something about it?"

He was provoking her, goading her into fighting him. Purposely.

Furious, she stomped forward, prepared to shove him out of her way but he dodged her attempt and she lost her balance, falling to the grass.

Her hands shook as she rose and tried to leave, but he stepped in front of her again. "That was pathetic."

Rearing her arm back, her fist shot through the air as she tried to punch him, but he caught her wrist. She tried to yank from his grip, but his hand tightened and he turned, pulling her back to him with her arm twisted behind her.

"That hurts, you brute," she said, struggling. "Let me go."

"Pax had you in this hold. Get out of it."

She tried kicking him, but he avoided her feet. Her anger was boiling over now, a violent mess of emotions. Anger mixed with grief of the past and fear of what was still to come.

"Take your anger out on me. Come on. If you refuse to talk about it, then hurt me. Do something."

She let out a snarl and tried to head butt him, but he wrapped his arms around her and twisted, throwing her to the ground. He pinned her wrists above her head and straddled her.

"Not good enough," he growled, eyes boring into hers. "Fight me."

Shaking with wrath, she glared at him, attempting to yank her arms away and kicking in frustration. "Let. Me. Go."

He was silent while she struggled a few seconds longer before her energy dissipated. Tired, she relaxed, the fight leaving her as quickly as it had come.

Casimir's eyes filled with concern. "You've disappeared these last few weeks," he whispered. "Come back to me, princess."

A lump formed in her throat as she fought to keep her tears at bay. But she couldn't get the words out. Couldn't say what she was feeling out loud. Everyone was dead. Her mother. Her grandfather. Eleanor. Zeph and the sailors. And she knew there would be more.

She couldn't bear it. Needed to get back to her room so she could bathe and take a nap. Needed a distraction. So, she would get past the general and escape what he was trying to do. She wasn't ready.

Casimir sat back and stood, allowing her out of the hold. He started to walk away, preparing to block her again, but before he made it out of her reach, she lunged and wrapped her arms around his leg and pulled as hard as she could, sending him crashing to the ground on his back.

"Shit," he panted, the air knocked out of him.

She rose and stood over him. "Asshole," she said before walking away, leaving him stunned on the ground.

She made it to the tree line and caught Quinn watching. "Nice," she said to Ava and grinned. Ava attempted to smile back as she passed, heading back to her suite.

THE GROUP WAS HAVING dinner at Kai and Jorrar's home tonight, and Ava was relieved to escape the castle for the evening. Now in a lighter mood after a long nap, she hoped a change in scenery would be a distraction from the fears about this war.

Cirilla finished tightening a forest green corset over her brown dress, and Ava touched the dazzling necklace of green gemstones around her neck, a gift from the Queens of Saxumdale.

"You look very pretty, Your Highness."

Ava smiled. "Thank you."

It had been a while since Ava had been in anything besides her training gear of pants and tunics, and tonight she felt beautiful.

She opened her door, finding Casimir standing with his back to her, leaning against the mantle above the fireplace. He was wearing a tan tunic with brown pants and looked utterly handsome as he turned to face her.

His eyes flared as he took her in. Clearing his throat, he said, "Let's go."

They walked in silence, Ava unsure what to say. They hadn't spoken since she had knocked him to the ground and she wasn't sure if he was angry about it, his face giving nothing away.

"So...how's your back?" she asked.

"My back?"

"Earlier. You know, when I tripped you and won."

Face stoic, he continued to walk down the hall and out of the castle. "You didn't win."

"What? You said if I got past you, I could leave. And I did."

The corner of his mouth curled up. "I let you."

"You did not! You are so frustrating. Sometimes I think you enjoy irritating me."

He looked down at her and his smile grew. "Maybe."

She couldn't help but laugh as they arrived at the stables,

meeting Thorne, Quinn and Raine. Assaulted with the smell of hay and horses, she took in the large structure. Vines crept along the roof, bright orange flowers releasing their floral perfume.

"Good evening, you two," called Thorne, his scarlet hair bright in the setting sun as he saddled a beautiful black horse.

"Hi." Ava fidgeted. "So...we're riding?" She looked at Casimir beside her. "You didn't tell me we were riding."

"You didn't ask."

"They live on the outskirts of the city," said her brother. "It will be too tiresome and take too much time to journey on foot."

"Oh," she squeaked as she regarded the massive creatures.

"What's wrong, princess? Never ridden a horse before?" Casimir asked.

"I had a bad experience once."

"These horses are easy. Don't worry about it," Quinn said, leaning forward to whisper into Ava's ear, "Your boobs look great in that dress, by the way."

"Umm...thanks?"

Casimir choked on a cough.

Quinn walked over to her own horse, a gorgeous chestnut mare. "I can't get Cas' expression out of my head since I saw you yank him onto his back this morning."

Raine and Thorne turned to them, adjusting their own horses' saddles. "You threw Casimir on his back?" Thorne asked, eyes wide in surprise.

Ava grinned. "Kind of."

"I let her," Casimir mumbled.

She pursed her lips and scanned the group, counting four horses. "Umm...we don't have enough horses."

Quinn's eyes were full of mischief, having already mounted her ride. "You get to ride with Cas."

"No thanks. I'll ride with one of you guys."

"Casimir's horse is the only one large enough to handle two riders. You'll be fine," said Thorne as he swung his leg over and settled into his saddle.

Grumbling, she walked over to Casimir, standing before a tall jet-black horse with white speckled socks.

She put her hands on her hips. "Are you going to put on the saddle?"

"A saddle won't fit both of us. We're riding bareback."

"What? No. Absolutely not." She backed away, dried hay crunching beneath her boots. "I'll fall off and get trampled."

He laughed. "You really are scared, aren't you?"

She looked at him and then his horse. "I can't even get up there."

"Well, come closer and I'll help you."

She stepped forward. "Now what?"

Without warning, Casimir grabbed her by the waist and lifted, setting her on the horse side saddle while he held her steady.

"What are you doing?" She gasped. "I'm going to fall!"

"Calm down," he said, amused at her discomfort. "Swing your right leg over. I won't let you fall."

"I don't have anything to hold on to," she exclaimed.

Raine called to her from atop his own horse, "Grab the mane, dainty human!"

"I'll hurt him!"

"You won't hurt him," said Casimir. "Swing your leg over."

She cursed to herself as she grasped his mane. The horse obediently stood still as she lifted her skirt high enough to get her leg on the other side.

"Now what?"

"Hold on and wait for me," said Casimir.

She took several deep breaths, looking over at Thorne, Quinn and Raine who couldn't stop laughing. "It's not funny."

"It's quite amusing actually," Thorne said. "Who knew the

princess who had such a connection with animals was terrified of horses?"

"They're so big and what if he bucks me off?"

"He won't," said Casimir as he gripped the mane and swung himself up.

"Ava, we literally rode an oceandrake a few weeks ago and you're scared of a horse?" Raine asked.

"I'm not *scared,* just nervous."

Casimir settled himself behind her, holding the reins with his right hand. He put his left hand on her stomach and pulled her against him. She sucked in a breath as the horse moved and she tried to hold onto something, squeezing his arm wrapped around her waist.

"Ouch," he said. "Please stop digging your nails into my arm."

She hunched her shoulders and let go, putting her hands in her bunched-up dress. "Sorry."

Raine rode up next to them. "Thank you for making my day. That was hilarious."

"I'm glad to be the source of your amusement," she deadpanned.

"Your boobs look great in that dress, by the way."

"That's what I said!" Quinn shouted from ahead.

Casimir tensed and cleared his throat.

"Enjoy your ride." Raine winked as he rode ahead, joining Thorne and Quinn.

"What an idiot," she mumbled.

"Tell me about it." Casimir laughed.

They made their way through town, passing the shops lining the streets. Lanterns glowed in the trees and the city was bustling with activity. Fae, goblins and pixies moved about, running errands and enjoying their evening. When they caught sight of the party, they waved, greeting their king.

Thorne led the way, followed by Quinn and Raine, with Ava

and Casimir bringing up the rear. The citizens pointed at her in awe, whispering among themselves.

Ava squirmed in her seat, trying to smile when she truly wanted to disappear. Her heart hadn't stopped racing, and she fidgeted with her dress as the horse continued to move down the road.

She could feel Casimir breathing behind her, muscled chest pressed against her back. His cedar and sage scent enveloped her, and his hand was warm on her belly, causing her insides to flutter. She so desperately wanted to lean back and nestle into him, but she remained stiff, struggling to relax.

"Take a deep breath," he said. "I can hear your heart racing."

"I can't help it. I'm nervous and everyone keeps staring at me."

"They're excited to see you. They heard about the attack and what you did."

"How do they know?" she asked.

"The animals talk. Word got around."

"Oh."

"Earlier you said you had a bad experience with a horse. Tell me about it." He pulled her a little closer. This time she couldn't help but settle against him.

"When I was little, like six or seven, my mom signed me up for horseback riding lessons. But the first day, another child pulled my horse's tail. The horse freaked out and bucked me off and I broke my arm. I refused to get on a horse after that and my mom had to cancel the lessons."

"Your nervousness makes more sense now. I won't make fun of you anymore."

"Why thank you, general."

"Pepper is quite calm. He won't run away or buck you off. I promise."

Ava laughed. "Your horse's name is Pepper?"

"What?"

"Nothing. It's...kind of a cutesy name for such a brutish rider."

Casimir leaned forward, pressing into her back as he adjusted the reins. "And what should I have named him?"

"I don't know." Ava shrugged. "Something mean. Like Nightmare."

"You think I'm mean?"

"No." She paused. "Well, you kind of were today..."

"I'm sorry. That wasn't my intention. I'm just worried about you. I thought taking your anger out on me would help."

"Don't worry about me," she said. "I'm fine. I'm handling it."

"It's okay if you're struggling. This is new to you. I—"

"Tell me why you named your horse Pepper," she interrupted.

"Don't think I won't bring this up again," he said quietly.

"Not tonight," she whispered. "I just want to enjoy dinner."

"Fine. Why did I name him Pepper? Do you see the black dots on his white socks? It reminded me of pepper and so that's what I named him."

"That's...cute."

"First, I'm mean. Now I'm cute. Make up your mind, princess," he crooned in her ear.

Straightening, she answered. "I didn't call you cute. I called your *horse* cute. You just have a big ego."

He chuckled and they continued down the city streets, now at the edge of town as she said, "You can let go of my waist you know."

He pulled his hand away. "Alright."

The moment his hand left, she felt herself sliding. Scrambling, she grabbed the horse's mane. "Never mind, I'm going to fall!"

His arm wrapped around her again. "I promise you won't

fall." He pulled her against him so hard, there was no space between them. "You're scaring yourself."

They continued in silence for a while, city turning to country as they wandered through open pastures and farmhouses. Ava was lost in the beauty of the rolling fields, lined by the mountains in the distance. Farmers were out in their gardens, some using magic to revive and care for their plants while others had tools as they dug into the earth, tilling it for their next crop.

"It's beautiful," she said as she marveled at the landscape.

She needed this. This quiet trek through the farmlands. This peace away from the stress of her daily training routine. Away from the reminders of the last few months.

"It is," he said. "I'd love to live out here someday. Right at the edge of town."

"Do you want to grow crops?" she asked.

"No. I just find the space peaceful. It's where Raine's father raised us." He sighed. "Maybe after the war, I won't need to be so close to the castle anymore."

She turned and glanced at him. He had a far off look on his face as he watched the farmers. "My grandfather's farm was like this," she said. "Peaceful."

"Do you miss it?"

"Yes and no. It was lonely. But I miss gardening, though I wasn't there for long."

Casimir's thumb lazily moved back and forth on her stomach and he continued to press close to her. Butterflies erupted in her belly as he asked, "You're good at growing things?"

"Yes," she replied. "Aren't all fae from Monterre good at that?"

"Not necessarily. Being able to raise vines from the ground and manipulate earth is different from growing crops," he explained. "Let's see...You're adept with plants and have special abilities with animals. And you're skilled with a bow and arrow."

"Yes…"

"But you're clumsy and scared of horses. What else?"

"What do you mean, what else?"

"I mean what else are you good at? Bad at?" he asked. "Hobbies, hopes and dreams. Desires. Weird quirks. I want to know you better."

"Why?"

"Because we're friends?"

"Oh we are?" she teased. She wanted to be more.

"We are…" The way he said it sounded almost sensual. He cleared his throat. "Tell me more about you."

"Well…I fidget a lot."

"I've noticed. And you get distracted easily."

"Yes," she said. "Or I get anxious sometimes and panic."

"I know," he said quietly.

"Um…I'm good at cooking."

"Really?"

"Yes. I'm a great cook. I always loved to cook for others back home. I would invite my friends over and make new recipes for them. I miss it."

"Cas is a terrible cook," Raine announced from ahead.

"Stop eavesdropping," Casimir shot back. Raine rode further ahead, leaving the two of them behind.

"I love to read but you already know that." She thought for a moment. "I'm also a bit of a neat freak. Cleaning helps with my anxiety. My hopes and dreams, you asked. I have no idea anymore. I used to want to settle down, grow flowers and live in peace… now, I'm not so sure."

She turned to look at him and his eyes were filled with affection. Interest. He swallowed and she turned back around.

"Your turn," she said, fidgeting and trying to stretch her sore legs.

"Well...I am *not* clumsy."

"No shit."

"And I'm not a neat freak, or whatever strange human term you said earlier." Ava stifled a small laugh. "My room is actually quite messy."

"That really surprises me."

"I'm good at wood carving. I like to whittle animals. You said cleaning helps you. Well, whittling helps me. Gives me an outlet. I also love to read, but you know that too...and believe it or not, I hate mornings. I'd rather stay in bed than get up early to train."

"That's also surprising, general."

"It's called discipline. Trust me, if we weren't in the middle of an impending war, I'd be sleeping in and lounging around for at least another two hours."

"Hopes and dreams and all that mushy stuff?"

"After we wipe Deidamia and Andras off the map? I don't know what I want to be honest. Peace. Land. Companionship," he whispered as he continued to stroke her stomach.

"The hopeless romantic general wants companionship, huh?"

"Mmm hmm."

They were silent for a while and Ava wiggled in her seat, legs and rear sore from being stuck on the horse so long. Casimir made a small grunting noise behind her before speaking. "Stop doing that."

"Doing what?" she asked, as she continued to adjust, trying to get comfortable.

"*That*," he said in her ear.

"Why?"

He yanked her closer and whispered, voice lowering as his lips brushed her ear. "You know why..."

"Oh. Sorry," she whispered, stomach dipping when she noticed the hardness against her lower back.

But she didn't want to stop. Wanted to stay flush against him on this horse for as long as possible. Overcome with need, she pressed into him, unable to stop herself. He groaned as his hand tightened against her.

"What are you doing?"

She didn't respond as she moved again.

He looped the reins around the hand on her stomach. With his other, ever so slowly, he brushed her hair behind her shoulder, fingers grazing her throat. She tilted her head, exposing her neck.

"This is dangerous, Ava," he murmured as he placed a small kiss below her earlobe.

She inhaled a sharp breath at the way he said her name and whispered back, "Then why aren't you stopping?"

"Because you're torturing me on this damn horse," he said, voice thick with desire, as his mouth moved lower on her neck, breathing her in.

"You almost kissed me that day with the blindfold," she whispered, closing her eyes as she leaned her head back against his shoulder.

"Yes," he rasped into her skin.

"Why didn't you?"

"I don't want to distract you from your training."

He kissed the curve of her shoulder and she whimpered, arching her back. He let out a throaty groan as his hand gripped her hip and squeezed. The ache of desire worked its way to her core as another whimper escaped her lips.

"But you're doing it now..."

"We're not training now."

She turned and looked at him. His eyes were darker, pupils wide as they roved over her face. He leaned in and their noses brushed against each other, when a voice sounded from ahead.

"We're here!" shouted Quinn, pulling them from the moment.

Casimir straightened and removed both hands from Ava, holding the reins as he steered them to the beautiful cottage at the edge of the forest. She cleared her throat, trying to slow her racing heart as they pulled to a stop near a fence.

Casimir dismounted and reached for her hand to steady her as she swung her leg around. He grasped her waist and lifted her to the ground, holding on longer than necessary as they stood facing each other. He tucked a strand of hair behind her ear with care before turning and leading the horse away.

19

The large cottage had a thatched straw roof and flowers of every kind filling the front garden. The fusion of pink, purple, blue and yellow blooms brought a cheery feel to the yard.

Kai and Jorrar greeted them as they entered with enthusiastic hugs, Ava following Quinn into the dining room. A long table sat in the center of the room with plenty of room for them all. An intricate lace runner contrasted the hand-scraped wood and a rainbow of flower-filled vases decorated the center. Wood beams crossed along the ceiling, holding colored lanterns to brighten the space.

Raine's sister, Fanya, was already seated, her black squirrel on her shoulder. "Hi, Ava," she greeted, her platinum curls bright in the light.

Ava leaned in to give her a quick hug. "It's good to see you." She looked at her animal companion. "And you too, Coco," she said, scratching the squirrel's head.

Two fae children burst into the room, laughing and chasing each other through the house. Both children had curly brown hair and umber skin. The girl—who appeared about seven years old—had Jorrar's silver eyes while the boy—who was a couple of years older—looked more like Kai. They were followed by their own animal companions, one of the small glowing foxes Ava had seen in the forest after escaping the daemons, and a bright pink hummingbird.

"Ava," said Kai, his black curls bouncing around the small horns on his head as he gestured toward the children. "These are our grandchildren, Griffin and Aria." Ava smiled as they disappeared out the back door into the flower garden. "I'll be in the kitchen finishing dinner. Make yourselves at home and help yourself to some wine."

Ava took her seat, Quinn to her right and Thorne to her left. Casimir sat across from her and she avoided eye contact with him as Raine plopped between him and his sister. Jorrar grabbed a pitcher and filled everyone's goblets as he made his rounds along the table.

Ava caught Casimir's eye and he turned red, taking several gulps of wine and looking away. Raine looked in between them and raised an eyebrow at their awkwardness.

"I'm going to go help Kai," she said, needing a moment to think.

She entered the kitchen and found Kai over a stove, stirring soup in a tureen smelling of rosemary, onions and other unknown spices. Moments later, a hand grabbed her arm and whipped her around. Raine had followed.

"Why is Casimir acting strange and why do you smell like a brothel?"

"What? I—" She shook her head. "I don't smell."

He crossed his arms and smirked at her. "The smell coming from you and Cas is strong enough to wake the dead."

"Yep," Kai said and her face warmed.

She stammered. "Wait...you all can smell..."

"Arousal, yes," Raine answered.

"Gross."

Raine laughed. "It's not gross. It's normal. No one will say anything, promise."

"Except Raine, of course," Kai interjected.

"Well, what happened?" Raine asked again.

"I—um...None of your business."

Raine narrowed his eyes at her, but his expression softened. "Cas is my best friend. Please don't break his heart."

"I would never do that."

"I know you wouldn't on purpose," he said. "Cas isn't so great with the whole 'talk about his feelings' thing. Like you."

"Hey...I talk ab—"

Kai let out a small snort.

Raine held his hand up and interrupted her. "Cas pretends he doesn't care, but he does. Deeply. He wants commitment, companionship. So, unless you're sure...don't lead him on."

"I'm sorry. I promise, I won't."

"Okay." He nodded, heading back to the dining room to join the group.

Ava remained in the kitchen with Kai. "Can I help? I'm a pretty good cook and I'm not ready to go back in there."

"Of course. Grab that knife and chop those vegetables."

BACK IN HER SEAT, Ava sipped on her wine as Kai and Jorrar finished setting the platters of food in the center of the table.

"Ava made a dessert," said Kai.

"You can cook?" asked Thorne.

"She sure can." Kai beamed as he carried in the rest of the food—a bowl of freshly baked bread in one hand and a tray of roasted potatoes smothered in herbs in the other.

"What did you make, Ava?" asked Jorrar.

"A berry pie."

"I love sweets," said Thorne beside her.

"Me too."

Jorrar corralled the children to the table, loading their plates with food. "But we want to wrestle with Cas!" Aria whined.

"I know, little one." He patted her head. "But you must eat first. Once you're finished, you may wait for Casimir and I bet he'll wrestle with you."

"Yay!" the children squealed as they dug in.

Kai sat at the head of the table and served himself food, the others following suit.

"So, Ava. We haven't had time to ask you...what was your life like in the human world?" asked Jorrar.

Ava leaned over, piling vegetables on her plate as she spoke. "Well...it was very different from here as you all might guess. There's no magic."

Griffin gasped. "No magic?"

Ava gave him a small smile as she continued, "It's kind of boring. People go to their jobs all day and come home and do it all over again."

"That sounds awful," said Quinn through a mouthful of food.

"It's not all bad," she replied.

"What was your job?" asked Kai.

She took a sip of wine. "I was a wildlife biologist before I inherited the farm." They looked at her in confusion. "I studied animals and their behaviors and wrote reports about it."

"Why?" asked Raine.

"Good question." She set her fork down. "To learn about their behaviors. And keep record of it. To protect certain species from dying off. That's a problem in the human world. People keep reproducing and having children. They use up the resources and tear down forests and other habitats to build their homes and end up killing or displacing animals. I wanted to help."

"That's awful," said Quinn.

"It is."

"Would you ever want to go back?" asked Kai.

Ava shook her head. "There's nothing left there for me anyway. Plus...I like it here...with you all."

Thorne looked at her and smiled. "You belong here. With all of us."

"Thank you." She smiled back and glanced across the table. Casimir was watching her intensely.

"Are you a princess?" Aria interrupted.

"Yes," she answered awkwardly. She wasn't good with children.

"You're pretty," Aria stated.

"Thanks."

"Can I touch your hair?" Aria jumped out of her seat and ran over.

"Um...sure," she said, tensing as Aria ran her fingers through Ava's long locks.

She met eyes with Casimir again who was holding back a smile at her obvious discomfort.

"Griffin, Aria," said Kai. "If you're done eating, why don't you go play outside until Casimir is finished?"

"Okay!" they shouted, disappearing down the hallway.

"You are terrible with children, Ava," said Raine.

"I know," she lamented. Curious, Ava turned toward Kai. "So...your grandchildren...they live here with you?"

"Yes."

"Their father died many years ago," Jorrar explained. "And their mother...Our daughter was with a party of healers, traveling to one of the outer cities when a group of Deidamia's soldiers attacked." Silence permeated the air as Jorrar told his tale. A tale she was sure the rest of them were all too familiar with. "Most of them were killed, but a few went missing. We never found her body."

"I'm sorry," Ava whispered.

"Thank you," Kai said.

Jorrar raised his glass. "Let's have a toast. Though the immediate future may be fraught with peril, may we never forget the importance of each other. And what we're fighting for. Our friends." He looked around the table. "Our family." Thorne looked at Ava and squeezed her hand. "Our beloved." Jorrar paused and smiled fondly at Kai. Casimir's eyes were bright as he watched her. An unwavering gaze that spoke volumes without saying a word.

"And for peace," Jorrar finished.

Everyone raised their glasses and repeated, "for peace," as they clinked them together. Ava couldn't help it as a tear ran down her face. The kindness and love she had been shown in such a short time by these fae who were little more than strangers months ago.

Mosshaven had filled the emptiness in her heart and soul, and she knew right then and there she belonged.

She belonged with them.

20

Casimir's arm vibrated as his sword met Raine's, the blade glinting in the morning sun. Strike after strike, jab after jab, he let his anger and worry out in the ring. And Raine let him. It had been two weeks since the dinner at Jorrar and Kai's house—since the incident on the horse—and though the dinner seemed to help that night, it hadn't lasted.

Ava was getting worse.

He had pulled back with the flirting, knowing she needed space as she figured out how to cope with and work through her traumas. They'd all been through the emotional aftermath of brutal battles. Of injuries and death. Of seeing their friends and loved ones killed in front of their very eyes.

But Ava was new to it. And she didn't seem to be handling it well, refusing to talk about anything whenever he asked. She hadn't said one word about Zeph's death even though she looked like she would burst into tears every time she met eyes with Pax as they walked into their suite. Her anger and irritation were rising. She was barely sleeping, and he had left a note for her this morning to sleep in and try to get some rest.

"It's time to take a break."

"No," Casimir said and continued swiping at his friend and dodging his blows.

"Enough," Raine said as he pulled a move, knocking Casimir's sword to the ground.

Casimir stood still, breathing heavily as his rage receded.

"You can't fix it for her. What she's dealing with. She must figure out how to do that for herself."

"I know that," Casimir spat.

"Stop taking it on."

"I'm not." He glared at his friend.

"We've all gone through it too. She'll be alright eventually."

They stood there for a moment, when Raine's eyes caught on something behind Casimir. "Shit."

Casimir turned around. Ava had just emerged from the castle, dressed in her training gear with her hair pulled back. She didn't even acknowledge them as she marched past the rings toward the obstacle course, a look of determination on her face.

He rushed to catch up with her. "Did you not receive my note? I said to take the morning off and rest."

She didn't look at him as she kept walking. "Andras doesn't take days off. Neither will I."

"You've barely slept. One day off won't hurt," he insisted.

She stopped and whirled toward him, her tired eyes full of steel. "One day makes all the difference." She turned and kept walking.

Accepting defeat, he followed her to the obstacle course and took his place at the sidelines. After a brief stretch, she took off to jog a lap around the field before taking her place at the beginning.

"Remember to focus," he tried to encourage.

"Stop talking," she bit back.

Running a hand through his hair, he remained silent and

let her figure it out on her own. She made it farther than she ever had before. Over the difficult wall and through the other obstacles. She was at the rope climb, the last obstacle. He watched as she pulled herself higher, eyes hard and flickering with anger.

Come on, Ava, he thought, as Aro lumbered up beside him, Luna at his heels. Titus was chasing butterflies in the trees as if he was in a game of tag. Casimir smiled to himself as he recalled the day Ava brought the firefinch home, Aro's fur soft beneath his fingers as he scratched behind his ears.

She's struggling, Aro said.

"I know," he whispered back.

It's going to get worse before it gets better.

"I know that too."

Don't do what you usually do.

"And what would that be?"

Lose your temper and say something you'll regret.

Casimir grunted. "As if I need an animal to give me advice."

Aro chuffed and ambled off to the trees.

Ava had almost made it to the top of the rope, a hint of triumph in her eyes, when she lost her grip and fell, cursing to herself.

Casimir ran over. "Are you alright?"

"I'm fine," she said, avoiding eye contact.

She rose and walked away, but he grabbed her arm and spun her around. "Why aren't you sleeping? Tell me about your nightmares. What are they about?"

"I don't want to talk about it." She tried to walk past him, but he stepped in front of her. "It's none of your business anyway."

Fury shone in her tear-filled eyes, mixed with pain, grief, and fear. He resisted the urge to whisk her away to take care of her, as he so desperately yearned to do.

"It's interfering with your training, so it is my business," he said, reaching for her. "Besides, I care about you. I want to help."

She was silent.

"Please. Talk to me. You can't keep avoiding it."

"Talk to you?" she said, voice rising as she looked back at him. "What about you? I know nothing about your past. Are you a hybrid? What happened to your parents? Who's Elara? Is she your old girlfriend? What happened? You want me to open up, but you've been a closed book this entire time."

He stiffened at the mention of Elara, the mention of his own traumas he loathed to rehash, hands clenched into fists as her words hit him. There was a flash of regret in her eyes the moment she said it, but his temper flared and got the better of him.

"You know what? I'm not going to ask anymore. All you know how to do is push people away." He turned and walked off, calling after her, "Train with someone else. If you want to spend your time feeling sorry for yourself, don't let me get in your way."

He walked back to the castle, ignoring Raine who had remained in the ring, gaping at him as he passed. He knew Raine heard everything and was sure he'd get a lecture later.

What was it you said moments ago? You don't need an animal to give you advice? Aro asked.

"Shut up."

Damn animals.

But Aro was right. He shouldn't have said that. He'd been pushing her to talk about her trauma for weeks. But it wasn't fair for him to expect her to do the exact thing he wasn't capable of.

He was a fool.

AVA TRUDGED to the woods and found a fallen log in front of a small stream. Collapsing onto it, she let the tears fall. She couldn't do this. Couldn't complete the training, would never make it to the Elderoak. And there was no way she could defeat a daemon queen. What was she thinking?

And what she said to Casimir; she regretted it the moment it left her lips. She never meant to hurt him, and knew he didn't mean what he said either. Knew deep down he cared about her; had known it from the moment he took care of her in Saxumdale. He was so tender that night, so calm. That this brutish warrior could have such kindness and compassion astonished her. She knew the stoic general was a mask. A necessary face to wear to get the job done. To make tough decisions.

"I'm fucking everything up," she mumbled, her head in her hands.

Something soft brushed against her hand and she raised her head to find Luna nuzzling her palm.

Are you alright?

"I don't know," Ava replied. *"I'm...tired. And sad. And angry."*

You should talk about it, Luna said.

"What? Are you my therapist now?"

I don't know what that means. But Jorrar's coming up behind you.

Luna settled on the lush grass beside Ava as the crunch of leaves sounded, Jorrar emerging through the trees. He gestured to the log next to her. "May I sit?"

She nodded, turning back to the water and watching it trickle along the rocks. They sat in silence, not speaking for several long minutes.

"I heard you've been having nightmares," Jorrar said at last.

"Yes."

"Do you want to talk about them?"

She whispered, "Not yet."

"Did you have one last night?"

She nodded again, wiping her eyes.

"War is a dreadful thing. It strips us down and reveals all our inner fears. The rawness of who we are at our cores. It changes us."

She didn't say anything as she listened.

"But...we get to decide *how* it changes us."

"I don't know how."

"You can't go around it forever. You must go through it. Face it."

She was silent for a long time, watching a butterfly as it flew from flower to flower, its turquoise wings shimmering in the dappled light.

"I feel..." she began, taking a deep breath. "Broken. Like every single part of me is scattered." She continued to watch the water as she leaned forward on her knees and clasped her hands. "I keep trying to put the pieces back together before more fall off but there's too many. Every time I reach for one, another one breaks. Ever since my mom died...I've been trying to patch myself back up." Tears slid down her cheeks. "But I can't. And now...after the torture, all of the deaths, that battle on the ship..."

She wiped her face and swallowed the lump in her throat.

Jorrar hummed his understanding. "There's nothing wrong with being broken. We all are in our own ways. How else are we going to be remade if we don't break from time to time?" He turned to face her. "You're trying to put the pieces back in the same places they were before, but they keep falling off. Do you know why?"

"Why?" Her voice was barely a whisper.

"They don't belong there anymore. It's time to try something new. To rebuild yourself. You aren't the same person. You will never fit into your old self."

"How do I even do that?"

"Everyone's journey is different. Talk about it. Admit you're struggling. Grieve. I also find that connecting with others helps. Doing things for those you love." He gave her a knowing look and clutched her hand in between both of his, eyes turning to steel. "Who you are is not the things that happened to you, Ava. Who you are is what you do about it. What kind of person do you want to be? Decide you won't let this war break you."

She heaved a big sigh as she absorbed his words.

"Ava," he added. "Did you know that I knew your mother?"

"You did?"

"Yes. You remind me of her. The kindness she always showed. The tenacity. She would be so proud of you."

Ava let out a sob, the damn bursting. She put her head in her hands and whispered, "I miss her."

"I know. But she's always with you. Never forget that. And never forget who you are. The woman who helped dying citizens in the tavern after only having been in Mosshaven a couple of days. The woman who rode a dangerous sea creature to save lives. The woman who fought back and stabbed Raine the moment we found you," he added with a chuckle.

Ava let out a small laugh, wiping her face with the hem of her tunic.

"It's okay to be scared. But let your strength overcome it. Let it guide you. *That* is who you are."

Jorrar departed on silent feet, leaving Ava alone to process his words. Her fingers found Luna's soft coat again as she slid down to the ground and sat beside her sleeping companion. Jorrar was right. Casimir was right. She had to stop avoiding the hard things or it would continue to devour her and stain her soul.

Avoidance was her bad habit, her way of coping. It was something she'd always done. When her mother had died, she threw herself into work so hard, she'd crash into bed with exhaustion so she wouldn't have to think about her broken heart. Back then, she didn't have anyone else in her life. She had only hurt herself. But now her inability to face her turmoil was harming those around her. People she'd grown to love and care for.

And it was time to stop.

21

For the next three mornings, Casimir was nowhere to be found. He spent most of the day in meetings as they increased their planning for the war and arrived at their suite well after Ava had gone to bed, rising before she awoke.

He was avoiding her.

Raine had taken over Ava's training during this time and he was angry. They barely spoke as she tried and tried again to complete the course.

"You're letting your emotions get the best of you," he said as she dusted herself off from falling on the rope climb yet again.

"I know."

"You know I'm angry with you, right?" he asked as they walked back to the castle.

"Yes."

"You need to fix this. Until you do, you'll never finish that course." He stopped and turned to her, crossing his arms, his hair bright in the sun.

She looked at him, devastated she hurt one of her favorite people. "I'm so sorry. I didn't mean any of it."

"I know you didn't. And don't worry, I gave Cas a lecture too," he said. "You do the exact same thing he does."

She shifted on her feet. "What do you mean?"

"Refuse to talk about your past until it spills over, and you say something you didn't mean."

"I know," she whispered. "What do I do?"

"Well, the first step is apologizing. You need to go talk to him."

She looked around and back at Raine. "He's avoiding me."

"I know."

"He probably doesn't want to talk to me."

Raine grabbed her face and turned her to look at him. "The two of you are so fucking stubborn. Go. Talk. To. Him."

She sniffed. "Alright." Raine pulled her into a crushing hug. "Ouch."

"You know I adore you. Right, dainty human?"

She pulled away and looked at him, overcome with emotion. He smiled as his humor returned, and tears welled in her eyes.

"Why are you crying?"

"Because," she said in between sobs, "you are all so nice to me..."

He flicked her nose and pulled her back in, letting her cry into him. "It's because you're our missing piece, Ava," he whispered and kissed the top of her head.

AFTER A QUICK BATH and a change of clothing, Ava searched the castle, unable to find Casimir anywhere. Dejected, she trudged back to her suite, hoping he'd returned unnoticed. When she entered, she halted.

A small wooden carving sat on the floor in front of her

bedroom door. She approached and gingerly picked it up, examining it meticulously. It was an exact replica of Luna.

"I made that for you."

Ava jumped and turned around to find him leaning against the open door to his bedroom, arms crossed. She swallowed thickly as she looked at the figure in her hand again, running her fingers along the ears.

"Thank you," she whispered. "It's beautiful."

She slipped the figurine into her pocket, avoiding eye contact with Casimir as she fidgeted with the hem of her shirt. She wanted to blurt out that she was sorry. That she was an idiot for avoiding talking about her struggles, and didn't mean the things she said. But she didn't even know where to start.

He strode to the couch and sat, one arm across the back. "Sit with me."

She took a deep breath and approached, lowering herself beside him. They sat in silence for a long moment, the gentle melody of birds outside the balcony drifting through the room. His hand moved to her hair, playing with it as they both waited for the other to speak.

"I'm sorry," she blurted. "I didn't mean what I said. I was exhausted and angry and—" She shook her head. "That's not an excuse. I shouldn't have—"

"Ava," Casimir cut her off. "Look at me."

She met his eyes.

"I know you didn't mean it. Neither did I. I'm sorry too. I never meant to hurt you."

"I know," she said.

"Please talk to me. Tell me about what's keeping you from sleeping. Why you're so angry."

She summoned her courage and turned away, focusing on the flames in the fireplace as she prepared to start at the beginning.

"I felt alone most of my life. It was just my mom and me. And Grandpa whenever we would visit him. We moved a lot, and it was difficult to make friends. The other kids thought I was weird and used to make fun of me. They used to tell me my mom was a witch."

She paused, inhaling deeply, while Casimir continued to stroke her hair.

"Then she died, and I was so lost. I didn't know what to do without her." She let the tears fall as she continued. "When my grandpa died and I moved to the farm, I was finally feeling some sense of peace. I had reconnected with my childhood best friend, and I was happy. At least...I thought I was."

She paused, preparing herself to say the rest out loud.

"I met Andras, who I knew as Henry, and he was kind to me. I think I was falling for him pretty hard...I feel so stupid that I let him trick me..."

"Ava," Cas whispered as he looked at her.

She kept her eyes forward as she continued, "As you know, it was all a lie. My best friend...Eleanor..." Her voice quivered. "Deidamia killed her. Slit her throat right in front of me and drank her blood. I tried to stop them, but I couldn't." She shook her head and sniffled, tears falling harder. "Sometimes I feel like it's my fault she's dead."

Casimir remained silent, seeming to understand her need to get it out. He didn't argue with her feelings as if he knew she needed to acknowledge her guilt.

"The dreams I've been having," she said. "I keep dreaming I'm back at their camp. Being tortured. I've been dreaming about Eleanor's death. About what happened on the ship. About Zeph dying. About Corvus. When I slit his—" She paused for a moment and closed her eyes. "When I killed him. The sound he made as he died...it was exactly how Eleanor sounded."

She let out a small sob, unable to stop it. Casimir reached

for her face, gently cupping it and turning her toward him. He swiped away her tears with his thumb.

"Eleanor's death is not your fault. You wouldn't have been able to stop it."

She sniffled. "I know that now. It's just…it still haunts me sometimes."

"I know, princess. I have things that haunt me too. Thank you for telling me. Please don't hide these things from me. I want to know when you're struggling. If you're hurting."

She nodded as she composed herself, his hand leaving her face and returning to her hair. She was about to speak when he held out another wooden figure. A fox.

"Elara was my little sister," he whispered. "This was her animal companion."

He hesitated a moment as he watched the flames dance in the hearth. "When I was a boy, daemon soldiers invaded the village I lived in with my mother and sister. Though Deidamia and Andras had already disappeared, some of their forces still attempted to take more land for themselves. They burned the houses and killed everyone they saw. My mother tried to hide us in the cabinets. She told us to be quiet and run as soon as we got the chance. I heard them enter the house." He paused, wiping away a stray tear. "Then I heard my mother die, trying to protect us."

She wanted to comfort him, wanted to touch him. To wrap him in her arms and tell him everything was alright. But she didn't.

His voice cracked as he continued, "My father hails from the astral kingdom and because of him, I have astral magic in addition to my earth abilities. So yes, I am a hybrid. I was scared. I was so scared, I started glowing. I tried to stop it, but I didn't know how to control it. They saw the light and found us. I watched as they killed my sister right in front of me. She was five."

"Oh Cas," said Ava as her vision blurred, hands shaking in her lap.

"They came at me too." He turned to her and pointed to the scar that ran from his jaw to his collarbone. "But for some reason, I didn't die. I got away and fled...like a coward."

She pulled his hand off the back of the couch and into her lap. "You were a child."

He remained still for a moment and placed the fox back into his pocket. "I know. But I don't think I'll ever get over the pain of that day. I escaped and basically lived on the streets for a while. I'd been stealing food from some of the local farms, sneaking in at night and eating their crops. Raine's father caught me and instead of turning me in, he adopted me."

"He sounds like a good man."

"He is. As I grew up, I fell in love with sword-fighting. I knew at a young age I wanted to be in the army. I wanted to fight against those who took my family away from me. I worked my ass off every day until I was named general and vowed to protect everyone in our kingdom, no matter the cost."

"You're a good man, too."

He looked at her. "I've killed a lot of people. So many, I can't even count."

"Did they deserve it?"

"Yes."

"And how many lives did you save by killing those people?" she asked.

"A lot. Hundreds... more."

"Then you're still a good man," she said as she squeezed his hand.

Casimir let go and put his arm around her, pulling her close. She laid her head on his shoulder and breathed him in. They sat in silence, absorbing each other's stories, another step toward understanding one another. Another step toward healing.

Ava knew she wasn't better, and she had a long way to go. But this was a start.

THE NEXT MORNING, Ava climbed through the course, feeling more confident after her talk with Casimir. He stood at the sidelines, coaching her through it. She didn't have a nightmare last night. In fact, she slept better than she had in weeks and had woken refreshed, determined today would be the day she would complete it.

Talking about her dreams had helped. Opening up about her trauma had relieved some of the pressure that had been building in her these last couple of months. Jorrar was right. She had to go through it and stop avoiding the hard things.

She made it to the rope climb and wrapped it around her leg.

"Remember, pull your legs high and use them to push yourself up. Stop relying on arm strength. Your legs do most of the work," Casimir called.

Pinching the rope between her feet, she pushed and made her way up. It was the last obstacle, and she was almost there. Higher and higher she climbed, sweat dripping down her back.

Her arms ached, ready to give out, but she focused on using her powerful legs to push harder. Her mind was brought back to her mother's words when her spirit visited her in the daemon war camp. She never knew if it was a hallucination or real, but she pulled her strength from it, remembering what her mother had said. 'Crush them, Ava.'

She channeled her anger. Her fury. *Crush them.*

With a shout and one last push, she reached the top and tapped the wood beam with her hand. She had done it. Finished the obstacle course.

Ava looked at Casimir who was beaming; the largest smile she had ever seen on his face.

He was beautiful.

She slid down the rope and landed on her feet. Casimir approached, still grinning. "Took you long enough."

"Oh hush, you brute," she replied as she shoved him, but he snatched her hand and held it.

Turning away, he pulled her along. "Come on. Let's go to the tea house to celebrate."

22

Drenched in sweat, Ava stood over the large stove in the castle kitchens. It had been a week or so since she'd completed the obstacle course and her newfound confidence had her excelling each day in her training. She'd turned a corner and while the grief was still there, she wasn't ignoring it any longer. Though it wasn't always easy, it was helping.

She'd spent hours with Casimir that afternoon sipping tea and talking. About the war, the upcoming Elderoak journey, the approaching Summer Solstice Ball where Ava would be presented to the kingdom. They talked about everything. Well, everything except them. That was something neither of them mentioned, both too stubborn or perhaps scared to acknowledge the elephant in the room.

Ava was covered in flour from rolling out dough as she prepared one of her favorite dishes. After her conversation with Jorrar, something he had said stuck with her. The part about doing something nice for others to heal. It had given her an idea.

So, she had asked her room attendant to introduce her to the kitchen staff and she did, though hesitantly. The head chef,

Derris, had said, "It's strange for a princess to do the cooking." She had to convince him cooking for others was something she did often in the human world, a way to show her love and gratitude, and he agreed to help.

The kitchen was enormous, the vast space almost overwhelming. The walls were made of the same pale stone as the rest of the castle, with large windows allowing in ample amounts of sunlight. She'd been there all day learning how to work the antiquated stoves and ovens, powered by wood and flame.

Then there were the ingredients. Although they had a lot of similar foods in Monterre, so many were new to her she'd spent two hours taste testing the unfamiliar herbs and spices to perfect her menu.

The center stone island behind her was laid out with the prepared dishes, the smell of yeast and spices hovering in the air. She wanted to make something they never would have tried here. Something unique to the human world. Settling on ravioli—her favorite meal she used to make with her mother—she hand rolled and cut each piece, filled with a unique cheese and local spices, and smothered in a rich tomato sauce.

She also made a special version of focaccia filled with tomatoes and Monterre's unique herbs, a fresh salad with homemade dressing, roasted root vegetables, and a lavender cake with sugared fruits and a honey glaze.

"Shall we take it from here, Your Highness?" Derris asked, surveying the spread before her. "You must be weary." He was a short gnome, his height only reaching about the level of her chest, and he had a long white beard obscuring the bottom half of his face. He spoke in a brittle voice full of warmth. "I must say, I'm impressed."

"Thank you." Most everything was finished, and the staff had promised to keep it warm while she washed up. "I'll meet you back here in half an hour."

He shook his head. "Oh no, Your Highness. We'll serve the food. You must wait in the dining hall with the king."

She looked at him with pleading eyes. "Please. I know it's not your usual procedure, but I'd like to help bring it out."

He huffed, but she caught a hint of a smile under his white mustache. "Oh, alright. Off with you now."

She left the kitchen and rushed down the halls, trying to get to her suite and back to the kitchen before anyone saw. Rounding a corner, she almost slipped and slammed into Casimir.

"Slow down," he said as he caught her arm to keep her steady. He tilted his head at her disorderly appearance. "Why are you covered in food?"

She pulled away and smirked at him before taking off down the hallway again, shouting after her, "No time to talk. See you at dinner!"

A rumble of his laughter echoed as she closed the door to their suite.

BACK IN THE KITCHEN, Ava carried the salad as she followed the staff out the side door entering the dining room. What if they didn't like it? What if they judged her for taking over Derris' duties? Was that disrespectful? She blew out a breath as she stepped into the large space, conversation ceasing when they saw her emerge.

Everyone was present, including Kai and Fanya, and they watched her with confusion as she walked in with the kitchen staff. Derris stopped before the table, and Ava stood next to him, waiting. She caught Casimir's eye, and he was looking at her with a hint of amusement, likely having figured out what she'd been up to after their run-in earlier.

"Your Majesty," Derris addressed the king. "Her Highness has something she would like to say."

She went rigid. "I do?" she whispered to Derris, glancing at him.

"Yes." He looked at her, ochre eyes bright with joy. "Go on," he urged.

Clearing her throat, she looked around the table and caught Raine on the verge of laughing. "I...um...I made dinner."

Thorne raised his eyebrows. "You did? By yourself?"

"Uh—" she began, but was cut off by Derris.

"She did everything, Your Majesty. We just followed her instructions if she needed help."

Everyone turned back to her, waiting for her to finish. "I made dinner for all of you." Her hands shook and she pleaded with herself not to drop the dish. "To show my appreciation."

Thorne grinned widely. "Thank you, Ava. Now why don't you sit before you pass out?"

"Yep." She nodded and leaned over the table, setting her dish in the middle.

She walked to her usual spot next to Thorne and across from Casimir and lowered into her seat beneath the glow of the chandelier.

"You look like you're about to throw up," Raine said.

"If I do, I'll make sure to do it in your wine," she replied, batting her eyelashes.

The rest of the food was brought in and laid before them.

"I take it you don't like talking in front of groups?" Quinn asked.

Ava shook her head. "I hate it."

"You did it in Saxumdale," Raine said.

"And I hated it then, too."

Jorrar chuckled. "Well, you'd best get used to it. It won't be the last time you have to address a group. Besides, you're being presented at the Solstice Ball soon. That will be a large audience."

"Don't remind me," she mumbled as she sipped her wine.

Raine turned to her, about to say something when he noticed her outfit. The dress was full of greens and browns, with multiple skirt layers and embroidered flowers throughout. It was the one Raine had picked out when he took her on a tour of the city.

"You're wearing my dress, dainty human!"

"It looks much better on me." She winked, giggling as she glanced at Casimir who had barely been able to take his eyes off her since she walked into the room.

"I think Cas likes it," Raine whispered.

She blushed and looked away.

Once the food had been laid out, Thorne asked her to explain the dishes. She listed each one, laughing at their attempts to pronounce 'ravioli' and 'focaccia' since there didn't seem to be any fae words for these, and waited for them to try it.

"Whoa," Quinn said as she took a bite of ravioli. "What's in this? It's delicious."

"The outside is a thin dough, and the inside has cheese and other herbs. Then you boil it in water and make a sauce."

"I love it," Quinn said, and everyone murmured their agreement.

"It's alright." Raine shrugged. She pinched him.

They continued their meal, everyone commenting on how much they enjoyed her 'human food,' and Ava warmed at the companionship and kindness hovering around the table. There was no talk of war, no mention of Deidamia, the Elderoak or their mission to retrieve the book, though she knew they were making plans.

They just enjoyed each other's company, and something more healed inside her at the laughter; the fellowship; the fondness everyone showed each other. Exactly like at Jorrar's house.

As they were eating dessert, Raine and Casimir devouring their second piece of cake, Fanya said from across the table in her bubbly voice, "Ava...Quinn and I were thinking about having a little fun after dinner. Would you like to join us?"

"Sure," she said. "What are we doing?"

Quinn took a sip of wine, giving her a mischievous grin. "Tavern hopping."

"I want to come!" announced Raine.

"No," said Quinn. "No fae brutes allowed."

Raine scowled at her, grumbling.

"That sounds amazing. Yes," Ava said.

"Do you know what tavern hopping is?" Fanya asked.

"We call them pub crawls, but I think it's the same concept."

Jorrar and Kai rose, saying their goodbyes before heading back to their house for the night, clearly not interested in partying with the rest of them.

"Well, I say we have a fae brutes night," Raine looked at Casimir and Thorne.

"What the fuck is a fae brutes night?" Quinn asked.

"It's where we get drunk and sword fight," said Raine.

Fanya frowned at her brother. "That sounds dangerous."

"That sounds sexual," Ava whispered to herself, already tipsy from the wine.

"Well, I'm not opposed to that either..." Raine started.

"No," said Thorne and Casimir in unison.

"Fine, fine." Raine waved his hand. "I'll find someone to play with my sword later."

Quinn rolled her eyes and rose, grabbing Ava's hand. "Time to go," she said as Fanya followed suit. "Goodbye," Quinn said as they made it to the door. "Enjoy your orgy."

A bark of Raine's laughter echoed as they disappeared down the hallway.

TWO HOURS LATER, they found themselves huddled in the corner of their third pub, taking shots of whiskey. It was a dark space. Warm wood surrounded them with flickering lanterns along the wall.

"And then," Fanya continued her story, "he kissed me."

"Who?" asked Ava, head fuzzy. "Wait...what're we talking about again?"

"Ava." Quinn slapped her arm. "Pay attention...Pax."

Ava squinted her eyes at Quinn across the table. "Pax! I love Pax," she drawled. "We fought on the ship...he's strong...and scary..."

Fanya giggled. "We know. You already said that."

Ava sipped her whiskey. "Fuck. Right. He kissed you?"

"Yes! I just said that."

Ava put her head in her hand. "Oh...sorry."

"I think we're going to have to carry you home," Quinn chided.

"Why—huh...Who?" She rubbed her face. "Why are *you* not that drunk?" Ava pointed her finger at Quinn.

Quinn lifted a shoulder. "It seems humans can't hold their alcohol."

Ava giggled as she reached for her glass, but Fanya swiped it away. "I'm cutting you off. Thorne will kill us if you drink yourself to death."

Ava groaned. "...more whiskey..."

"No." Quinn looked at her across the table. "What's the deal with you and Cas?"

Fanya gasped. "Cas? Oh...do tell us!"

Ava chewed on her lip. "There's nothing. I...uh...he's...what was the question?"

"Are you two sleeping together?" Quinn raised an eyebrow.

Ava pointed in between Quinn and Fanya. "Are *you* two sleeping together?" Then burst into laughter.

"No, but Quinn *is* sleeping with your brother," said Fanya.

"What?" Ava straightened.

"It's not a big deal. We have fun sometimes, that's all. He's quite good in bed."

"Eww." Ava shook her head. "I mean...good for you."

"So, about Cas," said Fanya.

"Uh—no." She tapped her fingers on the table. "We are not...have...not...done the sex. We haven't even kissed. But...he was getting all kissy on my neck on that damn horse."

"So *that's* why you were acting weird," said Quinn. "And nothing's happened since?"

Ava flopped her arm on the table. "No. He's a gentleman or something...Oh...look at me..." Ava sat up and crossed her arms in poor imitation of Casimir. "I'm the honorable gen— general. I'm waiting for the right time...or whatever. Oh...Ava wants me to throw her on the bed and fuck her brains out? No no no." She waggled her finger. "Can't do that. She's the princess."

Fanya burst out laughing.

Quinn gave her a naughty grin. "I'm telling him you said that."

"Oh...no. Please don't." She shook her head. "Why did you ask about him? Did he say something?"

"No." Quinn said. "But the way he looks at you when you aren't paying attention..."

"How?" interrupted Fanya.

"He *gazes.*"

"He does...does not gaze," slurred Ava.

Quinn gave her a flat look. "I've known him since we were children. I've never seen him look at anyone like that."

"Well." Ava giggled as the alcohol coursed through her

body. "He needs to gaze all over my naked body." She was laughing so hard she almost fell out of her seat.

"I don't even know what that means," said Fanya as she brushed her platinum blonde hair over her shoulder, shaking her head.

"Me neither," said Ava.

Quinn stood and grabbed Ava under her arm. "This is pathetic. I'm taking you back to the castle now."

"No! More! We—need more...whiskey."

"No more whiskey," she scolded, dragging her through the tavern.

The three of them exited into the night, the moon blurry above Ava as she looked at the stars. Fanya bid them goodnight and headed to her home in town near her bakery and Quinn practically carried Ava to the castle.

They made it back and walked through the gardens to the back entrance. Casimir and Raine were sitting outside on the ground against one of the low walls surrounding the training rings.

Quinn stopped before them, her arm around Ava's waist while Ava leaned into her for support. "Hullo, fae brutuses," Ava drawled.

Raine burst out laughing. "Oh, fuck. It seems the dainty human can't handle her alcohol."

"She's pathetic. But said some interesting things," Quinn said, looking pointedly at Casimir.

Ava put her finger on Quinn's lips. "Shhh...secrets."

Quinn rolled her eyes and stepped away. "She's your problem now."

Ava grabbed Quinn's face and yanked her closer, placing a kiss on her cheek. "Thank you, lady warrior...for a...uhh...a nice evening."

Quinn's eyes went wide as Raine couldn't control himself, doubling over. "We have her, lady warrior," he teased.

Casimir rose and wrapped his arm around Ava's waist as Quinn let go and walked off, grumbling under her breath.

"I think she likes me," said Ava.

Raine stood and shook his head.

Ava looked in between them. "How was...man night? Uhm...sword orgy?"

Casimir laughed beside her as Raine answered, "You *are* pathetic. It was a lovely evening, thanks for asking."

"How much did you have to drink?" Casimir asked.

"Umm...whiskey. Lots and lots of whiskey."

"Okay then," said Raine as he walked inside. "I'm going to leave you to it. Good luck, Cas."

"Goodbye wolf-man!" shouted Ava, leaning into Casimir, as Raine's laughter echoed through the castle doors.

Casimir began to walk her inside when she said, "I can walk."

He let go and crossed his arms, looking down at her. She swayed but remained standing as he cocked his head to the side and nodded toward the door. "Go on then."

She turned and tried stomping toward the castle, but her feet tangled with each other, and she tripped. Before she hit the ground, she was lifted and thrown over a broad shoulder.

"Hello!" she shouted. "What are you doing?"

"Shh," Casimir said as he carried her inside. "It's the middle of the night. You'll wake the whole castle."

"The princess is being taken away...the general captured her," she mumbled to herself. "Taking her to his room...to do naughty things." She giggled.

She thought she heard Casimir laugh but her brain was fuzzy and limbs heavy. They made it to their suite, and he set her on the couch. "Stay," he ordered, disappearing into his room. He returned moments later with a small tonic. "This will prevent you from getting sick."

She took it and choked it down. "That tastes like ass."

"I don't even know what to say to that," he said, standing in front of her.

She looked at his feet and raked her eyes along his body, pausing on his muscular thighs and what she imagined was between them. She continued higher, inspecting his toned forearms peering from the sleeves of his shirt. His golden eyes were predatory when she met his stare.

"What are you doing?"

"Picturing you naked." She giggled. "You know, you're a giant. Like a giant tree that I could climb. Can I climb you? Fuck...I didn't mean...Did I say that out loud?"

"Yes, you did. And you can climb me another time," he said, a smirk on his face. "But now it's time for bed." He lifted her and walked to the bedroom.

"You know, you carry me a lot...like my own personal chauffeur..." she mumbled.

He gave her a confused look as he laid her on the bed. "Chauffeur?"

"Never mind...human thing..."

"Alright then. Do you need help changing?"

"Yes...no...I don't know," she said, head swimming. "What was the question?" He grabbed her calf and removed her boot. She tensed. "What are you doing?"

A corner of his mouth lifted. "Do you want to sleep in your boots?"

"Do *you* want to sleep in my boots?" She couldn't control the giggles again.

Casimir shook his head in exasperation as he released her leg and grabbed the other, pulling off her remaining shoe. He rose and walked to her wardrobe, removing a white linen night dress and laid it on the bed.

He reached out a hand. "Can you sit up?"

She grasped it and let him pull, vision fuzzy as she tried to keep herself upright. He reached behind her and unclasped the back of her dress, fingers brushing her bare skin.

"Are you trying to seduce me, general?" she crooned, though it didn't sound as sexy as it did in her head.

He paused and leaned over her, forehead almost touching hers, hands braced on the bed. "If I were trying to seduce you"—his eyes gleamed—"you'd know it." He backed away. "Hold out your arms."

She did as he asked and huffed in frustration. "Why not?"

He raised an eyebrow as he pulled her sleeves, removing the top of her dress, revealing her torso. Her breasts were bound in stretchy fabric, but he didn't touch her, staying respectful of her bare skin.

"Because you are very drunk."

"So?"

With her dress pulled down to her waist, he eased the night dress over her head as she slipped her arms through the sleeves. "I don't take advantage of drunk women," he said in a matter-of-fact tone. "Now, stand."

She stood and he let her dress fall as he pulled the night-gown on with care. "That's what men in the human world do," she mumbled.

He grabbed her chin, tilting her to look at him. "Well, I am not like human men," he growled. "Besides," he said as he stepped closer and leaned in, lips barely brushing hers. "I want your head clear, so you'll remember every moment when I finally spend all night worshiping your body."

She shivered. "All night?"

"All...fucking...night," he said hoarsely.

"So, if I wasn't drunk...What exactly would you be doing?"

"I guess you'll have to find out another time," he leaned in to whisper in her ear, and she whimpered. "But it involves figuring out how to get you to make that sound again. And again. And again."

She closed her eyes and sucked in a breath as she ached with desire, his thumb brushing her bottom lip. When she opened them, he was watching her greedily, but backed away and pulled back her covers.

"Time to sleep," he ordered.

She huffed as she stumbled the two feet of distance to the bed. "You're no fun."

He tucked the blankets around her and brushed her hair out of her face with care. "Sleep, princess."

"Bossy general," she mumbled.

He walked to the door, pausing with his hand on the handle. "I'll see you at training tomorrow. A hangover is not an excuse to miss."

She swore she heard him groan and curse under his breath as he shut the door.

23

*A*va sat alone in her living room, reading next to the fireplace as Casimir finished yet another meeting. Turning the page, she pulled the throw blanket higher, when Raine barged in. He was wearing a velvet brown tunic with emerald green embroidery, thick pants, shiny new boots and his hair was even more impeccable than usual.

"Get up and get ready," he said, a mischievous look in his eye.

"Can't you see I'm busy?"

"You're never too busy to go dancing."

She set down her book. "Dancing? Nope. I don't dance. I'm a terrible dancer."

"That will make it easier to tease you." He brightened. "Therefore, making it more fun for me." He grabbed her hand and yanked her off the couch, pushing her toward her room, and followed her inside. "Let's go, dainty human. Get changed."

She stood in the middle of her room, staring at him. "I don't know what to wear. What kind of dancing is this?"

"The fun kind." He turned to her wardrobe and shuffled through her clothing, pulling out an outfit.

"There is no fun kind of dancing."

"Here," he said, handing her the clothes. "Hurry. Everyone else is already headed that way."

She took the clothes and walked to the bathroom. Raine had chosen a forest green velvet top with long sleeves and a sweetheart neckline. She pulled on the taupe skirt with vines embroidered along the hem. A pair of green boots completed the ensemble along with a green jade teardrop necklace.

As she finished getting dressed, she called out to him, "Who is going?"

"Everyone," he called back. "Yes, even Cas. Since I know you were going to ask."

"I was not," she said as she walked into the bedroom, finger combing her long hair.

"By the way," he asked. "Have you two fucked yet?"

She coughed, looking at him. "What? Of course not. We aren't—I don't—he doesn't want that."

He raised his eyebrows at her. "He most definitely wants that."

"I—it's...complicated."

He laughed as he grabbed two combs from her wardrobe and went around behind her, pinning her hair back on the sides. "Complicated? The only thing that's complicated is you two are still holding back. You both want to. You should get it over with to spare us all from the sexual tension. I don't think I can stomach another dinner with the two of you catching stolen glances from across the table."

She scoffed, putting her hands on her hips and turning around to face him. "There are no stolen glances," she said, emphasizing the last two words.

"You keep telling yourself that." He looked her up and down and beamed. "Perfect. Let's go."

WOODEN TABLES LINED the open room in the tavern, leaving space for a dance floor where citizens were twirling cheerily as a small ensemble played upbeat music with fiddles, flutes and mandolins. Lanterns hung from the rafters, illuminating the space, and the smell of ale and roasted meats hung in the air.

The joy was palpable, the sounds of boisterous voices blending as groups of friends sat together, drinking and gossiping as their worries faded away. This was one of Ava's favorite things about Mosshaven. The camaraderie among the residents in town. Never did there seem to be unhappiness or strife, even in the midst of a brewing war.

She looked around, hands fingering the sides of her skirt as she took in the sights and sounds of the tavern. Raine grabbed her hand and tugged, leading her to a large table in the back where everyone was already seated.

"Sit," he said. "I'm going to grab us drinks."

She took the closest open seat which happened to be in between Quinn and Kai.

"Ava!" drawled Thorne.

"Already drunk, big brother?"

"Perhaps." He chuckled, taking a sip of ale.

It was refreshing to see Thorne outside his role as king. And she hadn't seen him much in the past weeks, he'd been so busy.

Casimir sat across from her, nodding hello as he took in her dress. "You look beautiful."

"Thanks," she replied as warmth crept up her neck.

He was dressed in an olive-green tunic and his hair had several braids along the sides, flowing over his shoulders. Raine took his seat next to Casimir and passed her a mug.

"Mead for the dainty human since you didn't like the ale the first time."

"And we all know what happens if Ava gets a hold of whiskey," Quinn said.

Ava grimaced as she sipped her drink, meeting eyes with Casimir. The corner of his mouth lifted and she looked away.

"I heard about that," said Thorne. "You kissed Quinn and called her 'lady warrior.'"

Ava winced. "I didn't realize how strong your alcohol here was."

Quinn glared at each member of the table. "If any of you brutes call me that, I will punch you in the throat so hard, you won't be able to speak for a week." She glanced at Ava and winked.

"That's not all she did," said Raine. "I'm too far away for you to kick this time." He gave her a naughty grin. "Ouch!" he exclaimed as Casimir kicked him instead.

The others got the hint not to pry and visited among themselves, but Quinn leaned in and asked, "What else did you do?"

"Apparently, I propositioned Cas," she whispered as quietly as she could.

"And?"

"Nothing happened. He was the perfect gentleman."

"Not surprising," Quinn said as her head snapped up, her attention landing on Casimir and Raine. "Stop eavesdropping, you oafs."

Raine laughed and Casimir continued to look at Ava, sipping his ale.

Quinn whispered, "Cas keeps staring like he wants to rip those clothes right off you."

Ava choked on her drink, spilling it on her chest.

She grabbed a napkin and dabbed at the mead, glancing across the table. Casimir's eyes flared as they briefly dipped to her low-cut neckline before he blushed and turned away.

"He is not," she whispered back to Quinn.

"Whatever."

Raine rose and held his hand out. "Ava, dance with me."

She hesitated, looking around. "I don't know how."

"Who cares? I'll show you."

She chugged her mead and stood, taking his hand. "Alright."

They left the group along with Jorrar and Kai, taking off across the dance floor together.

"Follow my lead," Raine said as he placed one hand on her hip and gripped her other. "You just have to follow the rhythm of the music and move across the floor." She tripped over his feet as she tried. "You're over complicating it. Just go with the flow. I'll lead and you do what I do," he said as they took off in a trot.

They spun through the patrons as the music played on. "So, who are you taking home with you tonight?" she asked, scanning the room.

Jerking his head to his left he replied, "See her over there? With the long black hair and exquisite breasts?"

She followed his gaze. "It looks like she's with that man next to her."

"So, both of them will join."

She laughed as he continued to lead her down the dance floor. "Can I ask you a question?"

"Sure."

"Do you ever want to...you know...settle down?" Maybe the alcohol made her bold, but she added, "This whole, 'I sleep with everyone' thing. Is it an act?"

His swagger faltered before he regained his composure, though something still lingered in his gray-blue eyes. "I once believed that was possible. It's too late now," he answered softly.

"Raine, I—" she began, about to apologize for bringing up a sore subject, when he interrupted.

"This isn't a topic for a night such as tonight." He smiled, sadness in his eyes gone again as he twirled her.

Quinn and Thorne were on the floor together enjoying each other as they spun by. Thorne released Quinn and approached Ava and Raine.

"May I cut in?"

"She's all yours," Raine replied as he let go and sauntered toward the couple he'd pointed out moments ago.

Thorne took Ava's hand, leading her to dance once more. Quinn had pulled Casimir out of his seat, and they were now trotting across the floor.

"You're doing a great job," Thorne said as he spun her.

"It's not as hard as I thought."

"How are you?" he asked.

"Better. But I'm still terrified of the Elderoak journey. And the rest of this war."

His expression hardened. "You are an Everwood, Ava," he said, ever the king. "You remember how tenacious our mother was." She nodded. "I've seen that in you as well. At times, you're unsure. But when you allow yourself to let go of your fears, determination comes out and you become unyielding. Unwilling to give up." They spun across the floor, and she looked at him, his eyes fierce. "I saw it the first time we met."

Her lips curved into a small smile. "When you thought I was threatening you?"

He laughed quietly. "Yes. When you stood up to a king even though you were lost in an unknown world. And I've seen it every time you stand up for yourself. I know that strength came out in Saxumdale. You can do this."

Her eyes glistened as her brother spoke. He believed in her. Truly believed in her and she hadn't realized she needed his reassurance until now.

"It's a lot of pressure," she admitted. "That I'm the only one who can banish Deidamia."

"It is," he acknowledged. "But the thing about Monterre is,

we don't do anything alone. Other kingdoms are not quite like ours."

"What do you mean?" she asked as he spun her and brought her back, leading them in between pairs of dancing revelers.

"We listen to each other's opinions. I have the final say but I always consult Jorrar, the advisors, and often the others," he explained. "Most of the other kings or queens demand blind devotion. They don't allow their decisions to be questioned. Some have even been known to punish those who do." He paused. "Our father was that way. A tyrant. I want to be questioned. I may not like it, but I respect it. I want all of you to call me out if you feel I'm being rash. It may not change my decision, but it makes me think about what's best for everyone."

Ava beamed at her brother. He was a leader who cared. "Why are you different from the others?"

"I don't care about power," he explained. "I care about peace." He looked at her intensely. "So, like I said. You are not alone. We are in this *together*."

She pulled him close, stopping their dance as she gave him a hug. "I'm proud to call you my brother."

They were interrupted by Quinn and Casimir approaching.

"Switch partners!" Quinn announced.

Thorne let go and continued his dance with Quinn as Casimir strode toward Ava eagerly. He grasped her waist and yanked her close, entwining his fingers into her other hand. She couldn't slow her heartbeat and he didn't break eye contact while he led her through the crowd, spinning and dipping.

The feel of his hand low on her waist shot warmth through her body as she lost herself in his eyes. Those eyes. They were beautiful. Everything about him was beautiful. His smile, his soft hair, the scar running from his jaw to his collarbone. She wanted to touch it, to kiss it.

They were so close, bodies barely a breadth away as he led her through the crowd as if no one else was present.

Breaking the silence, she whispered, "You've been quiet tonight."

"I've had a lot on my mind."

His eyes dipped to her lips as she cleared her throat. "Like what?"

"Wouldn't you like to know," he answered as he pulled her closer.

She inhaled sharply. "Yes, I would."

He dipped her low and pressed his lips right above her collarbone. Her skin came alive as she gasped. He lifted her and spun her around.

"Does that answer your question?"

"Yes," she breathed, her stomach tightening. "But—"

"But what?"

"You haven't acted on anything since dinner at Jorrar's house."

"I was respecting your boundaries." He leaned in and whispered into her ear. "This is me acting on it." He placed a kiss on her neck, and she arched into him, eliciting a quiet growl from his throat. They looked back at each other as they continued their dance and Ava remained silent.

"Say something," he whispered after several minutes, concern in his eyes.

"I—" She had no idea what to say. Why couldn't she talk to him? Tell him how she felt? They've talked about so much together, opening up about their pasts, but they've never talked about this. About them.

"I'm sorry," he said. "I didn't mean to push you." He let go and took her by the hand. "Let's go sit down."

He led her back to the table, this time sitting next to her. Arm on the back of her chair, he toyed with her hair, sending goosebumps down her spine. The way he was so gentle when he touched her made her want to cry.

The rest of the group joined, seats all switched around. Thorne and Quinn could barely keep their hands off each other as she sat in his lap, kissing him. Ava glanced around and saw no one cared that the king was in the tavern, making out with one of their captains. As if this was normal.

"They're cute together," she whispered to Casimir.

"They are. They'll never make it official though. Too complicated."

She glanced over at Jorrar and Kai, who were whispering with the promise of pleasure in their eyes. Raine had brought over the couple he had pointed out earlier, the woman in his lap while he was kissing the man's neck sitting next to him. It seemed everyone had their own personal plans for the rest of the night.

"This is..."

"Getting awkward." Casimir chuckled. "Would you like to leave?"

"Actually, yes."

Casimir rose, Ava following suit, and they both said their goodbyes.

Raine caught Ava's eye and winked. "Don't do anything I wouldn't do, you two."

"That means nothing's off the table," said Quinn.

Raine grinned. "Exactly." He turned to the woman and kissed her.

Ava led the way through the crowd, Casimir's hand on her lower back. They left the tavern and walked through the streets, quiet now that it was late. He took her hand, interlocking their fingers, as her stomach fluttered with nerves.

"What's the deal with Raine?" she asked.

"What do you mean?"

"When we were dancing, I asked him about his love life. If

he ever wanted to settle down. He got quiet and said something about it being too late for him and changed the subject."

"Oh. He doesn't like talking about it."

"What happened?"

Casimir sighed. "I'm not going to tell his story. Just know he lost someone very special to him many years ago."

"Did he love them?" she asked.

"Yes. They were supposed to be married days after it happened."

"I should never have asked."

"It's alright. He'll tell you about it when he's ready. You didn't upset him."

"He hides it well."

"He does."

They walked along the cobblestone street, hand in hand, savoring each other's silent presence. The buzz of insects hovered around them as the leaves rustled, tickled by the cool breeze. Ava shivered and Casimir let go of her hand and placed an arm around her waist, pulling her to his side.

"Did you have fun tonight?" he asked, breaking the silence as they approached the castle.

"Yes. I'm a terrible dancer but that wasn't too bad. I enjoyed it. Do you all do that often?"

"We used to do it all the time. But not as much recently."

They continued through the entrance and made their way to the suite. Ava smiled at Pax and he nodded back as they entered the living room and walked toward Ava's bedroom door. Casimir turned to her and placed both hands on her hips. Her heart sped up as she looked into his eyes.

She desperately wanted him to kiss her, but she was terrified of what it would mean. Where it would lead. He stood before her, eyes taking her in, and cupped her face.

He leaned in, their noses touching but she tensed. Noticing her hesitation, he pulled back and gently smiled at her. Before she had a chance to change her mind, he kissed her forehead and pulled away. "Goodnight, Mi'ra Vässa," he whispered, turned and walked into his suite, closing the door with a soft click.

Dammit. Why did she hesitate?

24

*A*va's arms vibrated with restraint as the sound of Raine's sword clashing with hers rang through the air.

"Good," he coached, their swords crossed in front of her. "Again."

She whirled around and brought her weapon down but he blocked the blow. She was getting quicker, and though she was no match for the warriors while still human, once she had her fae strength and speed she'd hold her own.

Casimir was in meetings most of the morning, so Raine had taken over Ava's training for the day. It had been a couple of weeks since the tavern, and he was yet again back to the quiet general as he pushed her harder every morning. While she respected him for noticing her hesitance, it also infuriated her, confused her.

"Block left," barked Raine as she barely got there in time to stop his blow to her leg. A trickle of blood ran down her thigh as his sword brushed her before she knocked him away.

"Dammit," she said, leg stinging.

"Kai can fix it," he said as he lunged at her again. She blocked the blow, but soon after, he hooked his leg under hers

187

and threw her on her back, his sword at her throat. "You're distracted," he chastised. She glared at him. "Get off your ass and fight me."

She climbed to her feet and swung her sword in her hand. "I am."

"You're holding back."

She lunged at him, but he blocked it, swords locked in an x near his throat. "No, I'm not."

He leaned. "Yes, you are, dainty human."

"I'm not dainty."

He shoved her off him and backed up, swinging his sword as he taunted her. "Prove it."

She whirled toward him, and they met blow after blow. Her arms were aching and strength waning, but she pushed on, barely able to keep up. Raine advanced, pushing her to the edge of the ring.

"Not good enough," he said. "What would Andras say?"

Anger coursed through her at the mention of his name. "Shut up."

Determination flared in Raine's eyes as he continued to goad her. "He'd call you a coward."

"I'm not a coward," she seethed as she knocked his sword away before it sliced her hip.

"He tricked you. Tortured you," he went on as he battled her. "He got your friend killed."

She screamed as she lunged toward him, a burst of strength pulled from her anger. "Fuck you," she snarled and increased her speed as Raine parried.

"There you are."

Though he blocked each and every blow she landed, she was faster, stronger and more determined than before. After several minutes of their back and forth, he called it. "Let's take a break."

She slumped against the wall, dropping the sword. Raine

sat next to her and handed her a water skin. "That was fucking amazing."

She frowned at him, panting. "You're mean."

"So is Cas."

"Yes, but you're meaner."

"He holds back because he lo—" He stumbled before correcting himself. "Because he's afraid of hurting the dainty human."

She narrowed her eyes at him. "What?"

"Nothing," he replied and changed the subject. "You're getting better. You're ready."

She shook her head, still wondering what he was about to say but didn't mention it again. "I'm not."

"If you fight like you just did, you are." He took a sip of water before handing it back. "You have the technique down. Once you have your fae strength and speed, you'll be unstoppable."

"But I won't have that on the way to the Elderoak."

"You won't need it," he encouraged. "You can do it now."

They sat quietly as they rested. Ava watched a family of rabbits dart into the forest, their silver fur a blur. Luna opened an eye from her nap beneath a nearby tree, seeming to debate whether she wanted to hunt them. With a feline sigh she went back to sleep.

"Hey Raine?"

"Hmm?"

"What does Mi'ra Vässa mean?" she asked, remembering the words Casimir said to her the night of the tavern. She'd been too scared to ask anyone what it meant, not ready to hear the answer.

Raine looked at her and raised an eyebrow. "Where did you hear that?"

She looked around, refusing to meet his eyes. "Umm...Cas said it."

"Oh, did he now?"

She turned and looked at him. "Well?"

"I don't know if I want to tell you. It's much too fun to watch you squirm."

"That's not fair." She scoffed.

"I should make you ask him. I'm assuming you haven't, right?"

"No," she mumbled.

"I'll tell you on one condition," he said as he rose and held out his hand.

"Okay." She grabbed it and stood.

"Beat me in archery," he replied as he walked toward the archery range.

She flung her arms down and stormed after him. They paused on the edge of the field, a dozen targets displayed at different distances across from them. Bright green grass swayed in the breeze like an emerald ocean and a blue lizard skittered away into a nearby shrub.

"You have better eyesight than me," she said. "I'm good, but not *that* good."

He turned to her and brushed his long blonde hair over his shoulder. "Get three bullseyes in a row, then."

"Easy." She grabbed a bow and nocked the arrow, about to warm up.

"Two rules," he said, putting his hand on her raised arm to stop her. She looked at him and his expression was full of mischief. "No warmup. And you must hit *that* target," he added pointing to the one farthest away. The one she had hit before, but never in the center.

"No warmup? That's unfair," she argued.

"Like you had time to warm up on the ship, dainty human?"

"Alright, alright. Point taken. You're going to have to come up with a better nickname, wolf man."

"I'm working on it."

She set her stance and drew her bow, lining it up with the target. Her hand brushed her cheek as she continued to pull back, eyes on the bullseye. She took a slow breath in, exhaled, and released the arrow. It hit right in the center.

"Speaking of," she said as Raine's giant silver wolf appeared.

She trotted to Ava and shoved her furry head under her hand, demanding scratches. Ava petted her as Luna joined and wound between Sabriel's legs.

"Are you friends with all the other animals, Luna?" Ava asked.

Of course I am. Sabriel plays with me. And Aro is so soft for sleeping.

"Is it normal for the animals to be so social with each other?" Ava asked as Titus appeared from the treetops, whipping between them and screeching as he landed on a nearby branch.

"I like that little guy," Raine said, then answered her question. "I've never seen them this social." He looked at Luna who settled near Sabriel in a patch of sun, enjoying the warmth on their fur. "They don't hate each other, but they don't ever play or snuggle. Except with Luna."

"Luna's obsessed with Aro." Ava turned to Raine. "And Cas. She lets him pick her up. She never lets anyone pick her up."

Casimir is special, Ava.

"I know."

Raine smirked at her, turning back to the targets. "Alright, stop stalling. Go again."

She drew her bow and released her second arrow. It landed on the edge of the bullseye. "That counts," she insisted.

"It does. Last one."

Taking a deep breath, she squinted at the bullseye—harder to see now that it was blocked by two arrows. She released, frozen as she watched it zoom across the field.

It hit its mark perfectly, splitting her first arrow down the center.

She set the bow down and crossed her arms, beaming up at Raine who appeared shocked. "You didn't think I could do it, did you?"

"I knew you could do it. I'm just impressed by that last shot."

"Answer my question now."

He studied her. "What exactly did he say?"

"He said 'Goodnight, Mi'ra Vässa.'"

"When?"

"The night we went dancing." She sighed. "He walked me to my door, kissed my forehead and said that before he went into his room."

"Hmm... You two didn't—"

"No!" She placed her hands on her hips. "We've done *nothing*."

"I see." He smiled. "Somebody's upset they aren't getting any."

"I'm not—I mean—whatever. Are you going to tell me what that means?"

They walked back to the castle, leaving Luna and Sabriel asleep in the sun. Titus screeched and landed on Ava's shoulder, nestling in her hair.

"It's an old fae term that isn't used often."

"What do you mean?"

"We reserve it for someone who means a lot to us."

"Have you ever called anyone that?" she asked, heart racing as she gathered his meaning.

"Only one person." He glanced at her, humor replaced by a sense of sadness on his face. She was silent, letting Raine decide if he wanted to say more. "It means dear one."

"Okay, and what does *that* mean?"

"It means you're important to him."

"I know. At least, I think I know," she said.

"There's a lot you don't know."

"What do you mean?"

"I'll only say this. Casimir probably won't make a move until he's positive you want it. He's too...honorable or whatever. You need to figure out what's holding you back. And talk to him."

"What am I supposed to say?"

"How about this? 'Hey Cas...I'm in love with you and I'm pretty sure you're in love with me but we're both too stubborn to do anything about it so take off all your clothes and ravage me my dearest general.'"

Ava's jaw dropped. "I'm not in *love* with him."

"Uh huh," said Raine as he patted her cheek and turned to enter the castle, leaving her alone on the steps.

25

*A*va paced in the living room of her suite, poring over each interaction she'd had with Casimir. The touches. The flirting. The almost kisses. Everything since the night at the tavern. After her conversation with Raine the other day, she couldn't stop thinking about what he'd said. Casimir had barely spoken to her outside of training since they had gone dancing. Since she basically turned him down.

Shit.

The door opened and Casimir walked in, halting in the middle of the room. "I can hear you pacing and mumbling to yourself down the hallway. What's wrong?"

She whirled toward him. "You're joking."

He smiled at her as if he knew why she was upset. "I don't make jokes."

"You insufferable oaf, what do you mean you don't make jokes?"

His smile grew as he took a step forward. "Why are you angry?"

"You!" She let out a sigh of frustration as she put her hands on her hips.

Raising an eyebrow, he crossed his arms. "And?"

"And? That's all you have to say?"

"What would you like me to say?"

"I don't know." She shook her head. "You're so hot and cold all the time. What happened the night of the tavern? Why have you ignored me since?"

He tilted his head. "Why don't *you* tell *me* what happened that night at the tavern?"

"Stop answering my questions with another question!" He stood there, grinning at her. "You're enjoying this aren't you?"

He shrugged. "Perhaps."

She glared at him.

"Use your words, Ava. Tell me why you're mad at me."

She pointed her finger at him. "Don't patronize me. Ever since the tavern, you can barely look at me, acting like nothing happened that night."

He walked a couple of steps closer and stopped. "So, tell me what happened that night."

"I don't know! You acted like you wanted to...and then you didn't and went into your room. And ever since you've been aloof."

"Acted like I wanted to what?" His voice lowered.

"You know..."

"Tell me."

She rolled her eyes. "Like you wanted to...you're purposely trying to irritate me right now, aren't you?"

His smile didn't falter.

She stared at him, willing him to say why he's been acting so strange. The breeze moving the curtains and the crackle of the fire were the only sounds as she held his gaze.

"Do you want to know why I've been avoiding eye contact with you?" he asked, his voice low and soft. "Why I look away every time you look at me?"

"Yes," she whispered.

He took one step closer and stopped, eyes full of longing. "It's because every time I look at you, I want to throw you against a wall and kiss you until my lips are numb. I look away because if I look at you too long, it feels like my heart is beating out of my chest. Like I will go mad if I can't kiss you right then and there." He took another step. "But I don't want it to be just a kiss. I want it to be more. I want you naked before me so I can run my hands along your curves. I want to worship your body until your legs are quivering and you're screaming my name."

Her stomach tightened as warmth bloomed low in her belly. "Then do it," she whispered.

"I want you to say it. I want to know you're sure you want it," he said as he took another step closer and ran his hand through his hair, barely restraining himself. "Say it, princess. Tell me what you want," he rasped.

She trembled as she stood there, unable to escape the heat of his gaze. "I want you to throw me against a wall and ki—" She didn't finish because he consumed the distance between them in seconds.

One moment she was standing there, looking at him. The next, her back was pressed into the wall and his lips were on hers in a searing kiss. The whole world seemed to fall away as Ava gripped the front of his tunic, pulling him closer. His lips were soft and warm against hers and he kissed her gently, as if savoring it. Memorizing every detail.

The way it felt to kiss him was everything. It was rain on a summer's day. It was a sunset, the light melting below the horizon as it set the world on fire. It was tender and passionate. Full of promises whispered on the breeze and unapologetic vows.

Her lips yielded to his as he coaxed them apart. Exploring. How had she lived her life without experiencing a kiss like this? How had she gone so long being in the presence of this powerful, incredible man and not felt his lips on hers?

He pulled away to catch his breath and looked at her, his chest rising and falling as he studied her face. As if gauging her reaction, ensuring that she wanted this. One hand was on the wall beside her head while the other cupped her face. Unable to pull away her gaze, she lost herself in his golden eyes.

Foreheads pressed together, she moved her hands up his chest to his neck.

"More," she whispered, as she pulled him back in.

This time it wasn't slow or gentle, but full of need. Of all the pent-up desire they'd been holding back for months. It was possessive. All consuming.

She gasped as his tongue parted her lips and explored her mouth feverishly.

One of his hands moved to her waist and pulled her closer, no space between them. She slid a hand into his hair and he groaned, kissing her harder. It was only them. No war or impending journey. No evil lurking about. Only the taste of his lips against hers; the cedar and sage smell of him; his hard body pressed against her soft curves.

A spark ignited as their restraint snapped from denying themselves of each other for so long. She pulled him closer, hands roaming his back. A moan slipped from her lips and he met her desperation. His hands moved possessively along her curves as he deepened the kiss even further, releasing a low groan.

"Fuck, Ava." He moved his lips to her jaw, then trailed kisses down her neck and up the other side. "You have no idea how long I've been waiting for this. You're all I can think about."

He paused, gripping her hips and pressing his forehead to hers yet again. "You're all I dream about. You consume my every thought."

Those words. The way he spoke to her. She was desperate to touch him. To feel him. She yanked his shirt over his head and dropped it on the ground as she ran her hands along his chest and his lips met hers again, swallowing her moans. Frantic. Feverish.

"Cas," she whimpered as she arched into him.

Saying his name unleashed him. His hand slid under her tunic and grasped her breast over the tightly wound fabric, squeezing and inducing another moan from her.

"This thing is in the way," he complained.

He lifted her shirt over her head, tossing it aside before unraveling the bandeau binding her chest.

"Better," he groaned as he palmed her full breasts and kissed her again, hard and fast. He journeyed his way to her chest and took her nipple in between his teeth, biting and sucking. Her head fell back and she whimpered.

"I need," she panted. "Cas...oh..."

He grasped her thighs, lifting her and she wrapped her legs around him as he ground her against the wall. "Tell me what you need," he growled into her mouth as his hard length pressed into her.

She moaned, the friction of him against her almost too much but not enough. Never enough. She could crawl beneath his skin and it still wouldn't be close enough. This frenetic, carnal need within her ached. It was urgent. Like fate was pulling them to each other in this very moment.

"Please..." she breathed, grinding against him.

"Please what?" he asked, starting to slip a hand beneath the front of her pants while the other held her thigh.

"I need you," she pleaded as she tangled her hands in his hair.

"You have me. You've had me since the day Aro rescued you from that monster," he added, kissing her deeper when a door opened, jolting them from their embrace. They froze and Ava looked over Casimir's shoulder, panting and meeting eyes with Raine.

"Jorrar found something about the Elderoak," he

announced. "Meeting in the dining hall in five minutes." He paused and his eyes widened. "Oh shit. Did I interrupt your maiden voyage?"

Casimir turned his head and snarled as if he was some territorial beast, "Get. The. Fuck. Out."

Raine smirked. "Nice tits, Ava. See you in five."

The door closed and he was gone.

Casimir was still holding onto her legs wrapped around him and looked at her with equal parts frustration and hunger, breathing heavily as if trying to calm himself. "I'm going to break his nose."

She ran her hand along his face, tracing his scar before she laid a light kiss on his lips. "Maybe we could be quick," she whispered.

Casimir shook his head and gripped her chin, eyes boring into hers with heat. "It will never be quick with us. I'll take my time learning all the ways to make you whimper."

He set her down, retrieved her shirt and bandeau, and handed them to her before putting his own back on.

After she finished dressing, he yanked her against him and kissed her one last time.

"Later," he said into her lips as he pulled away.

She straightened her clothing and smoothed her hair before Casimir grabbed her hand and led her out of the suite.

They made their way down the hallway in silence, fingers interlaced. Ava didn't know what to say, heart racing from what had been about to occur and the anticipation of what Jorrar found. The guards opened the doors, and they entered the dining room.

"What's this about?" Casimir fumed.

Raine suppressed a smirk as he sat at the table, but the rest of them pretended not to notice their disheveled clothing and hair. They were the last two to arrive and sat next to each other. Casimir scooted his chair close, and placed his hand under her hair on the back of her neck, his thumb shifting back and forth.

Ava looked at Jorrar. "You found something about the Elderoak?"

Thorne and Jorrar looked grave, and her gut twisted as he answered. "Yes."

"Well?" said Casimir, concern in his voice.

Jorrar spoke, "We learned you must go alone past a certain point."

"What happens if someone comes with me anyway?" she asked.

"They die," said Thorne.

They all tensed as Jorrar continued, "The journey appears to be a combination of physical and emotional strength, which we had already assumed."

Ava remained quiet, biting her lip as she tried to keep calm. Casimir's hand clenched on her neck in silent comfort.

"The path to the tree will try to confuse you. There will be tricks and illusions. Some you must battle with your weapons, and others with your mind," said Jorrar.

"What tricks and illusions?" asked Quinn.

"It's different for each individual."

"I can't do that," Ava whispered.

"You can," Casimir said and turned to Jorrar. "What else?"

"We knew the journey was an annual occurrence. We learned when."

"And?" Casimir urged.

Thorne shook his head. "It's the day before the Summer Solstice."

"That's the day after tomorrow!" Raine exclaimed.

"What happens if I get there and I fail?" Ava asked.

Jorrar said, "If you're able to find your way back, you go home and try again next year."

"And if you can't?" Casimir said.

"You lose your mind and the forest takes you."

Ava popped out of her seat. She wanted to run away. To run to her room and start the day over and pretend she never heard this news. Her lips were going numb, and her heart was beating out of her chest. She was going to have a panic attack in front of the whole group. She tried to leave, but her legs wouldn't obey. She couldn't do this, wasn't ready yet. She needed more time, more training.

"I'm not ready...I'm not ready," she repeated to herself.

Her head spun as she gripped the back of her chair and tried to focus. Air. She needed air. At some point Casimir had risen and was talking to her, but she couldn't hear him. The room darkened as dizziness took over and a wave of nausea washed through her.

"Ava, breathe," Casimir said from far away, as if she was in a well. Her vision faded and she swayed on her feet.

Then the room went dark.

26

*V*oices whispered in the distance, though Ava didn't know who they belonged to. Her head was on someone's lap and a hand stroked her hair. A cool rag was being dabbed across her forehead, her face and her neck.

She opened her eyes, vision clearing, and Casimir's face came into view.

"Where am I?" she whispered as he continued to stroke her hair.

"In my suite," said Thorne, sitting in a chair on her right. "It was the closest."

"Where's everyone else?" she asked.

"They're still in the dining hall, giving you space," her brother said.

She sat up and Casimir moved closer, rubbing her back. "I can't do it."

"Yes, you can," they said in unison.

Thorne pulled his chair close and grabbed her hands. She raised her eyes, meeting his. "Ava, listen to me. You *can* do this. You must."

"I'm not strong enough. I'm not ready. I—I need more time."

"Where is that woman who never gave up on the obstacle course? Or the one who fights and argues with me every step of the way? The one who rode a dangerous sea monster with no fear? The one who gives Raine's shit right back to him? *That* woman is strong enough."

She sat in silence, unsure what to say as she mulled on Casimir's words.

"Ava," said Thorne. "You *are* fae. Take your rightful place. *Demand* it. Do you remember what I told you at the tavern?" She nodded. "We don't do anything alone. But more importantly, you belong to us. All of us." He brought his face closer to hers. "What would Mother say?"

"Crush them," she whispered.

"What are you going to do to Andras and Deidamia? The ones who stole everything from you. Who are trying to steal more," his voice rose. She had never seen him like this. This was the king. The leader of her kingdom. Of her home.

Her *home*.

Fury rose as she thought of what she'd lost at their hands. Of what else she stood to lose in the future should she fail at her task. She was terrified of facing the Elderoak journey, but she was more terrified of losing this. Her friends and her family. The peace and belonging she'd found at last. And that's what she would lose if she didn't do this.

What *everyone* would lose.

"I'm going to crush them," she answered with determination as she stood.

They watched her. The king and the general, pride on their faces.

"Are you ready to go back to the meeting?" asked Thorne.

"Yes."

Thorne led the way. Casimir took her hand, interlocking

their fingers, and squeezed before bringing it to his lips and kissing her knuckles.

They returned to the dining hall and took their seats, Casimir placing a hand on her leg. Ever since they unleashed themselves on each other earlier, he couldn't not touch her. As if he was scared if he stopped it would all disappear. She reveled in it and let it steady her, keeping her calm as she prepared to face this insurmountable task.

"Are you alright?" Raine asked from across the table.

"No." She looked at him, steel in her eyes. "But I will be."

Pride flashed on Raine's face as he nodded.

"So, let's say I pass."

"You *will* pass," said Casimir.

"*When* I pass. What happens next? Will I be different? Will I suddenly have magic? What will it feel like?"

"We don't know," Jorrar said. "In our records we've never had a fae born in the human world before. Therefore, a human has never attempted the journey."

"We can only assume," said Thorne. "I'm positive you will feel different. And you may even look different, more fae. You'll have magic but probably not a significant amount."

"Because I still have to go through my great tribulation, huh?"

It was the ordeal the strongest fae often went through, causing the well of their magic to increase. It was what Deidamia was trying to induce during Ava's weeks of torture.

"Yes," Thorne responded. "When your blood opened the portal, you obviously had enough magic in your lineage to do so. But it wasn't enough for anything else."

Ava shook her head and rambled, words spilling out as the memories of her imprisonment assaulted her. "They tried everything to get my magic to erupt. Burning me, pulling out my fingernails, slicing me with knives. They even rubbed some type of acidic powder into my wounds once—" she stopped when she saw everyone staring at her. "Sorry."

"How did you not die?" asked Quinn.

Casimir snapped at her, "What an insensitive question."

"Sorry. I worded that poorly. What I meant was, even though you're technically fae, your body is still human. I don't think most humans would survive torture like that. Some fae would even succumb."

"I'm not sure, but they never took it far enough to kill me, I guess. Most of the time I passed out from the pain. She had healers come in and patch me up enough to make it to the next. Though one time...the worst time...she had the healers give me something to ensure I wouldn't pass out. To prolong it to see if that would work. That was when she whipped me over and over." She paused, taking a breath. "I gave up that day. I was hoping she would go ahead and kill me."

Casimir was shaking, wary eyes watching him around the table. She rubbed his arm, trying to calm him.

"Exactly how long were you there?" asked Jorrar.

She thought for a moment. "I don't know. I lost track of time. When we arrived in Eorhan, they put me in shackles and threw me into a prison wagon. I have no idea how long it took to get from the portal to their camp. I was there for a long time. A month? Maybe longer."

"Do you know how often you were tortured?" Raine asked.

"I think every couple days," she whispered.

The heat of power emanated from Casimir. Jorrar called his name. "Casimir. You must calm yourself."

Vines by the windows grew larger, snaking their way around the room. Casimir gritted his teeth, and Ava grabbed his face and made him look at her.

"Hey," she whispered. "I'm here now. I'm fine. I'm safe."

A muscle ticked in his clenched jaw, violence in his stare as he trembled, vines writhing more aggressively and growing around the room.

"Take a walk, Casimir," said Thorne. He turned to Thorne, fury in his eyes as if he was about to push back. "That's an order."

He stood and left the room, flowers blooming behind his feet as he walked away. The vines receded and the room returned to normal.

Ava turned back to the table, heart racing with worry. "Could someone please explain?"

"I've never seen him like that before," Quinn said.

"Ava, I don't think you're ready for this conversation," said Thorne.

"What?" She looked at her brother. "That's not fair. Tell me."

He sighed. "When powerful fae become very angry, they can lose control and their magic erupts. He was on the verge of that. It's something we must learn to manage or there could be consequences."

"Why was he so angry?" she asked.

Raine looked at her, dumbfounded.

"I know it was hard to hear about what I went through, but none of *you* were on the verge of losing control."

Raine shook his head at her. "You're blind, Ava. You really can't see it, can you?"

"Can't see what?"

Jorrar cleared his throat. "Since fae are historically primal creatures, this anger sometimes comes out when someone they care about is harmed. Someone they care about romantically."

"Oh. And you're saying he cares about me. I know," she said.

Raine narrowed his eyes. "He cares about you a *lot*."

"You've already told me that. There's something else you aren't telling me."

Raine scanned the silent room. "Fine. I'll explain since no one else will."

She focused on Raine across the table, her heart racing with anticipation.

"There's a term we use. It's an old fae word. Different from the one you asked me about." She fidgeted in her seat. "Miraêl Li'ra it's called."

"What does that mean?"

"Soul-bonded," answered Thorne.

"Okay...oh. Oh wow," she said, reeling. "Like...a soulmate thing?"

"Yes." Raine looked at her pointedly.

She bit her lip. "Are you saying Cas and I—"

"Yes."

"Does he know?" she whispered.

"Yes."

"Why hasn't he told me?"

"You think you would have reacted well to that conversation?"

She opened her mouth and closed it again. He was right. If Casimir had come out and told her they were soulmates too soon, she probably would have panicked and withdrawn further.

But for some reason, she wasn't panicking now. It made sense. The way they seemed to be drawn to each other.

"So, what does this mean?" she asked.

"We have complete choice in our relationships," Jorrar explained. "You don't have to accept the bond." He paused. "But if you do, that bond is powerful. More than you can even imagine."

"I have feelings for him," Ava said. "Strong feelings. But I haven't felt any unique sensations. At least I don't think I have."

"It will likely happen after the Elderoak blesses you," said Raine. "And be prepared because it will be intense. Did you notice how angry he got when I walked in your room earlier?" She blushed at the reminder and nodded. "I'm lucky we're friends. If it had been a stranger, he probably would have attacked them."

"Why?" she whispered.

"There's a sense of possessiveness. A need to protect. During times of vulnerability, or if the other is hurt...or hearing about people hurting them..." he trailed off.

"Like me describing my torture."

"Exactly."

"How long has he known?" she asked.

"I'm not telling you. You need to talk to him about it," he said.

"Do you know anyone else who is soul-bonded?"

"It's very rare," said Jorrar. "Kai and I are not. Astrid and Soren are the only ones we're close to who are."

"Okay," Ava said, mind still reeling with the news.

"Sorry to change topics," interrupted Thorne. "But we need to finish our planning for the journey."

Footsteps echoed in the dining hall as Casimir returned. He reclaimed his seat and grabbed Ava's hand, pulling it into his lap.

"Are you alright?" she whispered.

He nodded. "I'd never heard the details before. It was...difficult." Ava squeezed his hand, and he turned to the group. "What did I miss?"

"We were about to finish discussing the journey," said Thorne.

"Wait," said Quinn. "Sorry to go back to this, but how did you escape the camp, Ava? You never told us."

She smiled, remembering the kindness of Remy, the hobgoblin she had befriended while there. Her fellow prisoner who she'd parted ways with on her journey to Mosshaven. She hoped he was alright.

"A healer," she said. "She helped me and another prisoner. I think she created a distraction." She turned toward Casimir. "That's when I saw Aro."

"Aro?" said Jorrar. "He was at the camp?"

"Yes," she answered. "The healer said something about hurrying because the distraction wouldn't last long." She paused. Something was nagging at her. "I still don't understand how Aro found out."

"Luna," Casimir whispered.

"What? I—yes. She said she was looking for help. Did she get Aro?"

Casimir nodded.

Something was still bothering her, but she couldn't put her finger on it. "The healer wasn't one of the daemons," she went on. "She said she wasn't there willingly, and she wouldn't leave with me. I tried to make her, but she refused. She said she had her own plans."

"Ava," Jorrar whispered, suddenly tense. "Did you learn her name?"

She looked at him and the healer's face flashed in her memory. Silver eyes like Jorrar's. *Exactly* like Jorrars. When she'd asked about his grandchildren, he'd told her their mother was a healer. And they never found her body.

Oh no.

"Her name was Isolde."

27

*A*va awoke to the sun streaming in her window. Unsure of the time, she assumed it wasn't early as evidenced by the daylight. Casimir had let her sleep in. Even Cirilla hadn't awoken her.

After her realization last night that the very person who helped her escape imprisonment months ago was the daughter of two of the kindest people she'd ever known, the guilt had overwhelmed her. Though Jorrar assured her she did nothing wrong, she still felt a pang of shame that she hadn't tried harder to get Isolde to leave with them. She should have dragged her away.

She rose and dressed before making her way to the living room where Cirilla had laid out breakfast. Ava took a seat, stomach in knots, but forced herself to eat a few bites of eggs and a pastry. Wondering where Casimir was, she knocked on his door but there was no answer.

"He's already at the training rings, Your Highness," said Cirilla, returning to clean the table.

"Thank you."

Luna trotted alongside her, Titus on her shoulder, as she

made her way through the castle, anxious to blow off steam and calm her nerves. Tomorrow was the day. The day she'd have to journey to their sacred tree and if she was deemed worthy, she'd take her true fae form and unlock her magic.

You're going to succeed, Ava. I know it, said Luna.

Ava looked at her companion as they emerged outside. "Thank you. I take it you can't come with me."

No.

"Figures."

Luna trotted off to Aro, who was snoozing under a tree, climbed onto his back and settled herself among his fur. Titus disappeared into the treetops in search of his own breakfast. Raine's wolf, Sabriel, and Quinn's panther, Bastien, were even hanging around—lounging in the sun instead of hiding in the woods like usual.

The conversation last night about her and Casimir being soul-bonded made more and more sense. The way Aro and Luna were attached to each other. How Aro had saved her life. The way any time the group faced danger, Casimir appeared in front or beside her, ready to protect. How he took care of her so gently in Saxumdale. Even when they were angry with each other, he still found a way to keep a watchful eye on her safety.

Ava reached the ring where Casimir and Raine were sparring. He was shirtless and hadn't seemed to notice her yet, his brow furrowed in determination.

She leaned her elbows onto the stone wall as she watched the two powerful warriors face off, this time using daggers. She couldn't peel her eyes away from Casimir as he lunged at Raine, who dodged his attack with grace.

Casimir's lightly tanned skin was coated in sweat, and she imagined herself touching him again. Taking a break, he paused. His back was facing her as he pulled his hair out of his face, muscles flexing in the sun. Her eyes drifted lower as she wondered what his muscular thighs looked like under those pants. Among other things. God, she wanted so badly to—

"Ava," called Raine. "Whatever you're thinking about, it's gross."

She straightened, clearing her throat as Casimir turned around and grinned.

"I wasn't thinking about anything," she choked.

"You're a shitty liar. I'll see you two later. I'm going to leave to protect my innocent eyes."

"Oh, go away," said Ava, blushing.

Raine left, laughing out loud, and disappeared into the castle.

Casimir strode toward her, a knowing look in his eyes, stopping a couple of feet away on the other side of the wall.

"You knew I was here the whole time, didn't you?" she asked.

"Of course." He smiled. "I heard you walk up."

She rolled her eyes. "Men."

"Alright, let's get started. In the ring."

"Now?"

He tilted his head. "Isn't that why you're out here?" He stepped closer and leaned in, whispering in her ear. "Or did you have other things in mind?"

She bit her lip, meeting his gaze as he pulled back. "Okay." She cleared her throat. "Let's train."

She climbed over the wall and stood in the center of the ring.

He chose two training daggers from the weapons rack, turned around and handed her one.

"You need to work on your grip again," he said.

He walked closer and wrapped his hand around hers, reviewing the hold and adjusting her fingers around the handle.

"Good," he said. "Now we're going over the basic moves."

"I know these."

"But you aren't very good at them."

He backed away, gripped his own dagger and swiped the air. She copied, but it still felt clumsy and foreign in her hand.

"Again," he said.

He strode around behind her. "Your stance is off." He placed his hands on her hips and turned them. "Lean forward a little, but make sure your weight is in your heels."

Her stomach fluttered at his touch.

"Better," he said as he walked away and came around to face her. "Now try that move again."

She did and it felt different this time. Easier.

They practiced for a while before Casimir changed tactics and asked her to get out of different holds. "If someone sneaks up on you like this." He was behind her, chest pressed against her and a dagger at her throat. "Remind me what you're supposed to do."

A flash of Corvus in the same position went through her mind but she pushed through it and turned her attention to the warrior behind her, focusing on his hard body, warm against her back.

"Ava." A shiver ran down her spine at the way he said her name. "Whatever you're thinking right now is very distracting."

"Well, you should put your shirt back on. *That's* distracting."

Using this distraction to her advantage, she stomped on his foot with all her strength, causing him to release her.

"Shit," he said as he grabbed his foot.

She whirled around while he was off balance and shoved him to the ground. Gripping her dagger, she straddled him, wrapping her legs around his as she held her weapon at his throat.

His eyes went feral as he took her in. "That's what I would do," she said, breathing heavily.

"Nice try."

He flipped her onto her back, pinning her arms above her. His eyes dipped to her mouth and he leaned in, running his nose along the side of her throat.

"Oh, fuck," Ava gasped.

His lips met hers in a hungry kiss. She moaned, arching into him.

"I thought you two were supposed to be practicing," Quinn's voice sounded from the sidelines.

Casimir backed off, mumbling, "Every fucking time."

"We *were* practicing," Ava said, breathless as they both rose from the ground.

Quinn crossed her arms. "Mmm hmm. Anyway, I came to check in and see how you were feeling about tomorrow."

Casimir put his shirt back on as Ava approached Quinn. "Honestly, I'm freaking out."

Quinn put her hands on Ava's shoulders. "Look, I know I'm not always easy to get along with. And I know I was unkind to you initially, but I believe in you. You *can* do this."

"Thank you," Ava said. "You have no idea how much that means to me."

"Also, I have something for you." Quinn reached behind her and handed Ava a dagger. A beautifully crafted silver dagger with a pommel ending in vines woven around a light green gem.

Ava's eyes watered as she looked at Quinn. "Are you serious?"

"Of course. I had it made for you. It will never fail you. As long as you remember my instructions," she added with a wink.

Ava wiped away a tear. "Thank you so much."

Quinn gave her a hesitant smile and pulled her into a brief hug. She released Ava and said, "It was nothing. And stop crying, you're making it weird."

Ava laughed, still speechless.

"Don't question yourself and you'll be fine," Quinn said as she walked away.

Ava turned around, sheathing the dagger, as Casimir approached. "I've never seen Quinn hug anyone."

"She just likes me more than you."

"That's probably true. Come on, I want to show you something." He took her hand and led her out of the training area.

"No more training?"

"I can tell you're still too anxious. I think I know how to help you relax."

She stayed quiet as they entered the forest and walked along a mossy path. Purple and yellow blooms in the grass hosted bees gathering pollen, buzzing from flower to flower. Beams of dappled sunlight warmed up the morning as they burst through the canopy above.

They walked deeper into the woods until they reached a dense copse of trees with a giant willow among them. The tips of the branches tickled the grass, swaying in the breeze. Casimir let go of her hand as he parted the leafy curtains and followed her inside.

She gasped as she looked above her. There were hundreds of shimmering purple butterflies fluttering around the canopy. A small golden pond sat near the base of the tree and brightly colored fish darted about in the water. The ground was covered with soft grass and brilliant pink flowers. It was dim, the branches filtering most of the daylight, but the bioluminescence of the creatures and flowers provided an ethereal light.

"This is beautiful," she whispered as Casimir stopped beside her.

"This is where I come when I need to think. Need to center myself."

She turned to him. "Is there where you went last night during the meeting?"

"Yes," he said reluctantly.

He walked to an area next to the pond where the ground dipped as if there were two seats made of grass facing each other. He sat on one side, legs outstretched and pointed to the other. "Sit."

She joined him, crossing her legs as she ran her hand through the velvety grass. A small golden snake slithered through her fingers, and she picked it up, murmuring to it as it stuck out its forked tongue. She released it, letting the reptile continue on its way and turned back to Casimir. He was staring at her with fascination.

"What?"

He shook his head. "You're not scared of snakes, but you're scared of horses."

She huffed. "I'm not *scared* of horses. They're just unpredictable."

He laughed. "Take off your boots."

"Why?"

"Because I want to give you a foot massage."

"My feet are probably smelly and sweaty."

"I don't care. But you can rinse them in the pond if it makes you feel better."

"Alright," she relented, and took off her boots and socks, dipping her feet into the cool water. She placed them back on the grass and he took one in his hands, pulling it in his lap, and kneaded his thumbs into her sole.

A sigh escaped her as she let the tension leave her body. Eyes closed, she leaned her head back on the hill behind her. They stayed silent as he increased the pressure, focusing on her heel.

When she opened her eyes, he was staring at her with wonder.

"You're...beautiful."

The way he looked at her made her breath hitch. Like his world began and ended with her. He'd always had such an intense gaze when he watched her, but now...now it was so much more. Like he was finally letting her see how he truly felt.

"Did you bring me here to seduce me?" she teased.

"No. I promise. There will be no seducing until after the journey." He rolled up her pants and his hands moved further up her leg, focusing on her calf muscles.

She relaxed into it as she bravely asked, "How long have you known?"

"Known what?"

"You know...us..." she said, blushing.

"So, they told you."

She continued playing with the grass as she looked around at the butterflies. "Yes, they did. I thought you were going to kill someone last night, you know."

"I wanted to," he said with a hardness in his voice. She looked back and met his eyes. "When we face Andras, I will break every bone in his body and listen to him scream as I dismember him. Then I will find The Scourge and burn him from the inside out." Her heart leaped in her throat at the violence in his words. "Anyone who wishes you harm will find themselves in utter agony. I won't hesitate to end a life if that's what it takes to keep you safe."

"That's...intense," she whispered.

"It's the soul-bond. Those who are blessed enough to have one will do anything to protect the other."

She swallowed. "Why didn't you tell me?"

"I didn't want to scare you. I was waiting until after your transition to fae when you'll likely feel the pull."

"What does it feel like?"

"I don't know how to explain it. Like my heart is on a tether, pulling me toward you whenever you're near. My soul aches if I see you're hurt or scared or upset. It's primal. Protective." They remained silent, staring at each other before he spoke again.

"You asked how long I've known? I suspected the day I pulled you from the water in the bog."

"What? We'd barely known each other for a week."

"Fate doesn't care about that," he said. "Sometimes soul-bonds know immediately and other times it takes years."

"And it took you a week."

"Yes. Well...I had a suspicion. When you disappeared and I realized you were being pulled under, I panicked. I didn't understand why I was panicking over someone I didn't know, but it clicked when I pulled you out...though I was in denial."

"I remember asking why you had a strange look on your face. That was the moment, wasn't it?" He nodded. "And we got into a huge fight later that same day," she added.

"We did."

"But you're sure now?"

He stared at her with intensity as he finished rubbing her calf. "Yes." He let go of her leg and started on the other. "I suspected that day in the bog, but the moment I knew for certain was when you fell asleep in my arms after Corvus attacked you. I knew then and there I would tear apart the world to protect you. It scared me."

She swallowed as tears blurred her vision. "What now?"

He stayed quiet for a moment. "Nothing. We can keep doing as we've done."

"Is that what you want?"

"It doesn't matter what I want," he said.

She narrowed her eyes at him. "Of course it matters. Why wouldn't it matter?"

"I'm not the one adjusting to a new world. I'm not the one who was stolen from their life, brutalized and hurt, and thrown into a war they never even knew existed. What you want matters more."

There was so much newness, and she was overwhelmed

with every aspect of this life. But she loved it here. And she wanted to be with him. That, she knew for certain.

"I'll wait as long as you want. I would wait for centuries if it's what you needed. And if you don't want anything at all. That's okay too," he added, which made her cry harder. He reached for her face and wiped away her tears. "Why are you crying?"

"I don't know," she sniffled.

He leaned forward and gathered her into his arms, pulling her to straddle him. She nestled into the crook of his neck as he brushed her hair out of her face and kissed her forehead.

After a few minutes, she gathered herself. "I'm scared."

"I know."

"I'm scared of everything. I'm scared of the journey. I'm scared of facing Andras and Deidamia. I'm scared of another horrible battle I know will be even worse than the ship. I'm scared of my magic. I'm scared of this...of us."

He lifted her chin and looked at her, placing a delicate kiss on each cheek where the tears had dampened her face. "Why are you scared of this?"

"Because...because everyone I've gotten close to has eventually died...and I'm afraid of losing you too."

"Oh, Mi'ra Vässa," he breathed, looking at her with a world of compassion. "I know what that feels like. We've both lost our families. But does the fear of the unknown mean we shouldn't try to be happy?"

"No," she said with a sigh. "No, it doesn't."

"It's okay to be scared. I'm scared too."

"Is that why you're a cranky brute?" She gave him a small smile.

He grinned widely. "That's exactly why I'm a cranky brute, *princess.*"

"That's the second time you've called me dear one, you know."

"Who told you what that meant?"

"Raine."

"Of course. He can't keep his mouth shut." He cupped her face before kissing her nose. "It's because you're dear to me."

Her heart warmed. "You never told me what you wanted."

"Yes, I did. Yesterday," he said.

"Yesterday you basically told me you wanted to take me to bed."

His eyes darkened. "I do."

"Is that all you want?" she whispered.

"No."

"You want more than sex."

"Yes," he rasped. She paused, waiting for him to say more. "I'll take any piece of you that you'll give me...but..."

"But?" she urged. "Tell me. All of it."

He looked at her with tenderness, one hand gripping her hip while the other was still cupping her face, his thumb caressing her cheek. "I want all of you. Every smile, every frown. Every kiss and touch. I want your good moods and bad moods and everything in between. I want to fall asleep next to you and wake up entangled with each other." She played with a strand of his hair as he poured out his heart. "I want to snuggle on the couch in silence as we read together. I want to wake up early and have tea with you on the balcony as we share our deepest fears. Or I want to lounge in bed and spend all morning holding you. I want to fight and argue with you and then I want to take you to bed to make up for it. I want to take you dancing to see the joy on your face as we spin around the room." He moved both hands to her face as he continued. "I want *all* of you. For eternity. I want the bond." He kissed her forehead. "And there's nothing I wouldn't give you to ensure your happiness."

She was in shock, unsure how to express the depth of her

emotions. Because she wanted it too. Wanted all of what he said and more.

Casimir held her chin and pulled her into a kiss. It wasn't feverish like last night, but slow and careful, like he was judging her reaction to his words. Her hands dove further into his hair as she kissed him back and couldn't help but start moving against him.

His hands clenched her hips, guiding her along his hard length as his kisses moved down her neck to her collar bone. He gave her a nibble, licked her skin and a whine escaped from her throat.

More. She wanted more. Grasping his shirt, she lifted the hem, but his hands clasped her wrists and he stopped her.

"Not here," he said.

She pouted. "What? We're alone and have time and you're saying no?"

"Trust me. We don't have time."

"Of course we do," she said. "You're ridiculous."

He moved to her neck again and said to her in between kisses, "Like I told you last night. We don't have enough time to do what I want to do to you. I want to go slow." She moaned as he continued. "I want to explore each and every luscious curve of your body." He moved lower, placing a kiss on the curve of her shoulder. "I want to learn what makes you whimper, what makes you moan, and what makes you scream."

That mouth of his. Those words. It would be her undoing if he kept talking to her like that. Like he venerated her. Worshiped her.

"I want all of you too," she said, trying to ignore the ache between her thighs as he pulled away.

"After the journey, when you're fully fae." His fingers traced her face. "We can talk about it. About us."

"I'm probably going to get irritated and argue with you sometimes."

"Good."

"And you'll get frustrated with me for getting distracted or not paying attention."

"I will." He quirked a brow.

They smiled at each other, and he kissed her again before scooting her off his lap and standing. She put her boots back on and stood, reaching for his hand.

They walked in silence, hand in hand, back to the castle to bathe, change and prepare for dinner with the group. The last dinner before she faced her darkest self tomorrow. The last dinner where she would be human should she succeed.

28

$\mathcal{A}$va dressed in her room, her stomach in knots as she pulled on her leather armor. Cursing to herself, she struggled adjusting the straps due to the shaking of her hands, when a knock sounded on the door.

"Ava," Casimir said. "Do you need help?"

She sighed. "Yes."

He walked in, stoic and reserved. There was no smirking or grinning. No flirting. No delicate touches or caresses. He was the general, preparing her for battle and he would not get distracted.

He stopped in front of her. "Let me," he said, fastening the buckles on her chest piece and adjusting the ties at her waist. "Is it too tight?"

She moved around a bit. "No."

"You need to eat."

She shook her head. "I'll throw it up anyway. I've been throwing up all morning."

A flicker of concern flashed in his eyes before he put the mask of the general back on. "Alright, let's go then."

They walked through the halls, Ava counting to four in her

223

head with each breath, striving to remain calm. Emerging outside, they were greeted by soft rays of the morning sun peeking over the trees. Ava pinched a bud of lavender as they passed through the herb garden and brought her fingers to her nose, inhaling the relaxing scent and trying to ground herself.

Waiting for them was the rest of the group. Thorne, Raine, Jorrar and Quinn. Even Kai and Fanya were there to give their support. Though their faces were hopeful, it wasn't enough to hide the unease beneath their masks. Every single one of them was nervous. The fate of their world depended on Ava's success.

They approached the group and stopped before them.

Raine gave a smile that didn't reach his eyes and said, "You two look like you're headed to a funeral."

The joke fell flat, and Ava attempted to smile back. He grabbed her and hugged her, whispering in her ear. "You'll be fine, dainty human." He pulled back. "That's the last time I can call you that."

"It is."

Raine reached behind him and handed her a bow and a quiver of arrows. "As your archery teacher, I decided you needed something better, so I had this made."

Ava removed her current bow and quiver, handing it to Quinn, as she looked at Raine in awe. "I can't believe you did this. I don't know what to say."

"Read what it says." He pointed to an inscription in the wood.

To our missing piece.

Her eyes filled with tears, and she hugged him again. "Thank you."

Pulling away, he shrugged. "It was nothing."

She turned to the rest of the group, giving them all hugs, Thorne holding on the longest and squeezing her tight. When he pulled back, he held her shoulders and looked into her eyes. "I have something for you." He reached behind him and presented her with a sword. "This was our mother's," he explained. "Its name is Silverglow. And now it belongs to you."

A lump in her throat, she touched the silver blade engraved with something in old fae. The grip was gold and the pommel ended with a motif of the Elderoak and a large emerald in the center.

"It's beautiful. What does it say?"

"Vaî l'ioh trenässe. Which means 'you belong to us.' I had it engraved a few weeks ago."

Ava's lip quivered at her brother's words. "Thank you," she whispered through her tears. She sheathed the blade at her hip before yanking him into another hug, resting her head on his shoulder.

"Alright, little sister. The next time I see you, you won't be human anymore." He pulled away. "Remember your training and keep your wits about you."

She let go, looking at the rest of them. "Thank you. All of you. I don't even know how to express how much you mean to me."

"Stop being so sappy and hurry up," said Quinn. "I'm ready for you to be stronger so you can help me kick the rest of the idiots' asses."

"Fine, lady warrior." Ava gave her a smile.

Quinn rolled her eyes but smiled back despite herself.

Casimir and Ava said their goodbyes and walked to the woods, heading in a direction she had never gone before. There was no path as they trudged through the brush and over logs, making their way through the dense forest.

"How far away is it?" she asked, about ten minutes into their journey.

"A couple of hours."

"The map you showed me yesterday made it look a lot farther than that."

"The forest is strange the closer we get to the tree. No one knows exactly where the Elderoak is, just that it's in that general vicinity."

"Then how will we know when we're close?"

"We'll feel it."

"Alright then," she said as they continued deeper into the forest.

Luna's voice spoke in her head. *I love you, Ava. You're going to conquer this. I know it.*

"I love you too, Luna. Watch over Titus while I'm gone."

He just wants to chase butterflies all day. He'll be okay.

It was a beautiful, yet strange journey. The woods remained dense the entire way and they barely spoke, both full of nerves and racing thoughts. The tree roots wove together, making their travel difficult as they clamored over them. Ava stumbled several times, but Casimir caught her and encouraged her to keep going as he held out his hand and helped her through the lichen-covered maze.

They walked through a group of smaller trees with branches so thick they blocked the sunlight. Bright violet mushrooms grew along the base of their trunks, releasing their spores as their feet disturbed the soil.

"How are you feeling?" Casimir asked, holding out his hand to help her over a fallen tree.

"Perfect. Great. Best I've ever felt. I'm not nervous at all. Cool as a cucumber."

"I have no idea what that last thing you said means. Another one of your human expressions?"

She laughed quietly. "Yes. But, I'm being sarcastic anyway. I'm terrified."

"I know," he said, voice full of tenderness.

She hopped down on the other side, about to say something, but out of nowhere Casimir shoved her against a nearby trunk and covered her mouth.

"Don't move," he whispered.

Her eyes widened as she nodded. He removed his hand, caging her with his body as if he was guarding her from something. Vines rose from the ground and twisted around each other, encasing them. Ava's heart leaped in her throat, on the verge of panic, but Casimir looked at her and whispered, "Those are mine. I'm camouflaging us." He put his finger to his mouth to remind her to be quiet.

She didn't move a muscle as the vines surrounded them, blending them into the tree. Though nothing seemed amiss, she could tell by his demeanor the danger had not yet passed.

Then, she heard it. Something moving through the forest. Massive, and taking slow steps through the trees. Branches cracked and the ground trembled as it trudged along, crushing the roots. Through a gap in the vines, Ava could make out something giant. As tall as the tallest trees in the forest, it walked upright on two legs with long arms dangling by its sides. Covered in roots and moss, leaves sprouted from its head. Its human-like face scanned the forest as it passed by.

Casimir pressed closer, reassuring her they were safe. The creature moved on and disappeared deeper into the woods, but they remained frozen under the vines for a while longer, ensuring it was gone.

Danger now passed, Casimir released his magic and they were freed from their temporary cage.

"What was that?" she whispered.

"Tree giant."

"I take it they aren't friendly."

"No," he said as he adjusted his sword at his side. "But they aren't very smart so they're easy to hide from."

She scanned the forest. "How much farther do you think?"

"Not far. I can feel the tree."

Her nerves were on fire as they resumed their journey. She was so close to her goal and yet it felt so far away. Unsure what she would even face in the hazardous woods surrounding the sacred tree, she urged herself to have courage. It would be over soon.

The rest of the forest remained quiet, and they saw no more tree giants, much to Ava's relief. Casimir stayed vigilant, scanning the trees for any other signs of danger.

Half an hour later, the woods opened up, trees thinning out though it was still dim under the canopy. Ava could feel something pulling at her, tugging her forward. She knew they must be close.

"I can feel it," she whispered.

He looked at her. "You can?"

"Yes. I had dreams about the tree when I was living on the farm. I could feel it calling to me."

"Then it's fate." He gave her a wan smile.

"It is."

Casimir continued in front of her when he abruptly halted, causing Ava to crash into him.

"What?" she said, looking around for another tree giant.

"We're here."

She walked around and stood beside him. Before them was a lake. Too wide to go around and surrounded by dense trees. The dark glassy surface of the water was beautiful, reflecting the lights of glowing insects buzzing among the leaves above them. Tempted by the cool liquid, she knelt and reached out, wanting to swirl her hand in it. No, not wanting. Needing. Needing to touch it. Casimir lunged and grasped her wrist, pulling her back.

"Don't touch the water."

"Why?" She blinked, realizing she'd been about to do something dangerous without thought, as if she didn't have control of her actions. Was the Elderoak already trying to trick her?

"There are foul creatures in there you do not wish to disturb."

She rose and turned toward him. "How are we getting across?"

His eyes flared with worry before the mask returned. "*We aren't.*"

Her hands trembled when she realized his meaning. "This is it?"

"Yes." He took her face in his hands. "I can't go any further."

She bit her lip as she tried to tame the pounding in her chest. Her heart was a drum, beating in time with her terror.

"Look at me," Casimir instructed. He took her hand and placed it on his chest as he placed his own on hers. "Take a deep breath. Feel my heart beating." She did as he instructed, not breaking eye contact. "Breathe in...and out...in...and out. That's it. Just like that. You're going to be alright. You can do this."

Her heart slowed enough to stave off the panic. She took one more steadying breath and nodded. "How am I going to cross?"

"I'll build you a bridge."

"Okay," she said. "I'm ready."

He grabbed her face again and pulled her into a frantic kiss. She returned the fervor and pulled him closer as she gripped the collar of his tunic. He released her, forehead touching hers as he traced her jaw. "I'll be waiting here for you, love."

She nodded as he pulled away and turned to the lake.

With a determined expression, he raised his hands as large roots burst from the ground, intertwining to form a makeshift bridge stretching across the water. Sweat dripped down his brow as he wove them together, ensuring there were no large holes she might fall through.

"I can't hold it long," he said, gritting his teeth. "I'll make another when you return. Go. Now. Remember everything we've taught you. I'll see you soon."

She kissed his cheek and made her way across the bridge, stepping over the uneven roots.

"A little faster please," Casimir grumbled as he struggled to keep the bridge intact.

She sped up, watching for any signs of danger. Halfway there. A little further. Small lights hovered among the dense canopy on the other side of the lake, as if they were urging her closer to the Elderoak. Mesmerized by the beauty, she continued to walk, unaware of her surroundings as if she was in a daze.

"Dammit, Ava. Pay attention!" Casimir shouted, breaking her trance.

She blinked through the fog in her head, looking behind her, and that's when she saw it. Something had slithered out from the lake and was barreling toward her along the bridge. A giant reptile with glowing white eyes, its scaled body covered in moss. Headed straight for her.

"Run!"

Only about fifty yards remained before she would reach the other side, but it felt like miles. Ava took off, sprinting to shore.

"Faster!" Casimir commanded, voice straining as he tried keeping the bridge steady.

She chanced a glance over her shoulder. It was gaining on her. Willing her legs faster, she pushed herself as hard as she could. Twenty yards to go.

Her foot caught on a root and she tumbled forward, shouting in surprise as she slammed into the bridge. The iron taste of blood filled her mouth, lip busted open on a sharp root.

She rolled over, scrambling to rise as the creature scurried faster, thirty feet away at most. Casimir bellowed her name as a root wrapped around her waist and hoisted her into the air. The creature jumped for her and she screamed, trying to reach her sword.

The bridge behind the monster folded in on itself, making a

cage around the creature and pulling it into the water. The root tossed her the rest of the way to shore, and she landed with a thud on the hard earth.

Ava got to her hands and knees and wheezed, trying to take a breath. That was much too close. She turned her head to Casimir who was panting on the other side of the lake.

"Are you alright?" he yelled.

She gave him a thumbs up as she rose from the ground, slowing her breathing with her hands laced behind her head. Eyes closed, she took a moment to steady herself.

Ava opened her eyes and looked at Casimir. Her soulbond. Her destined one.

Her heart swelled as the warrior regarded her with steel in his eyes and determination on his face. He dipped his chin and she returned the gesture, squaring her shoulders. It was time.

Turning away, she walked into the woods.

29

The forest was dark, only lit by minuscule luminescent fungi on the bark and the glowing plants scattered among the roots. Ava unsheathed her sword, preparing for any horrid beings residing within these woods. It was light in her hand and she swung it around, getting used to its feel. Perfect. Like it was made for her.

Warmth bloomed in her chest at the connection she felt with her mother through the cold metal. Her mother's sword. Now in Ava's hand.

She's here with me. And so is everyone else, she reminded herself as she pressed on.

Her eyes darted around as she picked her way through the trees when the shrubs trembled and began to move. Halting, she watched, scanning for a threat, when a small path appeared out of nowhere, giving her room to walk between the dense underbrush.

Strange, she wondered.

As she continued on the footpath, the trees changed. No longer bright green and teeming with life, the trunks were weathered and gray, topped with glossy black leaves. They loomed over her, an ominous warning of what she would face. Glowing blue flowers hung from vines wrapped around their branches, providing a hint of light. There were no creatures, no insects or other animals moving about. It was silent.

She was alone.

Truly alone for the first time since she parted ways with Remy after escaping her imprisonment. She hadn't realized how comforting the presence of her new friends—her new family—had been until now. Alone most of her life, she had found her true home in Mosshaven and she ached to be back with them. To be back with Casimir.

A faint hissing whispered through the trees around her. Gripping her sword tighter, she searched for the source of the noise.

The volume increased and Ava prepared herself for a creature to come racing at her from the darkness. She kept walking, looking high and low, when tendrils of an eerie fog reached for her. Vaporous fingers emerged from the forest, blanketing the ground so thickly, she couldn't see her feet.

Some type of mist.

There was nowhere to go to escape the haze, now swirling mid-thigh and rising still. Trapped in the twisting vapor, she froze, as if allowing it to touch her flesh would harm her.

What if it's poison?

Within a few minutes she was enveloped, unable to see her hand in front of her face. This was worse than the mist in the bog, denser and thicker. She couldn't see anything at all besides the thick white clouds.

"Shit," she murmured, unsure what to do.

She had to keep going.

Ava walked with her hands in front of her, feeling for any obstacles. The toe of her boot caught on a root and she slammed into the ground, a sudden sharp pain in her forehead.

The warmth of blood trickled down her face as her head throbbed in rhythm with her heart.

"Dammit."

How was she supposed to get to the tree if she couldn't see anything?

Trying a different tactic, she remained on her hands and knees and crawled. It was slow going, but she made it work for a few minutes until she repeatedly tangled herself in what felt like unruly vines. Climbing over a large root, she placed her hand on the ground and a sudden agony ripped through her palm. She'd placed it on a razor-sharp thorn, so large and deep it had pierced all the way through the top of her hand.

"Fuck!" she shouted. "Oh god."

Tears pricked her eyes as she tried to ignore the pain. Her whole hand was on fire, the sensation creeping up her arm. Swallowing against the nausea trying to work its way into her stomach, she braced herself for what she had to do next.

With a strangled yelp, she pulled her hand off the spike, panting through the excruciating pain. The mist was still too thick for her to get a look at the injury, but she could feel blood running down her forearm. Holding her tunic taut with her injured hand, she tried to ignore the throbbing as she cut a piece of fabric off using her dagger. She sheathed her blade and wrapped her injury, whimpering through her tears.

"No more crawling," she panted. "I have to figure something else out."

As she rose, an idea formed. Casimir had made her complete the small obstacle course blindfolded. This was just like then. She had to use her other senses. Inhaling deeply, she nodded to herself.

She shut her eyes, removing the temptation to look around as she listened to her surroundings. After a few moments, she took a tentative step forward, feeling with the sole of her boot.

A rock lay before her and she scooted around it, taking another step.

Step by step she plodded forward, now trusting herself and letting go of her nerves. Strangely, the path revealed itself in her mind and she could see the trees around her, faint outlines of what was truly there. Each rock, root and obstacle appeared, though her eyes were still closed, and she avoided them with ease.

Trust.

All she had to do was trust herself and the way became apparent. A curious trick of The Elderoak.

After half an hour, something changed in the forest. Stopping, she opened her eyes to the mist receding. She was in a small clearing, surrounded by the black trees, blocking her way forward.

Sword in her un-injured hand, she walked the perimeter of the clearing twice. The path that led her here had disappeared, trees now in its place. As if they had moved.

"What the hell?"

She was trapped.

Something rustled behind her, pulling her from her thoughts. Leaves crunched and boughs creaked as the trees parted, inviting in her next test. A snarl reverberated and terror sank its claws deep within her gut. She recognized the monster that appeared from the gloom.

One of the flying abominations from the attack on the ship.

Black skin hung off its skeletal frame as it stalked toward her on unnaturally long legs. Its arms hung to its knees, ending in razor-sharp claws. It assessed her with red eyes and opened its mouth, revealing fangs dripping with pale green poison. Poison? She didn't remember them having poison. And had they been this tall before? It was easily ten feet. As it crept closer, bat-like wings flared out and it leaped into the air, hovering above her.

Was this real? How was one of Deidamia's creatures in the Elderoak forest? Maybe it was an illusion, a manifestation of her fears to prove her worth. But before she could think on it any further, the being swooped for her and she ducked in time to avoid its claws.

She swung her sword and readied herself as the creature dove once more, and this time her blade met its target. It screamed with fury as one of its wings was ripped open, and the monster fell to the ground. Ava took a step forward, ignoring her fear, and prepared to lunge again when more wing beats sounded behind her.

She whirled as another beast aimed for her. Unable to dodge it, she screamed as claws impaled her shoulder. She'd been lucky her injured hand was not the one she favored for her sword, but now her right shoulder was injured. Useless.

Ignore the pain, Ava. You have to use your arm, she pleaded with herself.

One creature hovered above her as the other pursued her on the ground, unable to fly but just as deadly. The one in the air dove again and she rolled out of the way, shoulder throbbing as blood poured down her arm. The pain was almost unbearable, but she shoved it away. There was no time to succumb to the agony.

On her feet again, she backed away to assess her foes. There was no escape. She must defeat them, or she wouldn't succeed. She needed a plan. Perhaps she could keep the trees close to her back, and they wouldn't be able to come around behind her. It was worth a shot.

She backed into the tree line, keeping the monsters in her line of sight, and waited for the one in the air to make its move. It wouldn't take the bait and hovered as the other lunged. She tried to dodge it, but her plan worked against her; the trees were too close and she had no room to maneuver. The sting of fangs burned as the monster's teeth sank into her thigh and her sword fell from her hand.

She screamed in pain, kicking its face and trying to pull from its strong jaws. Retrieving her dagger, she jammed the blade through its eye and it released her with a snarl of rage, backing away. Ava dropped her dagger and snatched her sword in time for it to charge her again. She spun to the side, avoiding the attack, and raised her blade, severing its head.

One down, one to go. Her leg was on fire, spreading as the poison entered her bloodstream. How long did she have before she'd succumb to its effects?

Sheathing her sword, she grabbed her bow and nocked an arrow, gritting her teeth against the pain in her hand and shoulder. The creature hovered, waiting. Probably for her to weaken so it could enjoy its meal. She had to kill it before her strength waned. She stomped her leg, causing more blood to run down her thigh to entice the monster as she whimpered in pain.

The monster's eyes zoned in on her wound, an apparent hunger on its face. As it flew for her, she released her arrow into its eye. A crunch sounded as it punctured its skull and crashed to the ground, almost on top of Ava. She turned and stabbed its chest with her sword and fell to the ground, panting.

Once both creatures were dead, they dissolved as if they had never been there in the first place.

Crawling, she made it to the center of the clearing, retrieving and sheathing her dagger along the way. Her leg was bleeding profusely, the pain increasing as the poison continued through her body. She sat on the ground and cut two more pieces of fabric from the bottom of her tunic. She gasped through gritted teeth as she wrapped one around her thigh, staunching the flow of blood as she tied it as tightly as she could stand.

The other she tried to wrap around her shoulder, under

and around her arm, attempting to keep it in place. Her pain was so intense, the warmth of tears streamed down her face as she rose, swaying on her feet. Though she still wore her leather armor, it was as if it didn't matter, the claws and fangs from the creatures had pierced right through it.

"How am I going to do the rest of this?" she croaked, worried she'd be dead before she even made it to the tree.

She had to hurry.

Limping across the clearing, she walked to a path which had appeared out of nowhere. The reward for completing the challenge. Back in the dense forest, shiny onyx leaves encapsulating the walkway, she trudged on. Nothing happened for almost an hour. Sweat drenched her tunic as she continued, slower and slower, taking frequent breaks to lean against a tree and catch her breath. Tremors racked her body and her muscles tensed. Feverish and hot, she blinked through her tears as she hobbled through the woods.

As she continued, doubts crept into her mind. Whether it was her own fears or worries, or some new trick of the tree, she started questioning herself. Could she do this? Would she ever make it?

You can't do it, Ava, her own voice sounded in her head.

You're weak. You're not brave enough. Not strong enough. Not good enough. You're anxious all the time. You're awkward. How could anyone love someone like you? How could Casimir want to be with you? You're pathetic. You will never be able to defeat Deidamia. Turn around. Go back. You'll never make it to the tree.

"No," she whispered as she shook her head and pushed herself further, through her tears. "I have to."

She walked down the path, ignoring the uncertainties brewing within, when someone appeared in front of her.

Andras.

She froze as he strode toward her. "Hello, Ava dear." He

tilted his head, black hair flowing over his shoulders as he gave her a feline smile. "Did you miss me?"

"You're not real," she whispered. But was he? No. This had to be another trick.

But then his hand was on her throat, and he was squeezing.

She clawed at his arm, but he was too strong. As her vision began to fade, he let go and she collapsed, clutching her throat and coughing.

"Come with me," he said as he turned and walked ahead. "There's something I want to show you."

What? She stood and turned around, considering returning the way she came. But there was no path back through the clearing, the trees blocking her yet again. Forward was the only way out. Andras' back was to her, and she unsheathed her sword and ran at him. Ava fell forward as her sword went through his body as if he was a wraith. His figure shimmered, and reformed.

He looked at her over her shoulder, eyes full of fury. "Come."

She limped behind him, hands trembling at the nearness of her abuser. Though she knew now it wasn't truly him, he was terrifying even in this form. The trees opened into another clearing and Andras waved his hand in front of him.

"Look," he said.

Before her was Mosshaven. But not the Mosshaven she knew. It was engulfed in flames, and citizens were running through the streets, screaming. Daemon soldiers marched in between homes and cut down anyone in their paths. The roads were bathed in blood and Ava sank to her knees as she witnessed the scene.

"No," she cried, reaching out as if she could help. As if she could stop the massacre.

Andras waved his hand and the scene changed. The castle sat before her, pikes in front of it. And on top of those pikes...

were heads. Nausea churned in her gut as she looked at the faces. Thorne. Raine. Quinn. Jorrar. She screamed. Fanya and Kai. Cirilla and Pax. Even the chef in the kitchens, Derris, and the gnome who ran the animal rescue.

All dead.

"Please...stop," she sobbed.

The scene changed again and there was Casimir, strapped to a table. Being tortured by The Scourge like she had been. He was barely conscious as they stabbed him in the gut with a dagger.

She rose and ran to the scene, but it disappeared, leaving her alone in the empty clearing. Her body trembled as horror overtook her.

"Ava dear," Andras crooned.

She turned and looked at him, unable to stop her crying. "What is this?" she gasped in between panicked breaths.

"The future."

"No." She shook her head. "I won't let that happen."

He walked in front of her, pacing, hands clasped behind his back. "Naïve girl. You think you can defeat us? Two ancient beings with an army of *thousands*?" he seethed, turning toward her and walking closer. "These plans are already in motion." She trembled at his words. "And when we arrive in Mosshaven, we will kill every single one of your friends and make you watch. Then I will torture your love in front of your very eyes. You are only one person. You can't save Eorhan. You're *weak*."

She collapsed to her knees and put her head in her hands. He was right. She couldn't do this. Everyone was depending on her and she would fail. She sobbed and slumped to the ground, curling around herself. Andras disappeared and the sky darkened as vines grew from the ground and slithered over her.

What was happening?

Unable to keep going, she continued to cry. She had failed. The forest was going to take her and there was nothing she could do. The scenes of Mosshaven continuously replayed in her head. She couldn't stop it. They would all die because of her.

Her fault. Her fault. Her fault.

Lost in a fog of uncertainty, she hardly noticed the vines working their way further around her body. It was a tender caress, the forest calling to her. Luring her in. *Join me*, it seemed to say. *Your place is in the earth with me.*

Yes. That's where she needed to be. Deep within the forest where she would be safe. She closed her eyes and allowed the vines to tighten.

Just go ahead and take me, she thought.

Because if she gave up, if she allowed the woods to take her body and soul, she wouldn't have to face her enemies. She wouldn't have to watch her loved ones being murdered and tortured. She could be at peace.

Out of nowhere, she heard a voice far away in her head. Jorrar. *"You can't go around it. You must go through it."*

She opened her eyes. Another voice. Thorne. *"Take your rightful place as fae. Demand it."*

Raine's voice sounded next. *"You're our missing piece, Ava."*

Her mother. *"Crush them. When they stand in your way, crush them."*

"Don't question yourself," said Quinn.

As the voices of her loved ones spoke to her, she knew she couldn't give up. Succumbing wouldn't stop the future. It would only ensure it.

A sob released itself from her throat as she struggled against the vines. Then she heard Luna, Fanya and Kai. All encouraging her, all telling her they believed in her. She fought harder, struggling against the vines and reached for her dagger.

Casimir's voice. *"I knew then and there I would tear apart the world to protect you. There's nothing I wouldn't give you to ensure your happiness."*

If she gave up now, she'd let him down. She would let them all down.

"I'll be waiting here for you, love."

And he was. He was alone in the woods, waiting for her to return. She couldn't surrender to her fears. Refused to.

Her lungs burned as she let out a deafening scream, full of rage and fury. All her traumas, doubts and insecurities; she let them escape. She writhed and fought against her bindings as she pushed past her terror. For too long she'd succumbed to her nerves. For too long she'd run from her fears. It was time. Time to take what was hers. Time to face her task and stop running.

Time to become who she was truly meant to be.

The conversation she had with her mother in Deidamia's camp revealed itself, a reminder of what she'd been through.

"My little bird," her mother had said. *"You've always thought you weren't strong enough. That you weren't good enough. But I'm going to remind you that you are. You are always enough."*

She was done questioning herself. There was no room for that any longer.

She was Ava Everwood, sister to the King of Monterre. Daughter of a powerful King and Queen. And Eorhan's only hope at survival.

Her fingers reached the dagger, and she cut herself free. With trembling hands, she pulled the vines off and stood. Dizzy, exhausted, and in tremendous pain, she limped across the clearing. A path appeared in between the trees.

She closed her eyes and yelled, "Where is this fucking tree?"

What was the purpose of that obstacle? That task? To face her fears and doubts, she supposed. To trick her into questioning herself and force her to surrender.

"Keep your wits about you," her brother had said. And she almost hadn't.

Ava blinked through her blurry vision as she kept on. She wasn't going to let those scenes come to pass. Refused. No more lives of her loved ones would end at the hands of Deidamia and Andras. She wouldn't balk at fighting them. Not when she knew what they'd planned. When she got out of here—and she *would* get out of here—she would learn how to use her magic and would banish Deidamia.

And kill anyone in her way.

She stumbled along the path, dizziness overwhelming her. The poison and blood loss were becoming dangerous, and she was running out of time. The further she went, the more the Elderoak pulled her. The tug she had been feeling all these months called to her.

It was close.

There. The trees opened around her, revealing the Elderoak. It was exactly as she saw it in her dreams. Massive. The trunk nearly twenty feet wide and two hundred feet tall, its canopy smothered the other trees. A golden light shone around it and vines hung from its boughs, pink and purple flowers blooming among the green.

She was barely twenty feet away when she collapsed, vision fading.

"No," she wheezed.

Victory was within reach; she was so close. Her shoulder throbbed and her leg was numb. She reached with her left arm and dragged her way to the tree, crying through the pounding in her head. She crept closer, nails digging into the dirt as she willed herself further.

Almost there.

With one last pull, she collapsed, fingers brushing a root peeking from the dirt. She shivered as the poison overcame her.

Breathing one last breath, her body stilled, her heart stopped, and then there was nothing.

30

asimir paced on the shore. It was taking far too long. It had been hours. What if she was stuck in there forever? He ran a hand over his face as he glanced at the forest every few seconds, willing her to appear. He would wait a bit longer before going in after her. It didn't matter if he died. All that mattered was her. He had to get her to safety, away from this horrible journey.

His life had been turned upside down the day they found her in the woods. This terrified, sassy, irritating woman had changed him. The woman who yelled at him within days of meeting. Who was full of anxieties and fear, yet capable of tenacity and strength when she let go. He never would have imagined the woman who had glared at him the moment he stepped out of his tent was his soulbond. The one he was meant to be with for eternity.

And now she was alone, facing who knows what kind of horrors, and he wanted to tear the whole forest down to get to her.

After another half hour, he readied himself. He couldn't wait another minute and raised his arms, preparing to cross the lake. But he paused as something moved on the opposite shore. Flowers. Tiny pink and purple blossoms burst open and spread across the soil.

Then...her. A hint of strawberry blonde hair as she emerged from the shadows.

"Ava," he whispered.

He collapsed to his knees with relief as he watched her across the lake. She was slightly taller and obviously stronger, more powerful, with the pointed fae ears. As she walked, a path of flowers bloomed in front of her, as if the earth was worshiping her very feet.

But she wasn't walking. She was limping, as if she barely had any strength. Cloth was wrapped around her thigh, hand, and shoulder and her clothing was torn and bloody. So much blood.

Panicking, he prepared to make a bridge for her to cross, but he didn't have to. Her own formed without her even trying. Bright green vines bursting with colorful flowers wove across each other in front of her as she continued limping toward him.

The flowers she created. He'd never seen anything like it. A delicate rainbow of colors. Bright yellows and purples and blues. Verdant green vines covered with leaves. Powerful and beautiful, like his princess.

His Miraêl Li'ra.

The warmth of tears streamed down his face as she approached ever so slowly.

"Cas," she breathed, then collapsed.

He caught her and looked her over, checking her injuries. "What happened? Where are you hurt?"

"I'm okay," she said. "It's already starting to heal."

He unwrapped the cloth on her leg, revealing punctures pink with fresh skin. He peeled off the fabric on her shoulder and hand to find the same thing and sighed with relief.

"I'm sore," she said. "But I'm okay. I think the tree healed me." She cupped his face, and he pulled her into an embrace.

"You did it." He smiled through his tears.

"I think I almost died."

"What?" A flare of alarm washed over him as he pulled back, searching her face.

"Creatures. I had to fight them," she rambled. "They had poison and there was so much blood. I lost so much blood." She was fighting tears. "When I reached the tree, I collapsed, and everything went dark."

His heart felt like it was going to burst out of his chest. "You *died*?"

"I don't know." She shook her head. "Maybe...or I almost did. The monsters...they were the same ones that attacked the ship."

"What?" He gasped.

She nodded. "But they were an illusion. Kind of. I mean, obviously they were real enough to hurt me but when I killed them, they vanished."

"What happened after you collapsed?" He tried to hide the panic he was feeling. She wasn't dead now. She was here, in front of him. Alive.

"Pain. So much pain. And there was light everywhere. Then suddenly I woke up. And I felt different. I *feel* different." She looked at him and touched his face. "I'm not dead. I'm here," she said, trying to comfort him.

"Okay. How do you feel different?"

They continued to kneel before each other. He refused to remove his hands from her as he stroked her hair. He couldn't stop touching her and though she was safe, he wanted to get her back to the castle as soon as possible. *Needed* to. Needed to take care of her. To get her assessed by Kai and clean off the blood and hold her.

"It's overwhelming. I can hear everything. And smell everything."

"You'll take time to adjust," he said. "Can you stand?"

"Yes."

He stood, helping her rise with him. He wrapped her in his arms, holding her as he kissed her forehead, and she laid her head upon his chest. They stayed there for a moment, and he peppered the top of her head with kisses, murmuring he would always protect her.

He pulled back, and Ava kissed the tears upon his cheeks.

"Do I look different?" she added.

"Not much. A little taller and your ears are different."

She reached up and touched them. "That's so strange."

He chuckled. "That's all you have to say? That's strange?"

"It *is* strange."

He let go and took her hand. "Let's get back to the castle. The others are waiting."

As they walked through the woods, over roots and under branches, Casimir felt lighter, hopeful. He could breathe easy knowing she had survived the journey. There would be more danger to come, but he put that out of his mind. For now, they would enjoy the peace, the upcoming ball and celebration.

"Do you feel your magic?" he asked as they continued to walk. He had let go of her hand for them to climb through denser brush and felt its absence, needing to touch her every moment.

"I think so," she said.

"What does it feel like?"

"It's hard to describe. I feel like something is living in the pit of my stomach. It's warm and writhing. Wants to get out."

"That's it."

"Does it always feel this way?"

"Yes, but you'll get used to it. And you will learn how to

wield and control it. You can't let it overtake you or it can become dangerous."

Ava climbed over a root, and he followed. As his feet hit the ground, he ran into her back. She had stopped, her body tense, and was staring ahead.

Sensing her fear, he whispered into her ear, "What is it?"

She pointed ahead of them, hand trembling. "What is that?"

At first, he didn't see it, scanning the trees. But out of nowhere, it appeared. It was one of Deidamia's insect creatures he had fought with Raine, Quinn and Jorrar in the small village of Oakshire months ago.

And it shouldn't be this close to Mosshaven.

"Get behind me," he said as he inched forward, stepping in front of her.

"What do we do?"

"We kill it. I've fought them before."

"So, it's easy to kill?" she asked, voice hopeful.

He tensed. "No."

She grabbed her bow off her back and retrieved an arrow from the quiver, nocking it in preparation.

"Stay here and keep that arrow pointed at it. I'll try to sneak around. I don't think it's spotted us yet. When I give you the signal, release the arrow into its eye."

She nodded as he crept through the trees. He made his way around, behind the black flying insect, its six legs dangling as it hovered thirty feet in the air.

He whistled, and the moment it focused on him, he yelled, "Now!"

The arrow hit it in the eye and it fell to the ground, twitching. Casimir unsheathed his sword and finished it off.

She joined him, standing over the creature. "What is that thing?"

"I'm not completely sure. But it's one of Deidamia's abominations and it shouldn't be this close. We must hurry and return to the castle."

They made their way further into the woods, when a buzzing sounded through the trees. There were more.

"Run!" he ordered.

Ava sprinted, her limp almost gone, and he took off after her.

Three more insects chased them through the woods, closing in. How were they going to fight them off? It took all four of the warriors to kill three back in the village, and they almost didn't succeed. The creatures were smart and quick, and Ava didn't have the ability to control her magic.

"Get your sword!" he yelled.

She unsheathed it and they both stopped, standing back-to-back with their weapons drawn.

"They're too fast. We can't outrun them," he said. "Go for their face or their bellies, those are the softest parts. And don't let one grab hold of you or it will carry you off."

The three monsters buzzed around them, out of reach of their swords. He called for Aro, hoping he was close enough to arrive in time to help, when one of the creatures darted forward.

He rolled out of the way, but Ava wasn't quick enough. She turned around just in time and swung her blade, slicing off a leg. It flew out of reach and hovered above them, pincers clicking together with ire.

"What do we do?" she asked, voice panicked.

"I'm thinking," he growled, standing next to her again. Remembering the technique he and Quinn had used at the village, he whispered, "I'm going to be the bait. When one flies at me, I'll roll out of the way and entrap it in roots. As soon as it's trapped, stab it through the head."

"Okay."

He sheathed his sword and retrieved a dagger, walking away

from Ava, and cut open his hand. She held her weapon in preparation. Casimir reached out and squeezed his hand to increase the blood flow, willing one of the creatures to take the bait as a ball of roots formed behind him.

Unable to control its blood lust any longer, one dove for him. He rolled out of the way and turned, raising his hands and encasing it in the trap.

"Now!" he yelled, but Ava was already there, faster in her new body. A crunch sounded as her sword impaled it, the creature now twitching. Dead.

Two more left.

"Are we doing that again?" she asked, breathless.

"No. They learn. They won't fall for it a second time."

One of them dove for her, the one whose leg she had dismembered, and hauled her into the air.

"Shit," he said as he ran after it, the other insect chasing him.

She screamed in anger and determination as he rushed to help.

But she didn't need him. She pulled out her dagger and shoved it into the belly above her, slicing it open and spilling its guts. The creature let go and Casimir ran, catching her before she hit the ground.

"Gross," she said, picking innards out of her hair.

He set her on her feet. One insect left.

Casimir scanned the forest, when out of nowhere it appeared behind him and bit into his shoulder. Ava screamed and he bellowed as its pincers pierced his flesh, a searing sensation tearing through his muscle.

Ava tried stabbing it with her dagger, but it let go and flew out of reach.

"Are you okay?" she asked, eyes filled with terror.

"Fine," he grumbled.

Reaching for his magic, he turned to the creature and tried

to grow vines to entangle it midair. Nothing. He felt nothing. He tried reaching for his astral magic, but he was empty. As if his magic didn't even exist.

He cursed under his breath as he pulled out his sword with his uninjured arm.

"What?" Ava said, voice panicked. "What's wrong?"

"I can't access my magic. Their poison must nullify it."

"Shit."

The creature dove for them again, but they dodged it. Pride flared through him at the ease which Ava rolled away like he'd taught her.

His shoulder throbbed in time with his heartbeat. An incessant thumping spread down his arm. Lightheaded, he wondered how they would kill the creature, when Aro emerged from the woods beside him.

You got yourself bitten, Aro said.

"Thank you for pointing out the obvious."

You're lucky I'm here since you obviously couldn't handle this yourself.

Casimir glowered at his companion.

Aro huffed and stood on his hind legs, swiping at the insect. But it was too high, staying out of the bear's reach. Ava faced the insect with determination on her face, retrieved her dagger, and held out her palm.

"Ava...what are you doing?"

Stop your worrying. The princess and I will take care of this abomination, Aro said.

Ava cut her hand, holding it out to taunt the creature. "Don't you want me?" she said to the monster. "Don't you want to take me back to your queen?"

"Ava," Casimir pleaded, dizziness overwhelming him as he swayed on his feet, poison coursing through his shoulder and spreading.

The insect dove but she didn't move. Didn't even try to dodge its attack.

"No!" he yelled as he stumbled toward her.

It was almost upon her, but Aro jumped and took the creature in his mouth, a crunch sounding as he bit it in two.

"There," she said. "All dead."

Don't pass out, Aro urged.

"Don't ever do that to me again," Casimir said as his vision went dark and the world slipped away.

31

*A*ro lumbered through the woods, Ava riding on his back as she held Casimir in front of her. It took every ounce of strength to keep him upright as his head lolled back onto her shoulder while he drifted in and out of consciousness.

"We're almost there," she assured him as they emerged from the forest and entered the training fields. He groaned in response, his eyes still closed.

Luna appeared, keeping pace next to Aro.

Is he okay? she asked.

"I think so," Ava replied. "I need to get him to Kai."

You're fae now. I knew you would do it. We all did.

"Thank you, Luna. Now let's get Cas some help."

I already told Ivy to tell Kai you're on your way.

"Thank you."

Ava tried to ignore her worry at Casimir's injury. She'd panicked when he was injured on the ship, but now it had increased tenfold. Was this the soulbond? Her heart physically hurt seeing him in pain and she was so on edge she felt as though she might attack anyone who came even remotely close.

She spotted Raine talking to some guards and yelled, "Help!"

He rushed over, guards in tow. "What the fuck happened?" he exclaimed, as the guards grabbed Casimir and put his arms around their shoulders, carrying him off.

"Be careful!" she barked at them as she slid off Aro and turned to Raine. "He was bitten. I think there was poison in its bite. I'll explain the rest later," she said, following the guards.

Raine grabbed her arm and stopped her. "Tell me now."

"No. I'm not leaving him."

He stopped, eyes wide and looked at her a moment before grinning. "You did it."

"Of course I did," she said as she hurried to catch up to Casimir. "I'm a big bad fae now, whatever."

He laughed. "Wow. And you call *me* insufferable."

She whirled on him. "Don't joke with me right now. Cas is hurt. We need to get him to Kai."

He held up his hands. "Okay, okay. Let's go."

She could barely control her rage and fear as she marched through the castle, Raine staying close. They made it to the medical wing, and she threw the double doors open and strode into the sunlit room, windows lining the far wall.

"Kai! Where are you?" she shouted.

Brown curls appeared as his head peeked out from his office. "I'm right here. What happened?"

He rose and gestured for the guards to lay Casimir on a bed. His animal companion—a beautiful deer named Ivy—headed straight for Casimir and hopped onto the bed, nestling in between his legs.

The guards left and Ava paced as Kai examined him. Raine stood back, watching her with concern.

"Well? Fix him," she snarled at Kai.

"Whoa," said Raine as he reached for her shoulder, trying to calm her.

Fury boiled over and she turned, pointing her finger in his face. "Don't touch me."

"He's going to be fine," Kai assured her. He paused, evaluating her. "Ava...you're...you did it." He gave her a broad smile.

"I need everyone to stop saying that and fix him!"

Kai tried to hide his amusement. "I am. Okay, I'm sorry. I won't speak anymore."

He bustled about in his robes, gathering supplies to extract the poison and help with the pain. Ava couldn't stop pacing, feeling like she was going to crawl out of her skin. Raine cautiously drew closer.

"Ava," he whispered, reaching for her tentatively like someone would approach a dangerous animal. "Take a deep breath...your magic...you're going to lose control..."

She froze and looked at him in confusion. He gestured to her feet. Flowers bloomed where she had been pacing and vines were twisting across the floor.

"I don't know how to stop it," she whispered, hands trembling.

He crept closer while Kai worked feverishly. "May I touch you?"

She took a deep breath and nodded. He stood next to her and rubbed her back. "Focus on breathing right now. Casimir is safe. I promise this is not a life-threatening injury. He's had much worse, as you've seen before. Breathe in and out and imagine a light outside of you. Close your eyes." She did as he instructed. "There you go. Now visualize the light being pulled back into you. Deep down inside your belly where your magic sleeps. Keep pulling. That's it. A little more. Good."

Visualizing the light, the warmth of magic coursed through her and ceased. It didn't feel out of control anymore. Her trembling stopped and she opened her eyes, relieved the vines and flowers had disappeared.

"What's happening to me?"

Raine shared a look with Kai before responding, "Remember how Cas freaked out the other day in the meeting? About you?"

"I was about to do that?"

"Yes."

Sighing, she walked over to Casimir and sat in a chair next to the bed, pulling it close and taking his hand in hers.

Kai looked at Ava from the other side of the bed. "He'll be fine. This poison is similar to when your leg was bitten, just stronger."

"I'm going to get the others, if that's okay. They need to know what happened," Raine said.

"Yeah," she said.

He left the infirmary. The room was empty save for the three of them, no other patients to attend to today.

"How do you feel?" asked Kai, suturing one of the wounds on Casimir's shoulder.

He had removed Casimir's shirt and Ava winced as she saw how deep the punctures were from the mandibles of the creature.

"Weird," she answered. "Stronger. And angrier. I can smell and hear things I never could before. It's overwhelming."

"It will take some time, but you'll get used to it. I promise," he said. "I'm so proud of you, by the way." He reached across and squeezed her shoulder. "You've come a long way since I first met you."

Memories flashed through her mind. When she'd met Kai, she was battered and bruised. Covered in injuries from her torture and being bitten on the leg by one of Deidamia's horrific monsters. Kai had shown her compassion as he healed her, providing reassurance in a place when she'd felt scared and alone. It was the first time she'd felt safe in weeks.

"Thank you. It feels like it was so long ago. I can't believe the journey's done."

"Yes. Yes, it is," he said. "I'm finished. He should wake within the hour. Are you injured? You seem to have quite a bit of blood on you."

She shook her head. "I was, but the Elderoak healed me. I'm fine, I promise."

"Alright. Let me know if you need anything."

"Thank you," she said as Kai left.

She scooted her chair even closer, butting it up against the bed. Holding Casimir's hand in her lap, she reached with her other and brushed a strand of hair out of his face, tracing his jaw with the tips of her fingers.

Moments later, the doors burst open, and Thorne barged in, Raine, Quinn and Jorrar on his heels. "What in The Mother's name happened?" He looked at her accusingly.

Jumping from her chair, she strode toward her brother. "Don't talk to me like that."

He stilled as he noticed her ears, her demeanor. "You did it." He pulled her into a hug, but she pushed him off.

"Don't touch me," she said as she backed away, adrenaline coursing through her again.

Raine placed himself in between them, his back to Ava. "She's...adjusting...and Cas is hurt..."

Thorne stopped, understanding on his face.

Raine turned around as the other three watched. "Are you alright? Do you need to take a moment?"

She took a deep breath. "No. I'm fine now, I think. Sorry."

Raine stepped out of the way and Quinn approached, stopped before her, and grinned. "I knew you'd do it."

Ava smiled back. Her eyes met with Jorrar and he nodded with admiration.

"You stink by the way," said Quinn.

Ava gave her an exasperated look and returned to the chair next to Casimir's bed, holding his hand again. The other three grabbed their own seats and pulled them around the bed, watching her.

"Alright," said Thorne. "What happened?"

"Well, I made it to the tree. It was...awful." She didn't want to tell them the details, especially the visions about the potential future should she fail. She couldn't bear the fear on their faces if they knew what Andras and Deidamia had planned. "Anyway, that's not important. On our way back home, we ran into these creatures. Like giant black flying insects."

Raine cursed. "Are these the same creatures we fought that day in Oakshire?" he asked the others.

"Cas said he fought them before. I think so," Ava answered.

"What are they doing here?" asked Quinn.

Thorne shook his head. "I don't know but they shouldn't be this close to Mosshaven. That's concerning."

"One of them bit him on the shoulder and he couldn't access his magic," she said.

Thorne turned to the others. "You never told me their bite could nullify magical abilities."

"We didn't know," said Jorrar. "None of us were bitten."

"How many were there, Ava?"

"Four."

Raine looked shocked. "The two of you killed four of them? The four of us could barely kill three."

"Umm...yeah. I guess we did."

"How?" asked Thorne.

"The first one, I shot in the eye with an arrow and when it fell Casimir finished it off with his sword. Another, he trapped in a root ball, and I impaled it. The third picked me up and tried to carry me away, but I was able to get my dagger under its belly and gutted it all over me." She grimaced at the memory.

"*That's* why you stink," said Quinn.

"Yes. It was disgusting. The last one bit Cas but Aro showed up and I used myself as bait. Then Aro killed it as it flew for me."

Raine gave a loud laugh.

"What?" Ava asked.

"You killed more of them than Cas," he said.

"I suppose I did."

He looked pleased. "Impressive."

A noise sounded from the bed. She whipped her head toward Casimir whose eyes were open as he quietly laughed.

"You're awake." She gasped.

Thorne stood. "It's time we leave them alone. We need to speak at dinner in a couple of hours about the ball tomorrow."

"See you later."

They left and she turned back to him. Alone in the infirmary, Kai was nowhere to be seen. He had bandaged Casimir's shoulder and put it in a sling to prevent movement.

"How are you feeling?" she asked as she squeezed his hand.

"I've had worse," he said, smiling at her. "How did you get me back?"

"I dragged your ass onto Aro's back and he took us home. You're really damn heavy."

"It's all the muscles."

She gave him a flat look. "Are you okay? Are you in pain?"

"Not much. I'm fine. Seriously. This will finish healing in a day and I'll be as good as new tomorrow. Are you alright? You look...stressed."

"I was worried about you. And I kind of lost control a bit... you know...I yelled at everyone. Yelled at Kai to hurry and heal you." Her face flushed with embarrassment. "And all the heightened senses are overwhelming. Everything smells and I can hear things I couldn't before."

"You lost control because I was hurt?" He raised an eyebrow.

"Of course I did," she said. "Don't look so smug."

He smiled even bigger as he ran his thumb across her hand. "Smell and sound aren't the only senses that are more intense, you know."

She pulled her hand away, crossed her arms and looked at him. "Nice try. You're injured. I smell like a pile of rotten garbage, and we have dinner in a couple hours."

"We still haven't gotten the chance to finish what we started the other day," he said, staring at her.

"I know," she whispered. "When you're healed."

"Alright then." He settled back into the bed.

She leaned over and gave him a light kiss on his cheek.

"You're right. You do stink. You should go bathe."

"Rude." She scoffed as she stood. "But you're right. I'm about to go do that. I'll see you at dinner."

32

*L*ater that evening, they were gathered in the dining hall. Casimir had moved to sit next to Ava, trading places with Raine who was now across the table. Her heart warmed at his insistence on being close to her. Everything was different now that he'd confessed his feelings under the willow tree two days ago.

Ava wanted nothing more than to be near him. To touch him. Hold him.

She'd stayed in the bath as long as possible, washing the guts from her hair and body until her skin was rubbed raw. After emerging, she'd smothered herself in lavender lotion to ensure the smell was gone.

Dressed in a taupe cotton tunic and brown pants, her still damp hair hung in a braid. Casimir had taken a quick bath and met them at dinner after resting and napping more, his arm still in a sling.

The table was laid out with the usual fares. Roasted meats and root vegetables, baked breads and jams, potatoes and other sides. Kai had joined them tonight and was sitting next to Jorrar, laughing with him about something.

As they filled their plates, Thorne cleared his throat. "Since you two were gone, we discussed the ball and the guests who'll be attending. Raine and Quinn developed our security plan and have been communicating it to the guards."

"So, who's coming?" asked Casimir as he sipped his wine.

"Oh, the usual," Raine said as he waved his hand, brushing Casimir off.

There was a nervous energy in the air and the others looked uncomfortable; tense. Ava tried catching Raine's eye across the table, but he avoided looking at both her and Casimir.

"Will someone tell me why you all are acting weird?" she asked.

"Nobody's acting weird," said Raine. "You're just overly sensitive right now with your big fae feelings."

"What?" she scoffed. "You guys are definitely acting strange."

Casimir had gone still and was staring at Thorne.

"What's wrong?" She looked at him, but he ignored her.

"Who is coming to the Solstice Ball?" he asked again, glowering at Thorne.

The whole table went silent as Thorne cleared his throat. "Well...all of the kings and queens are coming."

"From *every* kingdom?" he asked.

"Except Frosthaven."

"Orion?" Casimir whispered.

Thorne nodded. "And Jareth."

Confused, Ava glanced at Casimir again. Why was he so angry?

"No," he said. "Uninvite them."

"We can't and you know that," said Thorne. "Our relationship with them is rocky at best."

"No thanks to you, Cas," whispered Quinn.

"And"—Thorne cast a sharp glance at Quinn—"we need to mend that if we're going to ask them for help in the war."

"I can't believe you would invite them," Casimir said. "After what happened last year."

Ava looked between Casimir and her brother. "What happened last year?"

"Casimir and Jareth got into a brawl and destroyed half a forest," said Raine casually waving his hand.

"Who's Jareth? And are you talking about Orion, the King of Caelestia?" she asked, trying to remember all the names she had studied.

Casimir remained quiet, still looking at Thorne.

"Well, if you won't tell her, Cas. I will," said Raine.

He didn't respond.

"Tell me what?" said Ava.

Everyone was quiet.

"Tell. Me. What?" she asked again and pulled on Casimir's arm.

He looked at her. "Orion is my father. Jareth is the heir to the throne, and my half-brother."

She froze, letting go of his arm. "Your father is *King* Orion?"

"I told you my father was from the astral kingdom."

"But you didn't say he was the king!"

"You didn't ask."

She threw her hands in the air. "Oh great. I was supposed to say 'hey, he's not the king, is he?' That's insane. Why did you lie to me?"

Raine whispered to Quinn, "Mom and dad are fighting again."

"Oh, shut up," Ava and Casimir said in unison.

"I didn't lie. I just...didn't tell you."

"And that's called lying by omission," said Raine.

Quinn snorted.

"Why not?" she asked Casimir. "Why didn't you tell me?"

"Well, like you...there are things I'm not ready to talk about, *princess.*"

"Oh, we're back to that now? Keeping secrets, *prince*?" Ava shook her head as she processed the news. She knew she shouldn't be angry with him, but she couldn't help it. Another secret. And this was a big one.

"Ava," Thorne began.

But she ignored him as Casimir leaned in. "Don't call me that."

"But you are one. A prince. I can't believe it," she said as she looked away from him and sat back in her chair, crossing her arms.

He turned away as well and sat still, drumming his fingers on the table.

"Well, that went well," said Quinn.

Silence descended on the room.

After a moment, Jorrar looked at Ava. "While technically Casimir is a prince, he is not heir to the throne, nor does he want it."

"And I take it he and Jareth don't get along," she said.

"That's an understatement," mumbled Raine.

Thorne replied, "Jareth is—"

"A prick," interrupted Quinn.

Thorne raised an eyebrow. "Yes. He's conceited, thinks he is better than everyone else and not pleasant to be around. We will need to keep a close eye on him. We don't need any brawls when we're preparing for war."

Ava sighed, still irritated but her anger was dissipating. She understood why he didn't want to talk about it, especially with how much he hated his astral magic.

"Not to change the subject and all," said Raine. "But we need to discuss our next steps now that Ava is fae."

She leaned to Casimir and whispered, "We're not done talking about this."

"I know," he bit back.

Thorne was silent for a moment, looking in between the

two of them before speaking. "First, Ava needs to train to use her magic. And continue training with weapons. While she's doing that, we'll finalize our plan to get the book and Isolde. As far as training in magic," Thorne continued. "You'll do that with Raine. He's the best at self-control. Casimir will continue with what he's already been training you in."

Ava looked at Raine. "I find it hard to believe you're the best at self-control."

"Oh, but I am, darling. And we are going to have loads of fun."

She laughed and the conversation returned to the rest of the ball guests. Everyone was shocked to learn the King and Queen of Igneothenia—who had been in hiding since their kingdom set in a range of active volcanoes was conquered—had been located and would be attending. No one had seen them in years and hope bloomed at their reappearance and the possibility they may still have part of their army after escaping the daemons.

No one from Frosthaven—the kingdom set in the icy mountains to the east—would be attending. Ava had learned in her lessons with Jorrar that Valeria, their queen, had allowed the daemons in and was working with them. Her desire and longing for power overarched any loyalty to the rest of the fae. Their kingdom had to be watched.

Ava and Casimir stewed in silence as the ball was discussed. Though she wasn't angry any longer, she was hurt he didn't tell her. And worried about what this meant for their relationship.

"Alright, let me have it," Casimir said as he shut the door to their living room.

Ava whirled around to find him smirking. "Oh, you think this is funny?"

"Not really," he said, but his smile didn't falter.

"You lied to me. How can I trust you if you're still keeping things from me?"

"It changes nothing," he said.

"It doesn't? I mean...you're a prince. From a different kingdom. Doesn't that change something with us?"

He took a step forward. "No. I won't inherit the throne. I don't even want it. It changes nothing."

"But you didn't tell me."

"And you've told me every single thing about you?" he asked as he walked closer.

"Yes...I think so. I mean, I'm not a secret princess or anything. It's not a secret anymore."

"But you were a secret princess. You kept things from us," he was still smirking as he looked at her.

"First of all, I didn't know I was a princess. Second of all, I didn't know you, prince."

"I said don't call me that," he said as he stalked toward her.

"Or what?" she backed up, hitting the wall.

He didn't answer as he stood over her, eyes full of mischief.

"Are you *enjoying* this?"

He leaned in, his forearm resting on the wall above her head and whispered in her ear. "Backing you against a wall? Yes."

Her breath quickened as she looked up at him. The way he was looking at her...like a man starved. As if preparing to devour her.

"I'm still irritated with you," she whispered, voice coming out hoarse.

"It's sexy when you're mad," he said as he leaned in and kissed the tender spot below her ear.

"You didn't tell me," she said.

His lips moved lower along her neck. "I'm sorry."

She sighed. "It's okay."

He removed his arm from the wall and tilted her chin, pulling her into a kiss. She put her hands on his chest, wanting more but afraid of hurting him.

"Cas." She stopped him and he paused, looking down at her, his hand cupping her face.

"Hmm?" he asked as his thumb stroked her cheek

"I...I want the bond."

He went still. "Are you sure?"

She brushed his hair out of his face. "I'm positive."

"You have no idea how relieved I am to hear you say that." He kissed her forehead.

"What now?" she asked. "Do we like...do something?"

"Not tonight. We won't have time."

"When?"

He leaned in, their foreheads pressed together. "After the ball. We cut our palms, join them together and say a prayer to The Mother."

"That's it? Do we need to have a ceremony or something?"

"Only if you want to. But most people prefer to do it in private because..."

She narrowed her eyes at him. "Because what?"

"Let's just say after the bond is blessed by The Mother it gets...intense. Very intense."

"Intense how," she whispered, heart in her throat.

He leaned in, brushing his lips against hers.

"I think you can imagine." He kissed her hard, tongue exploring her mouth as he moved his hand to her hip and yanked her closer.

Casimir's body pressed against hers as he deepened the kiss. His hand slid from her hip, under her shirt and palmed her breast. She let out a sigh against his soft lips, the smell of him surrounding her. The hint of cedar and sage. It had been a comfort the moment she first smelled it. That night when he offered his tent for her to sleep in. The faint scent on the bedroll had wrapped her in a safe embrace, lulling her to sleep when she'd been so lost and scared.

And now they were here. Their souls yearning to be bound.

She ran her hands along his chest, avoiding his shoulder and pulled away momentarily. "You're too injured. You only have one good hand."

"I can do a lot with one hand," he said as he squeezed her breast again and kissed her once more, harder and more feverishly, pinching her nipple.

He placed gentle kisses along her neck, starting under her ear and making his way to her collarbone, whispering about how soft her skin felt, how perfect she was. His hand left her chest and worked its way down her stomach, then between her legs over her pants.

He rubbed back and forth, creating the perfect friction. She reached down and palmed him over his own pants. A groan slipped from his lips as she slid her hand lower and gripped his length.

"I want to touch you," she whispered against his mouth as she reached for his buttons.

He caught her wrist. "Not yet. Let me take care of you tonight."

Letting go, his hand slipped under her tunic, squeezing her hip as he worshiped her neck with his lips. His fingers skimmed along the waistband of her trousers, taunting her as he moved beneath the fabric. Lower and lower, he reached between her legs as his teeth grazed her shoulder.

"Fuck," he groaned as he slid his finger through her slick arousal, circling the sensitive bundle of nerves.

She leaned her head back and released a whimper as he continued.

A finger slipped inside her and she gasped as he curled it toward him and claimed her mouth again in an urgent kiss. He added another and she moaned as his thumb found her clit and circled it in time with the pumping of his fingers.

She never wanted this to end. Wanted to strip naked and lead him to the bedroom, spending all night with him inside of her. The only thing stopping her was his shoulder, knowing he'd refuse until they were both healthy enough to let go.

"Please," she pleaded, as she clung to his tunic.

"Please what?" he said, licking and nibbling her earlobe.

"Please," she barely got out. "Don't...stop..."

"Never." His eyes roved over her face, greedily watching her expression.

He continued his rhythm, the slow buildup of her release nearing with every second. She bucked her hips, grinding onto his hand shamelessly as he continued his perfectly timed movements. Sensing her release was near, he increased his speed and her legs almost gave out at the sensation of being so close to the edge.

"Hold onto me," he growled into her ear.

His voice sent shivers through her and she gripped his neck as she teetered on the precipice, catching him watching her. A slight increase in pressure sent her tumbling over the edge, waves of pleasure sending tingles along her skin.

"Let go, princess," he whispered with reverence.

She cried out, closing her eyes as heat exploded through her, desperately pulling him closer. Tremors racked her legs as she fought to keep herself upright, her soul on fire. He slowed his pace, continuing to work her through the last of her climax as she trembled against him.

Pulse racing, she could barely catch her breath as she met his gaze. Removing his hand from her pants, he kissed her gently. Tenderly.

She broke the kiss and stroked his hair. "Sleep in my room tonight."

He shook his head. "If I do, I won't be able to control myself and I need both arms to do what I want to do." She swallowed and stared at him. "And I need to go to bed right now before I lose complete control."

"What if I want you to lose control?" she asked.

"Tomorrow. After the ball." He pressed his lips to her brow before he reluctantly walked to his room. "Goodnight, princess."

33

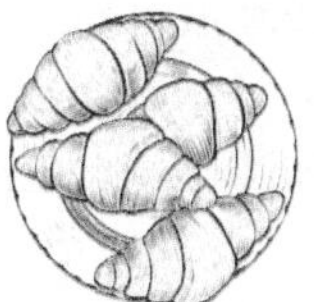

va was awoken by a light knock at her bedroom door. It was early, the sun peeking above the trees, and she groaned and pulled the covers over her head, attempting to ignore the wake-up call. Titus snuggled under the covers with her, obviously trying to get more sleep as well.

Someone's knocking, Luna said, stretching at the foot of Ava's bed.

"I know. Maybe they'll go away. I don't want to get up yet. I'm so damn tired."

The knock sounded again.

Answer it. They're waking me up too.

Ava rolled her eyes.

"Come in," she called, assuming it was her attendant. She lay there, surrounded by the plush bedding calling her back to sleep, and pulled the comforter down.

The door opened and in walked Casimir, shirtless, his arm out of the sling. He stopped before her bed, looking at her with amusement.

"What are you doing in my room?" Ava asked.

"I must work all day, but I wanted to have breakfast with you."

"But it's so early," she whined.

"Well, I'd rather snuggle with you in bed all morning. But unfortunately, I only have an hour before I'm busy and I want to spend time with you."

"Snuggling sounds like a much better option."

She threw off the covers and he stepped back, allowing her to walk to the bathroom. Luna had gone back to sleep and Titus crawled to where she lay, nuzzling into her fur.

"Let me get dressed."

"It's just us. You can come naked if you want," he said.

She peeked her head out from the bathroom and looked at him. "You'd like that wouldn't you?"

He grinned.

"I'll just grab my robe," she said as she walked back into the bedroom.

The cotton nightdress she wore was short, stopping mid-thigh, and it was sleeveless, showing off her toned arms and shoulders. The dress left nothing to the imagination as it revealed her muscular thighs and curved ass. She caught him watching her intensely and she turned toward him.

"What?" she said.

"I like that thing you're wearing," he answered.

"You've seen me in a night dress before."

He stayed still as he looked at her across the room. "Yes, but the circumstances were... different."

"Right," she said. He had seen her in a nightgown. The night Corvus attacked her. He'd also seen her naked, but she remembered he'd never looked at her body, always keeping his eyes at her face and above.

It was different now. Now they'd confessed their feelings and unleashed themselves on each other. She was about to turn around and grab her robe hanging on the wall when his eyes dipped lower and caught on her thigh.

"Tell me the story of that," he said, eyes full of concern.

It was a scar. A large one from her time imprisoned in Deidamia's camp.

"Didn't I already tell you?"

"It was briefly mentioned, but tell me now."

She cleared her throat. "Andras...he jammed some type of jagged knife in there and...twisted and...I don't know, he said something about it being something to remember him by and then I don't remember the rest because I passed out."

His eyes widened as fury crossed over his face and he approached. When he reached where she stood, he knelt before her and lifted her gown, revealing the entirety of the scar. He traced his fingers over it, and she sucked in a breath as he leaned in and placed a light kiss where it lay.

He rose and gripped her face. "He's going to regret every single thing he did to you."

She shivered at the violence in his voice. He kissed her on the forehead and walked out, leaving the door cracked for her to follow. She retrieved her robe and wrapped it around herself before following and taking her seat at the small dining table.

The table was laid out with eggs and bacon and a dozen fruit-filled pastries along with a bowl of fresh berries. Ava was starving, but before she could grab her plate, Casimir took it and piled it with food.

"I know you're going to be too anxious to eat tonight, so make sure you eat enough now."

She smiled at the reminder of him knowing her quirks and hang-ups. No one had ever noticed her interests or anxious tells. But he did. He noticed everything. And not because he was in charge of her training—like he had insisted several times before—but because he wanted to take care of her. He set her full plate before her, poured her a cup of tea, and handed it over.

"Thank you." She clutched it and took a sip. "So, what do you mean you have to work all day?"

Casimir filled his own plate. "Well, being the general comes with certain duties. Like overseeing security for the ball tonight. I'll be spending the day reviewing protocols with the guards to prepare for any potential problems."

"Oh." She took a bite of eggs. "I take it everyone else is busy too."

"Yes. Sorry."

She shrugged. "It's okay. I'll wander the castle or something. Maybe read in the library."

"Fanya's going to be here in a couple of hours to spend the day with you."

"Oh, good! That'll be lovely."

"And..." he added. "I'll be on duty during the ball."

"Seriously? So now I don't have a date?"

He raised an eyebrow. "I was to be your date?"

"Of course."

"You never asked me." He grinned mischievously

"I thought it was assumed."

"Sorry, I can't be your date."

Frowning, she took a sip of tea.

"But," he continued, "I will make sure to sneak away for a dance. And I'll be sitting next to you at dinner."

"I'll take what I can get I suppose. So, about the ball. What's it like? How does dinner work?"

"The first hour or so is mostly mingling. Dinner will happen after that, then the tables will be cleared and put away to open the ballroom for dancing and lounging."

"And where will you be?"

"First, I'll be stationed with you and Thorne as you greet

the guests. Once everyone's inside, I'll be in the ballroom with the others, monitoring the crowd."

She swallowed a bite of pastry. "And what will I be doing?"

"You'll be with Thorne most of the time. You two will stand at the castle entrance and greet the guests as they arrive. Then you'll stay with him as he announces the start of Solstice and through most of the night. Stay close to Thorne and you'll be fine."

"Do the other kingdoms know about me? I mean, besides Saxumdale."

"Yes."

"Any tips?"

He thought for a moment. "I've never met the rulers of Igneothenia. They disappeared when I was very young. Thalia, the queen, is said to be kind and Aelerion, brash and boisterous, but a good ruler. Of course, Astrid and Soren will be friendly."

"And what about your father?"

"My father is an asshole," he said. "He will probably be rude, but he won't harm you. Politics are too important to him. His wife is fine. She'll likely stay quiet, like he wants her to."

Ava grimaced. "And your brother?"

"Stay away from him," he said with sudden intensity.

"Why?"

"He delights in making people uncomfortable and will find any weakness he can and thwart it. Just for fun."

"Great."

They both ate in silence for a moment before Ava asked, "What happened with your father? Why didn't you grow up in Caelestia after...you know?"

He looked like he wouldn't respond, staying quiet, so she reached out and touched his arm. "Please. No more secrets."

He gave her a nod. "My father had an affair. Well, he's had

many affairs. He doesn't respect women and his wife looks the other way. When he found out my mother was pregnant, he threatened to kill her if she didn't promise to keep me away from him. Hybrids used to be looked down upon and he still carried that prejudice, though most of the other kingdoms—besides Frosthaven—moved past it. So, my mother raised me in a small village in Monterre, where she was from. That's where she met my sister's father, but he died soon after she became pregnant with her."

"And you eventually went to live with Raine and his family."

"Yes."

She grabbed his hand, lifting it, and kissed the top. "You are nothing like your father."

"Thank you," he said, sorrow in his eyes at the memories of his childhood.

"So, other than glowing, what else can your astral magic do?" she dared to ask.

He looked at her for a moment, a sudden glimmer of playfulness in his eyes. Before she knew it, she was floating, along with a few nearby items, as if he had turned off the gravity around her. She gripped the seat of her chair as it rose with her and hovered several feet in the air.

"Cas! I'm going to fall!" she exclaimed. "Put me down."

He laughed and she rose higher, shrieking. "Casimir!"

Everything stopped and her chair fell to the ground, her following suit, but he caught her in time.

"Don't do that again," she breathed.

He kissed her before setting her back in her chair, then reclaimed his own seat. "Well, I can do that." He nodded toward her. "And shoot starlight from my hands. Also, if I'm touching someone, I can burn them from the inside out."

"Oh," she said, eyes wide. "That's why the creature was a pile of ash on the ship, wasn't it?"

"Indeed," he replied. "Some fae from Caelestia also have powerful healing magic but that isn't usually passed down to hybrids. They can even bring those back from the dead if they're quick enough."

"Really?"

"Yes, but at great cost. They must give up all their magic."

"That's incredible," Ava said, still in awe of the way magic worked. "Do you know anyone who's done that?"

"No." He took a sip of his tea. "By the way, I'm sorry I didn't tell you who my father was."

"It's okay. I understand."

A knock sounded at the door, jarring them from their conversation. "I'm coming in!" shouted Raine from the other side. "If you two are fucking, you'd better cover up!"

Ava's face turned bright red as Casimir chuckled.

Raine opened the door and entered, plopping in an empty chair. "Ah good, the room is free of the smell of sex. What are you two talking about?" he asked as he grabbed a plate for himself.

"Who invited you?" asked Ava.

"I invited myself. Actually, I was here to see if Cas was ready." He looked at Casimir. "Which he obviously isn't, and then I smelled the food and thought I'd eat."

"You haven't already eaten?" Casimir asked.

"Of course I have, but I'm still hungry," he retorted.

Another knock sounded, this time Quinn shouting through the door. "Cas, are you ready to go?"

"He's not ready yet!" Raine called back.

Quinn walked in and took a seat next to Raine. "Oh, breakfast!" she exclaimed as she snatched a pastry.

"Could the two of you be any ruder?" asked Casimir. "What if we were having a private meal?"

"Oh, shut up," said Quinn. "Ava doesn't mind. Right, Ava?"

Ava shook her head at the two of them but couldn't help smiling. "I don't mind."

"What are you going to wear tonight, Ava?" Raine asked.

She paused. "Oh gosh. I don't know. Am I supposed to know that?"

"They'll find something for you. Have Fanya take you shopping. There's a wonderful dress shop in town that can get anything ready and altered for you in time for tonight."

"I don't have any money."

Raine waved his hand and scoffed. "Your brother's the king. They'll charge it to the royal accounts. No problem."

"Well, okay." She took a sip of tea before turning to Quinn. "You could come shopping with us. If you want."

"First of all, I have to work," she answered. "Second of all, dress shopping sounds like my worst nightmare."

After a few moments, Raine rose. "Thanks for the second breakfast. Cas, you've got fifteen minutes before we need to be downstairs."

Quinn followed. "See you there."

They bid Quinn and Raine farewell.

"Well, I guess I should get dressed," Casimir said, rising from the table. "Have fun today." He planted a kiss on her forehead. "I'll see you later tonight."

34

A bell chimed as Ava pushed the wooden door open to the dress shop nestled among the trees in town. Fanya followed behind her as they entered the warm space.

Dozens of dresses were displayed along the walls; an amalgam of silk and chiffon; of blues and greens and purples. Jewelry sat upon tables in the center of the shop, emeralds, rubies and other gemstones glistening in the light of the lanterns above.

An orc rose from her spot behind the wooden counter to greet them.

"Fanya!" she exclaimed in her low rough voice, black curls bouncing as she approached. "It's so good to see you. What can I do for you?"

"Hello, Ghorza," Fanya replied. "We're in dire need of a dress for the princess tonight."

Ghorza turned to Ava. "Oh! Your Highness." She curtsied. "I didn't realize it was you."

"It's alright. It's nice to meet you."

Ghorza turned and gestured for them to follow her. "I have

several dresses that would be perfect for tonight, and they're close to your size, so they won't require too many alterations."

She led them to the back where she pulled aside navy velvet curtains covering a doorway. The room had several settees in the center, facing a wall of mirrors with a small platform sitting before them. Ghorza walked to a table with wine goblets and a pitcher, poured two cups, and handed them over.

"You two have a seat and I'll be right back," she said, disappearing through another door.

Ava sat next to Fanya on a plush navy couch and took a sip of wine. "So, are you bringing a date tonight?"

Fanya shook her head. "Unfortunately, no. Pax is working."

"Oh, right. Pax!"

"Yes. I'm surprised you remember. You were quite inebriated when we spoke about this."

"Don't remind me. That explains why he was looking at you like that when we left the suite."

"Yes," Fanya said with a small giggle.

"Speaking of Pax," Ava said. "How's he doing?"

"You mean after losing Zeph?"

She nodded.

"As good as he can be, I suppose. They'd been assigned to that suite for the last thirty years. She was his best friend."

Ava swallowed the lump in her throat as the memory of Pax sobbing over Zeph's body flashed through her mind. They hadn't assigned another guard to their suite, apparently due to Pax's protests and the reassurance Casimir was in there as well. Ava didn't want a new guard. She wanted Zeph.

"But let's not talk about that now," Fanya said, interrupting Ava's thoughts. "We must get you a dress that will take everyone's breath away."

Ghorza emerged, carrying several gowns which she placed upon an empty rack. "Alright, Your Highness. I think one of these will do nicely."

Ava set her goblet down and stood. She undressed and Ghorza helped her step into a deep blue gown. She ran her hand along the sweetheart neckline and the bodice where thousands of beads blended into the shimmering skirts.

"It's lovely," said Fanya. "But that's not the one."

"It's not like I'm getting married," Ava said as she turned around.

"True. But this is the first time you're being presented to the kingdom. Your dress must be perfect."

"Oh. I haven't thought of it that way. This really is a big deal, isn't it?" she asked, fidgeting with the beads.

"Very much," said Ghorza. "It's quite exciting, too."

Ava gave her a wan smile. "Well, let's try the next one then."

She tried on three more dresses, all different colors and styles, but none of them seemed to stand out the way she and Fanya wanted them to. Feeling defeated, Ava stood before the two of them, this time wearing a golden gown she hated. The color washed her out and made her look paler than she already was.

A light appeared in Ghorza's eyes. "I completely forgot. I think I have just the thing! I'll be right back."

Ava took a seat, uncomfortable in the scratchy material. "This is a bust, isn't it?"

"No. We'll find something. I promise."

Ghorza returned, holding a stunning sage green gown. "This is the one," she said. "I know it."

It was beautiful. Ava rose to slip out of the golden eyesore, ready to be free of the itchy fabric. After Ghorza helped her adjust the back and sleeves of the new gown, she turned to Fanya.

Fanya clapped her hands. "Ghorza, you're a genius."

Ava turned back around and looked in the mirrors. She was speechless. The dress was perfect. Sheer fabric formed the tight bodice with a plunging neckline while lace detail covered her breasts and stomach, continuing into the chiffon skirts. The open back dipped to the curve of her rear, and off the shoulder sheer sleeves flared as they flowed along her arms, ending in more lace.

And though it was as revealing as the dresses she wore in Saxumdale, she didn't care this time. Because she'd begun to grow proud of her scars. "They're badges of courage," Casimir had said. Ava's heart warmed at the memory.

"I love it," she whispered.

"Cas is going to lose his mind," Fanya said.

"The general?" Ghorza asked.

Ava turned around and smiled sheepishly as Fanya answered, "Oh yes. He is smitten with her."

"He's a good man. And very handsome." Ghorza winked and approached to make small adjustments, pinning the fabric in the waistline. "This won't take me long. I'll have it delivered to the castle within a couple of hours."

After getting the measurements and alterations, Ava dressed into her original clothing and thanked Ghorza profusely. She and Fanya headed out the door for lunch when they ran into someone entering the shop.

Ava looked up. "Cas?"

He stuttered, like he was caught red-handed as he stood in the store, face bright red. "Uhh...Hi."

Fanya looked at him with her hands on her hips and eyed him suspiciously. "What are *you* doing here?"

He rubbed the back of his neck as his eyes darted between the two of them. "I...um...I just had to pick up my uniform. Ghorza was doing some alterations on it for me."

"Ghorza doesn't alter uniforms. This is a dress shop." Fanya raised an eyebrow.

"She's doing me a favor," he blurted, fidgeting.

"Mmm hmm," said Fanya. "Well, we must be off." She

looped her arm through Ava's and dragged her out of the shop. "Goodbye!"

Ava met his eyes and smiled as Fanya dragged her away. Once outside the shop, Fanya whispered, "He's lying."

"I gathered as much."

AVA WAS IN HER ROOM, pulling on the gown with Fanya's help, fingers shaking as she tried to adjust the waist. Cirilla had woven her hair into an intricate braid wrapping around her head, interspersed with tiny white flowers and green crystals.

Fanya wore a beautiful deep green dress with a tight beaded bodice and wide organza skirt that bounced when she walked. Her hair was left down and curled along her back.

Fanya took a step back and inspected her. "You need jewelry."

"I don't have any."

"I'll be right back," she said as she left the room.

Ava admired herself in the mirror. Fanya had put a small amount of rouge on her cheeks and lips and lined her eyes with kohl. She touched her pointed ears, still startled when she saw them.

A part of her remained in disbelief. How she went from a wildlife biologist to a lost fae princess. It felt so natural to be here. In her home. But other times it was overwhelming. And it was times like these she wished her mother were here to guide her.

A light knock at the door startled her. "Come in," she called, expecting Fanya with jewelry.

She looked in the mirror over her shoulder and met eyes with Casimir as he walked in.

He stilled in the middle of the room, at a loss for words. Ava waited for him to speak as she watched him in the reflection.

After a moment, she turned to face him. His throat bobbed as he evaluated every inch of her.

"Ava..." he rasped. "You're absolutely breathtaking."

She marveled at him, jaw-droppingly handsome in his uniform. He wore a forest green jacket embroidered with the gold emblem of the Elderoak tree and the general insignia underneath, brown pants and polished boots. Leather armor adorned his shoulder caps, and he was armed with his sword at his side. A forest green cape flowed behind him lined with golden thread and moved as he walked toward her.

"You look...quite handsome yourself." She smiled as she shifted on her feet.

He stopped a couple feet away and cleared his throat. "I have something for you," he said and held out a box.

"What is it?"

His hands trembled as he opened it, revealing the most beautiful necklace she had ever seen. Gold branches wove together, leading toward three teardrops of dangling peridot gemstones. A larger peridot hung at the bottom layer of more golden branches as they met together in a point.

"Oh," she gasped as she reached to touch the necklace. "It's...beautiful. I don't know what to say. You didn't need to do that."

"I wanted to," he said. "May I put it on you?"

"Yes," she whispered.

She turned back around. Setting the box on the table next to the mirror, he picked up the necklace and draped it along her collarbone, attaching it at the back. It sat perfectly, accentuating her decolletage and bringing out the green in her eyes.

"Is this why I ran into you in Ghorza's shop today?" she asked as he was fastening the clasp.

"Yes. I had her help me pick something that would go with your dress since she knew what you were wearing."

"That was very sweet of you."

Ava heard the door open and caught Fanya's eye in the mirror but as soon as she noticed Casimir, she winked and backed out of the room. He didn't seem to notice as he watched her through the reflection. His fingers trailed down her spine and she shivered. Reaching around, he adjusted the large gem, brushing her collarbone.

"Perfect," he whispered in her ear.

She sucked in a breath as he placed a kiss below her ear, one hand on her hip, still watching her in the mirror. He stepped closer and yanked her flush against him, digging his fingers into her hip as his other hand traced the curve of her neck and shoulder blade.

"I'd like to rip this dress off you," he said.

She turned around. "You can do that later. At least let me wear it first." She traced the emblem of the tree on his jacket with her fingers. "I like this uniform."

"It's the official one. We don't wear it often."

"I hate that you have to work."

"Me too." He traced the lines of her face with his fingers. "You are going to be a challenging distraction for me tonight." He stepped closer, touching his forehead to hers. "You. In that dress."

He shook his head and kissed her. Ava sighed into his mouth as she ached for his touch, hands moving along his chest. He deepened the kiss briefly before pulling away.

"I must go."

"I know. I'll see you soon."

He placed a light kiss on her lips again, backed away, and looked her up and down one more time. He ran his fingers through his hair before turning and leaving the bedroom.

Ava shook out her arms as she prepared to meet Thorne. She walked into the living room just as he was entering her suite.

"Oh," she said. "I thought I was meeting you down there."

"I brought something for you. Besides, I assumed you were nervous and thought I'd accompany you."

He looked fantastic in a dark green velvet top lined with gold, and brown pants. He wore his golden crown of vines decorated with emeralds and the stark green of his eyes stood out against his bright red hair.

"You look beautiful, sister," he said as he opened a velvet box, revealing a tiara matching his crown.

"You don't look too bad yourself." She smiled as she looked at the box. "What's that?"

"Your tiara."

"I didn't even think about that. I guess I must wear it, huh?"

"Yes. Sorry. I know you're not excited about all the attention. But it'll be fine," he assured her.

She stood still as he lifted it out of the box and placed it atop her head. Golden vines wove to a point on her forehead with an emerald dangling from it. Dainty gold chains interspersed with tiny emeralds hung in U-shapes, framing her pointed ears.

"Wow," she said as she inspected herself in the mirror above the fireplace. "This is beautiful."

"It was our mother's," he said.

She turned around and hugged him.

"Are you ready?" he asked, pulling away and holding out his elbow.

"As ready as I'll ever be, I suppose." She placed her hand on his arm and took a deep breath as they left the suite and made their way downstairs.

35

"Stop fidgeting," Thorne chastised.

They stood outside the entrance to the castle and down the steps, waiting for the guests to arrive. The sky was bursting with glittering stars, adding a magical touch to the ambiance of the ball. At the end the walkway was an arch made of willow branches, lights hanging near the top with a warm glow, welcoming the guests to the castle grounds. As Ava looked at the archway, she was reminded of the first time she passed beneath it. Her very first day in Mosshaven.

How far she had come.

She stood between Raine and Thorne, Casimir across from them with Jorrar. Quinn and Pax monitored the guards in the ballroom and would be joined by the rest of them later.

"I can't help it," she said. "The anticipation is killing me."

"You're not very sophisticated," Raine said.

"No. I'm not. Consider yourselves lucky I haven't already tripped over this dress."

"Please don't trip," said her brother. "You'll embarrass us all."

She scoffed. "I'll try not to. Okay, remind me what I'm supposed to do again?"

"Smile and greet the guests. I'll introduce them as they come through. You don't even have to talk other than simple things like 'nice to meet you' and so on. Also, when we greet the other royalty, make sure to curtsy."

"I forgot how to fucking curtsy," she whispered harshly, scratching her arm.

"And don't curse," he scolded. "It's unbecoming."

"I'll show you, Ava," said Raine, dipping low.

Ava and Casimir snickered.

"Why can't I have a serious court?" Thorne lamented.

"Because you'd be a boring king with a stick up your ass and everyone would hate you," said Raine.

Thorne pinched the bridge of his nose as Ava practiced her curtsies and mumbled, "it's so nice to meet you," to herself.

"What are you doing?" said Casimir, an incredulous look on his face.

"I'm practicing."

"You look ridiculous," he said.

"Oh hush."

A guard approached from the streets. "Your Majesty. The guests are starting to arrive in town. The first ones should be here within a few minutes."

"Thank you."

Ava closed her eyes, trying to calm her racing heart. She wiped her sweaty palms on her dress as she prepared to shake people's hands.

"Wait," she said to the group. "Do you shake hands here? Is that a thing? Do I need to hold it out or what do I do? Oh god, I'm going to be sick. My—"

"Ava," Raine interrupted. "You're so anxious you're making *me* anxious."

"I've never done anything like this before."

"We don't shake hands. The curtsy and bow are in place of that," said Thorne.

Sighing with relief she said, "Good because my hands are sweaty."

"Though some of the bolder men may kiss your hand," he added.

"Ugh, okay." Casimir's eyes flashed, as if he was jealous. She smirked at him. "What? You don't like that idea, general?"

"Not one bit."

Moments later a group of high fae approached, all dressed in elaborate dresses and gaudy tunics, the colors of green and gold on display. "Not royalty," Thorne whispered into her ear. "Smile and welcome them."

Ava did as he instructed. The group bowed and curtsied their greetings before they turned and ascended the stairs, headed inside.

"See?" he whispered. "That wasn't so bad."

She nodded, staying quiet as more guests filled in the streets and approached. They spent a while greeting citizens from both their kingdom and others. Orcs, goblins, fae and pixies. Everyone was welcome at the Solstice Ball.

Ava's heart no longer raced and she was beginning to get the hang of things, smiling at the guests and welcoming them. She could do this.

Thorne leaned in and whispered, "Soren and Astrid have arrived."

She looked down the line, finding the queens holding hands and smiling at the other guests as they made their way through the crowd. Soren's red hair was beautiful against the deep blue gown she wore, and Astrid's purple sequin dress sparkled in the lamplight.

They stopped before them, giving Ava and Thorne a curtsy. "Hello, dear friend. It's so good to see you," Soren said, voice low and sensual.

Thorne bowed back and kissed her hand. "It's good to see you too, Soren."

Ava curtsied. "It's good to see you again, Your Majesty."

Soren smiled warmly. "It's lovely to see you again too. I am truly sorry about the troubles you faced during your visit," she added with a hint of sadness in her eyes.

"Thank you," Ava whispered. Soren stepped away as her wife approached.

Astrid's dark blue eyes sparkled as she took Ava's hands in hers and leaned in, whispering, "You're doing great. I hate these types of things. If you need a companion to escape the monotony, come find me later. I'll give you all the royal gossip." She pulled back, winking. "Good to see you again."

Astrid turned back to Thorne. "I do hope you sat us near you all for dinner. The other courts are so boring."

Raine grinned. "Of course. I know you already miss my excellent sense of humor."

Astrid and Soren walked away laughing, hand in hand.

"I really do like them," whispered Ava.

"I do too," Thorne whispered back.

After greeting a few more guests, a voice called Ava's name. A familiar voice. High pitched and scratchy.

"Ava! Princess Ava! Miss Ava!"

Ava scanned the crowd, looking for the source, when she spotted him. Remy. The hobgoblin who had befriended her when they were both prisoners of Deidamia. The last time she'd seen him, they'd parted ways as he headed to his home with his brothers and she'd made her way to Mosshaven, saying their goodbyes. That was months ago.

She crouched to address her short friend, her eyes brimming with tears. "Remy!" she exclaimed as he waltzed up to her.

Opening her arms, she pulled him in for a hug and squeezed, a small sob leaving her throat. The two of them held each other for a long while, reveling in their reunion. She felt everyone's eyes on her, but no one said a word. They broke the hug, and she met his stare.

He looked so much better than when she last saw him. The pallor of his green skin was gone, and he had filled out; no longer bony and starved. A clean tunic and pants replaced the rags he wore in camp and his smile was genuinely happy.

"I can't believe you're here," she whispered through her tears.

He placed a gnarled green hand on her face and looked at her with his globe-like eyes. "You're a princess now. Yes yes yes. I'm happy to be here. To see you, my friend."

Three other hobgoblins came up behind him, looking almost the same save for their different statures. Remy's brothers. They bowed in unison.

The tallest one spoke as he regarded Ava with awe. "You saved our brother. Yes, you did."

"We are forever grateful," a short round one said.

Ava wiped her eyes. "He saved me too."

"Pardon the interruption, but you're holding up the line," Thorne said, leaning down.

Ava rose.

"I'm sorry Your Majesty," Remy said. "Your sister is special. Yes, she is. I was just so excited to see my friend again. She saved my life, you know. I shall go inside now." He bowed again and trotted off, his brothers in tow.

"Who was that?" Thorne asked.

"The hobgoblin who was imprisoned with me." Her eyes flicked to Casimir, who was watching her with admiration.

Thorne gave her hand a squeeze and smiled warmly. But moments later, he stiffened. "The astral royalty is here."

The rest of their group immediately tensed, Casimir going rigid as they waited for the trio to approach.

Ava's nervousness returned with a vengeance, her pulse

racing. It was obvious who they were by the way they were dressed and the air of self-importance hanging around them. They barely acknowledged Casimir other than a brief nod. Though the one she assumed was Jareth sneered at him and said, "Brother."

Casimir did not look like his father at all except for his golden eyes and his size. Orion was tall and imposing and instantly made Ava nervous. He had blonde hair cut above his shoulders, sprinkled with silver. Very few wrinkles were visible on his otherwise perfect face and he wore an all-white outfit lined in gold.

"Strange customs you must have in the human world," he said in a deep voice, looking at her with disgust. "A princess kneeling before a hobgoblin? It seems your time here hasn't cured your obvious disregard for propriety."

Raine stilled and Casimir trembled with restraint at the insult but remained quiet. Speechless, she curtsied, trying to hide her shaking hands.

"We respect all citizens of our kingdom, Orion," Thorne interjected. "Something you could learn about, I think."

He turned to Thorne, now ignoring Ava. "Your Majesty. I hope the members of your court have learned some manners since the last ball," he said, then strolled away.

The Queen curtsied, remaining silent, her pale blue gown shimmering with the movement. She regarded Ava with intense violet eyes, bright against her pale complexion and golden hair.

As she finished her greeting, Orion barked at her, "Come, Seraphina. We best get inside."

Bringing up the last of the trio was Casimir's half-brother, Jareth. Leaner and shorter than Casimir, he had his mother's deep purple eyes full of mischief and disdain. Honey blonde hair brushed his shoulders and his flawless alabaster skin shone in the lamplight. He was dressed similarly as his father; all-white trimmed in gold.

He stalked toward Ava with a feline grace and reached for her hand. Not knowing what to do, she let him pull it to his mouth, kissing it sensually as his eyes locked with hers. Her skin crawled at the way his gaze moved lower, stopping on her breasts.

"You may be ignorant but at least you're a sweet morsel to look at," he said after he let go. All the men around her tensed at his words. He leaned closer, inches from her face. "I wonder what you taste like," he whispered as his eyes dipped low.

Nausea brewed in her gut as she took a subtle step backwards. Casimir, Raine and Jorrar's hands had moved to their swords, ready to defend her at a moment's notice.

"Stand down," Thorne said, before turning to Jareth. "One more comment like that to my sister and I'll have you thrown in the dungeons, Jareth."

Jareth backed away and raised his hands. "Fine, fine. I was just teasing. All in good fun." He sauntered away, hands in his pockets.

"Are you okay?" Raine whispered.

"Fine."

Casimir's hands clenched into fists at his sides, on the brink of losing control. She raised her eyebrows and gave him a slight smile, trying to assure him she was alright.

The rest of the greetings went smoothly. She met the king and queen of Igneothenia. Aelerion was huge and tall with brick red skin and bright yellow veins on his hands and neck disappearing below his clothing. His vivid orange eyes twinkled as he greeted her boisterously, his booming laugh sounding over the crowd. Thalia was lovely, with the same complexion as her husband, neon yellow eyes, and long gray hair. They both donned black clothing, Thalia's ebony gown sprinkled with glimmering crystals.

The guests were almost done filtering in, and relief washed over Ava that this part was over. She hoped to do everything in her power to avoid Orion and Jareth and promised herself she would get through the night unscathed.

Once the guests had finished making their way inside the castle to the ballroom, Casimir approached. "Are you alright?"

"I'm fine," she replied. "Your family is something else."

"If he says one more thing like that to you, I'll have his head on a pike."

"No, you won't," said Thorne. "We must play nice this time."

"He's not the one that threatened to throw him in the dungeons," said Raine.

"I shouldn't have said that. You two go ahead inside." He nodded to Raine and Casimir. "We'll be there shortly."

The two warriors disappeared with the crowd, leaving Ava with her brother and Jorrar, who would announce their entrance into the ballroom. Heart in her throat and stomach in knots, she readied herself to be presented to the crowd.

36

*A*va was immediately overwhelmed by the sights and sounds of the ballroom. Lively music played from within, mingling with the conversations from the crowd. She tightened her grip on Thorne's arm.

Here goes nothing, she thought.

The commotion died down and the crowd parted, noticing their entrance. Jorrar stood before them and cleared his throat.

"Presenting, His Majesty King Thorne Everwood and his sister, Her Highness Princess Ava Everwood of Monterre."

The crowd clapped as they made their way along a forest green rug. Twinkling lights floated near the high ivory ceiling —blues, greens and golds scattered among the thick canopy of vines above. One wall of the ballroom was open to a large formal garden, archways leading to the outside where guests could enjoy the flowers and plants of Mosshaven in the evening breeze.

Dozens of tables sat around the perimeter and in the garden, preparing to host their dinner. Each bore a sage green tablecloth lined with gold, stunning centerpieces bursting with yellow and orange flowers sitting on top.

The kingdom's colors of green and gold were present everywhere. In the banners hanging from the walls bearing the Elderoak insignia, on the tables, in the guards' uniforms.

They walked through the crowd, citizens bowing and curtsying as they passed. Ava smiled and scanned the attendees for any familiar faces. She caught Pax's eye—who was standing guard near the back of the ballroom—and he gave her a subtle nod of encouragement, knowing how much she disliked being the center of attention. Remy and his brothers waved enthusiastically from their spot in the crowd.

She recognized the other advisors—Vivienne in a stunning navy gown bringing out the blue in her eyes, and Desmond a few feet away, gripping a wine goblet in his hand.

They reached a small dais where Thorne's throne sat, the back carved with the Elderoak. Next to it was another similarly carved throne for Ava. Upon the platform, Thorne turned around and raised his hands to address the crowd.

"People of Monterre, we welcome you to the annual Summer Solstice ball, where we honor the traditions of our kingdom and celebrate the beginning of the season. I want to give a special welcome to our guests from the other kingdoms. King Aelerion and Queen Thalia, who have been in hiding for decades. We're honored to have you back with us today. King Orion and Queen Seraphina, Queen Soren and Queen Astrid. Thank you for gracing us with your presence on this joyous occasion. I also want to welcome my sister, who as you know, had been missing for almost one hundred years. We welcome Ava Everwood back home to our kingdom and celebrate her return."

Someone shouted, "Here here," eliciting cheers from the crowd.

"Thank you all for coming, and enjoy the celebration!" Thorne finished.

The crowd cheered again and went back to mingling as Ava

and Thorne took their seats. Casimir appeared and took his place behind Ava. Quinn followed suit and did the same on Thorne's side, flanking them and prepared for any signs of trouble.

Ava whispered to Thorne, "How long do we sit here?"

"Just a little while in case anyone wishes to speak with us. You may get up and socialize in a few minutes, if you'd like."

Socialize? No thanks. Not when the only people she knew here were working. Though maybe she could find Kai or Fanya and stay by their side for most of the night. Or even take Astrid up on her offer.

No one approached, the guests busy enjoying the revelry and drink. Bored and antsy, Ava spotted Fanya in the crowd. "I'm going to mingle," she said as she rose and descended the steps, headed toward Raine's sister.

Casimir and Quinn remained with Thorne while Ava pushed through the throng of guests.

"Ava!" she exclaimed as she looped her arm through Ava's and pulled her to the edge of the crowd. "How are you holding up?"

"It's a lot," she said. "Casimir's father and brother are horrible."

"They're awful. If you haven't noticed, they treat women differently there. It causes a lot of problems between them and the other kingdoms."

"You don't say," Ava deadpanned.

"Where did you get that necklace?" she asked, noticing the jewelry she bore. "It's gorgeous."

"Cas bought it for me." She touched the gemstone hanging at the center. "That's why we ran into him at Ghorza's shop."

"Well, *that* is romantic."

"Where's Pax?" Ava asked her. "Has he seen how stunning you look yet?"

Fanya giggled. "Oh yes. I've been waltzing by him all evening, taunting him. It's great fun."

Ava laughed as they walked along the edge of the ballroom and ran into Kai.

He gave her a big hug. "You look fantastic."

"Thanks. So do you."

The three of them continued to visit and fortunately, Ava didn't have to mingle with any of the other royals. She was too intimidated to do so, unsure what she would talk about with them. Guests' curious eyes landed on her as they walked by. Ava fidgeted, trying to ignore the stares.

Vivienne approached, Desmond at her heels. "Good evening, Your Highness," she said.

Though Ava hadn't interacted with the advisors often— much too busy with the Elderoak preparations—she had instantly warmed to Vivienne. She gave off a motherly aura and Ava felt drawn to her.

"Hi Vivienne," Ava said. "You look beautiful tonight."

"As do you. How are you feeling now that you're fae?"

"It's an adjustment."

"Your Highness," said Desmond, ready to talk business. "Now that you've completed the Elderoak journey, will you be joining our war council meetings?"

"That's a good question. We haven't had a chance to discuss it yet, but I'll talk to Thorne about it," Ava answered.

Desmond grumbled. "I don't know what you'll bring to the table, but I suppose you should, since you're the princess."

Vivienne gave Desmond a pointed look. "She was right there in Deidamia's camp, Desmond. She has more knowledge about that than we do. She should attend."

"Right. Well, I'm going to go find some more wine," he said before disappearing again.

"What a grouch," Vivienne said as she scanned the crowd.

"Oh! I need to go speak to the chef about the dinner timing. Enjoy your evening."

They bid Vivienne farewell as she headed in the direction of the kitchens. Turning back to Kai and Fanya, her gaze caught on Casimir. He had moved positions, now standing near a wall, observing her with intensity. When she met his eyes, he jerked his head, gesturing for her to come speak to him.

"I'll be right back," she said to her friends, pushing her way through the guests.

Stopping before him, Ava raised a brow. Casimir's lips brushed her ear as he whispered, "Meet me in the north hallway in five minutes."

He walked away.

What? The north hallway? She remained frozen to her spot, confused, when she noticed Astrid eyeing her. Ava smiled and Astrid gave her a knowing wink, walking off to visit with the others.

Five minutes later, she made her way across the ballroom to the north hallway, slipping through an open door. It was quiet. No guests had wandered this way.

"Cas?" she whispered, searching the corridors.

A hand grasped her wrist and yanked her into a dark alcove, a hard body pinning her against a wall.

"What are you doing?" she whispered harshly, now face to face with the general.

"This," he said as he leaned in and kissed her with vigor, grasping her face with his hands. She grabbed his jacket and pulled him closer, sighing into his mouth before breaking the kiss.

"Someone will see us," she said as he kissed his way down her neck. The faint sound of music drifted from the ballroom as she reveled in his touch.

His lips found hers again. "So?"

He didn't stop, hands roving along her body, palming her

ass. "You...in that dress...have me distracted." He moved to her neck again as he lifted a hand and grasped her breast. She moaned, arching her back. "I want to rip it off and take you right here."

"Yes," she whimpered.

He continued, trailing heated lips along her shoulder, nibbling and licking, as his hands moved lower and gripped her hips.

He groaned into her neck and inhaled. "You smell so damn good."

Ava sunk her fingers in his hair and pulled his lips to hers, kissing him deeply as her breathing sped up. Someone cleared their throat in the hallway right next to them and they froze.

Ava glanced over to find Astrid standing there grinning. "I'm sorry to interrupt but your brother is looking for you, Your Highness."

"Oh," she said, the heat of embarrassment creeping up her neck.

Casimir backed away, straightening his jacket, and smoothing his hair. Ava attempted to fix her own as they both emerged from the alcove and faced Astrid awkwardly.

"You go back first," Astrid said to Casimir. "I'll walk Ava in. Tell Thorne she and I were getting some fresh air."

He nodded and kissed Ava on the forehead before starting to walk off, when Astrid called after him, "Casimir." He paused and turned around. "I'm happy for you," she said. He smiled and turned away, leaving the two of them alone.

"I need to fix your makeup," said Astrid, pulling out a small pot of rouge she had hidden in her dress. She dabbed it on Ava's cheeks and lips while she spoke. "I've known Casimir for a long time. I've never seen him shirk his duties for a woman before. You must be something special to him."

"Thank you."

"You're soulbonds, yes?" Astrid asked as she fixed Ava's hair.

"How did you know?"

"We can usually recognize each other."

"Right. Jorrar said you and Soren were soulbonds," Ava said.

"Yes. I had guessed the two of you were when you visited us." Astrid backed away. "Okay, I think it isn't too obvious you were just ravaged by the general. Ready to go back?"

"Yes."

She stayed beside Astrid as they headed to the ballroom, the sound of the music and voices growing louder as they approached.

"Don't be embarrassed," she said. "Soren and I sneak away at these things all the time. Something about getting caught is exciting. I didn't want to interrupt, but I knew someone else would end up finding you and it wouldn't go as pleasantly."

"How did you know where I was?" she asked.

"He hasn't taken his eyes off you since the moment I arrived. When I overheard Thorne ask where you were and noticed you were both gone, I figured it out quickly."

"I'm glad you found us instead of my brother," she replied. "That would have been awkward."

"Indeed."

They walked through the crowd and found Thorne speaking with Soren, Thalia and Aelerion—the latter's boisterous laugh booming across the ballroom.

"Sorry, Thorne," Astrid said. "I had asked Ava to accompany me to get some fresh air."

Ava smiled as they approached the group and caught Thorne's eye. He looked at her with suspicion but kept quiet.

"So, Ava," said Aelerion. "What do you think of Eorhan? Of Monterre?"

She instantly liked him. "It's beautiful. People are kind here."

"Monterre does have some of the most welcoming fae.

Much more pleasant to be around than those astral bastards," he said, laughing at his own joke. "If they give you any trouble, let me know. I've been wanting to go toe to toe with Orion for centuries."

His queen gave him an exasperated look and grasped Ava's hand. "We're so happy you're here."

The dinging of a glass chimed through the ballroom noise, the volume lowering as the music paused.

"If the guests would make their way to their tables. Dinner will begin shortly," Vivienne announced.

The crowd moved as the attendees trickled to their assigned tables. Some meandered outside, searching for their seats under the starry night, while Thorne led their group to a large table at the front of the ballroom.

He took his seat at the head and gestured for Ava to sit at the first seat to his right. Casimir appeared and pulled out her chair, taking his seat next to her after assuring she was comfortable. Raine sat to the right of Casimir, Soren and Astrid on the other side of him. Quinn, Jorrar and Kai took their places across from them.

As Raine lowered in his chair, he leaned over and whispered, "What have *you* two been up to?"

Astrid huffed a laugh under her breath as Ava rolled her eyes.

Jareth strutted to the table and took a seat right next to Kai, followed by his parents. Next to them sat Aelerion and Thalia, irritation on Aelerion's face at the astral royalty stealing their assigned seats.

Thorne leaned forward to address them, "Orion, I had the seating chart arranged with care."

He scoffed. "No one tells me where to sit. Besides, we are too curious about the new princess, we just had to be close."

"This is going to be bad," Soren whispered.

Orion looked at her across the table and sneered. "Good to see you too," he said sarcastically.

Ava felt Jareth's eyes on her and tried to ignore him as she scanned the table. Raine was watching Casimir out of the corner of his eye with concern. Likely pleading internally for him not to flip the table when his brother inevitably said something horrific. Casimir's hand moved to her leg, as if he was trying to protect her from any discomfort.

"Ignore them," she whispered. "They're going to try to rile you."

He looked at her and leaned in. "I'd rather be back in that alcove right now," he whispered back as his hand moved higher.

His thumb traced circles over the fabric on her inner thigh. She shifted in her seat, squeezing her legs together. "I'd rather be back in our rooms...doing other things..." she replied.

"And what might those other things entail, princess?" he crooned in her ear.

Thorne cleared his throat and gave the two of them a pointed glare as he sipped his goblet of wine. Casimir removed his hand and winced at her brother before looking away.

The first course—a blended root vegetable soup topped with basil—was placed in front of them, the scent of herbs and spices tickling Ava's nose. Though her stomach was still in knots, she was starving and scooped a bite into her spoon, humming to herself as her taste buds were overwhelmed with flavor.

"So, Ava," Orion said across the table, evoking cautious looks from the others as they waited for the insults to leave his mouth. "How is it we never knew about you? Thorne has been king since Vardan and Aurelia died and no one knew there was a long-lost *sister*."

Ava set down her spoon. "My mother escaped into the human world while pregnant with me and I was born there. I didn't know about any of this. Apparently, no one else knew she was pregnant besides her father."

"Ah yes. Lord Pellas. Your grandfather was an insufferable bastard. He was supposed to send Deidamia back to her realm...and yet he abandoned us...to protect you." He gave her a withering look.

What Orion didn't know was Pellas hadn't abandoned them; he knew Ava was the only one who would have enough power to banish the daemon queen, so they fled to raise her in safety until she could return to Eorhan.

Aelerion interjected from down the table, "It doesn't matter, Orion. That's in the past. She's here now, so we must move forward."

Orion waved his hand. "Yes yes, I know. You can't fault me for being curious," he replied as he sipped his wine.

Ava took another spoonful of soup as Orion turned and conversed with other guests, now ignoring her.

Soren leaned over Raine and Casimir. "Well, I'm glad you're here. It will be nice to have another woman among these tiresome fae brutes."

"They're aggravating, aren't they? Especially this one." Ava jerked her head to Casimir who looked at her, feigning offense.

Soren leaned over and whispered, "You two are very sweet together, by the way." She grinned knowingly, likely having been informed by her wife what she had caught them doing earlier.

Ava smiled. "So are the two of you."

Staff removed their dishes as the first course came to an end and Jareth spoke for the first time since the dinner began. "Ava, sweetheart," he said condescendingly. "When you get your fill of male brutes, come visit our kingdom. I could show you a thing or two about how true royalty behaves."

She eyed him, trying to think of a response, but he continued.

"You know we've had a strenuous relationship with Monterre, thanks to my beastly brother." Casimir tensed beside her, and she glared at Jareth. "My father has talked about an alliance between us, you know."

The people seated around their end of the table had gone quiet, Thorne eyeing Jareth with ire.

Her brow knitted, anger rising at the insult toward Casimir. "And?"

"Well, I shall have to explain it to you in simpler terms, I imagine. You having been raised in such an oblivious household." He sipped his wine. "I'm talking about marriage. I'm single and not getting any younger. The other women my father presented have bored me. You, on the other hand, will do nicely, I think. You won't even have to do anything. I'll do all the work and you can sit back...and take it." He leered at her.

Casimir lunged across the table and grabbed his brother by the collar of his shirt, slamming his head on the wooden surface and holding him down. A vine wrapped around Jareth's wrists behind him, ensuring he couldn't use his magic.

Raine cursed under his breath as the rest of them tensed, watching the interaction.

"You will do well to remember who you are speaking to and whose court you are in," Casimir seethed. "Don't ever talk to her like that again or I will shove this goblet so far down your throat, you will be unable to speak at all."

Thorne whispered, "Let him go, general."

Casimir released his brother and sat back in his seat. Ava touched his arm and whispered, "I'm fine. He's trying to get to you on purpose."

Jareth rubbed his head and straightened his jacket, eyeballing Casimir with hatred.

"Is this how you allow your general to behave, Thorne? Like an animal?" Orion barked.

Thorne looked at Orion. "I see no problem with the general

of my army defending his princess. It is you who must control your son."

Jareth looked between Ava and Casimir, putting two and two together, and laughed. "Oh, I know what's going on," he said. "The two of you. Really? Of course, you filthy semi-human would choose to be with a doltish hybrid. All the mingling in this kingdom has made you all soft."

Rage coursed through Ava and before she had a chance to stop herself, she said, "Don't insult him or I will make you wish you never stepped foot inside this ballroom, you narcissistic worm. It's pathetic you resort to demeaning women to convince yourself you aren't a small-dicked asshole with no prospects at all."

"Oh fuck," Raine whispered.

Everyone turned to her, aghast at the normally quiet woman ready to brawl with the astral prince.

"Control your woman," Orion barked at Casimir who looked at him with boredom.

"I am no one's woman," she said as she narrowed her eyes at Casimir's father.

Aelerion's boisterous voice interrupted the tension. "Well, I think we've had enough of you and your son's insults, Orion. Let us be done with his subject before I lose my appetite at your cruelty."

Orion scoffed but remained quiet, as did Jareth and his mother. Everyone went back to their dinner and nothing more was said about the tiff.

Ava caught Quinn grinning at her and even Thorne, though trying to hide it, looked proud.

Casimir leaned in and whispered, "That was hot."

"You know, Ava," boomed Aelerion from across the table. "I think I like you."

She smiled broadly. "The feeling's mutual."

37

The music sounded, violins playing a slow dance, as the royalty in attendance took their places at the center of the floor. Plush brown and gold couches sat in the corners of the ballroom to allow for casual conversation and the lights were dimmed for a more intimate ambiance.

"It's customary for the royalty to dance the first dance," said Thorne, leading Ava to join the other dancers.

"I don't know the steps," she whispered.

Taking her hand in his, he placed his other on her waist as she laid her remaining hand on his shoulder. "Follow my lead," he said as he led them in a waltz.

The other royalty danced around them. Orion with Seraphina, Soren with Astrid, Aelerion with Thalia. Jareth had found some attendee, a high fae woman whose breasts were practically pouring from her tight red dress, and he sneered at Ava as they moved past.

She ignored him and focused on learning the steps.

"Well, they definitely don't like me," she said to her brother.

"They don't like anyone but themselves. Don't worry about it."

"Why did they come then?"

"Good question," he replied. "I think they wanted to meet you and they take pleasure in insulting others. It makes them feel powerful, the morons."

"Do you think they'll join us in this war?"

"I don't know," he said. "Dinner didn't help with that."

"I'm sorry. I didn't mean to, it just came out," she lamented.

"Don't be sorry. I was on the edge of losing it as well, you just did it quicker than I." After a moment he added, "You remind me so much of Mother."

She tilted her head as they moved across the dance floor. "How so?"

"She was like you. Kind, caring, warm to all the creatures and citizens of town. But insult her loved ones and she would turn into a formidable opponent. The Kingdom loved her. She was a fair and kind ruler," he said sadly. "Unlike father."

"I'm sorry you had to deal with him," Ava said. "And that I wasn't here with you."

"You're here now. That's all that matters."

The dance came to an end. Ava scanned the crowd, when she noticed a man standing in the back, staring at her. Something about him seemed familiar...but she couldn't put her finger on it.

"What is it?" Thorne asked, noticing the direction of her stare.

She looked at him, then back to where the man was standing. He was gone. Shaking her head, she replied, "Nothing. I thought I saw someone. It was nothing."

But she couldn't shake the strange feeling that she knew this person.

The royalty split apart, the rest of the guests now taking their places for the next song. Ava parted from Thorne and made her way to a group of couches where Remy sat with his brothers. She yearned to know how he'd truly been these last few months.

"Princess!" he exclaimed. "Come sit. Sit sit sit."

She lowered onto the velvet couch next to him. "How have you been, Remy?"

"Oh, just wonderful." He rocked in his seat as his brothers watched her with curiosity. "I've been enjoying my home. So happy to be reunited with my family, yes."

"I'm so happy to see you," she said.

"And you're the Princess! I knew there was something special about you. Yes yes yes."

They visited for a bit, exchanging stories from the last few months. Remy had gone back to his exploration of the forest, sticking closer to home, not wanting to draw the attention of the daemon army again. Ava told him about living in Mosshaven, her training and the Elderoak journey. The ease of which they fell into conversation was a comfort Ava hadn't realized she needed. The first friendly face upon her arrival to Eorhan.

"I'm sorry to interrupt," Casimir's voice sounded. Ava turned to find him standing before them. "May I borrow the princess, Remy?"

"Of course, general!" Remy bounced in his seat. "You found love, Miss Ava. Yes, you did. Love love love. Someone who understands your big heart," he whispered loudly with a wide grin.

Her face warmed as she smiled at Remy.

Casimir extended his hand. "Dance with me."

She took it and he pulled her to stand. She waved to Remy over her shoulder as Casimir led her to the dance floor. With a tug, he yanked her close and rested his hand low on her back as he led them into another waltz.

"Thank you for standing up for me at dinner," he said, intensity in his eyes.

"I'll always stand up for you. No one gets to call you a brute but me."

He chuckled and pulled her flush against him. "You can call me anything you want," he said, voice low. They continued their dance, making their way through the crowd, spinning and twirling. "I can't wait for this night to be over," he said.

"Me too. This is exhausting. Would it insult everyone if we left now?"

"Unfortunately, yes. Especially since this is your first ball. Don't worry, only a couple more hours and we can escape to the suite."

"Hours?" she whined.

He leaned in and whispered in her ear, "Why are you so eager to get back to our rooms, princess?"

"To finish what we keep trying to do every time we get interrupted."

He gave her a subtle kiss on the neck and pulled back. "Not much for fancy balls?"

"It's fun to get dressed up every once and a while," she said. "But honestly, I'd rather be curled up next to the fire, reading a book and sipping tea."

"Me too."

Casimir twirled her out and back in again, dipping her along with all the other guests. His lips met her collarbone as he pulled her closer and continued leading them between the guests. His hand trailed lower, resting atop the curve of her behind and she shivered at the unspoken promises in his eyes as he lowered his gaze to her lips. She moved her hand from his shoulder to rest on his neck and swirled her thumb along his throat.

Casimir dipped his head, brushing his lips against the shell of her ear. "You're making it extremely difficult for me to get through the rest of this ball, love."

Ava scanned his face, her eyes half-lidded with lust, unable to look away as they continued the rest of their dance in silence.

The dance ended and Ava glanced around as Casimir slowed. There he was again. The man. In a different spot this time.

She froze.

Noticing her alarm, Casimir gripped her chin and turned her face to him. "What is it?"

She looked back but he was gone yet again.

"I—I don't know...I thought I saw someone," she replied.

He was instantly on alert. "What do you mean you thought you saw someone? Who?"

She shook her head. "I don't know. I think it's someone I've seen before in town. He looks familiar. It's nothing."

His eyes were full of concern.

"It's nothing. I haven't slept well in days, and I just completed the journey yesterday. I'm exhausted and imagining things."

He left it alone, but she could tell he didn't believe her.

"To be sure, I'll alert the guards to be extra watchful of anything suspicious. Go find Thorne," he said as he walked off.

Ava sighed and pinched the bridge of her nose. Who was this man? Was she hallucinating? She spotted her brother in a corner speaking enthusiastically with Aelerion and Thalia. Leaving the dance floor, she joined them.

Their words were muddled, conversation not registering as her mind still raced about the stranger. But she feigned interest and tried to participate when possible.

"Ava, are you alright?" Thalia asked, noticing her silence.

"I'm fine. Actually, I think I'm going to go get some air. I'm quite tired."

"Would you like company?" Thorne asked.

"No. I'll be back in a few minutes."

She headed toward the gardens, passing through an archway, and wandered along a path framed by purple flowering trees. There were guests mingling about, but it was much less crowded than the ballroom.

The steady trill of insects hummed in the bushes as the stars sprinkled the night sky with their diamond lights. Ava continued further, passing a fountain, the flow of water soothing in the quiet space. Reaching the other end of the garden, she found a bench hidden behind a row of shrubs.

Relieved at the privacy, she took a seat and closed her eyes, thinking over what had occurred tonight and readied herself to face the rest of the evening when someone cleared their throat behind her. Startled, she stood and turned around—face to face with the mysterious man.

"I'm sorry I startled you, Your Highness," he bowed, holding two goblets of wine in his hands.

"It's alright," she said. "Do I know you?"

"I didn't mean to make you uncomfortable. I just wanted to say thank you in person."

"Thank me for what?"

"I was on the ship that day," he explained. "May I?" he asked, gesturing to the bench.

"Oh, sure." She reclaimed her seat and he sat beside her, holding out a goblet. "You seem stressed, I brought you some wine."

She took the glass and thanked him, but something told her not to take a sip, so she held it in her hand, remaining alert.

"You were one of the sailors?" she asked with hesitation.

"Yes...you saved our lives that day. And I never got a chance to thank you." He gave her a warm smile, dark eyes admiring her.

"You're welcome," she said. "That was a horrible day."

"It was. How are you handling all the attention tonight?" he asked.

"It's a lot to take in."

He sipped his own libations. "I can only imagine the stress you must be under."

She sat with the stranger and continued speaking with him for a few minutes, but something felt off and she looked for a way to end the conversation and leave. No one could see her behind these shrubs and her instincts were screaming at her to get away.

"I'm so sorry, but I must get back. My brother is probably looking for me."

"Of course, of course." He rose from the bench. "I'll walk you."

"That won't be necessary," she said with feigned kindness.

Get away from him, she urged herself.

She rose and tried to move around the man, but he stepped in front of her, blocking the only way out from behind the shrubs. He pinned her with a hard stare, something vile dancing in the depths of his eyes.

"You should have drunk the wine."

"What?" she asked, backing away a step.

"Luna," Ava spoke to her companion.

What is it?

"Something's wrong. Alert the others. I'm in the garden with a strange man. I think he means to harm me."

Okay, I'm telling them now. Try to get away.

"Please move," Ava said, trying to keep her voice steady.

He continued closer, sizing her up. Ava backed away and stepped around him, but he grabbed her arm at the last second and shoved her against the stone wall, the goblet in her hand falling to the ground. He pressed in close and as she was about to scream for help, something hot burned in her stomach, and she gulped a sharp breath. A choking sound left her lips.

What happened? Why couldn't she breathe?

"Deidamia sends her regards," he leaned in and whispered

in her ear as he twisted his hand and her abdomen burned even hotter, a yelp leaving her lips at the pain.

He backed up, yanked his hand away, a bloody dagger clutched in his fist, and vanished into the shadows.

Ava looked at her stomach, hands moving to the white hot pain. Within seconds, bright red blood spread from a puncture in her dress. She'd been stabbed.

She pressed her hands against the wound as it hit her. She knew why she'd recognized him. He'd been one of the soldiers at Deidamia's camp when she was a prisoner. And he was here, in her home, in her castle.

A wave of dizziness almost overcame her as she stumbled through the gardens. Help. She needed help. Her stomach was on fire, and she struggled to breathe steadily as something coursed through her body. Was the dagger poisoned?

She leaned against a tree to steady herself, her vision beginning to waver.

38

Casimir scanned the ballroom, unable to find Ava. He'd alerted the guards of a potential threat and went back to look for her, but she had disappeared. Finding Thorne, he interrupted his conversation with Aelerion and Thalia. "Where's Ava?"

"She went out to get some fresh air, she'll be right back."

"When?"

Noticing the panic in Casimir's voice, Thorne frowned. "Oh, I don't know...about ten minutes ago. Why? What's wrong?"

He shook his head. "Nothing. I don't know. Something doesn't feel right."

"What do you mean?"

He ran a hand through his hair. "She said she saw someone in the crowd but brushed it off. I have a bad feeling."

"She's tired. She told me the same thing," he said, unconcerned. "I'm sure it's nothing. She'll be back soon."

"Alright," he said. But his gut was telling him something was amiss.

Get to the gardens, Aro said. *Now.*

"On it," he replied as his worry turned into full blown panic.

He hurried outside and jogged through the landscaping, searching the dark paths for some sign of her. As he passed a large tree, a weak voice called his name.

"Cas."

He whipped around to find Ava leaning against the trunk. Beads of sweat along her neck glistened in the moonlight. A crimson stain marred her dress, her skin pallid, lips white.

"What happened?" he asked, rushing closer.

"The man," she whispered, barely able to keep her eyes open. "...Deidamia...poisoned dagger..."

Casimir caught her when she passed out and lifted her in his arms. Her head lolled back, her body limp in his grasp. Breaths came in short bursts, slowing down with each second.

No no no.

He shouted at the closest guard, "Secure the ballroom. No one leaves until we find the person responsible."

Carrying her through the crowd, he searched for Kai. Gasps and shouts of fear sounded as guests noticed the motionless princess in his arms covered in blood. Raine spotted Casimir first and grabbed Kai, who happened to be next to him, rushing over.

"What happened?" he asked, eyes wide as he took in Ava.

"Someone stabbed her."

"Get her to her room," said Kai. "We can secure it better than the medical wing. I'll meet you there in five minutes."

"Hurry," he demanded as the healer took off running.

Turning to Raine, he said, "Make sure the guards have sealed off every exit. Find who did this and get them to the dungeons."

Raine nodded.

Casimir sprinted, cutting through the ballroom and down the corridors to his suite. Thorne caught up to him, shouting, "What happened?"

"I don't know. She said something about a poison dagger and passed out," he answered as he willed his legs faster.

He reached the suite and rushed into her bedroom. Kai entered seconds later, carrying a large apothecary box.

Casimir remained standing and pulled her closer, afraid to let her go.

"Lay her on the bed," Kai said.

He did as instructed, staring at her lifeless body. "Is she dead? Please tell me she isn't dead."

There was so much blood. Too much. She should have started to heal, at least a little, since she was now fae. But if there truly was poison on this dagger, there was no telling what was now coursing through her body.

His heart was gripped in a vice of panic, fighting the urge to destroy everything around him in fury. She can't be dead. He wouldn't allow it. Pacing the room, it took all his energy to keep control of his magic writhing to get out.

A hand gripped his shoulder. "Come, sit," said Thorne, trying to remain calm, though terror shone in his eyes at his sister's condition. "Give Kai space to work."

Reluctantly, he sat in the chair in the corner and watched as Kai examined her, feeling for her pulse. Thorne paced in Casimir's place, rubbing the back of his neck and muttering to himself.

"Well?" Thorne demanded, looking at Kai.

"She's not dead," he said. "But her pulse is weak."

"You need to save her," Thorne thundered, his voice rising.

"I need more details. I need to know what happened. Do you two know anything at all?" Kai asked.

"She said she thought she saw someone familiar," Thorne explained. "It seemed to spook her, but she brushed it off. Then she claimed she wanted fresh air and went into the gardens. That's all I know." He slammed his hand against the wall. "Fuck! I should have taken her seriously."

"You couldn't have known," Kai said. "Cas, anything?"

"I went to look for her. I had a feeling something was wrong. I found her leaning against a tree. She said something about Deidamia and a poison dagger and then passed out," he answered, hands trembling as he continued to try and keep his magic under control. Effort fruitless, he gripped the arms of the chair, the wood cracking under his hold.

Thorne turned to him at the sound. "You need to stay calm, Casimir."

"I'm fucking trying," he snarled.

"Thorne," said Kai. "I must know what kind of poison it was. I can keep her alive for a while with basic tonics, but I can't reverse the effects without knowing exactly what we're dealing with."

"Are you saying she'll die if we can't figure it out?" asked Casimir.

"It's possible," whispered Kai.

"I'll have a team search for anything that can help us," Thorne said and rushed from the room.

The ache in Casimir's soul burned; terror churning with anguish and barely contained wrath. He took a deep breath, approached Ava, and sat at the edge of the bed.

Brushing the hair from her face, he whispered, "Please don't die."

Kai placed his hand on Casimir's shoulder. "I'm going to do everything in my power to make sure that doesn't happen." He ripped open her dress and placed his hands on Ava's abdomen. "I'm going to try to stop the bleeding with my magic."

Casimir nodded, throat tight as he fought back tears, furious with himself for leaving her alone. He should have stayed with her when she told him about the man. It was his fault she'd been stabbed, and he'd never forgive himself if she didn't make it.

They'd had no time together. He'd had no time with his

love, his soulbond. His Miraêl Li'ra. He wanted to take her to the animal rescue and see those smiles again; to drink tea and read books snuggled on the couch; to make love to her and spend the rest of the night wrapped in each other's arms.

"Can I sit here while you work?" he asked, vision blurring.

"Of course."

Kai opened a vial filled with brown liquid. Casimir scooted back to give him room and held Ava's hand as Kai lifted her head and used a dropper to release the liquid down her throat. She coughed and Casimir tensed, but swallowed and was silent again.

"Good," said Kai. "That's a good sign."

He looked at her perfect face as she took shallow breaths. An hour ago they were dancing and enjoying themselves. How did this happen?

Kai gave her various tinctures and monitored her pulse, Casimir watching attentively. At one point, he put his hands on her chest and closed his eyes, searching for any clues with his magic to what the poison could be.

After what felt like forever, Thorne entered with a guard at his heels. "We found this in the garden. It seems some of the poison dripped off the dagger."

Kai stood and took a leaf from the outstretched hand of the guard and smelled it. His eyes went wide as he set it down and rummaged through his apothecary kit.

"What? What is it?" Casimir said. His chest was so tight it ached.

"It's strong. I can't even pronounce it and it's very rare. It kills quickly but we caught it in time and fortunately I have the antidote." He found the vial and uncorked it, leaning over her. Parting her lips, he tilted her head forward and poured the purple liquid in her mouth. "Come on, Ava. Drink."

Thorne hovered nearby, watching Kai carefully.

Her throat moved and she swallowed, taking the antidote.

She coughed and Casimir panicked, running his hand along her face, whispering encouragement to her. The coughing stopped and she stilled again.

"She'll live?" he asked.

Kai nodded. "But I don't know how long it will take her to wake. It could be days."

"Okay," he said. "Thank you."

Thorne leaned over his sister, squeezing her shoulder, a pained look on his face. He turned to Casimir. "I must go check on the guests and talk to the advisors about ending this ball early. Please let me know if she wakes."

"I will," he answered as Thorne left the room.

Casimir stayed with her for hours, sitting on the bed and holding her hand. He didn't move from his spot as Kai came in and out to assess her vitals. The rest of his friends left him alone, giving him space to be with his love. For he knew he loved her; he'd known for a while. And though he'd confessed his feelings, he hadn't said those three words yet, not wanting to put pressure on her.

And now she didn't know.

CASIMIR JERKED awake from his spot in the chair as someone entered the bedroom. Titus was asleep by Ava's head and Luna at her feet, both refusing to leave her side.

Raine strode forward and stopped. "We found him."

He stood. "Where is he?"

"The dungeons."

Kai entered to check on Ava and Casimir turned to him. "Will you please stay with her? I need to go interrogate this assassin," he said, voice cold.

"Of course."

Casimir kissed Ava's forehead and left the bedroom, Raine following.

"Who is he?" he asked as they walked the halls to the stairs leading to the bowels of the castle.

"Someone sent by Deidamia. He's not telling us much."

"I'll make sure he speaks," said Casimir, fury coursing through him.

He'd tortured prisoners before. Rarely, but he'd done it. Not usually one to enjoy it, this time he would. He'd delight in watching the daemon's eyes fill with terror at the realization of what he could do.

They reached the stairwell. Dark stone steps spiraled into the depths of the mountain lit by torches along the damp walls. Descending further, the floor evened out and they walked through the corridors of empty cells, currently devoid of prisoners aside from the daemon soldier. The damp smell of earth and a faint tinge of iron hung in the air, growing stronger as they reached their destination.

Quinn's voice carried down the hallway, speaking to the prisoner who was refusing to tell her anything.

Casimir approached the cell and Quinn asked, "Is she alright?"

"She's still asleep but she'll live."

She breathed a sigh of relief as she opened the cell. "Have at it."

Casimir stalked in, flipping a dagger in his hand. He stared icily at the man—the daemon soldier—sitting on the floor with his arms chained above him against the wall. Dark hair hung in greasy strands, brushing his bare shoulders.

Casimir knelt before him. "Who are you?"

The man spat in Casimir's face and laughed. Raine walked up behind him, followed by Quinn.

He jammed the dagger into the soldier's thigh as he wiped his face with the back of his other arm. The soldier screamed as

Casimir twisted the blade, black blood flowing out of the wound. "Want to try that again?"

"I'm nobody," he seethed. "Doing my duty for my queen." His voice slithered along the walls as he spoke.

He yanked the dagger out and ran it along the daemon's chest, painting him in his own blood. "And what is your duty?"

"Like I would tell a filthy fae that," he spat.

Casimir backed away and sheathed the dagger. Sharp roots grew out from between the cracks of the stone floor, and he willed them to snake around the man's legs, creeping higher.

"You think your useless plant magic will get me to talk?" He sneered.

Casimir gave him a feline smile and clenched his fists. The daemon bellowed as hundreds of needle-like thorns burst from the roots and impaled his legs.

Casimir knelt again. "One more time. What is your duty?"

The daemon moaned but remained silent, still refusing to answer.

Clenching his hands again, the vines thickened and squeezed, bones crunching as he broke the soldier's legs. A bone chilling scream burst from the daemon's mouth. Before he could recover, Casimir grabbed the man's hand and sliced off a finger, eliciting another scream.

"Okay! Okay," croaked the soldier. "To ensure her success. She has the book, you know. To let more of her armies in."

Quinn looked at him. "Why kill Ava if she needs her blood to open the portals?"

"I don't know," the daemon hissed. "I only do what she tells me. I don't ask questions."

"Liar," said Quinn before she kicked him in the jaw.

Casimir whipped his head to her.

"Oops," she said as she lifted a shoulder.

"We won't get answers if he's unconscious," he said.

The soldier groaned.

"See? He's fine," she said.

The daemon eyed the three of them before stopping on Casimir and grinning. "I was there, you know. When your bitch of a princess was being tortured. When The Scourge pressed the hot poker against her flesh. I heard her screams and smelled her fear. Heard her begging for death as she was whipped. It was delicious."

Barely a moment to think it through, Casimir lunged and slit his throat, black blood spurting from the wound. The daemon soldier went silent, body twitching as he died.

"What the fuck, Cas?" said Raine. "I have that nasty creature's blood all over me now."

He stood and wiped the dagger on his pants. "He was getting on my nerves."

"We won't get answers if he's unconscious," Quinn mocked him. "We won't get answers if he's dead either." She strode out of the cell mumbling to herself about men and their impulsiveness.

They shut the door behind them and left. As they walked down the corridor, they ran into Thorne who eyed them with disgust at the black blood covering their uniforms.

"What is that smell?" he asked.

Quinn crossed her arms. "Daemon blood. Cas killed him too quickly before we could get much out of him."

"You didn't find anything out?"

"Just that he was there to kill her," said Raine.

"They need her blood to open more portals. Why kill her?" Thorne responded.

"My guess," said Quinn, "is she's better off dead to them if they're unable to capture her again. If she's alive and not in their clutches, she's a huge threat since she's the only one who can defeat her. Especially now that she's fae."

"And they've already tried and failed taking her back how many times now? Three?" said Raine.

"Four," Casimir answered.

"You've counted?" asked Raine.

"Of course I have. The hounds back at camp when we first met her; the snakes and soldiers at the tavern; Corvus; the attack on the ships. They've come after her four fucking times."

"How did he get into the castle? I thought your security plans were impenetrable," asked Thorne.

"They were," Quinn replied.

"Which means…" Raine said.

"We may have a traitor in our midst," Thorne whispered under his breath.

39

*V*oices spoke from far away. Just out of reach. Everything was muffled and dark. Cold.

So...so...cold.

A door closed. Silence.

No, not silence. Footsteps. Loud and echoing, they hurt her head.

Back and forth. Back and forth. Someone was pacing.

She was so cold. Why was she so cold?

Slowly, the darkness waned. Faint light made its way into her vision. Her head pounded; body shivered. A hand grasped her own. Warm, large, and familiar.

Her name. Someone was saying her name. "Ava? Can you hear me?"

Yes, she thought. *Yes, I can hear you.* But the words wouldn't come. Her eyes wouldn't open.

"Are you there, love?"

I'm here. I'm here!

But darkness returned, and she was pulled under once more.

AVA COULD FEEL HER BODY, the darkness and cold now replaced by warmth. Softness surrounded her. The voices had been clearer, more distinct, but were currently silent. Sometimes she heard them speaking in hushed tones, but could never make out their words. Who were they? Her friends, maybe. Her family. Her love.

She released a shuddering breath and opened her eyes. Vision met with bright and painful sunlight, she squinted. Clenching and unclenching her fist, she tried to lift her heavy hand.

The ceiling came into view. *Where am I?* Vines hung above her. She turned her head. *Ouch.* It was like a vice, squeezing. There. A man, asleep in a chair. With long brown hair and a scar down his neck. Tall and large, hunched over uncomfortably. Worry etched on his face, even in slumber.

"Cas," she rasped. Her voice. It hurt.

He sat up and looked at her. His golden eyes meeting hers, he sighed with relief and moved to the edge of the bed, hand stroking her face.

"Hi," she said to him.

"Hi." He smiled, holding back tears.

"What happened?" she asked, wincing at her dry throat.

He clutched her hand and stroked the back of it. "You were right. There was a man at the ball. He stabbed you. He was one of Deidamia's soldiers. Sent to assassinate you."

"Where is he?" she whispered.

"Dead," he said, voice cold.

"Did you kill him?"

"Yes."

"Good."

She tried to rise, but he shook his head. "Rest."

She looked around the room, eyes catching on Luna asleep near her feet. Titus was curled up in her fur.

"They haven't left your side," Casimir said.

"How long have I been asleep?"

"Four days," he answered.

She closed her eyes for a moment, taking a deep breath and opened them again, catching him still watching her. "I could hear you sometimes. All of you, talking. But I couldn't get to you. It was so cold and dark," she rambled.

"It's okay." He brushed a strand of hair from her face. "You're safe. It's alright."

The door opened and Kai entered along with Raine, who was grinning.

"Welcome back, little frog," said Raine.

Ava frowned at him. "Is that supposed to be my new nickname?"

"It is."

"How in the world did you come up with that?" Ava asked, voice still rough.

Raine laughed. "We have a frog that lives in the marshes near the coast. It's called vilär'setis, which translates to little frog."

"And..." Ava said.

Casimir scowled and finished for Raine. "This frog has a defense mechanism where it basically 'dies' to trick predators. When the danger has passed, it comes back to life. Raine thought it would be funny to call you that."

"Because that's kind of what you did," Raine said.

Ava burst into a fit of giggles, Raine along with her. Casimir glared at them which made her laugh even harder. Even Kai had a subtle smile on his face.

"It's so stupid. I like it," Ava said.

"I don't," said Casimir.

"Well, the princess approves. I must get going. Glad to have you back," he said as he walked out the door.

"How are you feeling?" Kai asked as he approached and examined her.

"Terrible," she said.

She almost said 'like I've been hit by a truck' but realized they wouldn't know what that meant and almost burst into another fit of giggles. How strange to be in a world where they've never heard of cars or trucks or phones or televisions. This almost made her laugh more. Maybe she was delirious.

Kai handed a vial to Casimir. "Have her drink this every day. It will rebuild her strength quicker." He turned to Ava and squeezed her other hand. "I'm so happy to see you awake."

He rose and left the room, leaving her alone with Casimir again.

"Kai said you would have died had you still been in your human body," he said, worry in his voice.

"Well, it's a good thing I kicked ass on the journey, isn't it?"

"It is," he said, holding out the vial. "Do you want to take this now?"

"Yes. Can you help me sit up?"

He leaned over and wrapped his arms around her waist, pulling her up to sit, arranging pillows behind her back. She winced and put a hand to her stomach.

"Thanks."

"What hurts?" he asked.

"Everything feels weak, but my stomach hurts the worst."

She lifted her nightdress to inspect the stab wound. It was mostly healed, but the skin around it was still angry and inflamed.

"I'll see if Kai has anything to help," he said as he began to stand.

She grabbed his hand. "No. Don't go."

"Alright." He reclaimed his seat and handed her the vial.

She drank it, wincing at the bitter taste. "What now?"

"Well, you continue to rest."

"I need to start training my magic as soon as possible," she said. "She's obviously getting nervous. Desperate if she sent someone to the ball to assassinate me. We don't have time for rest."

He shook his head. "A few more days won't make a difference. You can't train if you can barely walk."

"Fine. We could...do other things..." she suggested. She wanted to touch him. To hold him. To feel his skin against hers.

His eyes darkened. "No. You're too weak. Soon, though." He leaned in and kissed her, then pulled away. "In the meantime, you need a bath."

She smacked him on the shoulder, and he chuckled. "Rude."

OVER THE NEXT FEW DAYS, everyone visited. Ava's brother had rushed in the moment he got word she was awake and had hugged her so hard, she thought her ribs would break. When he pulled away, he had tears in his eyes and was smiling with joy at her recovery.

Fanya came and gossiped with her, keeping her company whenever Casimir had to work and even Queen Thalia dropped by. She and her husband were staying at the castle now. Thorne had offered them an empty wing until they could reclaim their conquered kingdom.

Jorrar and Quinn had come, the latter chastising her for not hiding a dagger under her dress for protection, and the former sitting with her calmly as he did with most people. Pax had stopped by several times, trying to hide the worry on his face as he told her funny stories to keep her entertained.

She knew she was missing out on the meetings and planning the King and Queen of Igneothenia were now a part of. Casimir informed her they had almost finalized their plan to retrieve the book and rescue Isolde and were developing a strategy to take back the volcanic kingdom. There was an abundance of work ahead and she could sense the anticipation and dread.

Cirilla had helped her bathe, and she was able to move around, feeling stronger each day. Raine told her he'd start training with her in a couple of days and she was ready. Ready for revenge for all she and her friends had gone through. Ready to face her enemy.

Ava and Casimir had briefly spoken about the soulbond. He wanted to wait until she was well enough, but she was done waiting. She was well now and ready to make that commitment to him. Ready to bind her soul to his.

Tonight, she was nestled on the couch in her robe after bathing, a soft white blanket pulled up to her chest as she read a book. Casimir was in another war council meeting, and she had promised Kai she would rest for one more day before venturing about.

Unable to focus, she slammed the book shut and leaned her head back on the sofa, releasing a frustrated groan as Casimir walked in.

"What's wrong?" he said, sitting next to her, slinging his arm across the back of the couch and toying with her hair.

"I'm so bored. I can't wait to get out of this room."

"How are you feeling?" he asked.

"Completely fine."

She raised her hand and cupped his face, her eyes roving over his features. She wanted him now. Didn't want to wait any longer. Casimir's hand moved to the back of her neck and brought her lips to his, cautiously parting them as if he was afraid she'd break.

Ava deepened the kiss, plunging her hands into his hair as

she climbed into his lap and straddled him. He groaned into her mouth and gripped her hips as they continued their eager exploration.

She pulled away, her forehead pressed to his.

"Are you trying to seduce me, princess?" he said with a smirk.

She placed a kiss on his jaw as she ground herself into his hard length. "Yes," she whispered into his skin, continuing her path down the side of his neck. "Is it working?"

"Yes," he moaned. "Are you sure you're alright?"

"Positive." She gripped the hem of his shirt and lifted, but in one fell swoop, Casimir reached behind him, grasping the collar, and removed it, tossing it on the floor. Leaning back, she let her eyes explore every dip and cut of muscle, running her hands along his abs, the dusting of hair on his chest. Exploring each and every scar with the brush of her fingers.

His breath caught as he watched her, raw need blazing in his eyes.

He stood, set her down and picked her back up, throwing her over his shoulder. He smacked her ass, and she shrieked as he carried her through the living room.

"Did you just spank me?"

"Yes," he replied as he pinched her rear and she yelped. "I've been wanting to do that since you taunted me in those tight pants the day we left for Saxumdale."

She let out a giggle. "Really?"

"Oh yes, love. Don't think I didn't notice you swinging your hips around."

Casimir laid her on the bed, looking at her with feral desire. Ava raised her hand. "Wait."

A look of guilt flashed over Casimir's face, as if he was preparing to apologize, but Ava interrupted him as she rose and walked to her desk. "One second."

She opened a drawer and dug around, retrieving the dagger

Quinn had gifted her, walked back to Casimir, and handed it over.

"What are you doing?" he whispered.

"I'm ready."

"Now? Are you sure?"

She stepped closer and placed a hand on his face. "Yes, now. We were going to after the ball and then I was stabbed. The war is brewing fast, I can feel it. We aren't promised tomorrow. I want to seal the bond as soon as possible. I want to be with you."

He swallowed. "Alright. Hold out your hand."

Ava turned her palm face up, heart racing with anticipation. He reverently grabbed her wrist, his own hand trembling as he sliced her skin. She winced and he apologized before cutting his own.

"Ready?" he asked. She nodded.

He placed his hand on hers and pulled her against him, hands clasped against his chest. His free arm wrapped around her waist, and she clutched his neck. The moment their palms flattened against each other, a tingle erupted and worked its way up her arm.

Her vision blurred as she lost herself in his eyes. Molten gold pools full of devotion. Eyes that said everything without him even needing to speak.

As they beheld each other, he recited the prayer, speaking in a language she didn't understand.

The words were beautiful and poetic. She watched him as he spoke, his voice low and smooth. As he continued, the sensation intensified, spreading through every fiber of her being. The rest of the world disappeared and there was only them. Only here and now.

Goosebumps peppered her skin and Casimir's eyes widened. They tightened their grip on each other as he finished and every nerve in Ava's body came alive. It was as if the whole universe held its breath while their souls met, and they both gasped at the sensation. Ava closed her eyes and clutched his hand tighter. They seemed to float in a suspended state, two glimmering threads heading toward each other. They danced around one another as their very essence melded together; souls merging.

A burst of power seemed to flood Ava's body as her eyes shot open, locking with Casimir's. Neither of them moved, staying joined as they searched each other's faces.

"Did you feel that?" he whispered.

"Yes," she replied, voice shaky. "Is it done?"

"I think so." He pulled back and released their hands.

The cuts had healed, light pink scars remaining on their palms. But it wasn't a straight line like a cut; it was a symbol. A small circle with two dots on top of it.

"What is that?" she asked as she traced it.

"The soulbond mark," he said.

His hand cupped her face, thumb tracing her lips. He leaned closer, their noses touching as he brushed his mouth against hers.

The sensations from the bond had been replaced by something else. Something primal. Lust. Desire. *Craving.*

"Cas," she whispered.

At the sound of his name on her lips, the last tether of his restraint broke. One hand clasped the back of her neck as the other clutched her hip and pulled her closer.

He claimed her lips. The kiss was incendiary, immediate warmth pooling in her core. Her hands moved over his chest and ran through his hair, and he released a groan into her mouth, kissing her harder.

The intensity of the bond was so strong, the desire almost unbearable, she couldn't slow herself. Couldn't wait any longer. She needed him.

She pulled away and looked up at him, memorizing his face.

"You're beautiful," she said as she traced his scar with her fingers, beginning at his jawline and working her way down his neck to where it ended above his collarbone. He watched her as she leaned in and placed a light kiss where it ended.

Backing away, she didn't break eye contact as she untied her robe. His throat bobbed, and his breathing quickened. The robe slid off her arms and pooled at her feet, revealing the entirety of her nudity.

Casimir trembled as his eyes took in every inch, painstakingly slow, as if he was memorizing her every curve and dip. Every scar and stretch mark. Her full breasts and wide hips and thick thighs. His eyes rose and met hers, full of passion and wonder.

"You are the most exquisite thing I have ever laid eyes on." His voice came out in barely a whisper. "Are you sure you're well?"

"Positive."

It took all of two seconds for him to cross the distance between them. His hands went to her thighs, lifting her to straddle him. She looped her arms around his neck as her lips crashed into his, full of need and desperation.

He carried her to the bed and laid her down, hovering over her as he continued to kiss her, tongue exploring her mouth. He ground against her, and she arched her back at the sensation of his erection through his pants rubbing in just the right spot.

She ran her hand along his length, and unbuttoned his pants, not breaking their kiss. He groaned as he pulled away long enough to remove his trousers and tossed them to the corner of the room. Upon her again, his lips met her own once more. Her hand moved lower, gripping him and he growled, kissing her harder.

His mouth left hers and moved to her neck, working his way lower. Taking his time, his lips left a trail of heat down her throat, the sensitive dip of her shoulder, her collar bone. Reaching her breasts, he squeezed one while he took the other in his mouth licking and sucking and biting at her nipple. Ava arched her back and released a guttural moan.

Every kiss, every touch was too much and yet not enough. It would never be enough.

Lower and lower he continued his gentle torment along her stomach, her hips, moving closer to exactly where she wanted him. He parted her legs and placed a kiss on each inner thigh, inhaling deeply. His eyes flicked up to hers and he grinned.

"You have no idea how long I've been waiting to do this," he whispered.

Hooking a leg over his shoulder, he lowered himself. The first flick of his tongue had her gasping, setting her core ablaze. He licked up her center, letting out a groan of satisfaction. She whimpered, and if there was any bit of restraint left, Casimir broke it as he clutched her tighter.

Then, he devoured her.

Licking and sucking, his tongue moved around in circles in a beautiful torture as he worked her perfectly, knowing exactly what she needed.

"Oh my god," Ava cried out, gripping the sheets.

He moved faster, flicking in perfect rhythm as waves of pleasure began to build. Writhing and arching beneath his mouth, heat rushed beneath her skin, her climax already building. He held her still, not letting her hips move as if he knew her release was growing closer.

She murmured his name as the edge drew near, unable to catch her breath. Sensing her approaching orgasm, Casimir increased his speed and pressure with the flat of his tongue as he plunged two fingers inside her and curled them at the perfect spot. He hummed amidst his tantalizing movements and that sound pushed her over the edge, the ache in her core unraveling.

"Cas!" she cried out, her back arching and legs trembling as he held her tighter, not allowing her to move away while maintaining his speed as she found her release.

He slowed but didn't stop, easing her through her orgasm as she whimpered, coaxing every last tremor from her. Pulling away, he kissed his way back up her body, paying special attention to her breasts yet again.

She panted and moaned through the aftershocks as he returned to her mouth and kissed her, the taste of her arousal on his lips. He pulled away. "I wonder how many more times I can get you to scream my name."

"Shut up and kiss me again."

He kissed her, gently this time, as he eased his way on top of her, stopping as his hard length brushed against her. She grasped him again, moving her hand up and down and he groaned. She let go and he slipped inside of her, slowly and carefully. Tortuously.

Ava gasped at the size of him and he paused, allowing her time to adjust. He watched her as he pressed closer, now fully seated to the hilt.

Her nails dug into his shoulders, and she let out a husky groan. The sensation of them merged was indescribable. Her skin tingled. Her breath hitched. Senses were heightened. Every touch set a blazing path along her skin.

She moved her hips, impatiently waiting for him to move with her.

"Ava," he whispered as he kissed her neck, slowly thrusting. "You feel," he murmured into her skin, nipping her earlobe. "You feel so fucking good."

It wasn't enough. None of it felt like enough as she clawed his back and tried pulling him closer. He wasn't close enough. He would never be close enough and she panted and moaned as his pace quickened. She met his fervor and they moved together, both frantic with need.

"I need more," she moaned. "Cas...I...I need more."

She could barely control herself as the bond seemed to take over.

He flipped them around, arranging her to straddle him as he sat up on the bed. His hands held her hips, guiding her up and down on top of him and she cried out at the feeling of him so deep. God, he was so deep.

"Fuck, Ava," he said, moving her in a glorious rhythm.

She pulled at his hair and his back and moved faster on top of him as she felt another orgasm building. He didn't slow as he moved with her, his hands gripping her possessively. So close. She was so close. Casimir leaned in, his teeth grazing her nipple.

A gentle bite sent her plunging over the edge yet again, crying out as the wave of pleasure soared. Throwing her head back, her eyes fluttered as she grasped his hair and rode him through her climax.

"That's it, love," he purred into her neck. "You're so beautiful."

Her whole body shook but he continued his relentless pace, moving her on top of him with no sign of stopping. Whether it was Casimir's speed, the bond, or the new sensations of being fae, her orgasm wouldn't cease. She gripped his shoulders to keep herself upright as white-hot pleasure shot down her spine.

He wrapped his arms around her trembling body, holding her close. Burrowing his face into her neck, he increased the pace for the last few thrusts. Ava's orgasm crested as he found his own release and stilled, groaning and whispering 'perfect' into her skin.

Hours later they were tangled up under the covers. Ava's head on Casimir's chest and his arm around her waist. He trailed his fingers along her spine as they reveled in their nearness.

Ava was barely satiated and after a short break, they made love again, Casimir working her through two more orgasms as he himself had found his release once more. He explained it wasn't always like this, but immediately after the bond, the desire for closeness and connection was so intense, couples often stayed in bed for days because they couldn't get enough of each other.

She wished they had time for that.

"Ava," he whispered, and she tilted her head to look at him. "Hmm?"

He brushed a strand of hair from her face, looking at her with tenderness. He rolled her over, meeting her curious gaze as he hovered above her.

After placing a kiss on her nose, he said, "I'm in love with you. I have been for a while."

She swallowed a lump in her throat as he traced her face with his fingers.

"I'm sorry I didn't say it sooner...I...didn't want to scare you away."

Her heart swelled. "Nothing could scare me away from you."

He hummed with satisfaction. "I knew I loved you when I saw you on that ocean drake in the middle of the sea. You looked like a goddess. Right then and there, I knew how hopelessly and utterly lost my heart was to you."

Her eyes filled with tears, and he leaned in and kissed them away, a light peck on each cheek. "We didn't know each other very well then," she said.

"I know. But I couldn't help it. Seeing your strength. Your determination...it did something to me."

She sniffled. "I love you too." She tucked a strand of brown hair behind his pointed ear, taking in every detail of his face. Memorizing it. Soft lips. Coarse beard. Strong jaw. His scar. The scar that told his story. "I think I fell in love with you the day you took me to the animal rescue...Every broken piece of my heart. It was yours. It *is* yours. You truly saw me that day. You knew I was struggling. You knew what I needed. And you *saw*."

He kissed the corner of her lips, his golden eyes glistening.

"I will always see you, love." He pressed his forehead to hers. "My life began the day we found you in the woods. Like I'd been searching for decades for only you. And then you appeared; battered and bruised; terrified, but trying to hide it. My world shifted that day, though I didn't quite realize it. And there is nothing I won't do to keep you safe. Nothing. You are *everything* to me. You're my dear one; my soulbond; my whole heart."

Tears spilled from the corner of her eyes. "Oh, love. Why are you crying?" he asked as he wiped them away with his thumb.

"Because I'm happy."

"Me too," he said as he settled back into the bed, pulling her close and pressing a tender kiss to her temple. "You have no idea how happy I am."

The sound of Casimir's heartbeat was a comfort as she laid her head upon his chest. A hand painted circles along her hip, lulling her to sleep. As her eyes fluttered closed, the scent of him surrounding her, she wanted to be nowhere else but here. With him.

Her friend.

Her lover.

Her soulbond.

40

"You're not concentrating hard enough," Raine instructed as Ava held out her hand.

"Yes, I am."

She'd been trying to conjure a flower in her hand for the last hour. Sweat dripped from her brow as she stared at her palm, willing something to appear, for anything to happen. It was the second day of training her magic with Raine and she hadn't summoned so much as a minuscule leaf.

Shoulders slumping, she let her hand fall to her side. "This is pointless. I can't do anything."

He glanced down and his eyes widened as he looked at her other hand, snatching it to inspect her palm. "Is that what I think it is?" He gasped.

She smiled sheepishly.

"You and Cas sealed the bond? And you didn't tell me? You fuckers."

She pulled out of his grip and put her hands on her hips. "Why would we tell you?"

"Because I'm your best friend. And his too. I'm offended."

He scoffed but wrapped his arms around her and spun her around. "I'm so happy for you!"

"Raine, put me down. You're hurting me." She laughed as he squeezed her.

"Sorry." He let go. "So how was it?"

"How was what?"

"You know...the whole...intense sex afterward."

"I'm not telling you that." Her face turned bright red.

"That good, huh?"

She rolled her eyes. "Yes. It was...quite good."

"Quite good? Hmm...not 'mind-blowing' not 'leg-quivering'...just quite good?"

"Okay, enough," she said. "It was...all those things. But I'm not telling you details."

"Damn. I'm jealous. I need Cas to take *me* to bed."

"You're ridiculous."

"Alright, alright, I'll stop," he said. "Regarding your power. Earlier you said you can't do anything. Well, you can. I've seen it. After the journey."

"That must have been a fluke. I used it all up or something."

He shook his head. "You're powerful, Ava. I can feel it. The others can too. You have more magic than you should at this point, and you still haven't gone through your great tribulation."

"So, what was your great tribulation?" she asked.

"Are you trying to distract me from your training?"

She crossed her arms. "No, but I'm curious."

"This is not a very happy tale," he said, eyes sad. "But I'll tell you."

He sat on the stone wall and gestured for her to sit next to him. Titus appeared from the treetops and swooped toward them, landing on Ava's shoulder and nuzzling into her hair. Raine gave him a scratch on the head, and he released a contented growl.

He took a deep breath. "It was decades ago. My..." He paused and ran his fingers through his hair. "I was in love with someone. His name was Finnick. We had taken a trip to another town when we were ambushed by a group of rogue soldiers. Finnick wasn't much of a fighter and a soldier had a knife to his throat. I killed them."

"All of them?" she whispered.

"Each and every one. My magic erupted so quickly, they barely had a chance to act before they all had vines speared through their throats."

She gaped at him. "Does the great tribulation always involve someone you care about being in danger?"

"Not necessarily, but there's usually some type of peril. Whether it's a loved one, yourself or even your home. A moment of desperation."

They sat for a moment before Ava dared to ask, "What happened to Finnick?"

Raine looked at her. She had never seen him so sad. "He died. Thirty years ago. A week before we were to marry, he was traveling back to Mosshaven after spending time in another town with his family. He was ambushed by soldiers again. But this time I wasn't there to save him."

A lump formed in Ava's throat. "I'm sorry."

"Thanks." He gave her a sad smile and turned away.

Ava grabbed his hand and squeezed it. "Was he your soulbond?"

"No," he said. "But I loved him."

"Would you ever settle down again?"

"If I found the right person...probably. Definitely." He turned to her again. "But for now, I'm having fun. Get up. Let's try one more time with your magic."

They stood and she faced him.

"Hold out your hand and close your eyes. Imagine that light deep down in your belly. Watch it glow and slowly visualize it making its way through your body, to your hand."

"You know, you're not fun in training. Serious Raine takes over," she lamented.

"I'll be fun when you can do something. Stop complaining and make a damn flower, little frog."

She huffed and closed her eyes, holding out her palm, and visualized the light like he instructed. Ten minutes of nothing.

Sensing her frustration, Raine said, "Let's end today's session. We'll try again tomorrow."

"Why haven't you shown me your powers since we started training?" she asked as they walked back to the castle from the training rings, passing through the herb garden outside the entrance.

"I'll show you mine when you show me yours," he crooned.

"You always make everything sound so dirty."

"It's what makes me so charming."

They wandered back inside, preparing to meet everyone else for dinner.

Since Ava recovered from her assassination attempt, Raine had been training her with magic after lunch while she continued combat and weapons in the mornings. Those sessions were much easier now that she was in her fae form. She was faster, more agile and had better vision which had allowed her to take Casimir down a handful of times, eliciting a sense of triumph at her improvement. She'd even completed the obstacle course again, a piece of cake compared to before.

"So, who's the most powerful out of all of you?" she asked.

"That's a hard question. If you're asking about raw magic, probably both Cas and me, though I have much better control. He's the best out of us at combat fighting and prefers it over magic. If he would use his astral powers every once and a while, he'd be unstoppable."

"Why doesn't he use them?"

"It reminds him too much of his sister's death. And of his father."

"That man is an asshole."

"He's horrible. But I must say, watching you go toe to toe with Jareth was incredible."

Smiling at him she said, "It was kind of fun."

He grabbed her, put her in a headlock and ruffled her hair.

"Hey!"

"I'm glad you're here." He let go as they entered the dining hall.

A week later, Ava was standing in the training ring, hand trembling as she willed a flower to form in her hand. *Come on!*

"You're trying too hard," Raine said.

"First I'm not trying hard enough and now I'm trying too hard?" She let out a noise of frustration. "This is impossible. Why did it come so easily that one night?"

"Because Cas was hurt. But you weren't in control," he answered.

She placed her hands on her hips. "I don't know how to do this."

"You overthink things. It's what you did with the obstacle course. You need to relax and let it flow through you." Raine paused, eyes brightening. "I have an idea. But you're not going to like it."

"What..."

"I'll be right back. Stay there and keep trying until I return," he said and left.

She closed her eyes and tried imagining the light again. No luck. Frustrated with her lack of abilities, she opened her eyes and glanced at Luna, asleep under a nearby tree with Aro.

"Lucky cat. You don't have to worry about magical training. You just get to nap all day in the sun," she muttered.

I heard that, Luna said, cracking open an eye.

Ava gave her companion an amused look as Raine returned, Casimir in tow.

"What's your idea?" she asked.

Casimir smiled at her and stood before Raine in the ring. Raine flicked his wrist and vines burst from the ground, faster than Ava could follow. The bright green tendrils snaked up Casimir's legs and tightened.

"What are you doing?" she said.

Raine didn't respond as he kept twisting the vines around Casimir, ensnaring his body and reaching to his neck. Casimir tried to move but couldn't; trapped by his friend.

Ava couldn't control the panic she felt and yelled, "Stop!"

Small thorns burst from the vines, piercing Casimir's skin. The moment she noticed blood dripping down his leg, something hot surged within her. "You're hurting him," she snarled.

Raine released the bindings, and the two warriors faced her.

"Ava, look," said Raine.

Fury at seeing Casimir injured coursed through her, but she looked at her feet. Small roots had grown and were making their way toward Raine.

"I wasn't going to hurt him," he said.

Casimir shrugged. "I'm fine."

"What are you feeling right now?" asked Raine.

"Like I want to punch you in the face."

He shook his head. "I mean regarding your magic. Close your eyes and tell us what you can feel."

She did as he instructed, evaluating her body. "I feel hot. Deep down, it feels like I'm burning. And it's coming up through my hands...and I can feel them. The roots. They're moving."

"Stay with that feeling. Let the roots move. Will them to do what you want," he instructed. "They're an extension of you. They only listen to you."

She kept her eyes closed and pushed the warmth through her hands, feeling the twists and turns of the roots.

"Ava," Raine whispered. "Open your eyes."

When she opened them, the roots were climbing Raine and Casimir's legs, stopping mid-thigh. They were both grinning at her.

"There it is," Raine praised.

She scanned the two fae men with a smirk on her face, and yanked her hands back, pulling their legs out from under them and landing them flat on their backs.

Casimir grunted and Raine cursed as the air was knocked from their lungs. She strode forward and stood over them, releasing her magic.

"See? All I had to do was use your bond with Casimir against you and it was easy," Raine said.

"You're just going to hurt him every time to make my magic appear?"

He sat up, pulling Casimir with him. "If that's what it takes."

DINNER WAS A SERIOUS AFFAIR, a departure from their usual routine. Desmond and Vivienne were present, along with Aelerion and Thalia, who'd been joining their meetings. Tonight, the group was discussing plans to get their kingdom back from Deidamia's rule. Though they'd taken as much of their army as they could when they escaped, they didn't have their full force and needed the help of the other kingdoms to reclaim Igneothenia.

Thorne had opened the rest of the Earth Kingdom for any refugees from the volcanic province who could make it. They had the space with their open fields and various towns protected by the Emerald Mountains enclosing the majority of Monterre, save from a few smaller towns. Though it was tough on their resources, they made it work, many of the refugees contributing various skills to farm and harvest more food.

"We need to get your kingdom back before we launch an attack directly on Deidamia," said Thorne, swirling the wine in his goblet. "And we'll need to try and secure help from Caelestia, though it won't be easy."

"Good luck convincing that bastard, Orion," said Aelerion. "And you're willing to risk your army to help us reclaim our home?"

"We have the numbers with Saxumdale's help," said Casimir. "Both Astrid and Soren have already agreed they'll assist."

"And what of the environment, Thorne?" asked Thalia. "Your kind aren't conditioned to be fighting among the volcanoes."

Ava had learned Igneothenia was nestled among a mountain range filled with active volcanoes, the capital built over rivers of lava. The fae who lived there were immune to the heat and ash but most others couldn't visit long without serious consequences. That's why it had been surprising their kingdom was conquered so easily. Apparently, the daemons' world was not much different from Igneothenia, and the heat had no effect on them.

"We have a team of healers making potions to give us immunity. They're making them by the thousands. Soren has a team working on it as well," Desmond answered.

"How long do the effects last?" asked Raine.

"One week," Vivienne answered.

"You'll need a lot of potions," said Aelerion.

"We should have enough within a month if production isn't slowed," said Desmond.

"Alright," boomed Aelerion as he clapped his hands together. "One month to plan before I can have my home back."

The sound of boots pounding echoed in the hallway, interrupting their conversation. The attention of the room turned to the door. Seconds later Pax burst in, out of breath.

Casimir stood. "What happened?"

"It's Oakshire. A team of Deidamia's soldiers has taken over the town and are gathering citizens to be executed. She's sending a message. Since she failed at killing Ava."

Vivienne gasped. "My sister lives there..." she whispered to herself, fear in her eyes.

Pax paused, scanning the room. "And Andras is with them."

41

They were saddled, equipped with supplies, and on their horses within an hour. Ava rode her own after having practiced to overcome her nervousness. Casimir had gifted her a beautiful white mare named Bella upon proving her confidence and ability to ride, and Ava leaned forward and stroked her mane, trying to ignore her nerves as they made their way out of the city.

In addition to their core group, they'd brought along a company of eighty soldiers and a group of healers.

Quinn and Raine led the party, with Ava and Casimir following. Jorrar, Kai and Thorne rode behind them with Aelerion and Thalia bringing up the rear, insisting on helping. The group was followed by the rest of the soldiers on their own horses, packed with tents, food and weapons.

They followed the road through town, passing shops, taverns and restaurants, before leaving through the tunnel under the mountains. Ava hadn't ventured here since she first arrived many months ago. Dark stone walls encased the path, illuminated by glowing fungi and insects, providing subtle light as they passed. The sound of horses' hooves echoed in the passage, mixed with fearful whispers of what they may find.

"How long will it take to get there?" asked Ava as they emerged into the forest.

"Two days," Casimir replied. "If we hurry and only stop to rest briefly."

Two days? Would they make it in time?

Ava learned Casimir and his friends used to frequent Oakshire when they were younger and were close with the innkeeper there, a funny older orc named Sugha who always mothered and chastised them when they were too rowdy.

The animal companions darted in and out of the woods as they continued their journey. Aro occasionally emerged, checking on Casimir before disappearing again, Luna riding on his back. Titus remained at the castle, occupied with catching insects throughout the forest.

"Are you not capable of walking, Luna?" Ava asked, amused.

Oh I am. But this is much more comfortable and Aro doesn't mind.

Raine's white wolf, Sabriel, stayed close to Quinn's black panther, Bastien, and dozens of other creatures who must have been companions to some of the other soldiers traveled through the woods. Large cats, hawks and other birds, wolves, even a giant snake.

Ava glanced at Casimir. His jaw was clenched, and his hands were tense on the reins as he led his horse next to her. "Are you alright?" she asked.

He turned toward her. "Yes. Just worried."

"Me too."

"And I'm terrified to have you with us. You just recovered from the ball and—"

Ava reached between their horses and grabbed his hand. "Cas. I'll be alright. We all will. We're stronger together."

He let out a breath, still obviously worried.

They continued for hours before stopping and making camp for the night. Ava dismounted her horse, legs aching from being stuck in the saddle for so long, and thanked the soldier who led her away. Casimir parted ways with her to direct the set-up of their camp.

Ava wandered through the soldiers erecting tents and lighting fires with efficiency. They'd chosen a large clearing in the woods, surrounded by tall deciduous trees with yellow flowers glowing in the night. As she passed a soldier preparing a pot of stew, herbs tickling her nose with the promise of a hearty meal, she scanned the group, searching for her brother.

He stood at the edge of camp, staring at the night sky with his arm around Quinn, a pensive look on his face. His giant eagle, Skye, had landed next to them and lowered her head. She gave her a scratch, ruffling her feathers, and Skye chirruped low in her throat, relishing the attention.

Ava stopped on the other side of Thorne. "Are you alright?"

He turned, a smile on his face that didn't reach his eyes. "Not really."

"He's worrying about everything as always," said Quinn, though she wasn't sarcastic this time, voice laced with her own concern.

"Is there anything I can do?"

"There's nothing anyone can do," said Thorne. "Not until we win this war."

She stood silent as the three of them watched the stars.

Thorne spoke again, "I fear this is only the beginning of horrific things to come. Death and destruction, hate and depravity."

The cool breeze whipped Ava's braid and she wrapped her arms around herself. "Do you think we will? Win this war?"

"We have to."

Quinn let out a sigh and Thorne pulled her closer. Ava

placed her hand on his shoulder and they stood in complete silence, worrying about their kingdom, their world.

AFTER TWO DAYS OF TRAVEL, they were close to Oakshire and would arrive within the hour. Most everyone was silent, preparing themselves for what they would find, though an air of anticipation and anxiety buzzed around the company. Ava had barely slept last night, Casimir also restless, tossing and turning as they agonized over the fate of their citizens.

They'd be split into pairs, with a group of soldiers to accompany them as they entered town and assessed the situation.

Casimir approached. "You'll be with Raine." He cupped her face and pressed his lips to hers. Pulling away, he said, "Please be safe, love."

She brushed a strand of hair behind his shoulder. "You too."

Casimir walked away to address the group as Ava paced, stomach in knots. Raine stayed next to her, watching her walk back and forth, trying to hide his own worry.

Making his way to the front, Casimir began his speech. "We leave the horses and healers here, guarded by a small group of soldiers and make the rest of the way on foot. It's about a half hour walk. Remember your positions and watch for my signal to split up when we get within range. Remain on the edge of town until you hear my whistle," he instructed as he stood before the army, hands clasped in front of him.

Ava had never seen him addressing his army before, not even on the ship. That had happened too quickly for speeches and this kind of preparation. His face was grave and determined, raw power radiating from him and sensed from where she was standing in the back.

This is why they called him The Bear.

"Leave none of our enemies alive. Do what you must to end

them. Do not let them overwhelm you, and stay with your team."

They began their walk to town, Ava staying close to Raine. The group was silent, save for a few whispers here and there, ensuring the element of surprise and avoiding as many casualties as possible.

Casimir raised his hand, halting their company. He waved and pointed his fingers, indicating it was time to split up. The animals had come along—Sabriel and Luna stayed with Ava and Raine while the others accompanied their respective fae companions.

"Luna, you're too small to fight," said Ava.

I'll hide in the forest but I'm here if you need to communicate something with the rest of the group.

Ava sighed, relieved her feline companion would not be putting herself in danger. Not everyone had a giant wolf or bear who could rip the arms off their enemies, though the smaller animals were used for communication and sending messages.

The dense woods were still, their group cautiously stepping over logs and through the underbrush. They took their place and paused, waiting for the signal to leave the cover of the forest. Ava's hands shook and sweat dripped down her neck, as uneasiness churned in her gut.

Casimir's whistle sounded, indicating it was time to enter Oakshire. She followed Raine to the north entrance, near the farmers' fields.

All was silent. There were no screams, no clinking of armor or yells of daemon soldiers. They heard no citizens or movement at all. It was eerily quiet.

Too quiet.

They broke through the tree line, archers at the ready, reaching what appeared to be a former farmhouse. It was now a pile of ash, cinders smoldering as white smoke carried death to the sky.

A tree sat in the yard, stripped bare of its leaves and branches, now a lone pole in the middle of the grass. And attached to the tree, was a body. A female orc, vacant eyes staring into the distance.

Raine gasped. Ava covered her mouth at the sight as they got closer. The body had been flayed. Skin peeled off and nailed to her sides along the tree. Ava took a deep breath, stomach curdling with breakfast, and closed her eyes, trying to stave off the nausea.

"Sugha," Raine whispered.

She turned to him. His blue-gray eyes filled with tears as his face was overcome with rage. Sugha was the innkeeper; their friend who had known them for decades. And now she was dead. Brutalized by Andras and his soldiers.

"Check for survivors," he ordered the team as he stood there, unable to take his eyes off the body of his friend.

They searched the remains of the farmhouse, but returned moments later, shaking their heads. Raine turned away and led the group closer to town. They didn't see any soldiers. No Andras, no indication anyone was here, other than the destruction left in their wake.

Gravel crunched under Ava's boots as they entered town. It was decimated. Almost every building and shop was either a pile of ash or still burning. The trees were stripped of their leaves, trunks black and scorched from fire. No survivors were found. Everyone was dead.

They were too late.

Ava's hands shook as they continued their exploration, fruitlessly searching for bodies. For anything. Raine grasped her trembling hand and squeezed as they paused and stood before a large building, only half standing now.

"Something's not right," said Raine.

"Yeah, everyone's dead," Ava said through her tears.

He shook his head. "I sense something else. I have a bad feeling."

"Bad feeling about what?" she whispered, fear taking root.

He whipped his head to her, eyes wide. "We need to leave. *Now*," he said, as dark figures emerged from the remains of the buildings surrounding them.

It was a trap.

42

*D*aemon soldiers emerged from their cover in the shadows of the ruined buildings, their ebony armor absorbing the light around them. As if it was a living, breathing entity, determined to squash all hope, all goodness in the world.

Mouths pulled into grins of triumph, they charged. Fae archers released a round of arrows, taking several down, but there were too many.

A stone dropped in Ava's stomach. They were surrounded.

Shouts in the distance from the other groups echoed, finding themselves in the same situation. Ava placed herself back-to-back with Raine, their group of soldiers circling them, as they prepared to fight their way out.

She had barely drawn her bow when the daemons were upon them. Roots and vines twisted together, building a blockade around the team, buying the archers enough time to release another round of arrows. Ava released her own into a daemon's eye, killing him instantly. She retrieved another arrow from her quiver, nocked and released it, only this time the black-armored soldier dodged her effort as it was deflected by his spiked armor.

They tried to keep the roots steady, keeping the daemons at a distance, but they were cutting through them faster than Raine and the others could grow new ones.

It wasn't long before their formation was split and Ava switched to using her magic to pull soldiers down so Raine's wolf, Sabriel, could finish them off. As quickly as she ensnared them, more came. Wave after wave. Several fae soldiers were killed in the chaos as they continued to fight their way out.

She took a moment to search for Raine, but he'd disappeared, lost in the melee.

Shit, she thought, as she unsheathed her sword and pushed through, her months of training and faster fae body paying off.

A daemon soldier lunged for her. She met his attempt, swords clashing, as she blocked the blow and whirled around, severing his head. Another threw a dagger she avoided at the last second, its blade nicking the leather armor on her shoulder cap as it sailed by. Her magic warmed inside her, aching to be released. Raising her hand, emerald vines erupted from the soil, snaking around the daemon's body, holding him in place as one of her own soldiers slit his throat.

From her left, an enemy charged. Ava turned to meet him, but didn't have to. Sabriel leaped into the air, canines clamping on his throat and ripping, painting her silver fur with black blood. The wolf growled in triumph, bounding away to maim another soldier.

Dodging and parrying, Ava made it with the help of her remaining crew, killing enough of the daemons they were no longer surrounded. Where was Raine? Was he okay?

Pax arrived with more soldiers to assist. His green skin was covered in daemon blood, a snarl leaving his throat as he helped finish off the remaining enemies.

Yells, shouts and the clang of weapons resonated in the distance, the rest of their forces still locked in their own battles.

"Go help the others," she instructed.

"Yes, Your Highness," said Pax as he barked orders at the group and led them through town.

Ava wandered through the rubble, alone in an isolated part of town, but she wasn't leaving without finding Raine and ensuring his safety.

"Raine!" she shouted. Nothing.

With cautious steps, she wove through the debris and scanned the wreckage around her. Hollow dread filled her gut. He was nowhere to be found.

"Luna, can you find Raine?"

He's safe. You need to get out of there. Something bad is coming, I can feel it.

Tension left her body at Luna's words. *Safe. He's safe.* Heeding her companion's warning, she jogged to the sounds of fighting to help the others who were still in battle. She rounded a corner when a rush of power nearby made the hair on the back of her neck stand up. Something dark. Familiar.

A deep sultry voice sounded behind her. "Hello, Ava dear."

A shiver went down her spine.

Unsheathing her dagger, she spun around and whipped it at the voice. But Andras caught it midair, an amused smile on his face. She froze in place, fear taking over as she looked into the eyes of her enemy. Her abuser. The man—no, the daemon —who tricked her. Beat her. Drugged her. Then stood by as she was tortured for weeks.

"Look at you," he said, tossing the dagger to the ground as he strolled forward, placing his hands in his pockets. He was dressed in all black, matching his long ebony hair and contrasting his pale complexion.

"You have magic," he crooned. "What a treat."

"You killed everyone here," she whispered, trying to hide her trembling.

He shrugged and continued to advance as Ava backed away.

A shout came from her left. "Ava!"

Raine appeared, bolting for her as he unsheathed his sword. But Andras threw out a hand and black shadow shot forth, covering her friend in darkness.

"No!" Ava screamed, lunging at Andras with another dagger.

He grabbed her wrist, stopping her blow, as the shadows writhed and swirled around Raine. She was barely able to see him through the darkness but caught a glimpse of platinum hair as his body trembled, starting to convulse.

"Please, no," Ava begged as she let out a sob, heart in her throat. "Stop."

Andras released his magic and Raine fell to the ground. Motionless. She couldn't even tell if he was breathing.

He couldn't be dead. She wouldn't accept it. She wasn't going to lose yet another friend. Andras tightened his grip on her wrist so hard, she yelped and dropped her blade, wincing in pain at his strength.

"Get up!" Ava screamed at Raine. He didn't move. "Get up!"

Still, he remained motionless.

White hot rage boiled inside her as she turned to Andras. "I'm going to fucking kill you."

Fueled by her fury, she pulled out of his grip and raised roots along his legs, attempting to trap him but he laughed as his shadows dissolved them in seconds. He was too strong.

Run, Ava, said Luna.

"No, I'm not leaving Raine."

Roots and vines twisted and turned, Ava using her magic once more. Her attempt was met with shadow and death, disintegrating them as soon as they reached Andras. She unsheathed her sword, prepared to fight, when Andras laughed again.

She lunged, prepared to cut his head from his shoulders, but his shadows burst forth so quickly, her body froze as she was ensnared. Dark smoke snaked around her like wispy black ropes, climbing her legs, her torso and around her throat. He lifted her into the air and grinned as Ava dropped her sword and panicked.

43

It had been a trap.

Casimir and Aelerion's group was surrounded as they hacked their way through with swords and magic. Andras had wanted them to find out. Had wanted them to try and save the village.

And they had played right into his scheme.

Twisting to his left, Casimir sliced the head off a daemon soldier with his sword, turning around to deflect a blow from another enemy. His foe turned, attempting to use the spike on the elbow of his dark armor to gut Casimir, but he ducked, grasping the enemy's leg. Using his astral magic, the daemon was a pile of ashes within seconds.

Pushing to his feet, he shook off his fear over Ava's safety. Raine was with her and would protect her with his life. But he still regretted letting her come. He would never forgive himself should something happen.

Dodging another attack, Casimir whirled around and jammed his sword through an opening in the brutal armor. Aelerion fought near him, a river of lava twisting and turning as he melted the daemons. Aro lunged, grabbing a soldier by his arm and ripping it clean off, screams echoing in the morning sunlight.

As they fought their way through, Casimir went into a place of killing calm, and unleashed himself into the fray as they finished off the remaining enemies.

Casimir had finished off the last soldier when Aro said, *Ava's in danger. The town square. Hurry.*

He shouted to Aelerion to follow and they sprinted to the center of the village, leaping over fallen soldiers and rubble. He had to reach her. He wouldn't be too late. Not again.

They arrived and ducked behind a wall to assess the situation. Raine was on the ground, not moving. A wave of terror overwhelmed Casimir at the sight of his best friend's still body.

Fuck.

Andras had his back to them, Ava ensnared by his writhing shadows as he held her in the air. Her face was full of fear and hatred as she tried to fight against him.

Seeing her in the hands of the one who had tricked and harmed her unlocked a wrath so deep, he trembled as he tried to remain calm. Impulsively attacking would only risk her safety. But once he got Ava away, he would rip out Andras' spine for everything he'd done to her.

He whispered his plan to Aelerion, who disappeared and took his position, remaining hidden. Casimir rose and approached Andras. Ava spotted him and subtly shook her head, urging him to run.

Ignoring her warning, he gave her a subtle nod and spoke, "Fancy running into you here, Andras."

Andras turned around, lowering Ava and bringing her in front of him. Shadows pulled her arms behind her as he took out an ebony dagger and held it at her throat, regarding Casimir with contempt.

"I've always wanted to meet The Bear," Andras said. "I've heard so much about you."

His voice was ancient, skittering across Casimir's soul with every word.

"Well, here I am," he said, walking forward. "If you want someone to play with, I think I'd be a much more formidable opponent, don't you think?"

"No," Ava rasped, voice filled with terror.

"I see she's already found herself a new lover. It sure didn't take her long to warm another's bed after me."

Casimir trembled at the words but forced himself to stay composed. He wanted to rip Andras' head off at the way he spoke; tear him apart limb from limb. But Ava was too close and would get hurt in the crossfire, so he didn't respond. Didn't say anything.

"I think I'll like seeing her blood paint the ground red when we're finished. We translated the book, you know. We know how to open more portals to aid us. And now that I have Ava, I will drain every drop needed to activate them and Deidamia will drink the rest of her until she's a husk blowing in the wind."

"It seems your queen needs to make up her mind," Casimir responded. "Are you trying to capture her or kill her? But even the assassins you send can't seem to do their job properly."

Andras' face twitched as if Casimir had hit a nerve.

Aelerion appeared behind Andras, making his way forward as lava crept across the ground. A few more seconds. Casimir needed to keep him distracted.

"Who's truly in charge, Andras? It seems like you want to be, but she's undermining you, isn't she? Making decisions you don't agree with. Ava told me the two of you often argued when she was imprisoned there. She's using you, isn't she?"

Andras' irritation turned to laughter. "Using me? You have no idea what you're up against, you fool."

He tightened his grip on Ava and moved the dagger to her

face, slicing her cheek. Ava whimpered as blood trickled down her face, the sound breaking Casimir's heart in two.

"You'll never defeat us," Andras said. "Never defeat *me*," he emphasized. "I am ancient. I am eternal. I am—"

Andras paused, eyes wide, and looked at the lava making its way up his legs.

Screaming with rage, he let go of Ava and Casimir shot out vines to catch her and pull her to him. The lava continued to rise and Andras bellowed, wrapping himself in shadow now hidden from view.

After a few seconds, the shadows disappeared along with their enemy.

He was gone.

44

One moment Ava thought her throat was about to be slit, the next, she was in Casimir's arms as he knelt to check her over.

"Are you okay?" he gasped, inspecting her cheek.

"I'm fine. But...Raine," she said, voice breaking as she pushed out of Casimir's arms and rushed over to her friend.

Collapsing to her knees beside him, vision blurry with tears, she checked him for wounds. Nothing. There was no blood, no visible injuries. Casimir joined her, performing his own assessment, brow pinched with worry. He was breathing. Barely.

A sob burst from Ava, unable to hold it in any longer.

"Wake up," she cried, shaking Raine's shoulders. "Wake up, you idiot! Wake up, wake up!"

Monterre's soldiers filtered into the town square, the rush of boots announcing their arrival. Ava looked up, meeting her brother's panic-stricken eyes as he carried Quinn in his arms, her leg covered in blood.

"What happened?" she and Thorne said in unison as he saw Raine's unconscious body on the ground.

365

"We need the healers. Now," ordered Casimir as he stood.

"Are there any daemon soldiers left?" asked Thorne.

"No," said Casimir. "They've all either fled or have been cut down."

Casimir sent out two teams, one to check for their own survivors, and the other to ensure any last enemies who may be hanging on to life were truly dead.

Within minutes, Skye arrived carrying Kai and two other healers. The rest were on their way on horseback and would join soon. Ava had pulled Raine's head into her lap, tears streaming down her cheeks as she stroked his hair.

"Please don't die," she whispered. "You were the first friend I had here. Don't leave me. Don't leave Cas. We need you."

They established the healing quarters in the center of the decimated square, using a large open-air tent they'd brought for this purpose, and stationed the remaining soldiers around the perimeter to guard their space.

Kai approached, trying to hide the strain on his face at Raine's condition.

"Ava," he said quietly. "Why don't you let us move him to a bedroll so he can be comfortable while I work?"

She nodded, shoulders shaking from her sobs as she backed away and allowed soldiers to carry him to the tent. They laid him next to Quinn, who was moaning through gritted teeth as Thorne hovered over her.

Ava sat on the ground between the two of them, holding Raine's hand as tears continued to fall. Thorne's face was a picture of rage and worry, eyeing the healers with irritation.

"If you don't hurry your ass up, I will have you strung up in the dungeons when we return," he growled.

"Yes, Your Majesty," the healer replied, rushing over with supplies.

A deep laceration ran from the top of Quinn's thigh to above her knee, muscle and fat visible among her blood-soaked leathers. Ava turned back to Kai as he was laying his hands on Raine, eyes closed, searching for whatever was keeping him unconscious.

He opened his eyes. "What happened?"

She sniffled, wiping her face. "Andras appeared and Raine tried to stop him. Then Andras shot shadows at him and he dropped to the ground. It's my fault. He was trying to protect me."

Kai shook his head. "It's not your fault. And he's going to be fine."

"He is?" she asked, voice hopeful. "Why won't he wake up?"

"I've heard of Andras' power but never seen it in action. His shadows can cause invisible injuries, such as internal bleeding. He has a laceration in his spleen, but I can heal it with help," he answered as he waved over another healer.

She blew out a breath, her pulse finally slowing. "Okay."

"You'll need to let go of his hand while I do this," he said.

She did as he instructed. Kai and the other healer laid their hands on his chest and closed their eyes, remaining that way for several minutes. Raine let out a cough and opened his eyes.

"Please don't tell me I've stained my leathers with that horrific daemon blood," he whispered hoarsely.

Ava laughed through her tears.

Raine turned and looked at her, a weak smile on his face. "Good thing you survived. Otherwise, Cas would have killed me anyway."

She smiled. "Welcome back."

Raine evaluated her face. "Were you crying over me, little frog?"

"Of course I was. I thought you were dead." She wiped her face with the back of her hand.

He gave her a weak roguish grin. "Not this time."

Ava turned to Quinn who was squirming in pain as the healer prepped her leg to be sutured.

"Can't you give her something for the pain?" seethed Thorne. "You're hurting her!"

"She's going to be fine. Let him work," said Kai.

Quinn looked at Thorne and said through clenched teeth, "Go have your hissy fit somewhere else. You're distracting me."

Ava stood and walked to her brother, placing a hand on his shoulder. "Come on, let's walk." He glared at her. "Now," she insisted.

He rose and glanced at Quinn one last time before following Ava out from under the canopy. She sat on what appeared to have been the edge of a fountain and patted the seat next to her.

"She's fine. Raine's fine. We're all okay."

He sighed as he sat beside her and leaned over, placing his elbows on his knees.

"What's going on? I've never seen you act like this," she said.

"I watched a daemon soldier slice her open like she was nothing. I thought she was going to die." His voice was tight.

She narrowed her eyes at him. Oh.

"You love her."

He looked at her with conviction, but didn't answer, turning away again.

"I thought...she said...you two just had fun sometimes," Ava said.

He still didn't say anything.

"You should tell her."

"She doesn't want to be queen," he whispered.

"Have you actually ever asked her that?"

He grunted, confirmation enough. Stubborn fae men. They were all the same. Rolling her eyes, she rose and patted his back.

"Think about it," she said and walked away, searching for Casimir.

She found him speaking with some soldiers, giving orders

before they walked off. When he spotted her coming toward him, he limped to her and grabbed her face. "Did you get assessed by a healer? Did they look at your cheek?"

She shook her head. "I'm fine. It's barely even a scratch. Your distraction plan worked, though you could have warned me."

"I tried," he said. "Sorry I had to keep him talking so Aelerion could sneak up on him."

Ava scanned the area. "Where is he anyway?"

"He and his wife are with a group of guards looking for survivors."

"Remind me to thank him for saving my life."

Casimir took her hand and led them back to the tent. "Please have a healer check you over," he repeated.

Ava searched the busy tent for Kai. Spotting him, she walked over. "Will you *assess* me so Cas can get off my back? Also, he's limping." She jerked her thumb at him.

He turned to her and frowned.

"Don't think I didn't notice, you brute."

AVA STARED into the flames of a small fire as it popped and crackled while the cloudy night sky promised rain. Casimir sat beside her—along with Thorne, Jorrar, Aelerion and Thalia—while Quinn and Raine slept off their injuries. Out of the eighty soldiers they had brought, twenty-one had been injured enough to need care and almost thirty killed. More than half their group.

Casimir had a minor slice in his calf, easily bandaged, and was already beginning to heal. Jorrar had a small cut on his forehead but was otherwise fine. The rest of them, while sore and exhausted, were injury free besides scratches and bruises.

"So Andras got away?" asked Thorne, deep in thought.

"He disappeared into shadows. Apparently, he can jump," said Aelerion.

"We'll need to make sure there are wards around the kingdom," said Thorne. "Who knows how far he can travel."

"Thorne," said Thalia. "Jumping is not a magic we've seen before. Even in daemons."

Everyone's attention turned to Thalia as shock and confusion made their way through the group.

"Are you sure?" asked Thorne. "Is this new information? Did he use that magic in the old wars?"

"I never heard about him using it, but it's possible. Maybe the information was lost? There aren't many of us left who fought back then and most of you were children or not even born yet," she said. "Aelerion and I never battled against Andras. We were too busy attempting to stop Deidamia's commander from taking over our home."

"What does that mean?" asked Jorrar.

Thalia shook her head, her yellow eyes full of concern. "I'm not sure. We must research it."

"Our archives have hardly any information," said Thorne. "King Vardan destroyed most of our texts."

"You've said that before," Ava interjected. "But do you know why our father destroyed them? Are you sure it was just because he went mad?"

"I'm not certain. I was young when it happened. And honestly, I avoided him as much as I could."

Ava sighed, but something still nagged at her. Something of great importance, just out of reach. She couldn't stop thinking about why her father would have done that. They were missing a vital piece of information.

"Our libraries are inaccessible at the moment due to those daemon bastards," Aelerion said.

"We can ask Astrid and Soren if they will search for information," said Jorrar.

"Good idea," Thorne replied. "We must also venture to Caelestia soon."

Casimir grumbled something inaudible.

"They have the most extensive archives in all of Eorhan," said Thorne, looking pointedly at him. "Besides, we need to approach them for help in the war anyway. We'll discuss a plan for this when we return."

"Fine," Casimir said. "There's one more thing."

They waited, Aelerion and Ava knowing what he was about to reveal.

"Andras said they've translated the book. This was another attempt to take Ava back," said Casimir.

"Capture me...kill me...their indecisiveness is exhausting," Ava said.

Casimir gave her a flat look, unimpressed with her attempted humor.

"We need to get the book as soon as possible," said Jorrar.

"And we'll rescue your daughter while we're at it," Ava reassured him.

"You aren't coming," said her brother.

"Of course I am. I have to help."

"As your king, I'm ordering you. You cannot come. If they get a hold of you, you're dead. We're all dead."

"He's right, Ava," said Jorrar.

"I'm sorry, but I agree with Thorne," Thalia added. "It's too risky to bring the one they seek most into the depths of their camp."

"When will you all be going on this suicide mission?" she asked, worried they would risk their lives and not even let her do the same.

"As soon as possible," said Thorne. "Once we're back, we need to ensure Quinn and Raine are recovered. Then we'll leave. Hopefully a couple of weeks at most."

Though she understood the reasoning, Ava's stomach

churned at the notion of her friends going into that camp. Didn't want to even imagine the possibility of them suffering the way she had.

Picking at a loose thread on her pants, Ava tried to ignore the dread as she listened to the plans being made.

45

"*E*xcellent," coached Raine as Ava pulled the vines back in.

They'd been practicing all afternoon while Casimir was stuck in meetings. A team would depart tomorrow on a small reconnaissance mission. Once they got as much information as possible, Casimir would send word through Aro when it was time for a larger team to meet them at a predetermined location near the daemon camp.

They'd retrieve the book, the healer, and return to Mosshaven.

Ava loathed this plan, terrified of something going wrong. But both Thorne and Casimir had assured her this was only a mission to gather information.

She still didn't like it.

"Let's call it a day," Raine said as he sat on the stone wall.

She plopped down beside him. "How are you feeling?"

"Back to my merry self."

It had been about a week since they returned from Oakshire and Raine bounced back quickly. She laid her head on his shoulder, savoring the breeze as it cooled her off.

"Don't ever do that again," she said, replaying how his body had slumped to the ground.

"What? Try to protect you?" he replied. "Don't count on that. You would have done the same for me."

She sighed. "You're right."

They sat in silence as a group of soldiers from Igneothenia emerged from the barracks, ready to do their own training.

Raine perked up. "Let's go watch," he said. "It'll be good for you to see other kingdoms' techniques."

They made their way to the field as soldiers lined up in formation. Sitting under a large tree, they watched the volcanic kingdom's warmup routine.

A woman with crimson skin covered in neon yellow veins, which moved and writhed as she walked, paced in front of the company with her hands behind her back. Black flames were tattooed on her neck, and her pointed ears were adorned with countless piercings. The sides of her head were shaved, the rest of her black curls sitting in a mohawk-like style.

Her short, muscular frame was dressed in black pants and a matching tunic, tied with a bright red belt signaling her rank. The rest of the soldiers wore gray outfits with yellow belts. Twin golden swords were sheathed on her back, glinting in the sun as she strode along the field. Authority radiated from her, barking orders at the soldiers in a subtly accented voice.

Raine tensed. "Who is that?"

"You haven't met her yet? That's Maeryn. She's the general of Igneothenia's armies. She's kind of scary."

He shook his head. "No. I haven't met her," he whispered.

Ava looked at him with curiosity, seemingly enamored with the general. Unable to take his eyes off Maeryn, he watched her lead her kingdom's forces with unwavering focus.

"Are you alright?" she asked, startling him from his wonder.

His eyes darted to hers as he cleared his throat. "Fine. I'm good. I'm great."

Raine was never at a loss for words. Ava narrowed her eyes at him before he turned away. The soldiers practiced their blocks and stances, moving in unison as if they were of one mind for two hours before they finished and went about the rest of their day.

Ava rose. "Let's go say hi and I'll introduce you."

Raine shot to his feet. "What? Now? I—shit. Okay."

"What is wrong with you?"

"Nothing," he said, smoothing his hair and regaining his swagger as they approached.

Maeryn turned to them. In addition to the jewelry in her ears, she had a golden ring pierced through her full bottom lip. "Your Highness." She dipped her chin.

"Hello, Maeryn. I'd like you to meet Raine, one of our captains," Ava said.

Maeryn's bright yellow eyes scrutinized him as she held her hand out to shake his. He took it in both of his own. "If I'd known Igneothenia's general was so exquisite, I would have introduced myself sooner."

Ava tried to suppress her smile at his attempt at flattery while Maeryn's eyes bored into his, her face devoid of emotion.

"And if I had known the captain was such a suck up, I would have said don't bother," she replied, pulling away.

"I—oh. I'm sorry, I—" Raine stuttered.

"Don't mind him," Ava intervened. "He's always like that. You must be busy. It was good to see you."

"Good to see you too." Maeryn gave Raine a small smirk. "And it was *interesting* to meet you, captain."

"Yep," Raine answered. Ava looped her arm through his and dragged him away before he could say anything else.

They walked into the castle, and she halted to face him. "What was *that* about?"

He grinned sheepishly, rubbing the back of his neck. "I don't know. She...wow. She's stunning."

"I've never seen you stumble over your words when you're hitting on someone."

"Fuck. I know." He glanced toward the door. "I should go apologize. I think I offended her."

"I think she was amused. It'll be fine. Though I don't think your usual smooth-talking will work with her if you're trying to get her to sleep with you."

His gaze snapped to hers. "I'm not trying to bed her. No, not her. I—I just want to talk to her. I need to. I must get to know her."

"I don't understand what's going on with you."

"Me either." He shrugged and laughed uncomfortably.

They resumed their pace, heading down the hall to dinner.

"Are you doing alright?" Raine asked, changing the subject. "You know, with Cas leaving in the morning?"

"No," she replied. "I'm not."

Their boots echoed in the corridor, occasionally interrupted by the sound of birds singing outside the open windows. First to arrive in the dining room, Ava took her usual spot to the right of Thorne's chair.

"He's going to be fine," Raine assured her as he took his seat across the table. "He won't let anything happen."

"I know."

The rest of the group trickled in, joined by Aelerion and Thalia, the sound of voices filling the room as everyone started visiting. Casimir kissed Ava's head, pulling his chair close and taking his own seat.

Ever since they sealed the bond, he made every effort to be near her when they weren't in separate meetings or training. Her heart warmed at the way he sought her out the moment they were in the same room; how he was always holding her hand or touching her. He wasn't shy with his affections, not caring who was around when he whispered how much he loved her or placed a gentle kiss on her temple.

Casimir picked up her plate and filled it with food, a habit he hadn't stopped. She tried telling him he didn't need to, but he insisted. It was one of the many ways he showed his love and something she'd learned about him the last few months. That he loved taking care of her, paying attention to the little things.

A few minutes into dinner, the doors opened and Maeryn entered, nodding her greeting as she strode to the table and sat next to Thalia, who was seated on the other side of Casimir. Ava turned her attention to Raine, trying not to laugh at the sudden change in his demeanor as he stole glances at Maeryn.

"What's with Raine?" Casimir whispered into Ava's ear.

"He's got a thing for Maeryn, it seems. Like he can barely function around her," she whispered back.

Casimir grinned. "This is going to be fun."

"Payback after all the shit he gave us," Ava said, and Casimir chuckled.

Raine glared at them and Ava blew him a kiss.

Thorne cleared his throat. "Is everything ready for tomorrow's mission?"

"It is. We leave at dawn," said Casimir.

"I still think he needs to take someone else," Ava started but Thorne held up his hand and gave her a look.

"We've already discussed this." He was irritated at her push back. She'd yelled at him the other day in his suite when she learned Casimir was going alone, and he obviously didn't want her protesting again in front of their guests. "You will not question me on this any longer."

She put her hands in her lap, furious he would shut her down, but remained silent. Casimir moved his hand to hers, pulling it to his mouth, and pressed his lips to her knuckles.

"I'll be alright," he said. "Try not to worry."

Ava was silent the rest of the evening, stewing in her anger and fear for Casimir's safety. Raine was also quiet, eyes finding their way to Maeryn throughout dinner, but even the entertainment of his awkwardness wasn't enough of a distraction from her thoughts.

Ava shivered in the brisk morning air, pulling the cloak she was wearing tighter. Golden light framed the treetops as the sun peered over the horizon. Horses whinnied as the soldiers prepared them to leave on their mission. Bags were packed, weapons were secured, and a sense of unease hung about the air.

Casimir approached and pulled her into his chest. Holding back her tears, Ava nestled into him as she inhaled his scent of cedar and sage. No words were spoken as they embraced each other, neither willing to let go.

"Sorry general," said an approaching soldier. "But we must be going."

Casimir pulled back and looked at her. She grasped his face with both of her hands. "Please come back to me."

"I will."

"If something happens..." she started.

"Don't, love. Don't worry."

"Easier said than done."

She pulled him into a quick kiss, his hands clutching her waist. They parted and he pressed his lips to her forehead.

"I'll return soon. I love you," he whispered.

"I love you too," she said through her tears.

He walked away and mounted his horse, Aro staying close to the group. Luna sat at Ava's feet while Titus landed on her shoulder as the group made their way out of the stables. Casimir looked back one last time and raised his hand, Ava mirroring his action.

She stayed until they disappeared down the road.

Are you ok? Luna asked.

"No," she replied, looking at her companion. "This feels wrong."

I know. But you must follow Thorne's orders. It's what he thinks is best.

"I know."

With a heavy heart, she turned around and dragged her feet back inside.

46

$\mathcal{C}$asimir sat in the woods at the edge of Deidamia's war camp, the rest of his soldiers scattered about as they observed the schedule and routine of the daemons. They were communicating through their animals about what they'd learned, memorizing the layout and attempting to locate where the book and Isolde were being kept.

The camp was much larger than he'd expected, hundreds of soldiers milling about. Though Quinn had gotten their numbers, it was overwhelming to see it for himself.

Ava had been kept here for weeks and rage surged through him at the thought of her in this camp. Of her being tortured in a tent by the daemons, surrounded by soldiers and monsters. How she had survived, how she endured it, he couldn't even comprehend. Especially when she had still been in her human form.

He was still in disbelief that he'd found his soulbond, something he never thought he would be blessed with but had always longed for. It was rare for fae to find their destined one, and he'd found his love starved, beaten and dirty, wandering

380

through the woods. And now being here, he wanted to tear apart every single daemon who'd harmed her.

An owl hooted overhead as he remained in the dark, sticking to the shadows in the thick trees. He continued to watch the soldiers move about, learning their patterns.

I still think this is a terrible plan, Aro said from where he was hiding close by.

"Bringing a small team brings less attention to us. This was the best way."

I disagree. You seem to think you know better than me. Your infernal stubbornness is making my fur fall out from stress.

"You disagreeing with me is nothing new. What would you have suggested?"

We should have brought a larger team and caused a distraction while the book and the healer are retrieved. Just like I caused a distraction to save your soulbond.

"Did you know then? Who she was to me?"

No. But I sensed she was important.

And she was. She was so fucking important. To him. To their world. He yearned to get back to her as soon as possible. Being separated was tearing him apart. But if this was what it took to keep her safe and out of their enemies' hands, he would willingly walk through the depths of the darkest realm if only to prevent Ava from having to do so herself.

"Tell everyone to head back to our camp to discuss our findings," he ordered his companion.

Casimir rose when a twig snapped behind him. He spun around and found himself face to face with a dozen daemon soldiers, arrows pointed directly at him. As he readied his magic to take them down, blinding pain exploded at the back of his head.

Then the world went dark.

CASIMIR AWOKE WITH A START, thrashing against restraints as water splashed over him in waves. Was he drowning? He strained to lift his throbbing head as he opened his eyes. Several daemons stood before him with empty buckets in their hands. Soaked strands of his hair fell across his face and the strain of his arms overhead burned.

"He's awake. Let them know," said one of the guards.

One left while the other leaned against the wall, apathetically cleaning his nails with the tip of a dagger.

Casimir's shirt had been removed and his wrists were bound in chains, attached to a rocky ceiling. He wasn't in a tent, but what appeared to be a cave. Dirt covered the damp stone floor. The blazing flames of torches danced on the wall, casting sinister shadows in the dreary space. The smell of soil mixed with excrement filled his nostrils, covering the scent of fear hovering through the air.

Shivering, he reached for his magic, but nothing would come.

Fuck, he thought. They must have given him something.

He tried contacting Aro but that didn't work either. Whatever they'd given him cut him off from being able to communicate with his companion. That hadn't happened when he was bitten by the insect. This must have been stronger.

Footsteps echoed in the distance, growing closer by the second. Two pairs; one light and quick, the other slow and calculated. He squinted, trying to see in the dark abyss before him. Moments later, two figures emerged from hollow depths.

Andras and Deidamia.

The daemon queen observed him, standing preternaturally still, her blue eyes boring into his. Her white hair swished along her back as she resumed her walk.

Andras stood with his hands in his pockets and grinned, pleased at their capture. "I was hoping I'd get to see you again, general. I just didn't realize it would be so soon."

"Fuck you."

"I would," replied Andras, looking at his nails in the torchlight. "But you're not my type." He stepped closer, grabbing Casimir's face with his hand. "Your girlfriend, however. She is."

He snarled, pulling at the chains, but Andras stepped back and laughed, looking at Deidamia who had finished circling him and returned to stand by his side.

"I heard you were snooping about our camp," she said. Her voice was ancient, low and sensual. "What were you doing out here?"

He remained silent.

Deidamia closed in and stroked his cheek, sharp nails dragging down his neck as she asked, "Where's Ava?"

Again, he didn't speak.

Andras smiled at him. "It doesn't matter where Ava is. Once she learns we have her love, she'll waltz right in here. No need to hunt for her any longer. Our spy was right. We needed to lure Ava here instead of chasing her."

Spy? It had to be the same person who'd snuck in the assassin at the ball. The traitor they had not yet been able to identify. Who was it? Were they still there among his friends? He had no way of communicating with them, of warning them.

He yanked on the chains with fury.

Because Andras was right. Ava would come the moment she learned he'd been captured. It didn't matter if Thorne tried to stop her. She would never listen. He had to find a way out before she arrived.

Another set of footsteps approached. Loud and pronounced.

"Oh good," said Deidamia, turning toward the sound. "You're here."

Casimir narrowed his eyes as a massive daemon soldier appeared. His greasy dark hair hung in strands around his face, and he gave Casimir a broken toothed grin. The Scourge.

"General," she said. "I'd like you to meet Vazgeth. I'm sure you're aware he's an old friend of your princess."

Casimir scowled at her, remembering Ava's torture at the hands of The Scourge. He would rip him to pieces with his bare hands the moment he was free of these chains.

Deidamia paced before him. "I'm sure you've figured out your magic does not work. We've also given you something to slow your healing. Injuring fae who heal too quickly is quite boring."

She waved her hand at The Scourge. "Begin."

47

"It's been almost three weeks," said Ava, pacing in Thorne's suite. She had sought him out after dinner to beg him to send another team to the camp. "We've heard nothing from them."

Raine, Quinn and Jorrar were present, sitting in the living room. Ava could barely function through the ache in her chest. Something was very wrong. She could feel it. Though she didn't know how to explain it, a sense of urgency pulled at her soul. As if Casimir was calling out to her.

"Sit," her brother urged from his place in a chair by the fire. "I'm sure they're alright. Casimir knows what he's doing."

"I can't sit," she said as she continued her pacing.

Thorne rose from his chair and approached. "Calm yourself."

"Don't tell me to calm down," she replied, voice rising. "I should have gone. We all should have. I know the layout better than any of you."

"It was too risky," her brother argued, leaning against the mantle. "What if they'd captured you again?"

"I know. But something went wrong. I feel it," she insisted, pressing her hand on her chest as tears pricked her eyes.

Thorne looked at her with resolve. "Alright then. Let's gather another team and—"

They were interrupted by pounding on the door. "Your Majesty. It's urgent."

Thorne strode across the room and opened it. An out of breath soldier stumbled in. One of the members of Casimir's group.

Ava's throat tightened, awaiting the news.

"What is it?" Thorne asked.

"Everyone's dead," the soldier panted. "I'm the only one who got away."

Ava marched toward the soldier and gripped his collar, yanking him closer. "Where's the general?"

"They have him," he said.

"Who?" asked Thorne, but Ava already knew.

"Deidamia and Andras," he replied.

She shoved the soldier away. Not sparing anyone a second glance, she left the suite, ignoring her friends calling after her as hundreds of flowers erupted across the floor in her wake.

HALF AN HOUR LATER, Ava was saddling up her horse with another group of soldiers, Raine, Quinn and Jorrar in tow. Pax and Maeryn had also joined, insisting they wanted to help. Thorne would stay behind to monitor the kingdom, but waited to see them off.

Their animal companions were restless, staying close by as they waited for the group to leave. Thorne's giant golden eagle, Skye, was coming along too. She'd be vital in case they had to make a quick getaway.

Ava hadn't said one word to him after she left the room.

She was furious at him for allowing the mission in the first place, though she knew it wasn't his fault. He hadn't tried to stop her when she insisted she come along on the rescue, knowing he wouldn't be able to keep her away from her soulbond.

Raine approached and placed a hand on her shoulder. "We'll get him back."

She didn't answer, couldn't speak for fear of what she might say to anyone, even if they were only trying to comfort her. She had never been so angry in her life, and she was trying not to take it out on Raine.

But it wasn't just anger. It was fear. Terror.

The idea of the man she loved being brutalized at the hands of her previous abusers was utter agony. It was as if her soul was splitting apart with every minute he was in danger.

Her head was full of memories of her own torture and what they might be doing to Casimir. The vision the Elderoak had shown her. It was coming to pass. And she felt as though she would crawl out of her skin if she didn't get there now.

The pain he must be feeling. The fear. Would she know if he died?

No. She wouldn't entertain the thought of his death. Refused. No one else would be taken from her. She pushed the fears away as she turned to her brother.

"I'm sorry we didn't involve you in this. We were trying to protect you and keep you out of their hands," he said.

"I know. And I understand. But you and Cas don't get to decide how to protect me anymore. Don't take that choice away from me. I'm capable of protecting myself. I want to be involved in the planning and decisions. I can help."

"I know."

"You know that I've been around Deidamia and Andras more than most of you," she said. "I eavesdropped on their conversations. I paid attention the best I could. I might have important information. Don't shut me out for fear of what might happen. Please." Her voice broke on the last word.

"Alright." He pulled her into a hug. "I know you'll get him back," he whispered. "Be safe."

Pulling away, she mounted her horse. The group said their goodbyes and journeyed through town, Ava riding in silence next to Raine who was stewing in his own anger. Worried for his best friend's life.

She felt for her magic and found it. Writhing. Ready.

Wrathful.

It took all her strength to contain it, keeping it locked away until they arrived at their destination. Ava allowed her rage to smother her fear and used it to fuel her mission. She would infiltrate the camp and find Casimir. She would rescue her beloved. Her soulbond. Her love.

And she wouldn't hesitate to kill every single daemon who stood in her way.

AFTERWORD

Welp, so sorry for the cliffhanger. Poor Cas. I know you're ready to find out what happens next. Book three is well on its way but it's a slog. Lots of moving parts with the war, some new characters and twists and turns. But it's coming. I promise. And maybe we'll get a little more insight into Raine and his awkwardness around Maeryn. And also... Raine's POV will be added. Yep. Get excited. His mind is a blast.

And it is so much fun! Even more adventure, more spice, an epic quest and some wild twists that will have you gasping.

The conclusion to the Daughter of the Earth trilogy will release some time in the spring of 2026.

Want more? For two BONUS chapters (Ava's early days of training), scan the QR code and sign up for my newsletter! There's also a link for my discord server where we chat all things Daughter of the Earth, obsess about characters and other books, and just have fun!

ALSO BY K.M. GORDON

Daughter of the Earth Trilogy

Whispers of the Elderoak (Book One)

Journey to the Elderoak (Book Two)

ACKNOWLEDGMENTS

Wow. This book was such a blast to write.

I had so much fun with the romance and slow burn between Ava and Casimir. And I have so many people to thank, so let's get to it.

Of course, thank you to my writing bestie, Christine. I love our chaotic emails, TikTok videos and chats about literally everything. Your humor and bluntness are my favorite things. The comments you make on my manuscript never fail to make me laugh, especially when you're threatening to throw your computer because I overuse a phrase. Still devastated you live so far away.

To my beta readers Morgan and Ashley. Thank you from the bottom of my heart. Your opinions and suggestions helped me transform this book even more.

And Ashley? I love how our friendship has grown. From our random texts about our characters, thirsting over our MMCs, and silly TikTok collaboration videos. It's crazy how you can meet someone on social media and instantly click with them.

I want to thank my lovely editor, Laë, who not only has been amazing with her edits and suggestions, but has become a dear friend to me. Our hilarious message threads never fail to make me smile and I value our friendship dearly. Some day I will come visit you in France.

Thank you again to my cover artist, H.M. Mast. Still amazed

at your talent. This book cover was absolute perfection and fits seamlessly with the series.

Of course, I want to thank Dalton, my husband, and my heart. My very own grumpy bearded man. You are always supportive and cheering me on, even when I'm incessantly talking about my characters. Thank you for brainstorming with me when I was feeling stuck. Remember, it was your idea that they visited a different kingdom in this book and the whole Saxumdale trip became one of my favorite parts.

Last but not least, I want to thank my readers. I am honored to have had such enthusiasm with this series from the very first ARC review that was posted for Whispers of the Elderoak, to today. I will never tire of your messages about my characters, excitement for what's to come, and your passion for this series. Thank you thank you thank you. I could never do this without you.

ABOUT THE AUTHOR

Katie is an author residing in Oklahoma with her husband, son and three troublesome cats. As a life-long bird and animal nerd (yes, she's the friend who everyone sends bird pics to asking what species it is), a lot of her books contain wildlife, animal companions and details of the natural world.

She writes stories full of friendship, romance, banter, and deep conversations all set within a fantasy setting.

When she's not writing, she's reading, hiking, gardening, birding, or daydreaming about even more story ideas.

www.km-gordon.com

Want to connect with me? Find me on Instagram and TikTok @author.k.m.gordon